D0308261

The Hurting: The Glasgow Terror

R J Mitchell

© RJ Mitchell 2016
The author asserts the moral right to be identified
as the author of the work in accordance with the
Copyright, Designs and Patents Act, 1988.

All characters appearing in this work are fictitious.
Any resemblance to real persons, living or dead,
is purely coincidental.

All rights reserved. No part of this publication may be reproduced,
stored in a retrieval system or transmitted in any form or by any
means, electronic, mechanical, photocopying, recording or otherwise,
without the prior permission of Fledgling Press Ltd,
7 Lennox St., Edinburgh, EH4 1QB

First published by Fledgling Press 2012
www.fledglingpress.co.uk
Printed and bound by:
Bell & Bain, Glasgow
ISBN: 9781905916511

PRAISE FOR *THE HURTING: THE GLASGOW TERROR*

"*The Hurting: The Glasgow Terror* takes all the elements of RJ Mitchell's debut novel, *Parallel Lines: The Glasgow Supremacy,* and places them on a bigger stage. The stakes are higher and the action scenes more thrilling, as the story expands out from personal vendetta to global terrorism: if you put a Glasgow cop with a death wish up against suicide bombers, you can be sure that sparks will fly.

As the body count soars and DS Gus Thoroughgood takes repeated beatings that would have Jason Bourne crying for a time out, Mitchell is careful to root his fictional creations in factual reality of the city of Glasgow. The locations ring true even as characters and scenarios take on violent and exaggerated twists, with the result that this is a timely addition to the Tartan Noir genre."

ALAN MORRISON, *Group Arts Editor, Herald & Times*

"A fast-moving thriller in which two desperate Glasgow CID officers try to thwart a Jihad on their own doorstep. A suicide bomber detonates a bomb at a shopping centre. The countdown has now begun – but how do you track down the other bombers when you have no idea where they are hiding?

It all leads to a showdown at Ibrox stadium, where the action off the field is even more explosive than the action on it."

RUSSELL LEADBETTER, *Glasgow Evening Times*

"RJ Mitchell's latest presents a truly chilling scenario: fundamentalist terrorists wreaking havoc on the streets of Scotland's largest city.

Keeping readers on the edge of their seats throughout, the author is a skilled exponent of the action set piece as outrage mounts on outrage and a rawly grieving DS Gus Thoroughgood faces a race against time to kick the legs out from under the evildoers before they can unleash their ultimate weapon.

Full of red herrings and false dawns – plus a leftfield "no way!" surprise return – this is a thriller packed full of blood and sweat that also has its human side: none more so than in the rendering of a Saturday morning, West End sniper attack that raises the pulse no question, but also left me with a surprisingly large lump in my throat besides. A welcome addition to the Tartan Noir fold."

GREGOR WHITE, *Stirling Observer*

For Arlene, Ava and Mum

1

THE FIRST shards of light splintered their way through the bedroom curtain as the greyness of the morning light started to fill the room and slowly Thoroughgood began to waken from a fractured sleep.

Turning over onto his left side he reached out across the bed searching for her presence but the sheets were smooth and the bed was empty. Slowly the stupor of his drowsy awakening gave way to the cruel reality that was his waking hours. She was gone . . . gone forever.

His eyes flashed as the feeling of blind panic that had marked the start of his every day since Celine had been taken from him gripped his mind and body anew. He sighed out loud and stared uncomprehending at the space in the bed where she should be lying, where she had been lying what seemed liked a moment ago, so alive, so real, so sensuous, so Celine. But now she was no more, forever consigned to his past, yet during his sleeping hours so much a part of his present.

He had taken the offer to come to Castlebrae, the Scottish Police Convalescence home, thinking that a break in the Perthshire countryside might help him escape the torment that had seemed to taint everything in Glasgow.

Glasgow. Where everything reminded him of Celine and the man who had ended her life and his hopes of happiness . . . Declan Meechan.

He ran his right hand through the strands of the jet black hair that was increasingly grey-streaked, sat up in the bed staring at the curtain ahead, and then the Hurting came and it was too much. Gus Thoroughgood buried his head in his knees and wept until his body was wracked with a pain he knew would never go away and all the time her face remained the focus of his mind's eye. Then the voice in his head spoke up.

"C'mon Gus get it together, a month up here and you still haven't got it under control, face facts: she's gone and she ain't coming back, you've got to start again.'

The problem was where did he make that start, when nothing seemed to work? It had been almost five months since he had found Celine at Meechan's place, shot dead by a hired killer, so still, so peaceful, never more beautiful and yet so dead.

Grief had given way to anger. Alcohol had provided a false balm for the pain that seemed to sear his very being. He had tried to throw himself into his work and find a way to occupy every moment of the day. Failed.

Eventually it had been too much and Superintendent Tomachek had summoned him to his smoke-filled room. There, with his partner Kenny Hardie adding some moral support, they had suggested he take a month's leave at Castlebrae.

"A change of scene might help you put some distance between what has happened down here and maybe get some perspective on it all. Help you decide how to start again." Tomachek had said, trying to find some advice that might kickstart the healing process by offering him a way forward.

The anger surged anew through his veins as he thought back to that day and his reaction to the best advice the old boy could come up with.

"Just what the fuck is there to start again?" He had leaned across Tomachek's desk and the old man had recoiled from the fury that had spread across his features.

"That bastard Meechan has murdered the only woman I've ever loved and gone scot free, so please enlighten me, just what do you think I can start again?" He had ripped his warrant card out from his jacket pocket and tossed it onto the table. "I've sacrificed everything for this fuckin' job and with it has gone everything that meant anything to me. You can stick yer fuckin' job up your arse. I can't give it any more."

With that he had charged out the office, almost taking the door off its hinges in the process and leaving the disbelieving Tomachek and Hardie stunned in a combination of silence and pity at his meltdown.

Now, Thoroughgood got to his feet, pulled the curtains open and stared out at the gently rolling hillside painted in pleasing pastel shades.

He looked at his watch and saw that it was Saturday and he had a visitor today. Hardie was coming to pick him up and take him back to the place he had called home – Glasgow.

But as the moisture filled his eyes afresh and he felt droplets trace down his cheeks and salt slither into his mouth the voice in his head asked: "How can you call it home when there's nothing there for you anymore?"

2

KENNY HARDIE eased through the gears of the Focus as he picked up speed, zig-zagging through the lanes of the M8, manoeuvring into the outside lane and flattening the accelerator. The rain lashed off the windscreen this bleak grey Saturday lunchtime, as the weather tried to make up its mind whether it was autumn or spring.

As well as the dampness that hung habitually in the air, wrapping around his body like some soggy old blanket, there was also a chill that made the DC shiver. As the car began to heat up his mind started to thaw out and he began to focus on the meeting that had been dominating his thoughts.

His destination was the Perthshire village of Auchterarder and the subject of his visit was DS Gus Thoroughgood or the shell of the man who had been Gus Thoroughgood; his governor and his mate.

As Hardie's mind replayed the previous months which had left the DS gutted and broken, living a life devoid of meaning, his hair-trigger temper broke its banks and he rapped his left hand on the Focus dashboard.

"Why the fuck did you have to go after her again Gus?" Hardie shouted out loud and found his mind focusing on the image of his partner cradling the lifeless body

of the woman he had put everything on the line for –
Celine Lynnot.

A love triangle that had imposed a grip on Thoroughgood's life; which had tormented and tantalised him in
almost equal measure for the best part of a decade. Ended
with Celine's pre-ordered slaying by her fiancé, Declan
Meechan; Glasgow's foremost crimelord and Thoroughgood's mortal nemesis.

But as Hardie continued to turn over the aftermath of
Celine's brutal demise he knew that all that mattered was
how to get Gus Thoroughgood back into the here and
now. That was the reason behind this trip to Perthshire.
Achieving just that, Hardie knew, was going to be far
from easy.

He reached for one of the Silk Cut cigarettes poised
half out of the almost empty pack of twenty, pushed in the
cigarette lighter on the Focus dash and a minute later was
filling the interior of the car with smoke.

"Fuck 'em all," said Hardie in defiance as his mind
briefly strayed to the string of complaints he knew would
head his way from the next users of the pool car when he
finally returned it to Stewart Street, City Centre office,
later that day.

The diversion from the events at hand was momentary and as he filled his lungs with a deep inhalation of
nicotine, Hardie tried to train his mind on exactly what he
needed to achieve from the visit.

No matter what happened he needed to get Thoroughgood back to Glasgow. The month's compassionate leave
granted by Detective Superintendent Tomachek was up
and it was time to somehow start getting his DS back into
the routine and structure of bog-standard coppering.

The fact that Thoroughgood had tendered his resignation by virtually slapping the old man with his warrant card was neither here nor there. Tomachek valued the services of a DS he had taken under his wing as something of a protégé far too highly to let a moment of grief-fuelled angst put the full stop on Thoroughgood's career.

Apart from anything else, by putting his life on the line and ultimately losing the woman he loved, Thoroughgood had also brought down the seemingly untouchable Meechan and smashed a multi-million pound drug operation filtering into the city from the Western Isles. Thoroughgood's warrant card had remained in Tomachek's desk drawer until the Detective Superintendent had handed it over to Hardie prior to his departure that morning, with a warning.

"For God's sake Hardie don't hand it back until you are sure the time is right."

But that, as Hardie knew, was only one side of the equation. It was all very well Strathclyde Police wanting to welcome the returning hero back into their ranks with open arms but did the prodigal son want to return? Only time would tell how things would pan out and Hardie had resolved that whatever decision Gus Thoroughgood ultimately came to, he would be there for him. He flicked the automatic window switch and as the glass panel lowered, lobbed the Silk Cut out.

"Fuck it! As if that isn't enough, I'm gonnae miss the Rangers game as bleedin' well. I hope you're grateful Gus," Hardie said out loud and tuned into Radio Scotland's coverage of the afternoon's football.

It was almost 2.30pm when Hardie arrived in the grounds of Castlebrae. The imposing sandstone building

6

immediately recalling memories of the twin visits he had made as he recovered from back and shoulder injuries sustained during separate incidents.He parked the Focus and eased out of the car, tried to fight back the sense of dread enveloping him at just what kind of state he would find his mate and colleague in.

His attention was diverted by ducks waddling past his feet and heading to the small pond situated in front of the imposing Victorian building. He had not forgotten about them and delved into his overcoat pocket to produce a paper bag he had had the 'missus' fill with bread crumbs. Then Kenny Hardie got on the end of the line and followed his feathered friends down to the pond.

After he had waited for a moment to let the birds immerse themselves in the icy water, the grizzled detective began to throw assorted crumbs and chunks of his breakfast toast into the pond. "There you go my beauties, fire into that why don't you?" A smile that would have warmed the coldest winter night covered Hardie's face as he enjoyed a moment of rare satisfaction.

Submerged in his moment of animal magic Hardie failed to hear the footfall on the gravel behind him.

"Hello old friend, come to save me from myself?" Hardie recognised the voice immediately.

He turned round slowly and tried to keep his smile welcoming as he took in the appearance of his partner.

"Aye, you and your birds, some things never change," said Thoroughgood as he gestured to the bench overlooking the pond, "Fancy a seat?"

Hardie nodded and took the half dozen steps towards the bench overlooking the family of water fowl with the silence between him and his partner deafening.

The first thing he had noticed about Thoroughgood were the hollows his eyes appeared to have sunk into, while his cheek bones stood out like the edges of a ski slope. The weight loss was blatantly obvious and the jersey he wore – a yellow number Hardie used to taunt his mate about as being primrose – hung from him like an empty sack.

Perhaps most stark of all was the grey, in places white, materialising in the DS's previously jet black hair. But there was something else, something about Thoroughgood and the way he moved that Hardie had noticed immediately but been unable to diagnose. It was as though Thoroughgood had become weighed down, aged by the pain of a loss that had drained the very sap of life from his being.

They sat side by side on the bench and watched the ducks. This time Hardie did not smile for he had no idea where to begin. Surprisingly it was Thoroughgood who broke the silence.

"Ah fuck it, any crumbs left in the bag faither?"

The mention of his nickname brought the smile back to Hardie's face. "Sure, help yourself."

Thoroughgood took the bag and filleted it for some morsels before lobbing the last few into the pond much to the delight of the attending drake and his little family. Still Hardie did not know where to begin and his attempt when it came was hardly adroit.

"Tomachek and the rest of CID back at Stewart Street send their best and the old man is . . .", but before he could complete the sentence Thoroughgood did it for him.

"Wondering when I am coming back?"

Hardie shrugged his shoulders and nodded uneasily as the gorging ducks soaked his scuffed brown suede shoes in spray.

"It's okay mate. I know my time at Castlebrae is up this weekend and you've come to take me back to Glasgow. No disrespect but I just don't know if I want to go back with you."

The DC had feared as much. The arts of gentle persuasion and skilful diplomacy were unfathomable to Hardie. He knew then there was no point in pursuing his objective in a manner that would have left him open to ridicule. Thoroughgood may have had his heart broken but his mind was evidently in full working order.

The DS leant forward and stared at the ducks. It was hardly an act of encouragement and Hardie sighed out loud before reaching inside his anorak and seeking to stiffen his resolve with another Silk Cut. One click of his Zippo and a deep inhalation and he launched himself into the matter at hand.

"Fuck's sake Gus, what the hell else are you gonna do man? I know you loved her, Christ I do, but she's gone and it doesn't matter where you are, the Hurting is still gonna be there with you. Sitting around moping, wherever you are intending running off to, isn't going to bring her back is it? What you need is to get back to what you do best, back among the boys, and get stuck in. In my opinion the last thing you need right now is more time to torture yourself with what if's and if only's."

Hardie stopped for another drag on his Silk Cut but was just too late to stop ash falling on his treasured brogues.

"Ah, piss off ya diddy!" He chastised himself before flicking his right foot in the direction of the ducks who were this time on the end of an unwanted shower of fag ash, and a volley of quacks soon let Hardie know what they thought of his not so fancy footwork.

9

Hardie's words of wisdom did however have the desired effect of gaining a reaction from his partner. Thoroughgood sat upright and turned his body towards Hardie before levelling those hollow, almost translucent green spheres on the veteran DC. Hardie felt uneasy under surveillance of his mate's disconcerting gaze.

"Straight to the point as always Kenny, eh? Maybe you're right but I just feel tired of it all, I don't know where my life is going anymore. One minute everything is there for me and we are making all these plans and now it's back to square one, start again, like some sick game of snakes and ladders. But what is the point? You tell me.

"Get stuck back into the job? What for? Where is that going to take me?" Thoroughgood saw Hardie remove his fag and held his hand up to stay any interruption from his partner.

"Before you say 'One day you'll meet someone else', well maybe, but she won't be Celine. Anyway the old man took my warrant card so the problem is no longer yours or Strathclyde Polis' is it now?"

Hardie cleared his throat and drew an enquiring look from Thoroughgood who was well aware this usually meant an uncomfortable admission was imminent.

"Well not quite, Gus." Hardie rummaged in the other pocket from the one housing his beloved fags and slowly produced Thoroughgood's warrant card.

"The old man may have accepted it but your warrant card has spent the last few weeks gathering dust in his office drawer. We both think it's time you took it back and returned to Glasgow."

Silence.

Thoroughgood got up and moved closer to the water's

edge, gazing across the pond and into the Perthshire hills ringing the horizon with their pleasing undulations.

"You're naw gonnae jump mate?" shouted Hardie from behind him and they both erupted in laughter simultaneously. An outpouring of relief as much as anything else.

"OK, old mate, I'll come back to Glasgow with you but you can keep the warrant card for now. Strathclyde Polis has had the best part of 15 years of my life and right now I'm not ready to commit any more."

Hardie allowed himself a smile and patted his mate's right shoulder.

"Good man. What do you say to a curry in Mr India's once we get back to the West End?"

"Good to see that at least you haven't changed Kenny, still always thinking about your belly eh? Well I haven't exactly got plans for my Saturday night have I? But listen, there's one condition for me returning with you; there is no way I'm gonna put up with you kicking every ball of the Rangers game on the drive back. No radio ok?"

"Fuck's sake Gus, at least let me get the half-times! What's the problem, have you finally given up on Thistle?"

The raising of the middle digit of Thoroughgood's right hand was indeed eloquent proof that he had not.

"Just get me to the West End in one piece faither, will you?"

3

THE FOCUS surged down the A90, a study in still life. Hardie had not had the guts to ignore his partner's wish, that, as far as the football was concerned Radio Silence was the only station he wished to be tuned into.

Conversation was non-existent and Hardie shot Thoroughgood a sideways glance that revealed his gaze was vacantly focused out of the passenger window. For once in his life Hardie decided that the continued quiet of the vehicle was preferable to the vacuous chatter of conversation for the sake of itself.

The red Focus pulled out to overtake a blue Audi estate as Hardie realised that the drumming of his left hand fingers on the dashboard was now becoming so incessant it was even beginning to get on his nerves. He stopped.

Thoroughgood's mellifluous baritone broke their self-imposed silence. "Fuck me, it's Felix Baker and two mates. Well, well. What do you suppose they are up to, 40 miles from Glasgow, in the middle of the Perthshire countryside?"

The surprise, not just down to Thoroughgood's shock discovery of his voice but the content of his comments, forced Hardie to strengthen his grip on the steering wheel to compensate for the tremor of shock which had almost caused him to swerve the CID car into the Audi.

Hardie could not help himself leaning slightly farther forward in his driver's seat to catch a glimpse of Baker, a prolific housebreaker whose speed on the prowl had earned him the nickname of Felix.

Baker had terrorised the private housing schemes of Bishopbriggs, an affluent suburb in the north of Glasgow, through his use of the "Creeper" housebreaking MO that saw houses targeted in the dead of night when their occupants were deep in their slumbers. Then of course there was Felix's penchant for violence that saw any waking householders invariably beaten with a frightening severity that had left one OAP on life support in the city's Royal Infirmary.

But that was long ago and Baker was known to have graduated to the theft of fine art items on a steal-to-order basis from the stately homes of Scotland's old aristocracy.

"Look faither, just keep going will you? Any money they will spot a CID motor and the last thing we need them to pick up on is that it's being driven by two of their oldest polis pals," barked Thoroughgood and the urgency in his gaffer's voice injected the first faint feelings of positivity into Kenny Hardie's damp dreich day.

"All right Gus, but they aren't on a day trip just for the sake of the scenery. How do you propose we play this one? Now we've gone past them we're hardly in a position to give them a tug," said Hardie.

Thoroughgood turned his full attention on his partner. "Just get into the nearside lane and crawl along like you usually do and they can take that decision out of our hands."

But Baker and his two mates didn't play ball and remained stubbornly 100 yards adrift of the Focus.

Clocking the Audi almost constantly in his rear view, Hardie provided a breathless commentary on its incumbents. "Baker is driving all right but I don't recognise the other boy in the front and I can't get a read on the punter in the back. You reckon they'll be tooled up?"

"A bad boy like Felix is always going to be looking for that little bit extra insurance. If it's not shooters then he is bound to have a blade or two in the motor. They aren't sitting back there because they are nervous of motorway driving. They know it's a CID motor. What they've got to be waiting for is to see if our arrival is mere coincidence or if we're on to them. Either by chance or design, it makes no odds. So it's up to us to keep them guessing."

Thoroughgood took a look in his passenger mirror and tried to sneak a glance at the front passenger in the Audi but the combination of spray and distance rendered his efforts pointless.

"We're maybe a mile or so from the roundabout just up from Bridge of Allan. That will give them four options. Either they go straight through and keep heading for Glasgow and see if we do likewise, take a left into Bridge of Allan, go past the Glasgow turn off and take the Denny road, or double back for Perth.

"Any of the last three means they have clocked exactly who we are and have something on board they don't want us having a butchers at. If they head for Glasgow, well I still wouldn't bet on them being clean, just that they haven't recognised us and reckon we are local Central Scotland CID."

"Fair enough," responded Hardie in agreement.

"Right, I can see the roundabout signs ahead Kenny,

slowly pull on the anchors and we'll see if we can force the issue."

With 200 yards to go to the roundabout the Audi darted into the outside lane and proceeded to close the gap on the Focus. Baker and his cronies had no option, as Hardie had dropped down to second gear.

As the Audi pulled parallel with their car, Baker and his two minions kept their eyes resolutely to the front; locked on the roundabout. Then the Audi signalled to pull in front of the Focus and continued to indicate left for Bridge of Allan.

With Thoroughgood and Hardie now behind them, Baker and his gang headed down the road that would take them into the old Victorian spa town.

Hardie was first to articulate his thoughts. "He's clocked us all right Gus, might be time to get on the mobile to Central Scotland plod?"

The Focus followed the Audi at a distance and there could be little doubt that Baker and his confederates had realised the Focus was a police vehicle, judging by the furtive and repeated glances into their rear view mirror.

About 600 yards from the entry into the main street the road became a mini dual carriageway just as it crested the bridge over the river Allan. It was then that Baker decided it was time to test the resolve of his pursuers.

As the mini roundabout that preceded the dual carriageway loomed, the Audi suddenly shot across the traffic island diagonally, narrowly missing a bottle green people carrier, heading straight into the oncoming northerly traffic.

"Fuckin' idiot, what the hell does he think he's doing?" roared Hardie, flattening the accelerator of the Focus but remaining in the correct lane. But Baker's change of lane wasn't the only surprise the criminal and his mates had in store for the detectives.

With the speedo showing Hardie was hitting 60mph, the Focus had almost pulled level with the Audi on the opposite carriageway; it was then that the rear passenger window rolled down and a sawn-off shotgun appeared.

Thoroughgood had been keeping constant surveillance on the Audi and spotted the shooter first. "Hit the anchors! Sawn-off stickin' out rear window."

Automatically Hardie did as he was told but a hail of lead unloaded into the bonnet of the Focus. The Audi was back in front and this time it crossed the next mini roundabout and sped back onto the south carriageway.

"Jesus H Christ!" just about summed up Hardie's thoughts on the matter but Thoroughgood said:

"We've got three hundred yards to the village and there's a pedestrian crossing just outside the Allan Water Cafe that's always teamin' with kids, grannies, Mum and Dad, the whole bleedin' lot. If he goes in there at 60mph it will be carnage. Say your prayers faither."

But Baker had other ideas and with the village main street and the café looming he tried an ambitious and almost 90 degree turn down a side road running parallel with the banks of the river they had just crossed.

"Fuckin' maniac, he's never gonnae make that!" exclaimed Hardie, and he was right. It was like watching a slow motion replay as time seemed to stretch its perimeters. No sooner had the Audi begun its attempt at an abrupt left turn than the back of the vehicle started writhing violently as the movement asked of it defied the laws of physics.

With tyres screeching the vehicle started to tip and the two wheels on the passenger side began to lose their grip on the road before daylight clearly showed under the vehicle as it began its flight into oblivion.

The Audi managed one complete rollover before it smashed into the side of the concrete wall encircling a small remembrance memorial and a bench looking down on the riverside road.

That bench was occupied by two white haired women defying the elements and licking two ice creams with some vigour. Their cones were soon dropped as the elderly ladies' shocked faces took in the approaching horror of the low flying vehicle which was heading their way and on course to smash into the wall in front of them.

Hardie managed to bring the Focus to a stop at the junction of the riverside road and the mini roundabout with some effort and as he watched the Audi intently for signs of life he could already see the driver making his way round the far side of the crumpled car and breaking into a run down the side road.

Thoroughgood spoke. "You got a baton with you faither?"

Hardie shook his head. "Nope, but there is a Maglite torch in the back somewhere. Why you askin'?"

"You're gonna call out Central plod and I'm gonna take the Maglite and see if I can catch my friend Felix. It looks from the lack of movement like the other two are fecked. It's up to you if you want to sit tight or have a look but I'd put the missus and weans first, faither."

With that Thoroughgood turned round in his seat and fished down into the webbing attached to the back of Hardie's seat. His fingers soon located the metallic surface of the Maglite: "Hey presto!"

Hardie opened his mouth and got as far as "C'mon Gus…" But his mate was already out of the passenger door, his back a receding image as he ran down the side road after Baker. It was then that Hardie connected the look he had seen in Thoroughgood's eyes when he had located the Maglite with the one he had encountered the first time he had seen his friend earlier that day. Two words escaped his mouth when the realisation dawned.

"Death wish."

Turning into the side road Thoroughgood scanned the area immediately in front of him and found it empty. He jogged over to the railings that ran along the top of the wall at the edge of the road which dropped down to the river banks, and looked along to his right.

There, scurrying along the sandbank towards some pine trees, he saw the back of a male clad in dark clothing. Thoroughgood was off again, this time making towards the steps that led up to the roadway from the river bank.

Descending them two at a time, he reached the bottom almost breathless and then began to jog along the sandy surface of the banks of the Allan. The figure had gone. Reaching the pines Thoroughgood cautiously stopped just short of entering their cover. If Baker had been watching his advance along the bank then he would surely have recognised Thoroughgood.

The voice in his head urged caution, but it was competing with another voice now; one borne of desolation with no concern for the consequences of his actions. Then he shouted.

"Felix Baker!"
Silence.

"Fuck it," said Thoroughgood and walked into the shade of the trees just yards from the river, fully aware but caring not that death may be stalking him on the banks of the Allan.

Twenty yards in and the copper's instinct seemed to be taking over automatically once again. Thoroughgood knew he was being watched. He decided to force the issue. Turning his back on the trees he moved towards the river and stood gazing into the green depths as it flowed past him, aware that if Baker was close he would be unlikely to resist the urge to wreak vengeance on his unprotected back.

"So what," he thought.

There was little or no wind down on the bank, sheltered as it was by the pines and so far below road level, so that when a slight rustling registered in his ears the feeling that he had company was confirmed. Then the muffled noise of a footfall was revealed by the slight shingling of the sand Thoroughgood had noticed ten feet from the water.

Slowly the DS turned round to face his stalker and five feet away stood Felix Baker. Thoroughgood's face remained blank. Baker grinned with dripping malevolence.

"Well, well. If it isn't Gus Thoroughgood. Everyone's favourite heartbroken copper."

Thoroughgood did not respond, but his eyes took in the object dangling from Baker's right hand and couldn't believe the information they were relaying to his brain. For the criminal appeared to be carrying an umbrella.

"I think all the time you're spending in our country houses has gone to your head, Felix. But I guess when he's out for a stroll every gent should take an umbrella with him."

Baker lifted the umbrella and appeared to examine its every fold of fabric as Thoroughgood assessed the particulars of his appearance and the threat Baker's physique posed him. Baker was balding now and looking a bit soft round the middle: the DS concluded that business must be good.

As if reading his mind Baker patted his stomach. "Aye ye'd fancy yer chances of catching me now Thoroughgood wouldn't you." He looked back at the umbrella he was holding out parallel to his body and clicked a small button half way up the handle. Simultaneously a shard of glinting metal flew out the end.

"But I never travel without an insurance policy Thoroughgood, and here it is, a true gentleman's friend. An 1872 antique swordstick sporting a blade of lethal Parisian steel which will gut you like the floundering fuckwit you are.

"I should have stuck you when I had the chance on top of that row of shops back in '93 but then I knew you'd never catch me. Now things have gone full circle and instead of running, this time I'm going to skewer you like an under-cooked kebab."

For good effect Baker slashed the six inch blade down. There was a cruel hiss as it cut through the air. He brought its tip out level in front of him, pointing it directly at Thoroughgood, and took a step forward.

The DS smiled. "So when exactly did you find you had balls Felix?"

The blade slashed on the diagonal, heading straight at the DS's left shoulder, but he met the strike full on with all the solidity of the Maglite and sparks shot out as metal rasped on metal.

Thoroughgood quickly moved to put space between himself and Baker's right hand. "Remember my Maglite, do you Felix? I seem to remember the last time it gave you one helluva headache."

But the wild look in Baker's eyes betrayed his lethal intent as this time he lunged forward, aiming straight for Thoroughgood's midriff. The detective only just managed to parry the blow and as he did so he felt his back foot give on the shifting sands.

Baker stepped forward and raised the swordstick above the DS as Thoroughgood inadvertently stumbled to his knees.

"It's time I put you out of your misery. Goodbye Thoroughgood!" said Baker as the blade glinted above Thoroughgood's head, began to hiss its death song and descended through the air.

<u>4</u>

HARDIE HAD only waited long enough to see Thorough-good disappear from sight before a combination of curios-ity and customary anger saw him climb out of the Focus and head over to the smashed up Audi.

Hurt he may have been at Thoroughgood's remarks when the DS had suggested he sit tight and wait for the cavalry, but Hardie had not lost all caution. Stopping twenty feet from the upturned Audi he squatted down to satisfy himself that there was no threat from the two oc-cupants trapped within. There was not.

In the back seat the rear passenger's eyes gazed out in a death stare with blood dripping from the side of his mouth. Moving up to the back window – or the space where it had been, Hardie observed that the unnatural angle at which his head was lolling suggested the ned rid-ing shotgun for Felix Baker had indeed suffered a broken neck.

"Aye, good enough for you mate," he muttered, just as his gaze located the sawn-off poking out from underneath the criminal's body. However, the groans coming from the front passenger seat suggested criminal number two was not as dearly departed as his mate.

Hardie moved forward to look in the front passenger window which was snapped in half, and mounted the crumpled door.

"Early 30's, nice Mars Bar down the side of the face, semi conscious and saved by his seat belt," mused Hardie to himself, before letting out an involuntary "Bugger."

Hardie's disgust brought an opening of the villain's eyes quickly followed by a call for help.

"For fuck's sake get me oot o' here copper!"

Hardie took a swift look round to make sure he was not under surveillance, then replied.

"Like fuck, shithouse," smashing his right hand off the criminal's jaw and letting out a self-congratulatory sigh as a state of unconsciousness was rejoined. He reached into the backseat, took hold of the sawn-off, stuffed it down his raincoat and headed for the river bank. The voice in his head said 'Hope you're not too late mate.'

As Thoroughgood faced up to the gravity of his situation he recalled a saying that time slows down when you enter your final moments; that memories from childhood and other surreal experiences replay themselves in your mind's eye as death approaches.

The cruel glint of the swordstick hovered and began its descent on his cranium and Thoroughgood closed his eyes and saw Celine again. His arms entwined her, the life not yet gone from her body, the warmth of their final good-bye, the first time he had met her on the Riverboat Casino all legs and self assurance and smouldering like a forest fire.

At last his torment was over and he would be with her again, and this time no one could keep them apart, for all eternity. He heard the strumming of the acoustic guitar and the words resonated in his head.

"Hush now don't you cry, wipe away the tear drop from your eyes . . ." There she was waiting in bed for him and he dived into the twin pools of chocolate silk that were her eyes. Almost as a reflex action to his impending oblivion two words escaped his mouth.

"My love."

Baker had waited for this moment for so long the saliva escaped from his mouth and dripped down the side of his heavily jowled face. But the savage delight that had absorbed his features was transformed to a look of surprise by Thoroughgood's supplication and apparent gratitude for the death rite he was about to perform.

All of which added so much more appreciation to the moment. Baker delayed an instant to savour the look on the DS's face so he could picture it in his mind's eye until his last day and make sure he could let the Glasgow criminal underworld know how Gus Thoroughgood had died a whimpering wreck.

But Baker's delay was indeed fateful, and not for Thoroughgood. As he brought the blade down, the silence engulfing the scene of impending mortality was pierced by a shout of one word.

"No!"

Hardie levelled the shotgun at twelve yards and prayed to God, the Queen, and upon the souls of his eleven heroes in light blue that he would not miss. Then he pulled the trigger. As he did so the single syllable negative seemed to ricochet around his head forever. But his aim was true and Baker, perforated like a teabag, slumped on top of the kneeling Thoroughgood, all evil intent vanquished.

Hardie burst into a trot and ran over to the slumped corpse of the criminal, hauling it off Thoroughgood, whose features had been spray-painted in blood.

"For fuck's sake Gus! Are you okay man?" Hardie almost screamed. Lying flat on his back with his eyes shut, there was no response from the DS. But nor to Hardie's trained eye were there any fatal wounds.

A mounting anger swept over Hardie and grabbing his mate by both shoulders he shook him with all his strength.

"Open your fuckin' eyes you bastard! You are alive and I'm going to keep you that way, whether you like it or not!"

"Why?" came the reply.

5

ONCE AGAIN they sat side by side in the Focus, heading for Glasgow, engulfed in silence. The laborious process of providing Central Scotland Police with statements had been duly completed. A search of the boot of the wrecked Audi had provided the answer to why Felix had been so keen to avoid their attention: a haul of oil paintings valued at around £100,000 and fresh from a series of three house-breakings sustained by the Perthshire gentry. Proof that fine art theft was as rife as it was unreported in the upper echelons of old Scottish high society.

Of the three travelling villains, the shotgun rider had met his maker while the criminal in the front passenger seat had sustained a couple of fractured ribs and would be around to pay the butcher's bill. Baker was 50/50 in Stirling Royal Infirmary.

Shooting Thoroughgood a sideways glance Hardie saw that his mate was gazing aimlessly out of the passenger window once again and into the darkness. As usual, Hardie's need to puncture the surrounding silence was growing by the moment and finally he said;

"I don't know about you Gus but all that has left me starving. You still up for a curry?"

Thoroughgood turned his head and applied an intense gaze on his mate. "I suppose I've got fuck all else to do with myself. But I think we could both do with a shower and a change of clothes first. Mr …"

"India's," finished Hardie for his mate, mightily relieved that Thoroughgood appeared none the worse for their afternoon's work.

"Aye, that would be great Gus and if you don't mind me saying so, a quick pint in The Rock would go down a treat beforehand."

Thoroughgood nodded his head and then returned to stare out his window on the world.

Hardie drained the last of his pint glass and slammed it down on the table for good effect but there was no movement from behind the pages of the *Daily Telegraph* sports section. The veteran DC cleared his throat and a slight rustle of the newspaper pages preceded their lowering and Thoroughgood's vacant stare.

"Sorry mate, you Hank Marvin'?"

Hardie's grimace indicated that he was. "Sorry to rush you Gus but ain't that the truth?" Leaving The Rock they walked straight into a gentle drizzle that had moisture streaming off their faces by the time they had reached Mr India's.

To Hardie's surprise the brooding silence that had shrouded their quick pint and the walk from boozer to curry house was willingly broken by Thoroughgood.

"Fancy a bet faither? Remember that Diner Tec Review I set up for my mate Kenny, at the *Evening Times*, the one they had pinned to the outside wall back in 2004? What money it's still up?"

Hardie liked his odds. "Nae feckin' chance, I'll take a tenner on that. Look Gus, maybe you had a wee laugh over the bit about the waiter being a Partick Thistle fan but it's done the job drummin' up trade and making sure you enjoyed a lifetime of freebies. Forget it and give us the tenner."

"I don't know… old India was pretty proud of it, I'm sure it was still up at the beginning of the year. But hey, here we are!"

"Bastard! If I didn't know you had been up in Castlebrae for the last month I would have said you set me up, boss." Hardie's indignation was of the mock variety and an attempt to hide his relief that his gaffer was at last starting to show signs that he was capable of moving on.

As they made their way through the understated entrance of Mr India's the thought crossed Thoroughgood's mind that it would be easy to walk right past the restaurant if you didn't know it was there, but then maybe that was what made it the West End's best kept secret.

They stood on the raised landing just inside the doorway with Hardie intentionally staying in the background. The dimly lit restaurant was half-full and a pleasant buzz of conversation filled the air. Hardie instantly felt the tension leave his body aided by Thoroughgood's unexpected conversation piece and anticipation of a pint of the excellent Lal Toofan beer.

As he relaxed the veteran DC could see Thoroughgood's shoulders relax too, for the first time since he had got into the Focus and headed for Glasgow at the beginning of the afternoon.

Hardie recognised the small dark Indian waiter – and the trademark lunar grin that came with him heading their way but he couldn't remember his name.

28

Thoroughgood had no such problem. "Suleiman my man, how are you?"

"Mr Thoroughgood. We have not been seeing you for a long while. Where you been hidin' boss? You left Glasgow because Fistle are so rank rotten?"

His accent, half Glaswegian and half Indian with some Cockney thrown in, introduced a comic element into almost everything the diminutive and darting-eyed waiter said, especially when he persisted in ending almost every sentence with 'boss' in old fashioned deference to Thoroughgood's professional status. Something, Hardie noted, his mate had not corrected the waiter over.

"All that from Glasgow's number one Jags-supporting Indian waiter!"

"Ah, come on Mr Thoroughgood, that joke of yours on the Diner Tec review, I still hav'nae lived it down. West Ham is the team of ma faithers and it will be that of Suleiman Khan until my last day. Now boss, you want the usual table down in the alcove? I made sure it stayed clear as soon as I got the call yous were comin'."

Hardie was even more surprised by Thoroughgood's response. "Allahu Akbar! That'll do nicely, Sushi son."

"Salam, boss," replied the waiter in an exchange that Hardie had no interest in deciphering although, judging by the reciprocal grinning between Thoroughgood and Sushi, Thoroughgood's name shortening had brought an equal amount of illicit mirth.

By 9pm the two detectives were wading thorough their pakora, with Hardie already anticipating the delights of his customary lamb dopiaza, while the Lal Toofan came thick and fast.

Hardie's attempt to create an air of normality around

the events of the afternoon had been met with no opposition by Thoroughgood. Leaning back on his chair the portly DC let out a raucous belch before quaffing the last of his third pint of house lager.

"Aye they make the Lal Toofan that bit flatter than your normal bog standard British lager. Brilliant really! It has a high proportion of rice and maize and not so much of the old barley and hops, you know Gus."

Thoroughgood's eyebrows shot up in mock surprise as he feigned interest.

Hardie was in full flow. "Bloody smart, our Indian friends you know, coming up with a flat lager that compliments the best dish money can buy. No gas, precious little air fizzing up inside you and cutting down on the space available for dopiaza. Think about that the next time you're quaffing a Stella, Gus. Brilliant stuff if you ask me."

"I didn't," was Thoroughgood's reply as he kept his gaze on the menu while trying to choose his own main course. They were seated in the corner of a dimly lit alcove that was even more understated than the rest of India's.

Putting down the menu Thoroughgood finished off his lager and gave a nod to Sushi, who had been dancing attendance on them from the minute they had walked through the doors – just the way Hardie liked it.

As the small wiry Indian trotted across to take their order, Hardie beat his mate to the punch. "Ah, Suddi, here's a question for you. What is the English for Lal Toofan?"

The waiter's features went blank and he shot a 'what the hell is this all about' glance over at Thoroughgood, who merely shrugged his shoulders in mock resignation.

"Ah dinnae know boss. And it's Sushi, by the way."

Hardie smiled benignly. "I thought so my friend. It means Red Storm and if you don't mind me saying so that's something you should know if you want to be boosting your beer sales."

Again Sushi shot Thoroughgood a glance but Hardie, in full flow, was clearly warming to his night's entertainment. "Anyway I'll have a helping of your excellent . . ."

This time it was Sushi who interrupted: "Lamb dopiaza, a portion of boiled rice and of course, a garlic Nan."

Hardie beamed. "Bang on Suddi, you never forget do you son? And that's why we keep coming back." By way of an explanation to Thoroughgood, Hardie added; "The missus is out on a hen night so my breath isn't going to be an issue – thank feck."

"And for you Mr Thoroughgood, still a chicken ginger bhuna and boiled rice?"

"I'm glad we've cleared that all up," replied Thoroughood, winking at Sushi.

"Thank you Mr Hardie, we will have it with you in no time." Now Sushi hovered, with an air of anxiousness that was tangible and totally at odds with his previous jovial presence.

"Mr Thoroughgood, I wonder if I could have a wee word in your shell-like before you leave tonight. I have some information for you."

Hardie's eyebrows arched involuntarily in surprise at the waiter's words, and also in anticipation of Thoroughgood's reply, for at this precise moment the DS had still to indicate whether he would take his warrant card back and return to duty.

Thoroughgood attempted a side step. "Ah, Sushi, I've

been off duty for a while now, on leave, and I'm not so sure I'm the officer to be speaking to."

Sushi's right hand fired up to his slick black hair and shot through it in an obvious sign of agitation. "I have something that you and Mr Hardie must hear, boss. It is for no one else's ears. I will not be wasting your time boss, believe me."

Hardie tried to pour oil on troubled waters with a placatory comment: "I tell you what Sushi son, you get myself and the boss here a couple more Lal Toofans pronto and let us have a wee chat about this and we'll see what we can do. That good enough for you?"

"Thank you Mr Hardie, I would not be botherin' yous if it wasnae important boss. But we cannae be speaking in here, can I come around to your flat in Partickhill Road? You hav'nae moved boss?"

Looking over at Hardie, Thoroughgood nodded in an almost resigned manner.

"Listen Sushi, I appreciate you are keen to help but I am not going to be in a position to do anything about anything until I have met with my Super. That will probably happen in the next 24 hours or so, so why don't you give me a couple of days to get back in the saddle and swing by a night next week some time? That do you wee man?"

Sushi smiled in affirmation and as the waiter headed off Hardie saw his chance to pin Thoroughgood down on his immediate plans for the future.

"So Gus, are you the officer Sushi should be speaking to? I mean first things first, you still haven't accepted this . . ." and Hardie slapped Thoroughgood's warrant card on the table taking care not to soil it on a patch of pakora sauce that had somehow escaped his mouth.

Thoroughgood stared at his image on the white laminated plastic card as if it was a ghost from the past, something that reminded him of a memory that was too painful to countenance. His right hand stayed wrapped around his lager and his left twitched at the edge of the table cloth. He said nothing.

Unperturbed, Hardie pushed on. "Listen Gus, the statements we gave this afternoon, that whole incident with Baker and his boys, well you've given your designation as DS StrathPol again. We are going to have to see old man Tomachek and rubberstamp all of that.

"But it looks like ..." Hardie stopped for a moment and perused Thoroughgood's features for confirmation he was not off on another one of his metaphorical wild goose chases, before proceeding. "You are back on the job? Well, I'm no' sayin' it is reason enough to take the warrant card back but right now, right here, what else is there for you do? Plus we don't know what Sushi has cooking up for us, pardon the pun; it could be tasty, eh?" Hardie quickly supplied one of his trademark winks to underline his point.

Thoroughgood's features remained blank, still unimpressed with the prospect of returning to his former life.

Hardie finished the dregs of his pint and ploughed on. "Look, I said I would bell Tomachek after we finish here and let him know if you are willing to come back on board. If it's yes, the old man wants you and me in his office at 10am Monday morning."

Thoroughgood leaned back on his chair, clasping his hands together and placing them on the back of his head, his face expressionless but irritation soon evident in his voice.

"Fuck me, nothing ever changes does it? How long you been waiting to spring that on me?"

Knocked off balance by his mate's response, Hardie tried a new angle. "Come on Gus, you said to Sushi yourself, two minutes back, you were going to speak to Tomachek. But hey Gus, if your bottle has crashed that bad you're only gonnae come back into the job so you can find a way out, like you tried with friend Felix, you can forget it. It's up to you but for fuck's sake say something man."

The volume of Hardie's voice had risen to such a level that there was a clatter of cutlery from the table five feet to their left. A fifty-something female with a blonde beehive, who had attracted a lingering glance from the wolfish Hardie earlier, had been given such a fright by the detective's increased decibels her fork had jolted out of her hand and hit the tiled floor.

At that point Sushi arrived with two further pints of Lal Toofan but with the temperature around the table rising, the waiter was smart enough to lay the beers down and leave in silence.

"I don't know what happened to me back there with Baker but it was like 'what is the point anymore?' But maybe I frightened myself, and I guess you're right faither, if I don't go back to the job what else is there? You would have been as well letting Baker split me."

Thoroughgood's left hand reached out and picked up the warrant card. He lifted it and looked at the image of the young Detective Constable he had once been.

"I reckon I'll need a new picture for this because no one is going to believe it is one and the same person, eh faither?"

Hardie smiled and raised his pint pot. "A toast then, to the return of DS Gus Thoroughgood!"

"I guess so," said Thoroughgood, but although he smiled Hardie could see his eyes were brimming with sadness.

6

SUNDAY MORNING dawned grey and wet. Thorough-good lay in his bed and listened to the rain explode off his window as the realisation that he was home alone for the first time in months, empty and aching all over again, ricocheted around inside his head.

He stared at the bedroom ceiling, fighting the over-riding inclination to retreat into the past and fix his mind on her features – her smell, her voice and those delicious brown eyes – and felt moisture dampen his own yet again.

The rage broke its internal dam and he screamed out, "For fuck's sake not again! C'mon on son let's be posi-tive, get out your scratcher and get some brekkie, the morning papers. Bloody hell you pathetic excuse for a man! Who were Thistle playin' this weekend?"

The thought drew a wan smile over his emotionally derelict features and he stumbled into the kitchen on auto pilot, sticking on Radio Two: but Steve Wright's 'Love Songs' was far from music to his ears and he switched the radio off, instead seeking some comfort from the familiar surroundings of his kitchen.

There was none.

This was it then; a day full of . . . what? No meaning,

no point, no nothing.'Aye, Hardie was right, if you don't go and see the old man tomorrow what the feck else is there to do?' demanded the voice.

Ten minutes later Thoroughgood sank into his favourite armchair, steaming mug of coffee in one hand, slice of toast in the other, his glazed expression bouncing off the walls of his lounge.

'Music, maestro. For pity's sake, Gus,' said the voice, and he stumbled over to his CD player and pressed the open button. It jammed.

The CD player's refusal to open was the final straw and he smashed his hand off it, wincing at the gash it opened in his knuckle. The tears started to flow once more.

"Jesus H Christ!" He raged at the ceiling and left the room, curtains still drawn, wreathed in darkness.

The sound of a voice continued to penetrate the engulfing silence where before only the rain beating off his windows had. Thoroughgood realised he had been talking to himself for some time now.

"I've lost it then," he said aloud in self-mockery. Retreating into his bedroom he looked for his old kit bag, the one he had taken up to Meechan's that night, the last time he had seen Celine alive.

He placed his hand inside and sought the only thing that could bring him the solace he yearned for above all else. At last his fingers clasped it and he pulled his grandfather's revolver out of the bag.

Returning to the lounge he saw that the CD player had opened and he shook his head in cynical amusement.

'Alright son, let's go out with a bang then. So what is your Desert Island disc gonna be?" asked the voice.

He rifled through the CD tower fingering all of his old heavy metal favourites. A faint smile crept over his features as fleeting memories associated with individual discs came back to him.Finally he was left with two. A toss up between AC/DC's *If You Want Blood* – the first metal album he'd ever heard – or the one that hooked him on Queensrÿche: *Hear In The Now Frontier*. He opted for the latter, the intelligence of Geoff Tate's lyric and the scything power chords of Michael Wilton and Chris de Garmo's guitars clinching it.

As the album opened with *Sign of the Times* Thoroughgood looked down through the track list and chose exactly what his musical accompaniment would be when he decided the moment was right to join her.

"Ah, *You*, perfect music to die to."

He placed the empty CD sleeve on one arm of his favourite Chesterfield and his grandfather's service revolver on the other and ambled over to the chiffonier cabinet where he saw to his relief that there was still a decent quantity of Lagavulin in the bottle.

Thoroughgood poured a generous glass and returned to the armchair enveloped in the semi-light piercing through his lounge curtains. He fired up the volume via the remote control.

Scanning the sleeve he saw that track two was now playing. "Five to go Gussy boy, better swallow a large one," said his voice out loud again.

He did so and shut his eyes, slouching back in the chair. The third track struck up; 'Get a life'. How ironic, and he smiled, raised the glass in mock salute and then to his lips once more.

His mind jolted back and forward, faces came and

went. Meechan's spitting hate at him; Celine's imploring him; Hardie cajoling him.

He started to imagine how it would all have ended up if she was still here and he'd managed to take Meechan out.

Would they have been able to bring up Meechan's bastard? Could he have swallowed the happy families scenario or had Celine been right when she'd said he was too eaten up with hate and bitterness?

Track four — *The Voice Inside* — started up with De Garmo's slide guitar and Tate asking; "Do you know the people fighting for your head?"

'What a fuckin' requiem,' said the voice. He shook his head. Once again his choice of funeral music had been perfect. Only three more songs until the big bang.

He picked up the revolver and held it in his hand, looking down at the barrel and chamber and wondering just what he would feel when it spat lead into his head. How often had his grandfather used it? Questions, questions and more questions.

He returned to the chiffonier and pulled out the black and white photo album that recorded his grandfather's life and times with the RAF in the Second World War and leafed through them. Track five, *Some People Might Fly*, filled the room. Thoroughgood marvelled again at the perfection of his final musical accompaniment as it fitted perfectly once more with his thoughts.

Again the questions:What would he have thought? Was the old man looking down right now?

'You are letting him down, letting Celine down, letting yourself down. But so what?'

The guitar began track six — *Saved* — and Thoroughgood had had enough. Something snapped inside.

"No fuckin' way are you getting off with this Meechan. Some day, some place, some time I will catch up with you."

Standing up, he raised his glass in the air. "I promise you're mine, Meechan." He took a final swig of malt and kissed the barrel of the revolver.

He placed the handgun on the armchair and strode over to the curtains, ripping them open and wincing as the daylight flooded in.

Staring out of the window the salt from his tears provided an odd contrast to the peatiness of the Lagavulin.

The phone rang. He turned round and stared at it like it was an object just landed from outer space. "Fuck it," he said and lifted the receiver.

"That you Gus? It's Dr Meths here."

His mind was slow to register but eventually recognition dawned. Doctor Graeme Goode, his old Uni mate.

"My dear doctor, how can I help you?"

"I heard you were back from your stay up the road and wondered if you fancied letting your old mate give you a thrashing on the squash court?"

Before he could get a word in Goode was off and running in his usual machine gun delivery style.

"Listen to your doctor, Thoroughgood. Exercise and endorphins are just what you need! Why don't you pick me up at the hospital, say 4 pm and I'll have you tickled up, off the court and in the Rock by half-five? A spanking on your home courts at Western squash club? You ready to take your medicine mon ami?"

"Do I have much choice Dr Meths?"

"You know the answer to that one. All the best, and don't be eyeing up any of my bloody nurses on the way in." With that parting shot the good doctor was off.

7

FIVE HOURS later Thoroughgood entered the city's
Western Hospital to meet the 'Goode' doctor, wondering
if he would wind up back there after they had done battle
on the courts.

As he walked into the hospital he found his mind
returning to Saturday afternoons in the late eighties during their time at Glasgow Uni. It was then that Meths had
insisted on introducing him to the delights of the game.
Those Saturday sessions had turned into peculiar episodes
of teenage masochism. Hangovers on either side of the
court were habitually so bad that bouts of prolonged nau-
sea were apt to break out and interrupt their contests.

Thoroughgood smiled as he recalled how Dr Meths
had been dubbed with his nickname during his studies as a
fresh-faced medical student. That had been after a legendary drinking session involving a bottle of bourbon and an
attempted moonlit walk over the roof of Dalrymple Halls
of Residence.

'Aye, happy days,' he thought.

But Thoroughgood's nostalgic reverie was abruptly
ended by the sound of raised voices and the pleadings of
an increasingly frantic female coming from A&E reception.

Before he turned the corner into the main waiting room the DS halted, trying to pick up what he could from the pandemonium he was about to walk into.

"Listen ya fucking cow, when is ma wean gonnae get seen? That's three hours you've kept us pissing about for and she's naw well. I want something done aboot it right fuckin' now," snarled a male voice.

"Look sir, if you'll just be patient you will be seen. Your child is next and we are aware of your wait but it's always busy at this time in A&E. We're doing our best. If you'd just take a seat we'll . . ."

The nurse's voice was silenced, the abrasive tones of her patient cutting in.

"Listen, ya cow, I've fucking had it. Me and the bird are needing oor methadone scripts and the wee yin needs to get seen. So fuck anymore of your waitin'! You see this, ya bitch?", the male produced a syringe from his pocket, "Well, it's one I used just the day and guess whit … I'm fuckin Hep C and AIDS. Come here ya bitch, and tell me where I can get some gear.'

"We're naw going cauld turkey jist because some lazy cow cannae do her fuckin' job. Where's the fuckin' medicine chest cos you're gonnae open it for us and we're oot o' here."

Thoroughgood took stock before turning the corner. The ned would know the instant he appeared that he was CID so a bluff was not an option. If the junkie was needing his smack, or the methadone substitute supposed to wean him off it, his judgement was sure to be non-existent, the desperation of his craving dominating every thought process. Where the fuck was the security guard who should have been patrolling the casualty area?

"Typical – pay these guys peanuts and what do you expect?" muttered Thoroughgood. Rummaging through his pocket the detective found one of the empty cellophane evidence bags he always carried as a matter of course. Opposite him was the room used as a tea area by the porters, on the table was a silver bowl with fine brown sugar in it. The DS filled the transparent bag and twisted the ends into a neat knot.

'Believable score bag?' wondered Thoroughgood, turning the corner. What a mess. Half a dozen petrified civvies, including an obviously stoned female in her early twenties with a howling little girl in a pushchair in front of her.

On his right was the ned with the syringe in his hand which was wrapped around the nurse's neck. Two feet away was a doctor who looked fresh out of medical school, his face radiating fear.

"Listen son, it isn't worth all that for a score bag. Especially when I can help you out nice and easy," said Thoroughgood calmly.

The desperation in the nurse's features, a dark goddess the DS couldn't help noting, was obvious as she begged, "Help me!"

"Will you shut the fuck up you stupid slut? Now what you talking about rozzer? You get me something and she's as good as gold. Don't fuck with me or I plunge the bitch!"

"That isn't going to help the wee one is it? Look, here's a bag I took off a boy up in Royston Hill the other day. It's yours if you let the nurse go and then we get your kid seen to and everyone is happy," said the DS.

The junkie was on a knife edge. The DS could see in

43

his sunken eyes that reason was a distant memory. Supply might be what he was demanding but that was not what was going to bring an end to the situation.

A coffee table, six feet to the thug's right, and half that to Thoroughgood's left, offered some middle ground for negotiation. The DS tossed the cellophane bag onto the table. "It's your call son, there you go, just what the doctor ordered."

The junkie eyed the table for a second, opening a mouth that was missing most of its molars and barked at his vacant female. That was just the moment Thoroughgood needed.

The police issue ASP baton inside his jacket came out in one movement, clicking to its full length immediately, and the DS brought it down with an overhand motion as he closed the gap between the two.

"Shona, gonnae ..." the words died in the junkie's throat as the baton smashed into the side of his head and onto his right shoulder, the syringe dropped to the deck and the young nurse sprang free.

Down on his knees, but not out, the thug attempted to grab his blood-stained syringe and ram it into Thoroughgood's advancing legs.

Thoroughgood, whose gaze had been magnetically drawn to the nurse, caught the movement from the corner of his eye. Bringing the baton back up in a diagonal sweep to the left, as he had been taught in all those mind numbingly boring hours spent in Officer Safety Training, Thoroughgood smashed the weapon off the underside of his attacker's jaw. The junkie hit the floor cold.

"You're under arrest pal, and I'll thank you to keep your thievin' hands off my brown sugar," pronounced Thoroughgood.

He snapped the cuffs onto the ned's wrists which he had placed in the small of his back, the prone figure now inert on the floor.

Over at the reception window the young nurse shook uncontrollably.

Thoroughgood's hearing was assailed by the continued howling of the junkie's little girl who was being comforted by her mother in between mouthfuls of abuse spat at her unconscious boyfriend, but his attention remained on the nurse and he liked what he saw.

The dark hair that swept out from just under her hat had a sheen to it that immediately grabbed your attention. Yet it was the opal flecks in her eyes, sparkling like small shards of the precious stone that hit Thoroughgood right between his eyes.

He approached the nurse cautiously. "You okay? I don't s'pose you sign up for that kind of thing when you join a caring profession like nursing. Is there anything I can get you?" He asked and offered her a handkerchief, the voice in his head already chastising him for his wooden line.

"Thank you," she managed between sobs and tried to find some humour in the bleakness of the situation, "I guess it's all in a day's work."

Inadvertently Thoroughgood's right hand reached out and touched her on the shoulder in a spontaneous gesture of compassion. "Maybe, but I bet you don't get any danger money for it."

She managed a smile. "Thank you again Officer, I don't know what would have happened if you hadn't come along, do you have a name?"

Thoroughgood was slow to reply, his mind taking in

the lithe shape of her body which the navy nursing uniform thankfully failed to hide, "Sure, it's Gus. Yours?"

"Aisha," she replied and held out her hand.

Thoroughgood reached out and took it in his grip, his hand lingering for maybe a second or so too long as he realised this was the first time he had engaged with another female, spoken to another female, since Celine.

Maybe the sadness in his eyes shone out but almost immediately he withdrew his hand guiltily with an abruptness that drew a questioning look from her.

He attempted a smile to salvage the situation, then said, "Well, I better get back to my friend over there before he comes to and kicks off again. But it was nice to meet you Aisha, just a pity about the circumstances."

'Feck me!' said the voice in his head, 'What's this? Speed dating?'

Again she smiled and then, as she dabbed at her eyes with the Partick Thistle monographed hankerchief he had given her, the action prompted the nurse into speech, "Oh, what about this, detective?"

"Don't worry about it Aisha, keep it as a memento of our meeting." This time they both laughed and with a weak smile he turned and headed back over to the prone figure of the ned.

Thoroughgood sat down on one of the plastic moulded chairs and placed his feet on the junkie's back.

He shot a glance at the girlfriend and then at their frightened wee girl, cowering in the corner waiting for the inevitable. Sometimes life just wasn't fair, he thought. What chance did the little girl have? She would be with social services within a couple of hours but what about the long term damage of her silent witness to all the drug abuse of her parents?

He soon concluded it wasn't his problem. Cold-hearted it may have been but as a young cop working in the city's old 'D' Division – known to everyone in Strathclyde Police as the North – Thoroughgood had learned his lesson early about not getting personally involved in his work. Detachment was the golden rule and one he had tried – not always successfully, he admitted to himself – to keep.

A voice perforated his reflections. "Need any help, detective?" asked the security guard, who, resplendent in full stabproof vest, had just returned from his teabreak.

"Cheers mate, but I think I've taken care of this one," replied Thoroughgood, with a wink, his feet still resting on the ned's back.

Minutes later the sound of a siren preceded the arrival of the nearest area Panda, and its two uniformed cops. Thoroughgood handed over his 'body' and told them he'd stick his statement through internal, marked for London Road Police Office, for the next day.

He felt a tap on his shoulder, "All right, Gus old mate, you just can't help it, you bugger!" joked Dr Graeme Goode. "You coppers are all the same, nothing better to do with your time. Aye well, they say there are only two certainties in life; a nurse and death!"

"Coming from you, my dear Dr Meths, that is priceless," replied Thoroughgood.

The Doctor winked: "Maybe I was wrong about the two certainties Gus, cos you'll be bloody lucky to get a game off me tonight, plod!"

They shook hands and headed for the exit as Thoroughgood took stock of the Female and Child Unit officers surrounding the junkie mother and her little girl, at the same time nursing a feeling that he was also under observation.

Turning to his left he looked back over at the reception window and there behind it was Aisha. She smiled and offered him a wave goodbye and he winced inwardly as he realised he hoped that would not be the last time he saw her smile.

8

TOMACHEK SMACKED the head of his pipe down on his desk and knocked the charred remnants of the tobacco into his bin, added fresh Condor, lit up, then reclined back into his chair and took a massive inhalation before releasing the smoke into his office.

His shrewd eyes scrutinised Thoroughgood intently; the Detective Superintendent managing to hide his shock at the change in his prodigy's appearance. The hollowness of his cheeks, the sunken nature of his eyes and the flecks of grey evident in what had previously been a head of pure jet black hair.

Tomachek couldn't help his gaze sliding over to Hardie, sitting next to Thoroughgood, both on the opposite side of his imposing mahogany desk. Hardie shifted uncomfortably. This was the moment he had dreaded, the moment of truth, and the bottom line was he still didn't know which way Thoroughgood would go; the fleeting glance between Tomachek and the veteran DC confirming that they were equally uncertain of how the unfolding conversation would pan out.

Tomachek's gaze returned to Thoroughgood and at last he removed the pipe from his mouth. "How are you Gus?

How are you really, son? No bullshit, just tell it like it is."

Thoroughgood shocked both his colleagues by producing a smile that was the last thing either Hardie or Tomachek had expected.

"Actually I can hardly fuckin' walk!"

"Pardon?" Was the best Tomachek could manage.

"Best of three falls with a crazed junkie at the Western A&E, then five sets on a squash court with a sadistic doctor make for a helluva welcome back to Glasgow."

Tomachek's discomfort continued with the unexpected nature of his subordinate's conversation. Hardie cleared his throat, uncomfortably aware that he had fed the 'old man' a lot of positives about how he was confident Thoroughgood wanted to get back on the job, equally conscious that the DS was not producing the goods in that respect.

Thoroughgood, aware that his initial reply had put both his colleagues off balance continued. "What the pair of you really want to know is am I likely to be topping myself anytime soon? The answer to that one is no." He couldn't help a sardonic smile as he thought back to the previous morning and his Desert Island disc moment.

"Ok, I've been better, but I'm gonna live. But I realise now I need this job more than ever if I am going to come through this whole thing. So if you don't mind boss, I've been through the whole post mortem thing with the shrinks up at Castlebrae."

Shooting Hardie a sideways glance, he added, "And with Strathclyde police's answer to Sigmund bloody Freud. Now I just want to get back on the job, get busy and put the whole Meechan thing behind me."

Tomachek's pipe had found its way back into his

mouth and the Detective Super was chewing furiously on the mouthpiece, hanging on to Thoroughgood's every word. At last he removed it and pointed the walnut stem at the DS.

"But that is just it my dear boy, are you ready to get back into the thick of it?" Before Thoroughgood could answer his superior's question Tomachek was off and running.

"Look, I know you have had a helluva weekend back, what with the Felix Baker business and then that episode at the bloody Western yesterday. Balls and buggery Thoroughgood, the plain truth is that wherever the feck you go trouble seems to be waiting there to kick you in the goolies. By the way Hardie, you can thank your lucky stars that Felix the cat burglar has not used up his nine lives and will live to tan another day! But blow me, Thoroughgood, how much of that, after what you've been through, can a man take?"

Thoroughgood smiled and clocked a smirking Hardie sticking a digit up his left nostril, his attention wavering at the protracted nature of what he had thought would have been a rubber stamped return to action.

"Pick a winner there faither?" queried the DS and the room erupted in relieved laughter.

"Listen boss, I've had my moments, and some of the worst were yesterday morning, but the bottom line is there is no way I am going to let Meechan win. If I quit and roll up in a ball of self pity that is exactly what I will have done.

"Sure it's tough and it will continue to be tough but he's not going to finish me." As an afterthought he added, "I owe that much to Celine but most of all, I owe it to myself."

Hardie couldn't help himself and before he knew it both his hands were warming each other in a round of involuntary applause. "Well Amen to that!"

Tomachek continued to appraise Thoroughgood's features and his words with a searching look. Satisfied that the DS had indeed spoken the truth and nothing but the truth, he fished into his bottom desk drawer and pulled out a manila folder, slapping it on the desk and pushing it over to Thoroughgood.

"I believe you dear boy, I believe you. I really do, Thoroughgood. This is the proof of that particular pudding. Your first case back on the job is a Missing Person!"

Thoroughgood reached forward and lifted the folder, opening it and perusing the contents. As he did so he could hear Hardie shifting in his chair and shot him a withering look sideways, "You know anything about this, faither?"

Hardie's eyebrows arched and he managed a wholly unconvincing reply: "Maybe's aye, maybe's naw, as the man once said."

Thoroughgood read out the most important parts of the file: "An Asian doctor, works at the Western and resides at St Vincent Terrace, failed to show up for his shift Friday and was reported missing yesterday when he failed to do so again . . . riveting stuff, where do we begin?" Thoroughgood met the assessing stare of his superior officer full on.

Tomachek, though, had plenty more to say on the subject. "Listen to me Thoroughgood, this case may be a bit more sedate than you're used to but I think it would be good for you to head up an investigation where every corner you turn there is not someone trying to splinter you in a hail of lead or carve you up like my favourite Sunday roast. You get my drift dear boy?"

Taking another puff on his pipe Tomachek apparently couldn't help himself. "Balls and buggery Gus, just get back into the swing of things and see where it takes you."

Thoroughgood closed the folder, pushed his chair back and said. "Well superintendent, if that is all then, myself and faither here have a Misper' to find."

"It is, and you do, goodday gentlemen," was Tomachek's parting shot and with that the two detectives left his office, relieved to breathe clean air again.

Descending the stairs from the senior officer's corridor at Stewart Street, city centre nick, Hardie was first to perforate the silence. "Where is our first port of call then gaffer, in the search for Dr Mustapha Mohammed, his work or his hame?"

"Let's check out his flat at 406 St Vincent Terrace. I noticed uniform had visited it Saturday night and couldn't get in but the factor has since dropped off the key, just half an hour before our meeting with Tomachek. How bleedin' convenient eh?"

They pulled up at the front of the address which proved to be a block of modern build flats. While Hardie parked the vehicle Thoroughgood got out and walked from the pavement up to the front door which was clear glass with security entry and intercom. As he reached the door he half-turned to see if the old boy had finally made it out of the Mondeo – it never ceased to amaze Thoroughgood how long his 'neighbour' took to park a vehicle.

As he did so he heard the bang of a door and snapped his head back round to take in the interior foyer of 406 St

Vincent Terrace. He immediately clocked a figure standing inside the the building, apparently having come from the right-hand ground floor flat.

Although there had been no picture present in Mohammed's file, the obvious inclination was to presume that the missing person would be of Middle Eastern appearance and the male, Thoroughgood quickly registered, was exactly that.

The DS stuck the key into the front door and as he did so the figure turned abruptly and saw him. Thoroughgood turned the key and opened the door. "Wait a minute mate!"

It was all Thoroughgood needed to present his mobile and snap him with the camera. But that was as much as he got as the furtive figure immediately opened the building's rear door, clear glass too, exactly like the front entrance.

Thoroughgood upped the ante. "Stop! Police!" but his quarry had bolted through the swinging door and was already taking to his heels. Thoroughgood did likewise.

Taking in the male's rearview Thoroughgood reckoned he was about 5' 11" and wearing a green waistlength waterproof that may have been running gear, but in any case he wasn't hanging about.

The male sprinted through the residents' car park and onto the nearest street, shooting across the road and just missing a council waste truck in the process. Thoroughgood knew that there was no point in shouting any further warnings – he was going to need all his breath. If this was indeed Mustapha Mohammed then he was not for turning.

Thoroughgood had hoped to try and pace himself, aware that his legs were shot through with lactic acid courtesy of his battle on the squash court with Doctor

Meths. They burned as he broke into a sprint and he ruminated that his general lack of conditioning was also going to count against him. A fit man all his adult life, he was disgusted at how quickly he was going into oxygen debt. With Mohammed obscured from his sight by the waste truck, he charged across the road to get round the front of it and make sure that he didn't completely lose his quarry.

Thoroughgood had never given up on a foot chase and this was not going to be the first time. But he needed Hardie's help.

The DS put the radio to his lips: "Hardie, get back in the car and get round to Charing Cross at Sauchiehall Street. Suspect is 5' 11" wearing green waistlength waterproof and of dark appearance, with denims. Looks like he has a beard and I'm bettin' he's Mohammed."

Taking in another gulp of air as he tried to keep Mohammed's green jacket in view, Thoroughgood added. "Am in foot pursuit and trying to push him up towards Sauchiehall Street. Alert all local units."

"Roger that," responded Hardie.

The pursuit continued up into Granville Street with the male turning right into Berkeley Street, Thoroughgood desperately trying to keep his target in sight and cursing the fact that, resplendent in black Loake brogues and a charcoal Felini suit, he was at a further disadvantage in pursuit of a suspect in trainers and running gear.

Turning into Berkeley Street Thoroughgood was aware that he had lost sight of his man and slowed to a walk on a pavement lined by grimy tenement buildings, their stained walls testament to the pollution problem in Glasgow's city centre.

He gulped in oxygen as he took in the street scene;

minimum traffic, precious little pedestrian movement and then the looming majestic form of the Mitchell Library towering at the end of the street and dominating all that it looked down on, like some everlasting memorial to the age of the Empire. He reached for his radio, his mind trying to formulate a new set of instructions for Hardie who was reacting to everything blind.

The impact was sudden and brutal. Green jacket smashed into him from the nearest tenement close. Thoroughgood was cannoned into a parked Citroen and immediately became aware that his assailant, dark haired and with a beard in the early stages of growth, was also carrying cold steel.

Thoroughgood's back was jammed against the car's nearside door but although he was winded he managed to grab the wrist of his assailant who was trying to skewer him with a blade of curved appearance which he held southpaw-style, slowly closing in on the left side of the DS's jaw.

Their faces only inches apart, Thoroughgood could not help but notice the blemish in the male's left eye which added to his sinister appearance. Then Green Jacket hissed something at him in what he took to be Arabic; while the meaning was lost on the DS the hatred that seethed through the words was obvious.

Although he had the advantage of size and strength over the slightly smaller man, the surprise of the attack combined with the impact of his body on the parked vehicle had hit Thoroughgood hard. They slithered along the side of the Citroen with the cop now sprawled over the bonnet. His attacker continued to put all his power into trying to spear the DS with the vicious-looking blade. The chosen point of impact was now Thoroughgood's right eye, through which the DS noticed at desperately close range that the dagger was crowned with an ornate jewelled handle, possibly made from ivory.

His assailant's determination was manic and his good eye radiated homicidal intent. Thoroughgood smashed his right knee with all the power he could muster into the male's groin and he staggered back against the wall of the tenement.

'Shit,' thought Thoroughgood as he saw that Blackbeard had not released his grip on the blade which, even in his agony, he held out in front of him.

Then Green Jacket hissed, "Allahu Akbar!" The poisonous venom in these two words shocked Thoroughgood but only momentarily, for the man the DS believed to be Doctor Mustafa Mohammed immediately launched himself at Thoroughgood again. This time the cop was ready for him.

As Mohammed charged forward with his blade glinting menacingly, now in his left mitt, Thoroughgood moved to his left and put all his power into an upper cut that smashed off his attacker's jaw.

Thoroughgood was right-handed and the impact of the punch coming from his weaker hand was not as significant as it would have been had it come from his strong side, but there was no way he could risk a orthodox shot, and having to take a chance going across Mohammed's knife-holding left hand would have left him all too vulnerable to a lethal injection of cold steel.

Mohammed once again recoiled, changing the grip on the blade as he did so, moving his fingers from handle to steel in a manoeuvre that suggested to Thoroughgood that he had done it before. He realised Mohammed was going to launch the weapon at him and the DS dived behind the rear of the Citroen.

Almost simultaneously the smash of the blade breaking the glass of the vehicle's tail light sounded out. Trying to pick himself up from the tarmac Thoroughgood could already hear the sound of fast-fading footsteps. As he regained his balance Green Jacket was once more off and running.

"Fuck me, of all the bastards in the world why do I have to end up chasing Forrest bloody Gump," groaned Thoroughgood out loud.

Before he began to break into a run once more he quickly scooped up the curved dagger and part-pocketed it as best he could inside his jacket.

The pursuit continued towards the Mitchell Library and the male again cast a nervous glance backwards at Thoroughgood, but with the gap at fifty yards and increasing, he reached the side of the famous Glasgow landmark with plenty of leeway.

Thoroughgood knew he needed to put an extra effort in or he would lose Mohammed before he had reached Charing Cross.

The sound of a siren gave him a renewed burst of energy, meaning as it did that Hardie had followed instructions and must be coming up towards the front of the Mitchell Library.

Thoroughgood surged on. Pedestrian traffic was also against him, increasing the closer he got to the city's main library.

As Mohammed cast another concerned glance back towards Thoroughgood he smashed into an elderly female pushing a bag trolley with one hand and holding a walking stick with the other.

They both crashed to the ground on impact, with Mohammed somersaulting over the shopping trolley, a favourite of the city's elderly ladies. Thoroughgood was now twenty five yards away from his quarry and he could see that Mohammed was badly winded but attempting to get to his feet again while the elderly female lay inert on the ground.

Green Jacket began to pick up momentum again, evidently not having suffered any real damage but he had dropped a leatherbound wallet or filofax, and as he took to his heels once more he momentarily hesitated. His decision though, was an easy one. Risk his own freedom for the filofax or cut his losses and resume his escape bid. He chose the latter.

Thoroughgood too was impaled on the horns of a dilemma. Continue his pursuit and leave the elderly female prostrate on the pavement or put her welfare first. Eyeing the leather wallet as he arrived at her still form, he chose the latter. With one last glance he took in the receding figure of the male he believed had been Doctor Mustafa Mohammed and turned his attention to the prone and distraught OAP.

Almost immediately Thoroughgood saw the looming portly shape of Hardie arriving as he reassured the badly shaken pensioner that everything was going to be okay and that she'd just been unlucky. One raise of his eyebrows ensured that Hardie's radio was already in action requesting an ambulance.

9

BY THE time the elderly female had been taken away via ambulance Hardie had put his governor in the picture.

"All mobiles and beat officers look-out posted but it would appear our man has gone to ground. I must have just missed him cutting round the front of the Mitchell. Bastard must have been fast on his feet though, not like you to lose a suspect, still I guess you aren't as young as you used to be. Resemble a scene from Chariots of Fire did it, mate?" Hardie sniggered with delight, taking particular satisfaction in putting the metaphorical boot in about his mate's age, given he himself was a standing joke in Thoroughgood's book regarding his own less than streamlined appearance and woeful fitness levels.

This conversation had taken the time it took to return to the hastily parked Mondeo and Thoroughgood shot Hardie a withering glare.

"Listen Michael bloody Johnston, you don't know the half of it." Thoroughgood then fished out the ornate ivory-handled, jewel-encrusted dagger and showed it to his mate. "Maybe I didn't get the man but that may take us somewhere. Plus, I was bleedin' lucky it didn't book me a berth in the city mortuary. That bastard was desperate enough to stick me with it."

A look of brief contrition enveloped Hardie's craggy features. "Shite! I had no idea. I take it you and the good doctor had a bit of a tango then?"

"Aye you could say that and then some. A nasty piece of work with a bad case of garlic-induced halitosis and a squint in his left eye. It's a wonder the Pavilion hav'nae signed him up for panto! But all we need is a photo from the Western personnel records to confirm him as our Doctor Mustafa Mohammed and there isn't going to be much chance of a case of mistaken identity there!"

The two detectives were now outside 406 St Vincent Terrace. It was then that Thoroughgood revealed the second product of his foot pursuit, pulling out the filofax and holding it up for Hardie to see.

The DC was obviously surprised. "Well, our friend has been a bit careless hasn't he? Wonder what this will reveal?"

Thoroughgood nodded in agreement.

"All will be revealed inside the flat, come on, it's time we went over this place with a fine tooth comb. If the elusive Doctor Mustafa Mohammed has a tendency to be careless with his belongings you never know what else we may turn up."

Immediately upon entry to the the one bedroom flat Thoroughgood plonked himself down on the cheap cream leather settee in the living room, filofax in hand.

"So, I wonder what we have here?" he asked Hardie who hovered over his colleague with avid interest.

"Go on then! Open the thing and put me out of my misery," said the DC, his impatience obvious.

Thoroughgood smiled up at his mate and began to leaf through the brown leatherbound wallet. Slowly a look of realisation dawned on his face.

"Well feck me! Looks like we have stumbled onto something here, faither! Under virtually every letter of the alphabet we have a row of asterisks on an otherwise empty page in a filofax that has the name Dr Mustafa Mohammed, Western Hospital, Accident and Emergency Department written in block capitals on the inside cover."

Thoroughgood fingered the pages in growing anticipation, having to force himself to slow down so he didn't miss anything of evidential importance.

"Under 'A' it's one row, under 'B' it's two rows," Thoroughgood continued through the indexed pages: "Yep, there are more on the page headed 'G' and a double set under 'S' and 'T' as well." Thoroughgood handed the filofax to Hardie whose outstretched paw underlined his desperation to cast eyes on the booklet for himself.

"Bloody hell! This is enough to leave you seeing stars all right. So what are they trying to hide? It's obviously a list of targets but what kind of bleedin' targets?" Hardie screwed his eyes up and continued to finger the booklet, "Aye, there are more under 'M'. What do you suppose we are talkin' here Gussy boy?"

The DS shook his head and held out his hand for the return of the filofax.

"Why don't you give me five minutes with this while you look through the rest of the place? I'm betting there must be something else of interest here," and, with a smile creeping across his pale features, Thoroughgood added,

"While you're at it, check the fridge for milk. I could murder a coffee after my attempt at breaking the sub-four-minute-mile in a pair of brogues; they should make it an Olympic sport."

Hardie faked indignation. "Aye, fair enough, wouldnae mind a brew myself. A bit of caffeine always sharpens up the senses. But we need to get onto Tomachek, this is no bog standard MisPer' enquiry that's for sure. You up to that, gaffer?" mocked Hardie as he raised his right eyebrow in homage, he thought, to his hero, Spaghetti Western star Lee Van Cleef.

Thoroughgood talked out loud to no one in particular as he leafed through the pages of the filofax. "Nope I'd say this has something of a terrorist flavour to it and the one thing you can bank on is that our friend Mustafa ain't working alone. These fuckers always set up shop as a cell and you can bet your bottom dollar that he's foot soldier and not commander. I'd say, dear faither, that there is a strong chance the shit is going to be hitting the fan big time somewhere soon, and probably somewhere bloody well on our doorstep."

Hardie re-emerged from the kitchen. "Kettle's on but all I could find by way of milk was that soya crap. Still, better than straight black; three sugars should soften the blow," announced Hardie, apparently oblivious to his superior's concerns.

"Feck me, faither! Never mind the bleedin' coffee! Did you hear one word of what I just said?"

Hardie's baggy features immediately straightened out and he nodded his head in admission that he knew exactly what the implications could be for Glasgow or any other of Scotland's major cities.

Thoroughgood continued. "It's hard not to to let your imagination run away with you on this one. But," Thoroughgood pulled out the ivory-handled dagger that Mohammed had tried to impale him with, "what do you make of this nasty piece of work?" and he handed his mate the blade.

Hardie's attention had been caught by something on the handle.

"What have we here? Some kind of inscription, written in Arabic I presume. We will need to get that translated, methinks. Anyway, I'll crack on and see what else I can turn up and leave you to the filofax," said Hardie, placing his mug down on the cheap coffee table next to the settee.

Taking a sip from his own mug Thoroughgood winced. "Bloody hell, how can it be that we put a man on the moon forty years back yet we still can't get a decent substitute for milk? And this stuff is supposed to be good for you. Aye, like a hole in the heid," then added as an afterthought, "By the way, I've already requested that the Western emails a jpeg of Mohammed across to Tomachek's office."

Hardie shook his head as the implication of what they had just turned up apparently sank home. "It makes you wonder though Gussy boy."

Thoroughgood's features creased in agreement. "Listen, I don't want to be jumpin' the metaphorical fuckin' gun but the ramifications are obvious. This could be the type of terrorist activity that'll make 7/7 London seem like an amateur night out.

"Better crack on here mate and get back to Tomachek ASAP. Wait till the old man hears what his boring little missing person enquiry has turned up. We better get an ambulance booked for him because he'll be a coronary waiting to happen!"

Hardie smiled but his mate's humour was, they both knew, a poor attempt to introduce some levity into a situation that had catastrophic potential.

10

THEY ENTERED Tomachek's office at 12.30 pm on the nose, armed with several interesting pieces of evidence taken from Dr Mustafa Mohammed's flat. Thoroughgood had phoned ahead to prepare his superior for their arrival.

The impact of the tobacco smoke from the Old Man's permanently smouldering pipe always surprised Thoroughgood, almost as much as the fact that Tomachek somehow continued to get away with his blatant flouting of Force Health and Safety procedures.

His treasured walnut pipe wedged in his mouth, Tomachek indicated for Thoroughgood and Hardie to resume position in the two seats they had vacated just over 90 minutes previously.

The superintendent pulled a watch from the waistcoat pocket of his customary three piece tweed ensemble and clicked it open. Hardie shot Thoroughgood a warning glance and the two detectives prepared for the hairdryer.

"Balls and buggery, Thoroughgood! Just how the feck do you do it? I put you on some bog standard Missing Person enquiry and all of a sudden it's turned into a terrorist Arma-bloody-geddon scenario!" Tomachek slammed his right fist onto his desk and a pile of papers in his in-tray shot into the air.

The Detective Super removed his pipe and jabbed the mouth piece at Thoroughgood. "Well, get on with it man!"

Thoroughgood took a deep breath and began his report. "You know the details of my foot pursuit and the attempt the man we believe is Mustafa Mohammed made on my life."

Thoroughgood then produced the ivory-handled blade and pushed it across the desk to Tomachek, the jewels encrusted in the ivory glinting, as if to underline his point.

The superintendent examined the blade. "Dear sweet Jesus H Christ! Just how can it be that you manage to turn a bally doctor into some kind of terrorist, knife-wielding maniac, right in the middle of the city?" He stopped in mid flow and had a look at the writing on the handle. "What have we here? I hope you're going to have this inscription translated the minute you leave this office?"

Thoroughgood nodded. Tomachek's right hand shot out and he waved it at Thoroughgood through the fog of pipe smoke, signalling the DS to restart. Thoroughgood complied in relief.

"The filofax is rammed with sets of asterisks which are obviously a cover for potential terrorist targets although of course we don't have a Scooby Doo what types of targets, given they have used the asterisk code. That means not only do we not know the nature of the targets but geo-graphically speakin' we are talking needle in a hay stack."

Producing the leather wallet Thoroughgood leafed through the pages showing the concise lines of asterisks. "I've been thinking about it on the way over," the noise of a throat being cleared in the background interrupted Thoroughgood." Sorry, we've been thinking about it on the way over and I wonder could that mean we are talking

67

shopping centres? They would be premium targets for Mohammed and his mates and given we don't know what order they would be prioritised, or for that matter are able to confirm it is indeed a list of shopping centres, in terms of an attack it's going to make it almost impossible to police them pre-emptively speaking. Otherwise, why the need for secrecy?"

Thoroughgood continued. "What was also interesting was the number of credit cards that Hardie uncovered in the flat. Mohammed has five major cards and has borrowed up to five grand on nearly every one. In fact his platinum Barclaycard is at its limit of ten grand.

"The obvious question is why does he need that kind of finance or who is he procuring the cash for, and obviously what for?"

Hardie couldn't help himself from interjecting. "In any case gaffer, it stinks to high heaven but that was not all we found."

This time it was Hardie's turn to produce evidence and shove it across the table at the superintendent.

Tomachek steepled his hands and stared down at the offering, at first refusing to dirty his mitts with the documents. But the look of disgust on his craggy features was perfectly articulate.

"Passports? Forged, eh? What's this? More Arabic literature? That is a picture of the Twin Towers if I am not mistaken!"

Tomachek was forced to remove his pipe from its usually permanent location at the right side of his mouth.

"Dear Mother Mary! I don't believe it, this takes the bloody biscuit!" and he quickly grabbed one of the leaflets for closer scrutiny, clearly astounded by the evidence of his own eyes.

"A leaflet called 'How to make the perfect bomb'?" Tomachek grabbed at another of the leaflets. "Blow me bloody senseless! This one's called 'What to expect in Jihad'!"

Thoroughgood nodded in agreement. "Yup. We'll get the inscription on the dagger translated but you don't have to be Albert bloody Einstein to figure out that it's the language of hate or the call to Jihad. It's there in black and white in front of you gaffer, and we found it in a Glasgow flat."

Thoroughgood stroked his chin as silence descended on the room; the fading smoke from Tomachek's pipe almost supplying an ethereal quality such was the feeling of doom that settled on the detectives; a doom pulsing with a sense of foreboding that radiated through their beings.

But there was more to come and Thoroughgood knew that the best form of delivery, just like that of a death message, was brutal and sudden. He ploughed on regardless.

"We have also taken possession of a computer with a couple of interesting emails, apparently all in code. Here is the one that is the standout though," Thoroughgood shoved a piece of printed paper towards Tomachek.

The superintendent read it aloud. "'Hi buddy, I am sure my email will find you in good health and that all your family members are enjoying themselves. My affair with Vena is now turning into family life. I have met with her family and both parties have agreed to conduct the Nikah.'" Tomachek stopped and added approvingly, "Which I see you have had translated as wedding, 'after the 15th and before the 20th of this month.'" Tomachek continued to read. "'I have confirmed the dates with them and they said you should be ready between these dates. I hope you can be here to enjoy the party.'"

Tomachek paused for a minute and pushed a hand through the remnants of his receding grey hair. "In the name of the wee man, this just goes from bad to worse. 'You should be ready between these dates? I hope you can be here to enjoy the party?' The bottom line is, as I am sure you know, that there is some kind of terrorist atrocity coming straight at us."

Tomachek turned round and pulled his Strathclyde Police calendar from the wall and slapped it on the desk in front of Thoroughgood and Hardie.

"This is Monday 8th November, as I am sure you are well aware. That means that on any day from next Monday onwards, until or before Saturday week, we are at risk of something very nasty. Something that our dear friend Dr Mustafa Mohammed and his colleagues, because let's face it there will be more than one of them, have cooked up for us." Tomachek stuck his pipe back in his mouth, leaned back in his swivel chair and let out a long slow whistle.

Thoroughgood interjected into the silence: "Boss, I have to say I think we should be alerting MI5 and the regional terrorist centre. This is way too big for Strathclyde Police to cope with."

"You think I don't know that dear boy? The minute you leave my office I will get on the blower to Five's OIC, Sir Willie Stratford. Hopefully we can get things moving quickly with them. Because by the rood; if we don't, carnage is going to ensue somewhere in Scotland or anywhere else in the rest of the UK, for that matter.

"Right now though, you two have work to do. I want all the evidence you removed from Mohammed's flat. Make sure the building is fine-combed by forensics, and it

70

looks like you need some translation work done. I'd like to know what the Arabic on that bloody kebab skewer says. It looks like it could have some sort of ceremonial importance and you never know, there could be a lead in that line of enquiry.

"There is something else, however, you need to be aware of," said Tomachek and slowly he slid a photo image across the desk to the two detectives. "Recognise this bugger?"

Thoroughgood looked at the photo and then glanced quizzically at Hardie but his features were blank. "Let me guess gaffer; that is the Western Hospital personnel pic of Dr Mustafa Mohammed?"

"Correct."

Thoroughgood cleared his throat nervously. "Want the bad news or the good, boss?" he asked.

"Just spit it out Thoroughgood, would you?" snapped the detective superintendent.

"The male I pursued from St Vincent Terrace had a nasty squint in his left eye and a black beard in the making. There is not the slightest resemblance between him and the good doctor here."

With that Thoroughgood fished out his mobile with the picture he'd snapped of Green Jacket displayed on the screen.

Tomachek picked it up and with contempt spreading across his face, said; "Nasty bastard. That eye makes him look like one real evil amigo. Aye, you did well not to get spitted by that blade of his. Have you done anything about this visual?"

Thoroughgood nodded. "Yep. A jpeg has been fired through to Interpol, and the Regional Terrorist Centre, so

71

MI5 and six will be alerted and hopefully there will be an Ident available to us ASAP."

"Good man," mumbled Tomachek and then lowered his head into his left hand and began to rub furiously at his temple with two fingers before removing the pipe from his mouth with his free hand.

Thoroughgood and Hardie readied themselves for the incoming broadside.

"Listen to me Thoroughgood, and you too Hardie, this is quite obviously a bally bloody timebomb — no pun intended — we're sitting on. We may only have days to save the lives of thousands. We are going to need all the help we can get from Five and the anti-terror boys but I want you shaking down your informants and pulling out every stop.

"One of the first questions I need an answer to is just who the knife-wielding maniac was, and where and what has become of Doctor Mustafa Mohammed? Amongst others, it must be said."

Drawing himself up in his chair as he recovered some composure Tomachek continued. "Time is indeed of the essence gentlemen. |Now get to work. I will be in touch and you should do likewise if anything tasty comes your way."

Thoroughgood and Hardie sat in the CID Mondeo in the back yard of Stewart Street nick, in momentary silence. Hardie was first to speak.

"Listen Gus, I know it's a long shot but I'm wondering if the man we should be talking to is our little Indian waiter friend. By the time we wade through all the stuff from Mohammed's flat and start putting the word out on the street we aren't gonnae be that far short of calling time for today. What are you thinking mate?"

Thoroughgood rubbed his fingers over his chin. "Yeah, let's face it, the Muslim community in Glasgow can't be that big. I think the old man may be onto something with that dagger. He could be right, it looks like it may have some sort of ceremonial significance; that has got to link it to religion, which is what this is all about, bottom line. That probably means it has come from a mosque.

"I just think this is all too much of a coincidence. That, and Sushi's desperation to talk to us means it ain't likely to be a case of 'fail to pay' at India's. That makes meeting up with the wee man tomorrow's priority I'd say."

"Absolutement, mon gaffeur," agreed Hardie.

<u>11</u>

0900HRS. HE stared in the mirror and finished trimming his beard. It was neat and tidy just like everything else about his appearance.

He stared at his reflection; the brown eyes his patients had told him were so full of kindness and so appropriate for a doctor. A frown spread across his forehead as he considered all the pain and suffering he had eased over recent months, all the people he had cared for, the joy he had gained from a profession he believed he had been born to enter.

It never ceased to amaze him how readily he had been accepted into his new community. But then it was the same for a physician in any society, people always elevated you, knowing that in many cases the healer possessed the power of life and death over his patient.

He supposed that being a member of a caring profession had played a large part in his acceptance and in truth he enjoyed the status and the respect that came with being a doctor. Once people knew you practised medicine and were there to help them it was amazing how they were prepared to trust you with that almost mythical power of life and death.

Their secrets poured out as if you were a trusted member of their family. His patients had wanted to please him, with some even showering gifts upon him. From the bottles of whisky which seemed to be the ultimate indication of gratitude in Scotland, to offers of clothing and even sexual gratification from some of the female patients who had found his smouldering yet soulful brown eyes hypnotic.

He replaced his spectacles. In truth he had no need of the glasses but they helped to make him seem that bit more studious, perhaps even vulnerable. Today he needed to appear the victim, not the victor.

Breakfast was something he was looking forward to that morning with particular relish.

He would wash the nashta down with kahwah; he welcomed the first drop as he scraped the roof of his mouth with his tongue and realised that nervousness had left it dry as the desert.

He took a bite from the khatchapuri and savoured its familiar charms as he waited for his omelette to cook. If this was to be his last breakfast before he entered paradise then he would make sure he left this world with a full belly. After finishing his food and washing it down with the last of the green tea he took an apple from the bowl and placed it in the pocket of his gown.

The satisfaction at having a full belly with which to go about Allah's work saw more memories of his stay in Glasgow flood back. Yet his chosen path beckoned. The path to paradise.

This was Allah's work and it had to be done.

Washed and cleansed, he walked back into the bedroom and dressed in simple shalwar kameez and placed his taqiya on his head. The only prayers from him today had been those said in private at dawn. But he would not answer the muezzin's call this Friday afternoon at the mosque. Instead he hoped prayers would be said for him by those who mattered. The true believers; the devout followers of the Imam who knew that what he did, he did for Allah.

Hassan Ressan took a glance at the chest of drawers in front of him and his eyes swept over the name badge belonging to Dr Mustafa Mohammed, S.H.O. A&E, Glasgow Western Infirmary. The man he had been for the past 18 months. Strange how he had begun to take pleasure in a life built on a tissue of lies; enjoyed the conventions that had come with his revered position in Western society. In truth he'd lived a double life but now at last he would find eternal truth. The deception would be over.

He had been careless leaving documents, and of course the filofax, at the other address but really, what did it matter? Here, ten storeys up in the Red Road flats, he was part of a burgeoning asylum community, anonymous and irrelevant: the two most important qualities for a man about to execute an act of Jihad.

1530hrs. Hassan wandered through the automatic doorway, his manner humble and non-threatening. He kept his eyes downcast in a manner that would ensure anyone taking the time to look at him would feel sorry for him rather than view him as a threat.

His day had been spent rehearsing his route to the shopping centre and exactly what he would do when he got there. All doubt, all guilt had been gradually erased from his mind. He was fully focused just like the brothers of the 9/11 attack must have been.

The voice in his head spoke. 'What is that phrase they use? In the zone. That is it! And now I am in the zone, the killing zone. And death is my companion.' Hassan allowed himself a smile at the realisation of the impact his work would surely have.

His mind flashed back to the training camp on the northwest frontier of Pakistan where he had been taught the techniques of the Jihadist. An impressionable teenager, meeting with the freedom fighters and teachers of al-Quaeda who had changed his whole way of looking at the world.

When one of the veterans of Afghanistan, Naif, or White Eye as he was known, had come to Glasgow and attended mosque Hassan had been captivated by his stories of the fight to the death being waged against the evil West. His growing awareness that there was far more to life than books and studies had hardened into a conviction.

It was at that point Hassan Ressan had been targeted by al-Quaeda, who had become aware of his brilliance as a medical student with a particular flare for chemistry, and one whose own perspective was becoming increasingly compliant with their own.

All that mattered were the words of the prophet and the Holy War against the infidel and now he was going to play his own part in taking that war onto Crusader shores. Yet he had enjoyed his four years in Glasgow. Perhaps, if he was completely honest with himself, he had secretly hoped that the day his training would be required would never dawn.

Today was that day.

He had been well trained; his teacher was the best, and he was a very good student. He knew how to assess a target in order to calculate the exact quantities of hexogen, a volatile explosive that would be required to be added to the equally unstable nytroglycerin to produce the desired carnage.

He remembered the words of his teachers as they explained the part oxidizers, desensitizers, plasticizers and freezing-point depressants had to play. Now Hassan believed himself to be every bit as skillful a bomb maker as those teachers four years back, and he had been very busy.

He placed his hand under his kameez and felt for the reassurance of the belt he had strapped around his middle which carried his deadly cargo, and he tasted the salt from a bead of sweat as it dropped onto his lip and entered his mouth.

'Nerves. Always a good thing. My senses are heightened as they should be, Allah be praised!' said the voice in his head.

Yet still the troubling images persisted. The kindness he had been shown by the family of the teenage female stab victim he had saved in A&E just ten days back; the warmth of the staff and the closeness that had evolved between them during his months in his post.

Another image seeped into his consciousness; the face of the nurse he knew that in another life he would have loved with all his heart. The voice in his head said her name over and over 'Aisha, Aisha.' With all the might of his willpower he quietened the voice and the seed of doubt that was beginning to gnaw through him.

What happened here today would send a message and

set the tone for what was to come. Mentally he weighed up the cost of his actions and the carnage that would ensue from them and the other Improvised Explosive Devices he had already placed in key locations in the centre. But now was the time for payback for the thousands that had died in Afghanistan and Iraq since the infidels had invaded. Countless innocents slaughtered for what?

The Imam had been right; it was time for the Crusaders to feel the pain and fear of Jihad within their own borders, in the heart of their cities, in the souls of their very beings. It was his role to make that happen.

He walked on, for he knew exactly where the detonation point lay. The position at which he must stop and slip his hand under his kameez and press the button that would set off the lethally positioned IEDs which would cause carnage and chaos in equal measures throughout Braehead shopping centre. Then he would pull the rip chord to send him and everyone else within a 100 yard radius to oblivion.

The prospect of carnage was at its maximum today for it was, as Allah had surely ordained, the opening day of the Davis Cup Tie; being played in the same building as the shopping centre, within the sports arena. The location he sought was the seat he had purchased only five rows back from the court which would, in 30 minutes be graced by one of Great Britain's most famous sportsmen: Murray Fury.

There, concealed in the crowds of people desperate to gain entry for the opening singles match featuring Scotland's finest sporting son, he would be completely anonymous. With the event unpoliced and only guarded by stewards, his entry to courtside would be simple and his admission to eternity guaranteed.

Gaining entry to the courtside and detonating himself within feet of Fury and in full view of the TV cameras beaming the tie against Belarus around Europe would guarantee that this was a moment of supreme triumph. A triumph that would send a shockwave around the globe, thanks to the death of one of the most famous UK sportsmen and Britain's finest tennis player.

As he arrived on the top floor and began his walk towards the arena doors he was aware that his senses were indeed heightened. Everything seemed to be viewed in high definition.

The scar running down the side of the track-suited male's face grabbed Hassan's attention as he passed by. His lingering look suggested that if their encounter had been away from the safety of the congested confines of Glasgow's busiest shopping mall Hassan would have indeed been the victim he wished to be perceived as. But the man moved on with no more than an evil leer at the downtrodden Asian male who looked hopelessly out with his comfort zone in the bustling shopping centre.

A young woman pushed a double buggy towards him, apparently determined to make sure that he moved out the way or was run down by her self-propelled juggernaut. Aware that there was some instability in the cargo he carried and warned by the female's harsh Glaswegian voice: "Get oota the fuckin' way will ye? Ya half-wit!" Hassan sidestepped the child-bearing express train with a dexterity that belied his appearance.

Now the fast food centres situated just outside the arena entrance came within his view. Pizza Hut opposite and McDonald's to his right and the sight of families enjoying lunch in a happy and safe environment sent a shiver of uncertainty, or was it guilt, through Hassan Ressan's soul. But it was a fleeting moment, for it was immediately replaced by images of the charred bodies of the Pakistani family. Victims of a US drone strike he had witnessed, murdered and butchered at a family wedding on a day that should have been filled with the greatest of family joys. He kept walking.

Now the yellow-vested stewards were just thirty yards away checking tickets. Hassan looked at the female steward who was about to ask for his ticket. Red-faced with dyed blonde hair and stinking of a heavy scent that was almost as cheap and tacky as the rouge on her cheeks.

"Ticket please, sir?" she asked and he duly passed his ticket to her, taking care to keep his eyes averted and offering a courteous "Thank you," into the bargain.

Then he was through and the doors to the courtside were just twenty yards on his left. He took a deep breath and walked on, silently reciting the Shahada over and over again: "Allah is the one true god." And he was about to meet him.

He looked at the gold watch on his left wrist, the one mark of ostentation he had allowed himself. Hassan had an obsession with time and today it was ticking fast. He saw that it was 15.45: Fury would be on court in less than fifteen minutes. He allowed himself a small smile of anticipation, knowing that all the training he had received, all the hours of self sacrifice and the time spent concealed within Western society had all been for this moment of maximum impact.

He had drawn level with the toilets when to his surprise he heard a voice in his right ear.

"Awright Gupta! Into the fuckin' toilets and get the fuckin' Rolex off pronto mate!" He turned and saw the track suit, recognised the cruel scar running down the face of the male he had passed in the shopping centre moments earlier.

He felt a fist smash into his side and knock him sideways, the impact of his body propelling him through the door as it gave way. In the background another voice shouted.

"Hey, what do you think you're doing?"

But none of that mattered anymore, for Hassan knew that his moment had come, perhaps prematurely, but he trusted in the skill with which he had crafted the explosive belt. He fingered the button then ripped the chord free.

As the device exploded he saw the look of fear and the light of the bomb blast envelope his attacker's face. Hassan uttered his last word: "Kafir . . . "

12

THE AFTERMATH of the explosion at Braehead and the carnage it caused had left everyone at City Centre office in a state of utter shock.

Thoroughgood thought back to 9/11. Sitting in the same police station with the radio blaring inanely in the background, until the implications of the information it relayed finally dripped into his subconscious.

He remembered the mad rush to get in front of a computer or a TV set to confirm that moment of awesome terror. Now here they were all over again. The scramble for phones and bickering that had broken out as everyone sought to contact their loved ones around Glasgow brought this horrific reality thudding home.

A moment of irony swept over Thoroughgood mixed, he supposed, with self pity. 'No need for you to worry Gus, no one there for you to care about, no one for you to miss, no one to miss you, why didn't you pull the trigger? Shitebag.'

Thoroughgood realised someone was missing. Where the hell was Hardie? The realisation dawned that Hardie had kids, and more importantly, a missus whom Hardie constantly moaned was a shopaholic who probably had shares in Braehead.

He tried calling his mate's mobile, got the engaged tone then made for Tomachek's office. He knew there was a television there where he would at least be able to watch the rolling Sky News.

He approached the door and heard a familiar voice coming from within. It was Hardie's and he was clearly agitated.

"Listen Davie lad, where the fuck is your mother?" then a pause: "Gone shoppin', aye son that's a big help, but where has she gone shoppin'? Haven't you heard about what's just happened at Braehead fifteen minutes ago son?"

Thoroughgood opened the door and saw his mate sitting in Tomachek's swivel chair. Even from the other side of the room he could see the beads of sweat on Hardie's brow.

"Listen to me you little bugger! I can't get her, her mobile is just going to answer machine. Now one last time, could she be at Braehead?" demanded Hardie, now on his feet.

Within five minutes they were in the Mondeo and on the motorway out of Glasgow, heading for Braehead, foot to the floor with flashing blue light in full luminous glow on the grill helping to clear their way. Hardie and Thoroughgood were not the only people in a hurry to make it to the shopping centre. Sirens pierced the air and billowing smoke from the devastated shopping centre filled them with dread.

There was no way they were getting within a mile of the ruined shopping mall and they abandoned the car on a grass verge just off the slip road to the centre. Hardie had said nothing for over five minutes. Thoroughgood could see the tears engulfing his jaded brown eyes.

The moment the car came to a stop Hardie was out and off at a pace Thoroughgood had not seen for years. As they reached the main approaches the crowds of people became deep and anger and despair filled the air.

Warrant cards already in hand, they hit the outer cordon that had already been formed around the mall and barely slowed down as they offered a quick identification and continued to the entrance. The acrid smell of smoke was now beginning to mix with the sickly stench that they both knew emanated from the remains of charred human bodies. Hardie's breath was coming in huge rasps and he was yanking at his tie in an effort to let more air into his heaving chest.Now they could see the first of the corpses being brought out on stretchers covered head to toe. Beyond the escalator that would take them up to the arena there were huge girders dangling down and wiring hanging loose.

They were about to hit the escalator when a uniform Police Inspector stepped forward and barred their way. Hardie was having none of it. "Listen Inspector, my wife is up there and neither you or anyone fuckin' else is going to stop me looking for her." For a moment the inspector hesitated but seeing the manic look in the DC's eyes he stepped aside.

Hardie took the escalator steps two at a time and reached the top, his body shaking with exhaustion.

Thoroughgood could hear his mate talking to himself.

"Come on Betty, come on Betty girl you're gonna be okay, I'm gonna find you, everything is gonna be ok."

Thoroughgood realised that he had never heard his mate call his wife by her Christian name before.

They could see a Pizza Hut sign hanging drunkenly

in the distance. Incongruously Thoroughgood observed an outsized tennis ball, obviously brought for Fury's post match autograph session, sitting on top of a chair; a kid's dream of meetingtheir hero ruined. Anger seared Thoroughgood's soul. All that could be heard were groans and screams and shouted orders from the emergency services.

Thoroughgood spotted a senior medic and made his way over to him at the double. "Listen mate, Detective Sergeant Gus Thoroughgood. I know all hell has just broken loose but we are looking for a Betty Hardie, where are you are taking the injured?"

The medic gave a curt reply: "They're all in the ice rink."

Thoroughgood turned to his mate: "Come on."

As they made their way to the ice rink they noticed that the stretchers being taken in were all carrying body-bagged corpses. At last Hardie spoke.

"Lockerbie must have been a picnic compared to this."

They pushed through the doors, dodging medics rushing out. At last, straight ahead they saw a group swathed in blankets, bandaging and tin foil sheets. The screams of the victims who were still alive were all pervading.

The two detectives arrived at the injured zone and immediately identified themselves to the medics, aware that they might be about to confront Hardie's worst nightmare.

The DC's eyes were darting around every human form with any movement coming from it. He searched desperately for his wife's straw-coloured hair, his despairing face awash with emotions that Thoroughgood recognised from his own torment. Then Hardie was off again, making his way from one injured person to another, until he had made his way through all of the survivors.

86

Thoroughgood remained with the medics, his glance turning to the rows of body bags over to his right. He saw Hardie begin to make his way back to him, in resignation and acceptance that any hope of seeing his wife in this life again was indeed over.

Thoroughgood could see his mate's shoulders shaking uncontrollably and he began to move forward to offer Hardie a shred of comfort that he knew from agonised experience was an act of total futility. The irony that he was about to offer him that which he had extended to Thoroughgood in the depths of his own torment was not lost on the DS.

Then a voice perforated the wails of the dying. One word. "Kenny!"

Hardie sprinted straight past Thoroughgood who turned and saw a moment that would remain etched on his consciousness for as long as he drew breath.

In a second of supreme emotion that Thoroughgood had never thought his mate was capable of, Hardie had grabbed his Betty in both arms and was spinning her round and round in the air repeating one word: "Darlin', darlin', darlin' . . ."

Tears rolled uncontrollably down Thoroughgood's face.

Thoroughgood was clock-watching again, his mind repeating the events of just over five hours ago endlessly, as if on some Sky News loop. Despite repeated calls to Mr India's restaurant they had not been able to contact Sushi, with the enigmatic waiter failing to reply to any calls. Nevertheless they had to exhaust all lines of enquiry and the events at Braehead had made their need to speak with the waiter even more pressing. Sitting in Thoroughgood's lounge their shocked silence, was all embracing.

Thoroughgood had tried to dissuade his mate from leaving his beloved Betty, who, although suffering a host of cuts and bruises, was relatively unscathed. But Hardie was now fuelled with a ravenous desire for revenge. Sushi, he now believed, was their only hope of gaining any intelligence on the perpetrators of the carnage that had left 133 dead and 48 injured.

The text alert on Thoroughgood's mobile grabbed their attention simultaneously. The DS checked the screen: "It's Sushi, says he will be here in fifteen. Thank God for that!"

Hardie was first to articulate the fear that was filling both of their minds. "I know we don't have any proof as yet and the scene is still being sifted over but ten to one, whatever Sushi wants to speak to us about has got to be wrapped up in this whole terrorist thing. I mean, we find a filofax with a list of what we suspect are shopping centres on it and hey presto, a bomb goes off in Braehead, 300 yards from where Murray bleedin' Fury is about to open a Davis Cup Tie? Fuck me gently Gussy boy, I can't help thinking if we had done more and done it a damn sight more quickly then this could have been avoided."

Thoroughgood met his sidekick's hypothesis with a metaphorical straight bat. "Look, Hardie, we got all that terrorist material and we made the powers that be aware of it. Tomachek passed it up the tree to the Intelligence Services and it was their business from then on. For fuck's sake faither, aren't you forgetting we are just a couple of bog-standard detectives following up a routine Misper' enquiry? Whose fault is it that it turned out to be your worst feckin' Jihadist nightmare?"

Hardie was surprised by the anger in Thoroughgood's pale, drawn, features and watched in silence as the DS moved over to the CD player and let out another curse, "Shit!", as he attempted to prise open the CD holder with little success, much to Hardie's amusement.

"What's wrong Gussy boy? Is your most prized possession experiencing mechanical difficulties? asked the DC. "Bit like yourself by the look of things!"

Thoroughgood grabbed a nearby bottle opener and inserted it into the side of the CD drawer, managing to prise the device open. "No problem at all there faither but thanks, as always for your help," and he quickly slipped in Van Morrison much to Hardie's satisfaction.

He had to admit he was experiencing an aching guilt that he had indeed lived to listen to another CD; the events of the previous Sunday morning remaining his own private property, while the dead at Braehead would never again enjoy their favourite sounds again. Yet he wasn't prepared to let Hardie in on his own very private guilt-ridden grief, especially when the DC had been through his own agonies of despair and relief only hours before.

Thoroughgood tried diplomacy. "Listen faither, you'd be as well chuckin' it and getting back to the missus' bedside. Even by your standards you look like you've been dragged through a hedge backwards. You look shite, faither, to be precise."

Hardie's Van Cleef eyebrow shot up in disgust.

"Listen to me, Gus bloody Thoroughgood, you may be my superior officer but there are 133 people dead and 48 injured because of a terrorist incident we may have the only lead on and he's about to walk through these feckin' doors! Do you suppose now the missus knows all that, she wants me home tending her scratches when she can have any one of half a dozen of her friends clucking over her?"

Hardie took a breath as he waited for the response. None was forthcoming. Triumphant, he rammed home the verbal advantage. "I thought not. Now, with the greatest of respect Detective Sergeant, shut the fuck up and gie's peace."

Thoroughgood gripped the arms of his chair and still said nothing.

As the silence stretched, Hardie guiltily reflected inwardly that perhaps he had gone too far. After all, Thoroughgood was clearly still not his usual self. Nursing the fresh torment caused by the Braehead bomb blast and their inability to do anything to prevent it, Hardie hoped his mate would not return to the suicidal state in which he had brought him back from Castlebrae.

'Fuck it,' said Hardie to the four walls, "don't know about you, but I need a drink." He focused his attention on pouring two rum and cokes and handed Thoroughgood his before inelegantly dropping his sagging body onto the leather sofa which let out a gasp of protest at the weight it had suddenly been asked to support.

Hardie leaned back and stretched out one arm along the back of the sofa before raising the dark frothing liquid to his lips. He raised his glass, "To Betty bloody Hardie, by Christ I love her!" and took a huge draught of the drink.

Thoroughgood stared at his partner and joined him. "Amen to that, my dear faither!"

"Poor bastards! I mean for cryin' out loud. I can tell you this Gus, I will be at the Kirk come Sunday to say a few amens and an even bigger thank you. Only the man upstairs knows why Betty wasn't killed. The only reason she didn't head for Pizza Hut for a coffee and a slice of her favourite salami pizza was because she thought it would be mobbed with tennis punters. She's funny that way, my missus, full of wee contradictions. Guess it's why I love her!"

Thoroughgood's phone sounded — an incoming text — "According to forensics it was a suicide bomber and a necklace of IEDs. A necklace? How poetic. How the fuck have they managed to get a whole string of IEDs in under the gaze of CCTV? That's it then. Just our bleedin' luck. What type of organisation uses suicide bombers? Not even the Provos go that far do they? It's got Jihadists written all over it."

But Hardie, finally exhausted by the emotional hell he had been through over the last few hours, now had his eyes shut although his knees seemed to have taken on a life of their own as they danced in time to the Irish crooner's classic 'Precious Time'.

Suddenly the DC's eyes twitched open and he stared straight at his mate who had been taking in the virtuoso but creaking performance of Hardie's lower joints, and they both let out a mutual laugh.

"Feckin' great lyric, eh Gussy boy?" as he belted out the first line of the Ulsterman's anthem.

They both laughed again, sharing a moment of levity in a day that neither would forget.

"Fuck me, how appropriate is that one? We just don't know how much precious time we have left," said Hardie.

Halfway through 'Here Comes the Night' the doorbell rang.

"Thank God for that! Friend Sushi, methinks," said

Thoroughgood. "Let's just hope this isn't a wild goose chase — we just don't have the time for that."

Hardie raised his glass in mock salute. "Ah Gussy boy, you should have learned to trust your old faither by now!"

13

SUSHI STOOD, dripping wet. His eyes met Thoroughgood's and the small dark darting pools were furtive as
they searched the DS' face for clues to his mood.

"Come in Sushi, and close the door behind you," said
Thoroughgood. Entering the lounge, Thoroughgood gestured to Sushi to take a seat at the opposite end of the sofa
from his portly colleague.

"Well, Sushi son? Where have you been hidin'? Don't
fuck about. You know what happened at Braehead this
afternoon. What have you got for us?" asked Hardie.

Sushi didn't know who to look at first, his head darting
between Hardie and Thoroughgood. The DS forced the
issue; much to Hardie's silent satisfaction, for the veteran
DC was applying as much scrutiny to Thoroughgood and
how he was going to handle the unfolding conversation,
as he was to Sushi's information.

'Please Lord, not some bloody breach of the peace in a
kebab shop', thought Hardie.

"Come on Sushi, whatever it is, it's obviously important to you and time is getting on a bit," said Thoroughgood.

Sushi seemed to relax for the first time since he had entered the flat and a tentative smile crept across his face: "Any chance of a fag?" asked the waiter.

Hardie reached into his anorak pocket and pulled out his ever-present packet of Silk Cut, before nonchalantly flicking one cigarette into his cavernous mouth and launching another two feet to his left where the waiter gratefully grabbed it.

By the time Hardie had finished lighting the cigarette and Sushi had taken his first deep drag the waiter's inhibitions had apparently disappeared.

Sushi exhaled and let it all hang out: "I'm sorry I hav'nae been round earlier but I needed to make sure I wasnae wasting your time. Boss, I'm worried that the shit has hit the fan, big time and I hav'nae a Scooby what to do about it, innit."

"Sushi, it is long past my beddy-byes and you know what happened this afternoon. Let's cut to the feckin' chase shall we? 'Cause if you need more time to think your way around whatever is giving you sleepless nights you are gonnae be wasting my time and yours." rapped Thoroughgood before adding, "On the other hand you've come this far, so if you're asking my opinion son, I'd get it over and done with."

The waiter shook his head and immediately slid the fingers of his right hand through his oily black hair before inhaling deeply on his cigarette.

"For fuck's sake Sushi, will you just get on with it son?" bawled Hardie, his exasperation clearly mounting.

"Okay, okay, boss. I know what happened at Braehead is bad but I believe it is just the beginning. What happened in London 7/7 was one isolated attack but I think

94

Braehead will be the first atrocity of a campaign of terror that will leave Glasgow in meltdown."

The shockwaves Sushi had expected to detonate around the room with his revelation did not materialise.

Thoroughgood shot Hardie an enraged look. "Look Sushi, we have just had almost the worst terrorist atrocity on Scottish soil and you say it is the green light for worse to come? Havers man! Pull the other one my friend, it has a bell on it," and Hardie lifted his leg and gave it a shake for good measure.

The waiter however remained undeterred: "Believe me boss, this is just the start of the nightmare." It was a statement of fact rather than a piece of guesswork, delivered in certainty. Thoroughgood reacted first.

"That makes the material uncovered at Mohammed's now more important than the crown bloody jewels."

Thoroughgood threw Hardie an enquiring glance as he sought to assess if the effect Sushi's words were having on his mate were similar to their impact on him. "OK Sushi, I want you to be very careful with this because it is going to set a chain of actions off that will be seismic if your information is true, and probably even if it ain't."

"In the name of Allah and all that I hold dear to me, what I have to say is the truth."

Thoroughgood gestured for Sushi to begin.

"We have a new Imam at the central mosque. When he first took over he seemed to be a real man of God, a teacher who cared for his people and was well versed in the Koran. But gradually his preaching has become more radical."

Hardie interjected, "That ain't no crime Sushi, we do live in a democracy, mate, and what about that boy Abdul

Muhaimin, or the 'Protector' as they are calling him, hasn't he been preaching a Jihad or whatever you call it down South and nobody has been doin' sweet FA about it for long enough."

Sushi shook his head animatedly: "But that is it Mr Hardie. I have now heard that the Imam has been preaching in private; in rooms at the back of a book shop, where he has been holding meetings with those who sympathise with his thoughts. He is developing a young and radical following and now that is beginning to alarm the mosque elders."

Now Thoroughgood questioned Sushi's concerns. "Okay, so what is your Imam called? What do you know about his private sermons and where he is preaching them?"

"His name is Tariq, which in English means messenger. The name is taken from the 86th sura of the Koran; Tariq Ibn Ziyad, who conquered Spain for the Moors and the man who Gibraltar was named after when it was first called Jabal Tariq, or mountain of Tariq."

"Blimey," said Hardie, "and I thought my explanation of Lal Toofan was interesting!"

Sushi shot the DC a quizzical look but was soon back in full flow. "Tariq has been Imam at the central mosque for eighteen months. Everything was fine for the first year or so but over the last six months there have been several new faces attending prayers and those people are not from this land.

"They keep themselves to themselves but I know they also attend Tariq's private meetings at the bookshop. They are brothers from our faith's homeland and I believe they are here to wage Jihad on you Christians."

Thoroughgood's mouth curled in acceptance that Sushi's revelation was almost certainly the real deal. "Okay, but I need a lot more than just suspicions Sushi, and I'll tell you why. After that terrorist attack at Braehead, this kind of shit could bury you and your people if you aren't careful," he said.

Sushi held his arms out in helplessness. "What do I need to give you to convince you it is real, boss?"

Thoroughgood, aware that he wasn't being entirely honest with the waiter, said, "For a start I would like one of these private sermons on tape so we can gauge the level of intent and get a feel for friend Tariq.

"Second, you say that Braehead is just the start and not the culmination of his planning? Well where has that come from? And have you got any idea what type of targets he is assessing, now that he has caused mass destruction and death in Glasgow's busiest shopping centre? You know that we uncovered a filofax from a flat earlier with a list of probable targets all filed alphabetically but by using asterisks? Given what happened at Braehead today does that mean we are talking shopping centres? Plus, where are these brothers holed up? 'Cause we are going to need to round them up tout suite mon ami."

Sushi appeared at a loss. "Sorry boss?"

"He means we need 'em hooked pronto mate," translated Hardie helpfully.

"Last Thursday, Tariq held a meeting with some of the Mosque elders and it was then that he really made his beliefs clear."

Sushi stopped and took a deep breath before continuing his tortured account. "One of our customers at India's is Professor of Middle Eastern Studies at Glasgow University and I have become very friendly with him over the years. You know how it is, you get talking to your regulars. But with Professor Farouk being an elder in the central mosque, which I attend myself, we have that bit more than the curry shop in common, innit?" Sushi finished in his bizarre mixture of Scots cockney.

"Anyway, the last time we spoke, the professor told me that he was becoming very concerned about Tariq, his views and where he was going with things, and that he was not the only one worried about the Imam.

"The professor is a learned man and deeply devout; if he is worried by what Tariq is saying or doing then we have a problem, boss, believe me."

Thoroughgood remained unconvinced. "So what is the bottom line then, Sushi? What did Professor Farouk say Tariq wants done?" demanded the DS.

"The professor told me last night that Tariq wants Jihad brought to these shores and he wants an act of vengeance that will make the whole of the Western world sit up and take notice — one that will commemorate the martyrs of 9/11 and all of the other brothers who are giving their lives in Afghanistan and Iraq in order to free the homeland of 'the Crusaders'. That is what the professor told me Tariq called the British and American armies."

Hardie interjected helpfully: "Bit like trying to bolt the barn door after Shergar has bolted out the back one, if you don't mind me saying, friend Sushi."

The waiter ignored him and continued. "The professor says that Tariq has vowed the attack will be at a venue that is at the very centre of 'infidel culture' in Scotland; one that will bring massive casualties. He wants a showpiece atrocity that will enshrine his name at the centre of Jihad against the West."

"You're too late wee man, or were the 133 people laid out at Braehead a figment of my imagination?" demanded an increasingly angry Hardie.

"He has a point, Sushi. All this info is a bit late in the day, after the events of this afternoon."

An awkward silence ensued before Sushi finally broke it. "I give you my word, boss. This is not a one-off. I think the evidence you uncovered in that filofax proves the point boss.You have to believe me."

The two detectives exchanged nervous glances, aware that Sushi's conviction was compelling.

"Okey dokey, so what the Bo Didly could top Braehead?" asked Hardie sarcastically; his eyebrows raised in trademark fashion at Thoroughgood. An obvious invitation for his superior to put Sushi fully in the picture.

Thoroughgood took a long swig from his drink and swirled it round his mouth, all too well aware that Sushi was staring at him, desperate for details. Unashamedly he enjoyed his moment of control. "Sushi, son, we haven't been totally honest with you." Thoroughgood slipped his hand inside his jacket and fished out the ivory-handled dagger and placed it on the coffee table between them."Recognise that, son?"

Sushi stared at the jewelled dagger, apparently transfixed by its presence; it was clear he had seen it before. The waiter picked it up and handled it with reverence as he read the Arabic words carved into the handle.

"The true believer will taste everlasting happiness in the death of every infidel."

This time the silence was deafening.

14

DOWANHILL WAS a prosperous middle class area in the heart of Glasgow's West End, populated by professionals, students and the elderly, who, immersed in its cosmopolitan make-up, would not leave until death did them part with their neighbourhood.

At precisely 9.30am Charles Rose kissed his wife Melissa goodbye, delighting in the delicious impact of the white musk that had been her preferred scent ever since he had met her. It had always been their ambition to own one of the imposing Victorian flats that topped the Dowanhill, and although their union had not been blessed by offspring, they were as happy as any couple they knew.

Charles left their sandstone flat in Crown Circus, crossing the road onto the slightly crumbling steps that would start his descent of Dowanhill Road. He took care to maintain the static position of The Herald jammed between his right arm and his side, still in a state of shock at what had happened the previous day. A suicide bomber blowing himself up at Braehead shopping centre, and a body count close to 150. It was truly shocking and Charles wondered what the ride in the Underground would be like this morning. People would either be in a state of shock or unable to stop talking about the atrocity.

His Saturday morning sessions in the office were something that Charles had had to become used to as he paved the way for what he hoped would be an eventual takeover bid by one of the big boys. Really, when you worked five days a week there literally weren't enough hours in the working day.

He stopped for a second and swept his eyes over the vista that spanned the West End and took in the imposing buildings of Glasgow University where, in the Uni chapel, he had been married all those years back. The thought swept through his mind, as it always did at this stage of his journey to work, that there was nowhere in the world he would rather live. As he walked, he followed the route he had been travelling for the last 15 years; to Hillhead underground and the journey that would take him to his insurance company in the city centre.

A hundred yards further down he stopped to pat the black and white cat who waited for him at this stage of his route every day. Almost as if it had some mystic power to predict the precise time of his passing. The tom purred and wrapped itself around his ankles and he smiled.

"Hey Jasper, how'd you do it?" He hunkered down and rubbed his index finger under the cat's chin. "Time for me to go, old pal. See you same time tomorrow, no doubt!"

Marching down the hill, his mind focusing on the claims and complaints that would be awaiting him, Charles smiled the appreciation of a man satisfied with his lot.

As he reached the bottom of the hill about 100 yards from its junction with Byres Road, a crack snapped out across the street and Charles half turned to his right. A window must have been smashed.

Lorna Welsh and Gordy Johnson had been together for just over a year, having met at the beginning of their Politics and English degree course at Glasgow University. Twelve months later they were inseparable and, against their families' wishes, sharing a rented studio flat in Crown Terrace. Unusually for a Saturday they had a 10am lecture in the Boyd Orr building. As they turned into Dowanhill Road on their way to the Uni arm in arm they exuded young love.

"What do you think the old ranter will have in store for us today, Lorn? My head's throbbing after the do last night. I hope he doesn't go off on one. No wonder people needed a bevvy after that business at Braehead."

Lorna, a lithe brunette with a smile that hinted at mischief, gave her boyfriend a playful punch in the ribs. "Yeah it's wild, a suicide bomber here in Glasgow, I can't believe it. But before you start blaming me for how many glasses of red you had, just remember you are 'an autonomous individual with extraneous interests'. Or have you forgotten your Ordinary Moral Philosophy 'B' from first year?"

Gordy laughed then groaned in mock pain at the dig in the ribs. "Fair enough, but what about we give the lecture a miss and you get Julie Brown to take the notes and maybe we could spend our afternoon doing something far more interesting?" he said.

As they approached the road's junction with Byres Road a sharp crack rang out and they both jumped in fright. "Jesus, where's the sniper?" asked Gordy, laughing.

Frank Harris finished his tea with a slurp then belched as he attempted to extricate himself from the armchair in his sitting room. He stood and turned to look at the photograph of his beloved Elsie on the imposing marble mantle piece. She had been dead for five years and yet he still missed her so much. He couldn't stop the tears welling.

He took his glasses off and, wiping them with a handkerchief, gave a snort and said to himself "C'mon Frank, Elsie would expect better of you than a load of pathetic sniffling."

Replacing his glasses, he took a deep breath and picked up the fading photo which had been taken on their honeymoon in Florence some 38 years back. The memories of the view from their room sweeping out and over the Florentine hills weaved through his mind; the afternoon they made love on the balcony and Elsie's red and white polka dotted dress that he'd almost ripped in the passion of the moment.

He groaned out loud at the memory. Life for Frank, 74 and alone, was all about memories. He wanted to remember his girl in her prime and not racked and ravaged by the cancer that had killed her after a long drawn out illness. He had prayed every night for the lord to end her torment.

He kissed the photograph. "Well girl I better go and water the plants, I don't want you getting angry with me now!"

Alone in his huge four bedroom ground floor Dowanhill flat, Frank's plant pots and the twin hanging baskets outside his door had become a panacea for the pain that had tormented him every day since Elsie's departure. The aroma of his prized pansies drew a smile from his gnarled features. He went through to the kitchen to fill his watering can then made his way through the hall. He opened the imposing green wooden door and walked to the top of the steps down to the pavement.

"C'mon me beauties it's time for your morning drink."

Suddenly Frank was startled by a crack that sounded like an exhaust backfiring. Something wasn't right. The former Argyle Highlander RSM drew on his military experience from Northern Ireland: That was no exhaust. The horror of his realisation dawning on him, Frank looked up the hill.

Charles Rose, immaculate in his black pinstriped suit, strode down the hill, the smile from his morning encounter with Jasper still on his face and the lingering traces of Melissa's White Musk in his nostrils. They were the last pleasures of the insurance broker's life.

The bullet smashed into his head, impacting square on the temple and throwing his body across the pavement into the black wrought iron railings 100 yards up from Frank Harris's flat. He was dead before he hit the concrete. The blood from his head wound pumped out onto the ground and ran down the pavement.

Walking 15 feet behind him, the student couple stopped in their tracks, shock spreading across their features as the implication of the noise they had joked about smashed home.

Lorna screamed "Oh my God! He's been shot!"

Gordy immediately grabbed her, pulling her over to the cover of a car parked at the side of the street. Just then a second bullet smashed off the railings to their left, where they had been walking a split second previously. Lorna screamed again and this time she could not stop.

Frank Harris took in the carnage and dropped his watering can. He had to get to the phone to alert the police. But, as he turned to go in, the chorus of screams in the background multiplying, a third crack smashed out. Frank felt the impact of the projectile in his right hip and dropped down onto the landing.

"Bastard!" the old soldier screeched, "Where are you, you dirty bastard?" Frank knew exactly what he was dealing with. He'd seen it all too often during his tours. "Fuckin' sniper!" He tried to drag himself up onto the first step but the sniper had other ideas.

The second bullet smashed into his back and he screamed out in agony, rage and realisation that his time was finally up. "Elsie, my darling ..." he murmured as the third and final bullet exploded into his head.

Dowanhill was bedlam. The screaming was endless as pedestrians dived for cover from the bullets raining down on them, from where nobody knew.

Suddenly another noise filled the air: the screeching of wheels as a black Volkswagen burst out from the line of parked cars that split the centre of the road. The vehicle squealed to a rubber burning halt next to the Vauxhall Astra behind which Gordy and Lorna were sheltering. Two boiler-suited figures jumped out. Both wore plastic masks, one depicting Tony Blair the other George W. Bush.

They walked in opposite directions around the Astra until they stood a foot away on either side of the terrified couple. The taller of the two, 'Tony Blair', took charge. "Le tet-Harak."[1] He levelled a gun at Gordy's head while his companion did likewise at Lorna's.

---

1   "Do not move."

"La it-qa makanak. WaHid waHid."[2]   The students
stared uncomprehending at the two figures .

Gordy made eye contact with Lorna as he tried to com-
municate some kind of reassurance to his girlfriend, but
a warm, wet sensation spreading down the inside of his
trouser leg revealed his true feelings.

Gordy underwent another strange experience as suddenly his throat seared with a burning sensation. He felt
his breath going and froth built in his throat as though he
was drowning from within. As jets of blood burst in front
of his eyes he realised his throat had been cut.

His eyes remained locked with Lorna's for one last
time. 'Blair' took the glinting steel that had replaced the
gun in his hand and ripped it across her neck. As Gordy
started to collapse he felt warm jets of liquid on his face
as the spray of his girlfriend's blood drenched him.

The masked figures dragged the lifeless bodies to the
pavement and laid them out for all to see, an open mausoleum.

Their killers jumped into the Volkswagen and it surged
100 yards down the road before one jumped out to pin
a piece of paper to Charles Rose's inert body. Then he
climbed back into the passenger seat and the car screeched
off as the sound of sirens filled the air at last.

No-one knew where the next bullet was coming from
or who the next victim in the sniper's sights would be.

---

2   "Stay where you are. One at a time."

15

THE PHOTO shoot had gone better than expected.
George Square had been transformed for one morning
only into a Saint Tropez beach and for once the sun had
shone.

It was Vanessa Velvet's crowning glory. The former
model and reality TV show star turned lingerie tycoon had
just launched her most seductive line ever under the new
brand name Bitch. The brand's byline was 'for the woman
who doesn't give a damn'.

Using her contacts in Glasgow City Council, in
conjunction with the Evening Times, which had recently
named her Glasgow's 'Businesswoman of the Year', she
had known she would be able to persuade Council Leader
Jim Fraser that her launch would bring a deluge of publicity the city's way. The hard part had been convincing
Fraser that it was all going to be positive publicity.

But Vanessa knew what she wanted and she knew how
to get it. The promise of a lunch date within the discreet
confines of Glasgow's most famous celebrity hotel, with
the hint of something more on the menu for afters, had
persuaded Fraser to sanction shutting off George Square,
despite the indignation and moral rapprochement ex-
pressed by some of the council fathers.

Her idea, Vanessa thought, was brilliantly simple. With Glasgow hoping to host the Commonwealth Games in 2014, and beach volley ball potentially to be included as a core sport for the first time, Vanessa planned for her models to hijack the campaign for its inclusion with an exclusive photo shoot based on an artificial beach volley-ball court created in the centre of George Square.

She knew it would create maximum impact both in terms of interest and outrage, because that was what she had specialised in all her life.

She watched the shoot wind up, taking in the elaborate set and smug in the knowledge that the pictures would soon be hitting the pages of glossy magazines around the UK and indeed the globe.

She picked up her mobile from the chaise longue on which she had been observing her models cavorting on the artificial sand. Knowing that her following of 10,000 were hanging on her every word, she tweeted; Well, I never knew how sexy beach volleyball could be. Hope they put it in the games! She finished with her trademark sign-off. Life's a Bitch. V.V.

The models trekked past and Vanessa watched the sand drop off their lithe, tanned bodies as the growing crowd cheered and catcalled. The cabbies who had parked up at their rank for most of the morning honked their horns, while cameras clicked and flashed constantly. Vanessa felt a stab of envy.

At 39, with two failed marriages behind her, one to a pop star and the other to an industrial entrepreneur, she had two kids but very little happiness in her personal life. Still, her alimony had funded her start-up in the business world and her feminine wiles and fame had made the rest easy. She had enjoyed almost every minute of it. The self-obsession that had blighted her showbiz career and almost led to its destruction had receded as she realised she enjoyed manipulating the media as much as she had enjoyed being the subject of their scrutiny.

It had taken her three years to extricate herself from her doomed second marriage. He had proven to be particularly spiteful after he had discovered that she had been enjoying a double life with a Premiership footballer. But look at her now – the unofficial Queen of Glasgow. Delicious in a pink silk blouse with a cream skirt that reached just above her knees, she played with her trade-mark blonde mane and her golden necklace. She was still a beauty and she knew it.

Yet … she was haunted by a now almost constant fear over the fading of her beauty's light. The pictures snapped at a myriad of award dinners, charity functions and Bitch publicity shoots would soon be marred by wrinkles. She dismissed the thought once more as the photographer approached her. Her personal snapper, Pete Johnson, was one of the most important members of her entourage, entrusted as he was with her priceless image.

"Hi Vanessa, how about a quick picture of you and the girls on a chaise longue? We've got one set up on the court."

Vanessa purred "Hey Pete, you know I'd never turn you down."

Over his shoulder she sawJim Fraser smiling wolf-ishly at her. He approached and took her hand warmly but delicately in his.

"Vanessa, another triumph for you and some fine PR for the Commonwealth Games bid too. I'm sure we'll have the beach volleyball in the games and sold out in 2014." Fraser leant forward to kiss either cheek, making her cringe inwardly.

He whispered "I hope I'll see more of your Bitch lingerie this afternoon," then pulled away, flashing his politician's trademark, a drippingly false smile with a full set of gleaming teeth. He underlined his growing anticipation with a wink.

Their Saturday lunch date was timed for 1pm and he was apparently ravenous.

Vanessa engaged first gear in her white Mercedes Sports, famous for its VVX1 plates, the roof already peeling off at the flick of a switch. She loved to drive open-topped through the city with her blonde mane flying behind her, the speakers blasting out classics from her favourite eighties bands. She didn't give a damn; she was the Bitch.

She looked for some musical accompaniment to help psyche her up for a wine and dine that would put the leader of Glasgow City Council firmly in her pocket.

It was all a game to Vanessa, and she was proud that no one played it better than her. She selected Duran Duran's Astronaut, slipped the disc in and waited for Simon Le Bon's smooth tones to open up with *Finest Hour*. She felt the shiver of excitement that always ran down her spine when the game was afoot.

Driving along Great Western Road she noticed that the carriageway was quiet for early Saturday afternoon. Vanessa didn't care; it allowed her to floor the accelerator giving a burst of power that enhanced the moment. As One of those days blasted out, she allowed herself a mischievous thought which transmitted into a wicked smile. 'How appropriate!'

She drove past Byres Road and noticed it had been closed off. The area was awash with police. Vanessa dismissed it as probably being caused by a traffic incident and floored the accelerator once more as the lights turned green.

She pulled up outside the hotel to the cool synth intro of *Point of No Return* and remained in the car, closing her eyes to listen and revelling in the music and the memories it set off in her mind.

As the song finished she opened her eyes and found the doorman standing next to her car. "Miss Velvet, can I take anything in for you this afternoon?" he asked in the slightly accented voice she could never place but could never be bothered to enquire about.

"No, I'm travelling light, Victor. Good to see you."

As she swept throughthe foyer she was met by the manager, Novak, who she knew was Serbian.

"Mr Fraser is in the bar if you care to make your way through, Madam."

Fraser was waiting on one of the comfortable settees, cradling his customary gin and tonic and surveying the lunch menu with an avid interest that soon transferred itself to Vanessa as she made her grand entrance.

He rose a shade too quickly, she thought, hinting at an impatience to get straight to the main course on the after-dinner menu. As she reached him he leant forward and kissed her on the lips lightly.

As they ordered, Fraser's hands seemed to take on a life of their own. One found itself on Vanessa's left knee which was crossed over her right leg in a provocative position that had brought Fraser's lust to the boil. She looked down at his hand and, just as he was expecting a scathing stare, she smiled. Her smile made him forget all about his wife and children and the party faithful who saw him ultimately as the next Scottish Labour leader and the man to bring to an end the growing SNP threat.

They made their way through to the tasteful oak-panelled tartan-trimmed dining room that provided such a classic understated backdrop to their sordid tryst. Fortified by their aperitifs neither cared about the need for discretion any longer. Fraser's hand playfully swept over her wondrous figure on its way to her waist and he was rewarded with another spine tingling smile.

They skipped straight to the main course, both going for the rack of lamb in a rosemary and blackcurrant jus, and washing it down with a bottle of the house reserve Rioja. By this time Fraser's minimal pretence at propriety had been dropped. His hand slipped across the fine linen table cloth and entwined itself around Vanessa's.

She knew she had him right where she wanted him. Now she could tease and how she could tease. "My, Mr Fraser, we are impatient and you haven't even had your dessert yet."

His smile almost dripped saliva. "I think I've been a very good boy Miss Velvet! As my dear old grandmother always said, every good boy deserves his reward!"

She smiled and playfully ran her hand through her blonde tresses. "Mmmm," she murmured seductively. Her leg moved under the table and slipping her stiletto off she ran her foot up his leg. Fraser reached for his Rioja and threw the remainder down his throat to distract himself from the thunderstorm of anticipation welling inside his body.

Vanessa rose, pushing her chair back slowly in perfect co-ordination, and walked round behind him teasing a hand across his shoulders and causing him to half-turn round in his chair like some love sick puppy dog. She walked out of the dining room and began to climb the stairs with the city's most powerful politician in tasteless hot pursuit.

Vanessa unlocked the door with the security card she had arranged to be discreetly placed on their table with the wine list. She entered the bathroom immediately and within seconds there was a knock on the door and Fraser's voice whispered "Room Service for Miss Velvet!"

She opened the door and Fraser stared. There she stood, resplendent in the most exotic Bitch lingerie. The last vestige of Fraser's control went and he almost knocked her off her feet with the intensity of the desire that poured out of him.

They landed on the bed and their bodies intertwined, living for the moment and caring nothing for the consequences.

Having lost all track of time and now satiated, Fraser propped himself up against a pillow and looked down at Vanessa. "Sweet Jesus, I've never met a woman like you!"

Vanessa purred her answer. "I know." And his blood rose again.

A knock sounded at the door and a voice said, in an accent Vanessa recognised as similar to Victor's, "Room service for Miss Velvet with the compliments of the hotel."

"Ooh, I love a surprise Jim," she cooed, all of a sudden acting like a little schoolgirl. "Would you mind getting the door?"

"For you my darling, anything," he replied playfully.

Fraser opened the door and stared uncomprehendingly. He only had time to take in the black swathing of the figures on the landing when something metallic lashed out and cracked against his jaw, propelling him onto the bed for the second time that afternoon.

The two men burst into room 69, levelling their revolvers at the heads of both the occupants and letting the door slam behind them.

"Shut the fuck up and we don't decorate the walls with your brains," said the first man.

Vanessa's face was framed in shock and she had lost the ability to scream. The first man, slightly taller and with what appeared to be a white blemish on one of his eyes, jumped onto the bed and cuffed her across the face.

"Make yourself decent, bitch." She pulled up the camisole top that had fallen down during her recent exertions. The intruder slapped tape across her mouth and grabbed her hands before binding them in a similar fashion.

Fraser had been stunned but not knocked out by the pistol whip and the second man had already completed a gagging order on the leader of the council.

"On your feet," commanded the man with the white eye. "It-Ha-rak!" he hissed and gestured for them to move. The door swung open and Glasgow's highest profile businesswoman and the leader of the city council were dragged along the corridor and bundled out the fire escape at the rear door of the city's most prestigious hotel.

16

BLINDFOLDED AND hands bound, Vanessa lay in the boot, her sobbing uncontrollable. It seemed like hours but she knew that they must have been held for a relatively short time. She had only instinct to go on as her captors had removed her gold Rolex. When Jim Fraser had tried to argue he had been belted over the head with a pistol and had his own watch taken before he was shoved unceremoniously in beside her.

Even in complete darkness Vanessa quickly realised that Fraser was out cold from the second blow. She shivered despite the close warmth of Fraser's body next to her own.

It was the ultimate nightmare for anyone in the public eye, to be kidnapped – by some kind of money grabbing blackmailers no doubt. Even if they were returned to their loved ones, ransom paid, their respective lives would be ruined.

Vanessa contemplated the spotless image she had tried to rebuild in the public's perception. Any blackmail case would attract the type of publicity her celebrity status would make unavoidable. 'Just another money-grabbing fame-seeking bitch,' she thought as her mind turned already towards a damage limitation strategy.

All the money she had poured into high-profile charities, the newspaper columns defending British business, British culture, British bullshit, anything to get on the right side of the establishment, to become part of the establishment. The big hearted businesswoman, who was proof that success could be grasped with hard work, but had never forgotten her roots, still had the common touch.

'Oh I've got the common touch all right, and if the shit hits the fan with Fraser then the truth will really be out there,' she thought. But she would keep a cool head and see what the bastards were after. 'Keep thinking on your feet girl,' Vanessa told herself.

The car came to an abrupt halt and Vanessa thudded into the inert body of Fraser. The boot suddenly opened and Fraser was manhandled out first and a figure, swathed so only his eyes were visible, grabbed her by the wrists and pulled her out of the boot before roughly shoving her down on what felt like concrete.

"Ta-aal wi-ya-ya,"[3] said a voice in a language that Vanessa thought was similar to the Egyptian spoken by the locals on her recent holiday in Sharm el-sheik.

She heard a door open then slam shut again and she felt hands on her shoulders and her body shivered with fear. Vanessa was forced down onto her knees and she heard Fraser's voice from a few feet away say, "Okay, okay!"

---

3   "Come with me,"

Her blindfold was ripped off and, blinking furiously for a second, she saw that they were inside a room with a domed ceiling. She wondered if they were in some kind of underground cavern.

Vanessa looked over at Fraser and saw that his right eye was almost closed and there was blood streaked across his face. She couldn't stop her concern pouring into words. "Jesus, Jim, are you okay?"

She was so focused on Fraser that she didn't see the man seated calmly on a chair at the end of the room until she felt something cold, something metallic jammed up against her chin, forcing it up and a voice said "If you wish your head to stay on shoulders, bitch, shut the fuck up."

The man who had spoken was the one with the hideous white blemish in his left eye. Vanessa also noticed an overpowering, nauseating stink of garlic.

She kept her mouth shut.

She noticed movement to her left as Fraser's body seemed to flicker with motion in a half-light that she realised must be coming from a candle. Then a thud sounded as Fraser keeled over onto the cold damp surface of the rough stone floor.

Another heavily swathed man bent over Fraser and attempted to lift him. He was stopped by a command from the seated figure.

"Take the kafir to his cell. It is the female I will have words with."

"Yes master," was the reply.

Slowly the pressure on her jaw relaxed and she was grabbed from behind by her bound hands and propelled upwards towards the voice.

Now she was able to focus her attention on the man sitting in the raised part of the room. He had a black beard and eyes that were as dark as the whirlpools of hell. Vanessa had met some intimidating and powerful men before, but the evil emanating from the individual in the skull cap and flowing robes of the Middle East reached a whole new level.

"Welcome to my humble abode Miss Velvet," he said and flashed a cruel smile. "Not what you are used to but it is now your home," he added. "Whether that is for the remainder of your life we will see."

Vanessa could not help her desperation betraying her "Why have you brought me here? Just name your price, for God's sake."

He smiled again then slowly rose from his seat and covered the few yards between them with languid menace. He took off his prayer cap and viciously slapped it across her face.

She recoiled and would have stumbled but for the strong hands that held her upright by her wrists. She tasted blood in her mouth.

"For God's sake?" he repeated with dripping sarcasm. "How appropriate, my painted whore."

He returned to his seat at the raised end of the room and indicated for Vanessa's guard to propel her towards him and onto her knees.

She couldn't control the sobs racking her body. "Why am I here?" she begged, "Please tell me. Who are you?"

The man leered and grabbed her chin in his hand.

"You may not know me Miss Velvet, but I know you. I have been watching you for months. The face that appears everywhere, the flowing blonde hair, the endless cultivation of publicity. You have no morals, you have no shame, you are everything that makes me and my people sick and now you kneel snivelling before me begging my mercy. You ask why you are here 'for God's sake'? Which God do you worship, bitch? The Western God of Capitalism? Everything has its price, there is nothing that can't be bought and paid for."

He stopped for a moment and took a breath, his eyes pulsing hate, a mere foot away from Vanessa who remained in the iron grip of her captor.

"Tell me, was that not why you were in the hotel? Everything and everyone can be bought, including the leader of Glasgow City Council," he paused before spitting out the last two words, "Miss Velvet."

He struck her again but this time with the back of his hand. The blow was cruel and vicious and administered with a force that snapped her head back and made her feel nauseous.

"It is I who is here for God's sake, whore. Here to do the one true God's work. You, slut, will help me bring about its successful completion. The price on your head is the freedom of a beloved brother kept captive for doing Allah's work, the work of Jihad against the accursed West … Can you comprehend the meaning of Jihad my Miss Velvet?"

Vanessa tried to regain her composure before she finally found her voice. "It is a religious war I think, waged by Islamists on the West in Afghanistan and the Middle East."

"As explanations go that is as good as I could have expected from a godless kafir such as you. Shortly, you will be taken to your cell, but first we have something you might enjoy, given your love of publicity. We are about to make you more famous than in your wildest dreams."

"In that room," Black Beard continued, pointing to a door "we will film you and the beloved council leader pleading for your lives at sword-point. The price, if our demands fail to be met, will be your heads." Once again he grabbed her jaw and forced her head round until she met his vicious eyes. "Is that plain enough for you Miss Velvet? Just think, your death would result in immortality. A fame never ending, even though your disgusting, shameless existence had been finally snuffed out."

The last vestiges of Vanessa's self-control disappeared. "No! No! I will do anything, meet any price you set, just let me go free!"

His face was temporarily awash with surprise then he laughed in cruel delight. "You offer yourself to me as a harlot, no? You tempt Allah's servant?" he laughed viciously again. "But the only price I am interested in you paying is your life."

Vanessa gambled: "Why me? Why not set me free and hold on to Fraser? He's the politician and everyone knows he will be the next leader of the Labour Party in Scotland and eventually the First Minister. Surely he is more important to your cause, more useful than just some businesswoman?"

The bearded man turned to the other captor who stood nearby in the shadows. "Give me your knife," he demanded.

He grabbed her jaw and held the glinting blade under her chin. "You have made me very angry Miss Velvet. A shameless harlot who will mount the cock of any man to get what she wants. Now she's prepared to sacrifice his life for her own snivelling existence. Before I turn your life into a pile of shit I think it is time I have some sport with you."

He moved the point of his blade down to her camisole top before ripping it down and exposing her breasts.

"What now, Miss Velvet? Would rape be a fitting punishment for a painted Jezebel, as your own holy book would surely call you, do you think? But then, I doubt if someone like you has a religion."

Vanessa steeled herself for what was coming.

Her captor lifted his knife point from between her heaving breasts and pressed it onto her cheek. "No, I will not sully Islam by such behaviour. I have other plans for you, Miss Velvet. But first I will have my fun. Should I slice that pretty face of yours so that no one wants to photograph it again? That would be cruel of me would it not? Almost mindless! But we are not here for anything other than to wage Jihad for the one true cause.

"I am the Imam Tariq and these men are members of the Spear of Islam. We are here to avenge the thousands of brothers who have had their blood spilt by crusader greed and cruelty."

He stopped and examined the curved blade, before slicing it through the air with hissing hate. Vanessa felt her heart pound. Then she felt a sharp searing pulse as her hair was slashed and her treasured blonde locks shorn viciously.

The Imam Tariq held a handful of her hair in his hand and taunted "A small memento of our time together Miss Velvet. Perhaps you will be lucky and leave with your life. But that is something I can not guarantee."

17

THE HUM of expectation was vibrant as a small group gathered in the private room at the back of the Half Crescent bookshop. The room was dimly lit with scented candles that diffused the sweet smell of cinnamon and apple through the air. At its rear was a raised platform with a wooden chair and a small table on which a glass of water and a copy of the Koran were placed.

As the audience's fervour grew, a beaded doorway to the left of the stage was brushed aside and a man exuding an aura of assured menace strode into the room. He wore a black shalwar kameez and a taqiya and when he reached the platform he held his right hand up for silence in a gesture of authority. At once the hushed chatter of the group was silenced.

The man on the platform brushed the fingers down through the beard that dropped almost three inches below his jaw. He lifted the glass of water to his mouth and sipped it slowly before returning it to the table. Then he focused his eyes, dark as the night, on his captivated audience.

"Allah be praised!" The man's right hand shot out, his index finger pointing at the group before his hand opened and swept from one side of the gathering to the other. Their attention did not waver.

Imam Tariq began. "The person who hinders Allah's rule, this man must be eliminated. We ask the devout to steel themselves and be ready for the call to arms to face the enemy down and give him death. The faithful can show no weakness in following the word of truth, the word of Allah. You, my brothers and sisters, must be strong from start to finish.

"Forget about weapons of mass destruction. Jihad is a war that must be waged in hand to hand combat, by dagger, by sword, by whatever means comes to your fingertips. It must be done face to face with the infidel so that you see the fear in his eyes, smell it coming off him. You, the faithful, should savour it as you wipe out the crusaders who have defiled the soil of our spiritual homelands all these years.

"You must penetrate the enemy with cold steel until he cries out no more and watch him bleed out like a pig before you. This is the first stage of Jihad."

Tariq drew a deep breath and took another sip of water, still closely watching his audience.

The crowd, made up of students and professionals, were youthful, pliable and enraptured. Tariq's chest puffed with pride as they hung on his every word.

"But we of the true faith face challenges too. Our young people are being infected with the ways of the West and the immorality of the crusaders' religion and . . ." His voiced trailed into silence.

He picked up the Koran and slammed it down onto the table, sending the glass of water flying. His voice seemed to fill the whole room with its power. "It must be stopped, this corruption of believers by the infidels. And I want you, my true brothers and sisters, to make sure it is. "My friends, let me tell you that no drop of liquid was loved by Allah more than blood!"

The fervour gripping the gathering now exploded into verbal force. "Allah be praised!" A round of applause broke over the room but Tariq noticed that not everyone was embracing his words wholeheartedly.

At the back of the room sat a white-haired man with a distinguished air about him. The Imam recognised him as one of the elders on the Mosque council, a man who disapproved of Tariq's preachings and the fervour he was beginning to foster in his followers and the wider Mosque. Now, however, was not the time to let the old man distract him from delivering and spreading his message. That was for another day.

"Brothers and sisters, our people are cheated and treated like cattle by the West."

There was a tumult of indignation now generating from the gathering. "It is the truth! The infidels must pay!"

Tariq continued. "The Nation of Islam must regain its dignity. But it will not be regained without blood."

Again Tariq's gaze was drawn to the white haired man sitting at the back of his avid audience who, unlike the rest of the gathering, was not applauding. The two men's eyes locked for a moment, long enough to reveal the disgust the old man felt. But there was another emotion in that gaze and Tariq was filled with satisfaction when he recognised it. Fear. The elder stood and walked through the door, back to the public part of the bookshop and Tariq knew that he must be dealt with soon.

"Now we must take action."

The group were on their feet and their voices filled the room in praise of Allah, but Tariq raised his hands and commanded silence.

"Now my brothers and sisters, as you know, we have started our Jihad here in Glasgow by punishing the unbelievers at Braehead and Dowanhill. The time has come for you to join us and execute on crusader soil."

Professor Farouk had reached the front of the shop and passed two imposing men flanking the doorway, when he realised he had left his spectacle case in the private room in his haste to get out of Tariq's sickening presence. He turned back but one of the guards barred his way. He noticed the man's left eye was ruined by the paleness of a cast.

The professor explained; "I left my glasses," and indicated with a motion of his hands that they were in the back room. The outstretched arm was removed and Farouk slipped back into the rear of the gathering. The audience, on their feet cheering and chanting, masked his return from the Imam.

Farouk watched with growing horror as the curtain behind Tariq shook open and five men filed out, their heads swathed in black linen keffiyeh with only their eyes left clear.

The applause died down as the audience took in the scene. The five lined up in front of Tariq were each carrying a firearm which Farouk recognised as AK-47 semi-automatic rifles. They presented them to the audience and once again the chant rose. "Allahu Akbar!"[4]

Farouk felt a sickening chill.

This was it then. Jihad had come again to a major city in the UK. It was being waged in Glasgow and Tariq's preaching in the Half Moon bookshop was proof, if any more was needed, that it was he who had been behind the atrocities at Braehead and Dowanhill. Farouk knew he had to tell someone before things got any worse.

An apocalypse now beckoned.

---

4   "God is great!"

18

THOROUGHGOOD AND Hardie, both still in a state of shock, arrived together outside Tomachek's office. Clouds of smoke were visible through the half glass door.

"The old man's going at it fast and furious this morning," Hardie remarked.

"No bloody wonder, what the fuck is this all about? Four more dead and apparently sweet FA to go on. It's everybody's worst nightmare. We don't even know 100% if it's terrorists, criminals or just some madman with a grudge against society. As for Braehead, I just can't get my mind around that."

As they entered the room the Detective Superintendent swivelled his chair round to face them. "When I ask you to be in my office at 4pm that's when I want you here!" he barked. "It's 4.03 – you're three minutes late." Tardiness was Tomachek's pet hate.

"The biggest act of terrorism on Scottish shores since Lockerbie. Murder and mayhem in the West End and you two bastards don't think it is important enough to attend a meeting with your senior officer on time? It's bally plain old buggery. It's also dammed disrespectful. Anything you want to say to that DS Thoroughgood?"

"Sorry gaffer. It's chaos in the backyard. We had to park outside on the street and then battle our way in past everyone and his granny. The media are crawling all over the place."

But Tomachek's irritation had passed. He waved his hand to waft the smoke out of his way, turned his world-weary eyes on his subordinates and gestured for them to take a seat. Leaning forward and placing his elbows on the edge of his side of the desk, he said "Sit down boys, we have a major problem."

Thoroughgood shot a sideways glance at Hardie and then looked back across the desk at his superior officer. "We're all ears boss," was the best he could do.

"Before I fill you in on new developments, Hardie, can I say I'm damned glad your missus came through Braehead with just a few cuts and grazes. Truly I am."

Tomachek slapped a copy of Monday afternoon's Evening Times onto his desk and pointed at the headline filling the entire front page. Friday: Braehead blown up. Saturday: West End carnage. Tomorrow: who knows? Glasgow in Terror.

"We have the media camped outside the office and it gets a whole lot worse because they don't know the fuckin' half of it, dear boys."

He tossed a single sheet of paper across the desk to Thoroughgood. "The first copper on the scene at Dowanhill found this pinned to the old boy who had his brains blown out while watering his flower baskets. Makes you think twice about taking care of your tulips don't it?"

Thoroughgood shrugged his shoulders and flattened the note out on the desk in front of him. Hardie took a look at it too before commenting "I'm not too fluent in the old Arabic, boss."

128

Tomachek exhaled a billow of smoke. "Indeed. And it isn't just bog standard Arabic, my dear Hardie, it is a code and we need to get it cracked tout suite."

Thoroughgood interrupted his boss. "I notice it's a photocopy boss. I assume Special Branch, MI5 and MI6 don't know about this duplicate?"

"Just so, Thoroughgood. I'll doff my bonnet to them in public but what my men get up to in private is another matter."

Thoroughgood could feel Hardie's eyes burning into the side of his face and he knew exactly what was going through his mate's mind. Friend Sushi and his tip off, should they tell the old man or not?

He threw Hardie a warning glance.

"Okay boss," before adding in a rush, "Is there anything else we can help you with?"

Tomachek's eyes almost popped at the question. "Of course there bloody well is! Firstly, I want to know exactly where some religious nut job got his hands on a specialist Soviet sniper's rifle. There could be a trail there."

Thoroughgood nodded in agreement but there were questions he needed answered. "Religious nut job? I take it that is the flavour of the poisoned prose before us?"

Tomachek inclined his head. "You can take it as bloody well read Detective Sergeant."

Thoroughgood met his superior's hardening gaze unblinking but it was Hardie who spoke. "While we're here do we have any intel' on White Eye from yesterday, boss?"

The question did little to lift Tomachek's spirits. "No we do not. The obvious conclusion is that he may not be from these shores. Ironic that, given his unusual appearance, we haven't got the slightest clue who he is. Which reminds me, do we know anything about the blade he tried to slice you into square sausage with?"

It was Thoroughgood's turn to provide information. "Aye boss, we've had the inscription on the handle translated." Thoroughgood hesitated, aware that what he was about to say was likely to send Tomachek into orbit.

The senior officer erupted. "In the name of the wee man will you spit it out Thoroughgood, before I have a seizure?"

Thoroughgood felt his lips curl as the words came out. "The translation is 'The true believer will taste ever lasting happiness in the death of every infidel.'"

"Great. Just bloody brilliant. What the bally hell we've got here the Lord God only knows," said Tomachek.

"Well if that's all, we better get goin' boss," Thoroughgood said. He started to rise but Tomachek gestured for him to remain in his seat.

"Not so fast, Detective Sergeant. The note was just the aperitif. Get ready for the pièce de resistance!" said Tomachek.

"At around 2.30pm on Saturday afternoon the businesswoman - I'll call her that for want of a more appropriate description - Vanessa Velvet, was taken from a hotel room at One Devonshire Gardens. By force."

Hardie couldn't help himself. "But wasn't she at that lingerie launch, the one with models playing volleyball on a fake beach in George Square? 'Bitch' or something I think she's callin' it. The missus told me about it the other day but I wasnae really listenin', as per . . ."

Tomachek surprised them. "Aye, 'Bitch. For the woman who doesn't give a damn.'"

Astonished at their superior officer's knowledge of Bitch lingerie, Thoroughgood and Hardie exploded with laughter as the tension engulfing the room fleetingly lifted.

"All right, all right, calm down. There's more ..."

Thoroughgood could not help himself interrupting. "Surely not boss! Has VV posted a YouTube clip and it was all a publicity stunt?"

Despite himself the DS grinned. Then he shook his head in dismissal of his subordinate's suggestion before continuing. "VV, as you call her, wasn't in the hotel room on her own. She was accompanied by none other than the leader of Glasgow City Council, the man Labour expect to lead them to the political Promised Land, Jim Fraser. The man they're callin' the next Tony Blair. Needless to say he has also disappeared without a trace into the bleedin' bargain, although I'd be prepared to speculate that dear Vanessa had well and truly put the va va voom back into his life before they were taken."

He picked up the remote control lying on his desk and pointed it at the TV. "Fasten your seatbelts and meet our new friends from 'The Spear of Islam'."

Thoroughgood and Hardie's eyes locked in on the TV screen in silence. The film that followed was brutally to the point.

It showed Jim and Vanessa kneeling in submission, partially clothed, in front of two men wearing the same Bush and Blair masks as used in the Dowanhill attack. The men were dressed in combat clothing and armed with vicious looking curved swords.

The figure masquerading as Bush made an emotionless and monotone speech in Arabic which Tomachek translated from a pre-prepared sheet. He threatened that if an activist known as Ismail Khan was not released from Guantanamo Bay within 72 hours, one of their captives would be decapitated.

The film ended with Vanessa pleading for the demands to be met. As she did so 'Blair' forced her chin up with the point of the blade re-iterating, this time in English – "Free our brother or the bitch and her pimp will lose their heads."

"We will provide filmed proof of their executions," he continued malevolently. "Be warned infidels, it is time for you to find out what the consequences of Jihad in your godless country are. We, the Spear of Islam, will make that happen. You have my word."

Then the screen went blank.

Tomachek was first to break the silence. "This film was posted on the Al Jazeera Arabic network yesterday evening. Your thoughts?"

"Have we got a make on it, a point of origin or anything like that from the Special Branch boys?" Thoroughgood asked.

Tomachek lent back in his captain's chair and shook his head. "No Gus, they've been too cute. We failed to get an IP address and we haven't been able to analyse the backscatter from one upload.

"They have us very much at a disadvantage. And because of the content of the broadcast we have the whole shooting match involved, from Special Branch to MI5 and 6 wanting to evoke their specialist procedures and to hell with good old police work."

Hardie was first to penetrate the prevailing awkwardness. "The design on the cloth at the back of the shot looks familiar. It's a similar geometric design to one I saw in an article a few weeks back investigating radicalised Islamic students."

Tomachek took another puff on his antique pipe and looked up at the ceiling. "Radicalised students, Hardie? Hogwash. This lot know exactly what they are doing and they have intelligence about the city that is helping them achieve their means. How the hell else did they get to know about the leader of Glasgow City Council meeting our highest profile businesswoman for lunch and extras to follow?"

Hardie retreated behind a grunt.

"And I thought dealing with that murderous bastard Meechan was bad. This mob are going to make him look like the proverbial pussycat. I tell you dear boys, this is it. Hell's bells are tolling."

Hardie pitched in. "Nice touch with the Bush and Blair masks, very fuckin' cute. So, let's get this straight, this 'Spear of Islam' lot, they've not come right out and taken responsibility for Braehead or Dowanhill have they? Obviously the masks seem to tie them into the latter. But this film is threatening to wage some type of Holy War in the UK, correct?"

The answer came from Thoroughgood. "Listen old mate, I'd say from the events of the last few days that we are already at war. The question is not can we stop them from inflicting Jihad. It's how quickly can we bring it to an end."

Taking their seats in the Focus parked outside Stuart Street Police Office, Hardie was first to puncture the troubled silence that had prevailed since they left Tomachek's office. "Looks bad Gus, don't it? The old man is right though, this has potential for disaster on so many fronts. I never thought I'd say it but thank fuck for friend Sushi.

133

Do you think it was the right call not to mention what he told us to Tomachek?"

Thoroughgood arched an eyebrow. "You kiddin' Kenny? No chance. Listen, even if we had followed up on Sushi's concerns there is no way we could have pre-empted this mess. Right now I need to make a phone call to a certain waiter because we need a meet as soon as possible."

19

THE GUESTS took their seats for an exclusive dinner none of them had thought would ever take place, but one which all hoped would pave the way to a powerful and profitable future.

Only one man in Glasgow could have hosted this particular gathering. The roof-terrace marquee had been specially reserved for a meeting that, it was hoped, would unify the city's drugs trade under the rule of that man. His name was Johnny Balfour.

Balfour had moved swiftly to fill the power vacuum left by the departure of Glasgow's underworld overlord and put an end to the never-ending battle for supremacy of the underbelly of Scotland's biggest city.

Since Declan Meechan had fled the city, and his nominal over-lord Jimmy Gray had died, the encroachment across the Clyde from the Southside had been incessant. Balfour's tactic had been simple. Divide and conquer. As the constant warfare between the local 'firms' had drained their strength he had exploited their weaknesses, playing them off against each other. Meanwhile he decided who he could work with and ultimately absorb into his organisation and who had to be eliminated.

Now Balfour stood at the head of a luxuriant dinner table on the roof-terrace at the private members club 29, on the cusp of complete dominance of Glasgow's drug trade.

The exclusive nature of the premises was ideal for discreet dining and Balfour, the son of an accountant, had never been one for ostentation and grand gestures - until now. Slowly, the 52 year-old surveyed the six men he had summoned to the meeting at which he planned to carve up the city almost as clinically as he intended to slice up the superb fillet steak that was 29's tour de force.

A ripple of a breeze whistled under the marquee but the weather was dry and decidedly better than usual for this time of the year. The autumn sunshine cast a pale shadow on the roof-top, an ideal setting for his guests to enjoy a smoke while they ate, drank and conducted the business at hand.

With entry to the roof-top sealed off by both club security and his own henchmen, privacy was guaranteed. Yet the unease among some of the assembled cast was palpable.

As he stood, the thought crossed Balfour's mind that some of his guests still did not appreciate what was at stake, what he was working towards. "Gentlemen, thank you for your attendance. I assure you that your presence today will benefit all of us in the weeks, months and years to come. You have my word on that."

The response was lukewarm, underlining the size of the task that awaited Balfour and his vision. But he received warm backing from an unexpected quarter. Frankie Green, the balding owner of a string of bookies and a private-hire taxi firm, got to his feet flashing an insincere, gold-glinting smile.

"Aye boys, it's time for us to put our differences behind us and unite. There is only one man who can do that and map out a future which will benefit us all." There was a vehemence in his words that was not lost on his fellow diners as he added, "Johnny Balfour is that man. This is our time boys, and with Meechan gone, if we don't seize the opportunity now it may be gone forever. I pledge my allegiance to Johnny Balfour. I suggest you boys do likewise."

At the opposite end of the table Balfour looked startled by this astonishing development but Green was not done. "If you don't mind Balfour, I'd like to propose a toast, 'To new beginnings!'"

To Balfour's relief and deep satisfaction the rest of the company scraped their chairs back and took up the toast.

The information that Balfour was planning a summit meeting at 29 had been confirmed only 24 hours earlier.

Checking the ropes and the claw-hammer grappling gear that would be used to scale the building, the man with the discoloured eye smiled grimly at the memories this mission was bringing back. The countless raids on embassy buildings and barracks which he had executed serving Sheik Osama, in the countries that Bin Laden would one day soon unite, flooded back.

Slipping a mask onto his head he held his hand up in the air with all five digits aloft. Turning around he looked at his companion to assess his readiness. Masks on heads, AK-47's slung over backs, ropes and grappling gear ready to be launched, he counted down his fingers in silence.

The concentration of cigar smoke had turned the air in the marquee an almost pastel shade as Balfour assessed his company. He pushed his chair back and raised his newly replenished glass of Chateau Neuf du Pape.

"My friends; a final toast before we get down to the business of the moment. I give you the reason we are all here today – dominance!"

As Balfour's glass reached his lips and his eyes shut momentarily, awaiting the satisfaction of glasses clinking together, he heard a series of metallic clunks. Opening his eyes and sweeping his gaze over his guests' faces, he saw their looks of concern turn to panic.

He turned to the source of their terror. Two figures had appeared at the edge of the roof and now quickly vaulted over the immaculately manicured mini hedgerow before ripping open the transparent doors of the marquee.

The intruders' features were hidden by Bush and Blair masks. Balfour felt a hot surge of anger and took a step forward. But as they gained their footing on the roof the figures unslung AK-47s from their backs, levelled them at Balfour and his company and advanced with obvious lethal intent.

Panic engulfed the company who, by mutual agreement, had come unarmed and had sent their henchmen to enjoy a drink in the bar below. Balfour signalled to Green to make for the door to the main restaurant and turned to face the gunmen. As Green started to move the area was filled with the sound of gunfire. He was mowed down in a staccato of lead which felled him three yards short of the door.

Balfour addressed their attackers. "Listen, I don't know who you are but we are all extremely wealthy men. Whatever you want we can make it happen . . ."

He got no further. 'Bush' let his AK-47 do his talking in a hail of bullets that ripped through Balfour and threw his corpse onto the table.

The other diners scrambled for the doorway but the second intruder had already made his way around the table. Dropping onto one knee he unloaded the entire contents of his AK-47 magazine into the four surviving men.

The man with the white eye lifted the mask from his head and pulled a glinting blade from an inside pocket before drawing it across his throat in mock instruction of what was to happen next.

The Blair caricature, his mask resting on top of his head, smiled viciously. The duo went from man to man systematically slitting their throats to the bone.

Their instructions had been that every guest must be confirmed dead. The survival of any one of the men would not be accepted by their backer. He had demanded the liquidation of Balfour and his intended crime cabal as the price for helping the group realise their dream.

The bloody work was done in seconds and White Eye savoured a job well done. Looking up into the clear sky providing a serene ceiling over the city centre roof-tops he said, "I promised you when I left your side that your will would be done, Sheik Osama, and now that day has come much closer. I, Naif, pledge to make it so. Allahu Akbar!"

Slipping his mask back on Naif gestured to his companion to do likewise. Then he typed a two word text on his mobile and pressed Send.

The pair grabbed their ropes and swung through the air back to the roof they had launched their bloody mission from, leaving Balfour and his confederates bleeding out across the roof-top of Glasgow's most exclusive eatery.

Meechan sat in the Adagio City Aparthotel room and contemplated the twists of fate that had brought him there. The building was close to the famous Sacré-Cœur Basilica, in the famously bohemian Paris district of Montmarte. With 76 rooms the hotel was big enough to provide the required measure of anonymity.

He ran an index finger round the rim of his grande tasse as he waited for the text message that would determine if he could set a chain of events in motion that would allow him to wreak the revenge he burned for. His slate-grey eyes took in the Soviet-make Makarov PM pistol in front of him which would help him take the first steps towards that cold revenge.

He raised the coffee to his mouth and sipped, glancing at the metallic attaché case which contained the deadly vials. Their seven figure value was the reason he was in France.

Meechan awaited clients who were far from ordinary, but then the wares he was hawking, on behalf of his new employers, the Rising Sun, were extraordinary too. The men he was waiting for were from Mossad, the ruthless security agency of the Israeli government.

If the text he waited for failed to materialise, he would do business with the Mossad – a deal that would remunerate his new employers and enhance their control over the former Soviet block underworld. It would also pave the way to a potentially lucrative business relationship with Mossad.

Meechan was all too aware of the chips that were being stacked on his imminent meeting. Yet, should he receive the text message he longed for, he would renege on the deal and embark on a venture that would place his

140

own life in continual peril and leave him hunted both by his employers and the Mossad. But it was a price he was prepared to pay.

His mobile's message tone punctured the silence of the room and he lifted the phone and checked the screen. Two words appeared: 'Subjects terminated.'

Quickly Meechan pocketed the mobile and took to his feet hoping he had the time to exit his room before the Mossad agents arrived. A rap on his room door indicated he did not and an accented voice followed it.

"Monsieur Marsaud, votre familie arrivez."

The coded phrase confirmed his worst fears. Meechan grabbed the Makarov and the case. He slipped the latter under the bed and took up a stance that would place him behind the door when it opened.

Pistol levelled, he said, "Trés bien mon ami. Entrez vous." The door swung open.

As the first dark-suited figure entered the room Meechan thudded in two shots, one high one low, ensuring at least one bullet would be debilitating. He immediately fired another double discharge through the door itself, which splintered pleasingly.

The first man toppled forward onto the floor, blood spilling from his mouth, the head wound inflicted by Meechan's first shot apparently lethal. But his attention was drawn back to the door as the vicious retort of returned fire scythed through it.

Meechan had anticipated not taking out the second man and was in the process of diving onto the deck as the bullets ripped through the door. He noted they came from an upward trajectory that meant the shooter was adopting a low firing position.

As he hit the laminated floor Meechan's momentum took him skidding across it to the cover of the bed. In a moment of fear he realised how close he was to the case containing his deadly cargo. Raising his head above the bed he saw that the second agent had taken cover in the hall. From the cursing coming from the corridor Meechan realised he had injured him.

Assessing his situation Meechan knew he had two options. One was to make his escape over the balcony and take a chance on the 12 foot drop to the cobbled courtyard. This option would leave his back momentarily exposed.

"No-brainer," he said to himself. He had to take the second agent out or at least disable him. He pulled the case out from under the bed, sprung the locks and pocketed the two vials, slamming the case shut again.

"Pour vous mon ami!" he shouted and skidded the case across the floor towards the doorway.

He was already on his feet and sprinting for the doorway as a hand dropped down to grasp the case. Off-balance, the agent was taken by surprise. Meechan's size 10 smashed into the agent's jaw and as he crumpled to the ground Meechan fired his remaining shot at point-blank range into the the man's head.

Meechan grabbed the case and the agent's gun and charged back into the room as his ears filled with screams from the corridor. He replaced the vials in the metallic lead-lined attaché case and made for the window. Ripping a curtain from its pole he tied it to the balcony railings, tested it would hold, then shimmied down to the court-yard.

Walking out onto the Place Charles Dullin, Meechan

smiled ferociously. The game was afoot and there was no going back.

The stakes were life and death and Meechan did not care whose.

20

BY 6PM Thoroughgood and Hardie were closeted with Sushi in the DS's lounge as Sushi spilled everything he knew about Tariq. The detectives hung on his every word. Handing Sushi the note which had been pinned to one of the shooting victims Thoroughgood asked, "Any ideas who could help us decipher this, Sushi?"

The waiter examined the note intently. "It is definitely coded, boss. Something about a wedding planned for the middle of November but as for the rest of it you need to speak to Professor Farouk. If anyone can set you straight on it he is the man.

"I'll phone him and tell him you'll be heading his way if you want boss. I think he'll be relieved to see you.

"I told you Mr Thoroughgood, Tariq wants Jihad and now he has begun he will not stop until Glasgow is in the middle of a religious war. Dowanhill and Braehead are just the start. It is not only yours but the Muslim community in the whole UK's worst nightmare and it's happenin' now."

Thoroughgood nodded in agreement then cleared his throat because he had something to else to say and no idea as to how Sushi would take it.

"How well do you know the Imam, Sushi? How hard it would be for you to make yourself useful to him and gain his trust?"

Sushi dismissed the idea with a shake of his head. "The Imam knows me through the mosque but his inner circle is a tight group. I would not know where to even begin to try and become close to him."

Hardie spoke up. "I may have the beginning of a cunning plan."

Thoroughgood flashed a sarcastic smile and then motioned for him to proceed. "The floor, my dear Hardie, is all yours."

"OK here we go. We already have in our possession something that friend Tariq treasures almost above all else, and which we could use to help put Sushi in this maniac's trust."

"The dagger," interjected Thoroughgood stealing his sidekick's metaphorical thunder.

"Indeed. You've already nearly had the life strangled out of you by one of his henchmen in an attempt to keep it. It obviously has great significance to him," continued Hardie.

"My plan is that we provide Sushi with the location of the dagger at a set time. He in turn furnishes Tariq with that info and we wait and see what transpires. Obviously we are up against the clock given Jim Fraser and VV have less than 72 hours before they part company with their heads.

"Plus we won't know what the contents of this note are until Professor Farouk translates. So I think friend Sushi has to be chapping at someone's door tonight with the info we need to get to Tariq."

"So Sushi, are you up for it?" finished Hardie.

Sushi's agreement was total. "Whatever it takes boss, innit," he said with his trademark nervous sign-off.

Thoroughgood added, "I take it that we will retain possession of the dagger? One other thing Sushi ... you realise that by the very nature of what we are trying to do, you won't see it but back-up will be around, believe me."

Hardie's grim nod provided further confirmation to Sushi that appearances in this case would most certainly be deceptive.

At 7pm Thoroughgood and Hardie drove into University Gardens heading for a meeting with Dr Basil Farouk at the Department of Middle Eastern Studies. The department was half way along University Gardens - a terrace of three-storey sandstone buildings almost all occupied by Glasgow University's various history departments, with the Department of Middle Eastern Studies being the exception. Thoroughgood and Hardie walked along the pavement looking for number 10.

"It's a bit bleedin' ironic Gussy boy, if you ask me, that we are going to meet some boffin to decipher a code left by a Tony bloody Blair lookalike, and the boffin resides at number 10," commented Hardie with an amused chortle.

"Hilarious, absolutely feckin' hilarious. Listen faither, you might try and show some respect for the professor. Not only is he absolutely vital to us but he is also an elder in the Central Mosque, a respected figure in Glasgow's Muslim community and a senior academic at Glasgow University. My Alma Mater, to be precise! You with me?"

The serious note in Thoroughgood's voice told Hardie that he had no option but to comply with the request. As they reached the door bearing Professor Farouk's name Thoroughgood reinforced his point with a burning stare at his colleague before he knocked on the oak-panelled door.

After a moment an accented voice replied, "Come," and Thoroughgood and Hardie entered the room.

The professor sat behind a huge antique desk. He held out his hands to beckon the detectives to fill the two empty seats on the opposite side from him and assessed the pair for a moment before letting his gaze linger on Thoroughgood. "Well, Detective Sergeant Thoroughgood, I presume?"

"Professor Farouk." Thoroughgood offered his hand to the academic and was met with a firm grasp. "I'm pleased to meet you. This is my colleague DC Hardie."

Farouk inclined his head to Hardie.

"Gentlemen, forgive me, but from speaking to our mutual friend young Suleiman, I feel the situation we find ourselves in demands expediency, does it not?"

Thoroughgood was disconcerted by the way the professor had taken control of the meeting but was in no position to bridle.

"Absolutely Professor," he replied pulling out the note. "This was found pinned to one of the two men shot dead in the West End. It appears to be in some kind of code which has baffled our translators. Sushi was confident you would be able to translate it and also that you would help back up his suspicions that the Imam Tariq is behind the recent atrocities."

Farouk placed a pair of half moon spectacles on his nose, before turning his intense gaze on the note. After a long moment he spoke.

"This is very interesting indeed. What we are look-ing at is a code cipher that was used in the Middle Ages wherein a message in one language was written using the alphabet of another to disguise it.

"I dare say that to your translators this message appears to be written in Syriac, but they would be quite mistaken."

Hardie's eyebrows shot up in bafflement. "Forgive me sir, but my knowledge of Islam is pretty basic. Can you provide an idiot's guide?"

Thoroughgood cleared his throat in a reminder to his colleague to show respect, but he need not have worried. A smile formed on the professor's face followed by a husky laugh that seemed incongruous with the academic's refined features and mannerisms.

The professor explained. "Tariq is a Shi'ah, so the obvious choice for his message would be Arabic. But what we have here is the use of the Jacobite script to encode an Arabic message. In layman's terms that means for every letter in Arabic he has used the corresponding letter in Syriac. Translated literally it means very little, but if each letter is turned back into Arabic then you have your message. Gaining a meaning from it is another matter."

Thoroughgood and Hardie remained nonplussed by the professor's comments and their vacant features warned Farouk that further elaboration was required.

"We know that it is written using the Syriac alphabet but must be reversed into Arabic before being translated into English to get the intended meaning." The professor took a sheet of paper from a drawer in his imposing desk and scrawled an Arabic translation. "Now let me turn it into English and we will see what we have." Minutes later the translation, if not the meaning, was complete.

'The day is coming when grief must at last break out across this godless land.

"There will be many days of celebration for the believers of the true faith. We have experienced the first of these and we look forward to our act of ultimate joy.

The grains of sand are slipping away like your hope. A feast awaits that will start your atonement for the evil and unjust war of imperialist greed.

Before the feast however will be staged a number of events that will bring joy to us but only despair and pain to the Godless.

For every day until the great day there will be an outbreak of grief and the Hurting will go on and on.

Know this, infidels, you are powerless to stop us in our purpose. Count your days.'

After he finished reading the professor frowned. "The warning appears to be of a whole series of atrocities causing uncontrolled panic and the deaths of hundreds. And make no mistake, time is not our friend."

"Too bleedin' right Professor," agreed Hardie. "Count your days, grains of sand slipping away and an act of ultimate joy! It sounds like a bombing campaign."

"Indeed it does, Detective Constable Hardie, and if we don't stop it we, and I say 'we' because my people will bear the brunt of the backlash, are facing our worst nightmare."

Thoroughgood broke the silence which descended on

the room. "Do you think that Tariq is behind this? Is he capable of carrying out what happened in the West End and Braehead? If so we will need more of your help, Professor."

Farouk, his consternation obvious, slowly nodded. "I have no doubt he is. Tariq is a man who burns with the fire of the righteous. There is no grey area with him, everything is black and white and in his mind his cause is the only true one." The professor took a deep breath, apparently having inwardly resolved to embrace his decision to assist the detectives.

He continued, "I have been aware of the increasing zeal in Tariq's preachings for some time, as have several of the other elders. Recently we have also become aware of strangers attending his preaching. Furthermore he has been preaching to select small audiences of mainly younger believers at a bookshop here in the West End called The Half-Moon."

Hardie exchanged a knowing look with his DS and Farouk's keen eyes did not miss it.

Farouk continued, "I can see that you are not surprised by any of this."

A momentary silence hinted at a slight reluctance in the professor to continue, but after a pause he spoke. "Last night I visited The Half-Moon looking for evidence to confirm my concerns over Tariq. The evidence was there – and a hundredfold, gentlemen.

"Tariq delivered an impassioned oratory on Jihad against the West. There is no other way to put it. But what confirms to me that he has the ability and the determination to carry out the atrocities we've seen was the presence of men armed with AK-47 assault rifles. So you see gentlemen, there can be no doubt that Tariq has both the desire and the capability to carry out more atrocities."

Hardie's inelegant summation of the situation broke the silence. "What a feckin' nightmare."

Farouk levelled his gaze squarely on Thoroughgood. "But now Detective Sergeant, I think you have information that you should share with me."

Thoroughgood shifted uncomfortably in his chair. "OK Professor, I appreciate all of the information you have shared with us and, yes, we have not been as candid with you."

Hardie cleared his throat, uncomfortable with his superior's planned course but Thoroughgood felt he could trust the academic and was not about to hold back now.

The DS said, "You know all about Braehead and Dowanhill. But you possibly don't know that hostages have been taken and their captors have posted a film on an Al-Jazeera website calling themselves the Spear of Islam. The film demands the release of a terrorist with links to al-Quaeda from Guantanamo Bay, or the hostages – the leader of Glasgow City Council and a high-profile Scottish businesswoman – will be executed."

Thoroughgood ploughed on. "What you won't know is that a doctor Mustafa Mohammed has gone missing from the Western Infirmary and when we went to his flat we uncovered literature about waging Jihad and bomb-making and a filofax full of what we think is info about shopping centres. I chased a man with a blemished left eye from the flat – who almost carved me up with – this."

Thoroughgood set down the ivory-handled dagger on Farouk's desk. He could tell by the academic's reaction that he had seen the weapon before.

The professor lifted the blade and stroked his index finger lovingly along the cold steel ending with the wicked curve.

"This is the ceremonial dagger worn by the Imam on great days. It is said to belong to the greatest Sultan of them all, Saladin. The legend is that when Jerusalem fell to Saladin in 1187, this is the dagger he used to inflict the first wound on Raynald de Chatillon, the Crusader butcher of Muslim caravans.

"I have heard it said that Tariq believes that whoever possesses it will succeed in his Jihad against 'the Crusaders'. I must warn you that if Tariq finds out you have the dagger he will stop at nothing to take it back."

Hardie opened his mouth to speak but Farouk indicated he had more to say. "You say that a man with a blemished eye tried to kill you with the dagger." Farouk turned the finely weighted blade in his hand and the steel glinted from the weak sunlight filtering through the office window. "One of Tariq's guards at the bookshop last night had such a blemish. I know that Tariq is capable of anything. I think his actions could cause the Muslim community throughout the UK great harm. I will do anything I can to help you. But … he is a clever man. He will know that the doctor's flat has been raided so he will be aware that you are in possession of information that will help you thwart his ambitions. That means, Detective Sergeant, that you must move with all haste."

This time Hardie could not help himself. "Amen to that."

Ignoring his sidekick, Thoroughgood asked, "Okay Professor let's cut to the chase. Where can I find Tariq?"

"Officially Tariq's place of residence is the Imam's house next to the Central Mosque but that is no longer where he stays. Over the past few months it has become a matter of some irritation for the elders that Tariq is never available when required. The best suggestion I can come up with is that he may be staying at one of his followers' houses."

Before Thoroughgood could speak further the door of Farouk's office opened and a vaguely familiar female voice from behind the startled detectives said, "Sorry, Father, I did not realise you were busy. Please forgive me I will . . ."

As Thoroughgood turned his head around to take in the speaker the look of surprise on his face was mirrored by hers. "Detective Sergeant Thoroughgood," she said, "What a small world it is! It's a pleasure to see you again."

Farouk looked uncomprehendingly first at his daughter, then Thoroughgood and finally at Hardie who shrugged his shoulders in equal mystification.

Thoroughgood smiled warmly at the nurse he had saved the day before and found himself inexplicably happy to be speaking her name. "Aisha, the pleasure is all mine."

After she had explained their previous encounter to the professor, Farouk adroitly asked his daughter if she would make his guests a coffee and the conversation quickly returned to the matter in hand.

"So gentlemen we are agreed that the sooner Tariq is confronted the better?" asked the academic.

Thoroughgood was once again disconcerted by the professor's directness but he knew that after Fraouk's revelations about the meeting at the Half-Moon, time was of the essence.

"Professor, we have a plan to lure out Tariq and also help us integrate Sushi into his trusted group of followers," said Thoroughgood.

The professor's eyebrows raised an inch and he indicated to Thoroughgood to carry on.

"You have just underlined the significance Saladin's dagger carries for Tariq. We plan to give him the information, through Suleiman, as to where he can locate it. We'll try to trap him or whomever he sends to get it. It's a gamble but if, as the note suggests, we are facing an ongoing bombing campaign and a race against time to save the hostages the stakes are high enough to demand we make it. What do you think Professor?"

"I can see the plan's merits. I am not sure that you will hook the fish you seek to catch through it, as Tariq is a shrewd and cunning man. But your idea of helping Suleiman gain entry into Tariq's favour may be more successful. There is no doubt that Tariq sets great store by the dagger."

Thoroughgood cleared his throat. He knew his plan had implications but right now what really bothered him were the revelations of the coded message the professor had just cracked.

Glasgow was now in the middle of a concerted campaign of terror and things were only going to get worse.

Apart from this lone long shot, Thoroughgood didn't have a clue where to start.

21

THE ROOM stank of damp, and scuffling and scuttling noises coming from the semi-darkness indicated that Jim and Vanessa were not alone.

The hostages were gagged, bound and strapped to chairs. Only the flame flickering from a small candle on a table at the side of the room provided any illumination. It was a scene worthy of anyone's worst nightmares. Fraser tried to provide some kind of encouragement to Vanessa with a strangled smile but saw that it was a waste of energy, failing to have any impact on the sobs racking Vanessa's body.

He looked at the old brickwork walls and what he could make of the ceiling. Despite the agony of his headache he took in every possible detail of their environment and had a feeling that they were underground. His last memory had been of the lights going well and truly out before he was presumably slammed in the boot of the car.

The men had spoken mainly in Arabic when they had taken the hostages. Their English, although spoken in a thick accent, was better than half the population of Glasgow's, thought Fraser with bitterness.

He returned his gaze to Vanessa's dishevelled and

swollen features. Fraser's mind flashed back to their passion earlier that day. A rendezvous that had promised so much and now would have disastrous implications for both of them even if they escaped with their lives.

Vanessa had been so beautiful, the object of all his desires. He had hoped the rendezvous might develop into an ongoing affair. What he couldn't understand was just how the gang had found out about their liaison. Who had tipped them off?

Fraser was also still in the dark over where Vanessa had been taken earlier. Time was now a blur, but he believed they may have been held overnight and that this was the second day of their enforced captivity. The truth was, he could not be sure of anything.

Fraser ached with hunger but his determination to escape from this disaster burned even stronger within him. After all he wasn't just anybody . . .

As a student he had once entertained ambitions of a career in the intelligence community although his lack of personal discipline, poor judgement and an opinionated mouth had rendered that no more than a pipe dream. Ironically, Fraser now supposed he would be relying on operatives from that very intelligence community to save their souls. This was way above the remit of Strathclyde Police.

Now he again tried to give a shred of comfort to Vanessa by rubbing his foot against hers, hoping the slight physical contact would somehow offer her a shard of solace. Sure enough it drew her attention to him and her eyes locked on his imploringly, searching for some reassurance. Just then the door burst open.

Fraser immediately focused on the man who entered

the room. His face was unfamiliar but his voice was not and the councillor had no doubt that he had been one of the men who had taken him and Vanessa captive.

The man was carrying a tray with two bowls placed on it which he put on the table with the candle. The flame flickered with his movement. A squeal from the semi-darkness once again made the hostages aware that not all the occupants of the room were human.

The man, dark-haired and swarthy, strode over to Vanessa and removed her gag. Into the silence her sobs broke and as she opened her mouth the guard backhanded her with a vicious swing of his hand. The ferocity of the blow knocked her and the chair over and she crashed to the floor.

For a second Fraser thought the man was going to kick her, his face, flickering in the candlelight, providing a study in cruelty. Then he bent over Vanessa, grabbed her chin and spoke.

"You listen, bitch. You do what told, give me no trouble. If you are good girl you get bowl soup to drink. Understand?"

Lying on her side, still tied to the chair, Vanessa managed to croak "Yes."

The man then pulled her to an upright position in the chair.

He moved towards the table returning with the bowl and held it to her lips. She drank hungrily, her desperation for liquid seeming to dull her senses to the scalding heat of the brown soup.

"Good bitch, good bitch," said their captor. He removed the empty bowl and snapped the gag back in the lingerie tycoon's mouth.

He replaced the bowl and returned to Fraser with the other one. Pulling the politician's gag down he proffered the bowl. Fraser curled his mouth round the rim and drank, ignoring the sting coming from his burning lips. The soup registered as similar to the Oxtail soup his mother had made him drink as a kid.

As the guard removed the bowl Fraser spoke before his gag was snapped back. One word echoed out. "Why?"

The guard registered surprise at the question. He spoke in his mother tongue. "La ila ha illa llah." He paused before translating in his thick English. "There is no god except the one God, infidel. You need have no worries because soon enough, dog, you will die. But first," and he gestured at Vanessa, "you will watch your bitch die." He drew his finger across his throat to leave the two hostages in no doubt of the fate that awaited them.

Fraser mustered the last shreds of self control and spat straight at his tormentor's face. "Fuck you!" he rapped as the soup bowl smashed into his face and the lights went out for a second time.

As Fraser and his chair toppled over onto the uneven, stony floor the door to the room opened again and a voice resonating authority uttered one word. "Out."

The guard left the room.

Vanessa stared at the door as it slammed shut behind their tormentor.

She looked over at Fraser lying inert in oblivion and a shiver of raw fear ran down her spine.

22

THOROUGHGOOD AND Hardie left University Gardens, their moods darkened by the conversation with Professor Farouk but their resolve stiffened to apprehend Tariq before he unfolded any further carnage on the streets of Glasgow.

Their journey back to Thoroughgood's flat was spent planning their next meeting with Sushi. He would be fully briefed over his new role as informer and trap-layer. But there were other pressing concerns to deal with, the first of which was bringing Tomachek into the picture with their plan and Sushi's role in it, as well as his background.

When they arrived at Gardner Street, Sushi was leaning against a lamp post across the road from Thoroughgood's flat, fag in mouth. Alighting from the Mondeo the DS signalled Sushi to follow them in.

As soon as they were inside the flat Thoroughgood opened proceedings. "Okay Sushi son I'm assuming you have been busy? Do we have a conduit for our 'information' for Tariq?"

The waiter's face lit up with a grin that could only mean he had had a productive evening in that regard. "Yes boss. Tonight is the Half-Moon's late opening, so I paid a visit while you were at the professor's office."

Sushi took a deep drag of his cigarette and continued. "It is owned by a man called Ahmed Omar, one of Tariq's biggest supporters. He knows me from the Mosque, where we are on nodding terms. I told him that I have information for the Imam's ears only, concerning the location of Saladin's dagger.

"I could see straight away that I had his attention and although he was cautious he agreed that one of Tariq's men will meet me later tonight. The location I suggested for that meeting was the outside the Conservatory at the Botanic Gardens."

"He warned me that if this was a trick I would face expulsion from the Mosque and eternal damnation and that Saladin's dagger was of massive importance to the nation of Islam; one of its greatest treasures. The bottom line is that we are meeting at 12 midnight tonight."

"Well blow me," gasped Hardie unable to contain himself, "Religious artefacts, a Jihadist death squad and a suicide bomb campaign. It's like something out of the Da Vinci feckin' Code, ain't it? You don't bloody well hang about Suleiman. The Botanics will be under lock and key by then but there are ways to get in. Ain't that right gaffer?"

Thoroughgood took time to find his voice but eventually responded. "Sushi, there are a lot of implications regarding this meeting. This might be the time to make you aware of them."

But Sushi held his hand up. "Listen boss, I know what they are; physical, mental and spiritual. But Glasgow is my home and if I can do anything to help you stop Tariq then how could I kip in me bed at night if I hadn't bothered me arse?"

160

Hardie responded by jumping up and shaking the waiter by the hand enthusiastically.

"Don't worry Sushi we will get your script sorted and remember you will have us watching your arse."

As soon as Sushi left Hardie brought the other pressing matter to a head. "OK Gus, so we have a point of contact with these nutters and a plan of sorts. But, and it is one hell of a big bleedin' but, what about the old man?"

Thoroughgood regarded his mate with a disdainful look designed to let him know full well he was aware Tomachek would take some convincing.

"Very good faither! How is it that for 90% of our time I feel like you are the boss man but every time there's an awkward phone call to make, a death message to be delivered, or the need to run the gauntlet of Tomachek . . ." Thoroughgood got no further.

"Privileges of rank mon gaffeur as I always say at these moments, when you are forced to earn your corn. Privileges of bleedin' rank. But hey, I'm happy to give you my thoughts on the matter . . . if you have a need for 'em?"

"Fuck off faither why don't you?" was the best Thoroughgood could come up with through gritted teeth.

"Drink?" asked Hardie.

"Aye, why not? After all if Tomachek doesn't leave me with my head in my hands then the chances are it will be removed from my shoulders when the clock strikes midnight and we are poncing about in the bloody Botanics . . ."

Hardie went on, "Listen, I know you're going to take shite from the old man but what else does he have right now? The other thing that concerns me, gaffer, is what the fuck are the intelligence services doing about all of this?

Don't you find it strange we haven't been called in to a joint meeting and a 'thank you lads but no thank you – there's a pair of good little plods now'?"

Thoroughgood's eyebrows rose in an admission that the thought had crossed his mind. "Exactly. But time is short, so you pour the drinks and I'll do the talking. Captain Morgan's and coke will do the job."

"Absolutement," was the reply from Hardie.

"OK, here we go. We have kept the auld man in the dark about Sushi but he knows we've been workin' on something. If he had anything better up his sleeve himself we would know about it by now surely? We'll be offering him something that will strengthen his hand and I think after the usual verbal arse kickin' he'll be crackin' open that bottle of Glengoyne he keeps in his desk."

His Gettysburg address rehearsed, Thoroughgood sat down in his armchair and accepted the glass of frothing dark liquid Hardie had offered him.

"Get that down you gaffer and then bell the old buzzard. Personally speaking I think we have him by the balls. One thing I would suggest is that you push him on the intelligence services. I just cannae get my heid around the fact they haven't had any intel' on Tariq."

After a final slug of his Morgan's Thoroughgood picked up the phone and keyed in the digits of Tomachek's home number. A thought crossed his mind.

"Feck me, it has just occurred to me that I know the auld man's number better than my own bleedin' number. How sad is that?"

The other end of the phone clicked into life and a voice boomed, "Valentino Tomachek. That you, Thoroughgood?"

"Yes gaffer. Sorry to bother you but I needed to talk with you urgently," said Thoroughgood.

"Balls and bleedin' buggery Thoroughgood! Get on with it then, I was almost in the land of nod," barked the detective superintendent.

Thoroughgood gave his commanding officer the bottom line. "Okay, boss. We've established a point of contact with Tariq's gang of Jihadists and we have a meet tonight, 12pm at the Botanic Gardens."

A bout of coughing broke out at the other end of the phone. "Bally hell, you've done what? How by the rood's name did you manage to do that?"

Thoroughgood felt somewhat disconcerted that he was going to have to admit to his earlier economies with the truth.

"I mentioned to you that we had someone in the pipe-line who may be able to help us with translations. Well it turns out he has been able to do a good bit more than that. Are you ready for the full Monty, gaffer?"

"Blow me senseless, Thoroughgood, at this stage I wouldn't want it any other way. Now get a bally move on man."

"The Spear of Islam are being masterminded by the Imam Tariq who is the main man at the Glasgow Central Mosque. His preaching has become increasingly radical-ised recently and he has sought to develop influence over the younger, more suggestible members of his congrega-tion." Thoroughgood halted for breath.

"Carry on," came from the other end of the blower.

Thoroughgood did as he was bid. "We have intelli-gence that leads us to believe he has also recruited a group of terrorists fresh from the al-Qaeda training grounds in the south western frontier of Pakistan.

"Tariq has been holding meetings for his radicalised followers at the Half-Moon bookshop. Earlier this week, witnessed by an informer, he preached Jihad. After he had done so he was joined by five of his brothers from abroad brandishing AK-47s.

"Although the two males who committed the Dowanhill atrocities wore masks, the description of their gear that day fits with that worn at the meeting by Tariq's Jihadist death squad. That is also the case with the terrorists who appear on the hostage film."

Thoroughgood finished the second part of his command performance and waited for reaction.

"In the name of the wee man . . ."

The detective sergeant quickly forced his voice into the silence left after Tomachek's reaction and proceeded. "We now have an informant who has made contact with the gang through The Half-Moon bookshop and used Saladin's dagger as bait to arrange the meeting with a member of the Imam's gang tonight.

"Our man will provide the location of the dagger in an effort, firstly, to lure Tariq – or at least some of his gang – out.

Secondly, we will try to ingratiate our man within Tariq's inner circle. Our man has been warned that he must come alone and he knows the risk involved but it is one he is willing to take."

"In the name of Mother Mary, tell me that is it?" pleaded Tomachek.

Thoroughgood could only disappoint his superior officer. "Nope. We have had the note attached to the Dowanhill corpse translated. We believe it suggests that the Braehead bombing was only the start of a concerted bombing campaign that is going to continue possibly at shopping centres all over Scotland and maybe even the UK. We do not have a bloody clue where or when the next atrocity will come."

"Before we go into how to handle the Botanics meet I have a question for you . . ."

"Fire away," Tomachek's replied tersely.

"Just where the hell are the security services in all of this?"

Tomachek cleared his throat. Clearly discomfited by the question and the information that he had no other option but to provide, he blustered. Badly.

"Indeed, dear boy, a legitimate question if ever there was one. Also it must be said one that leads us into an absolute bally bloody minefield."

Thoroughgood forced the issue. "Come on boss, I think you owe me, Hardie and the boy putting his life on the line tonight, the bottom line."

"Without doubt, Thoroughgood, without doubt. Alright here it is. MI5 have been monitoring Tariq and his group from the inside. Until the Braehead bomb they thought he was a firebrand with a big mouth but no terror portfolio.

"Their man on the inside believed that there was no real hard and fast threat. Just 'chatter' as they like to call it. So they made the call that rather than expose an informant who had taken months to get in under deep cover they would let him lie a bit longer. A calculated risk but one that the boys had to make. With me so far, Thoroughgood? Hardie?"

"We are," was the chorused reply.

"The problem is that their man on the inside has disappeared off the map since Braehead. MI5 suspect he has turned double agent. So, from MI5/M16 believing they had everything under control up here they have discovered within the last few hours that they have likely been completely misinformed and we are, to put it politely, up shit creek without the proverbial paddle."

Hardie's voice came over the line. "Fuck me boss! Does that mean that we are the only show on the road?"

"Yes and no is the answer to that one Hardie. I am meeting Sir Willie Stratford at Stewart Street tomorrow morning; I want you two in attendance. Your man's meeting is vital, and after tomorrow's conference we'll have the full backing of the London based intelligence services including surveillance, but until then we're on our own. So you fellows take no chances tonight and likewise your man. Is there more?"

Thoroughgood's voice burst into life. "Yes there is. Tariq appears to have sleepers in key positions all over the city. He must have learned through them, of the liaison between Jim Fraser and Vanessa Velvet. Can I confirm that every available security measure has been adopted round all possible targets - the airport, hospitals and the like?"

"What do you take me for Thoroughgood? A bally amateur? The chief has made sure that he has done everything to ensure that Glasgow sleeps safely tonight. We have the army out and their bomb disposal experts on 24 hour standby. Glasgow is in a ring of steel between the army and our own armed response units. All leave has been cancelled indefinitely with the rank and file. God willing we come through tonight with something we can build on bloody quick.

"As of tomorrow I'd expect the intelligence services to

166

take control of the whole shooting match, pardon the pun, but if we can hand them over some key intelligence and a route to Tariq then I think, Detective Sergeant Thoroughgood, I may be able to guarantee you a couple of pips on your shoulder. As for you Hardie, instead of that bloody great big chip you carry on each of your shoulders how would a set of stripes go down?"

At the other end of the phone Tomachek took a gulp of something that was clearly not air and added, "As if all of that wasn't enough Johnny Balfour and several of the city's most notorious 'businessmen' were mown down at an exclusive rooftop restaurant this afternoon. CCTV footage has shown the killers to be dear old Tony Blair and George W."

Thoroughgood could not help his incredulity. "How the hell does that all add up?"

"I have not the slightest clue, but I do know that I will see you in my office at 11am tomorrow morning for the meeting with Stratford. Don't be trying to get yourself killed to avoid it now dear boy."

"I'll do my best," replied Thoroughgood.

23

BY 11PM Sushi had been fully briefed by Thoroughgood and Hardie about the information they wanted to put Tariq's way.

A phone call earlier that evening to Professor Farouk had arranged for the dagger to be relocated to his office the next day and round the clock surveillance mounted to keep watch on the premises thereafter. The Intelligence services were to assume control of the operation and Farouk would ensure that his department was closed for the day.

As locations go it was less than perfect but at the same time the risk of collateral damage had to be weighed up against the need to have Tariq believe that the object of his desire was located somewhere it was attainable and not an obvious trap.

With 24 hours having ticked away towards the execution of Vanessa Velvet and Jim Fraser, unless the Al-Qaeda Jihadist in Guantanamo Bay was released, any arguments against the plan were flimsy.

Thoroughgood and Hardie would be inside the Botanics grounds, on surveillance duties, while both of the garden's entrances would be watched by trusted men.

Thoroughgood had enlisted the help of his old mate DC Ross McNab, the perma-tan prince of the Serious Crime Squad. Hardie had called in a favour to ensure that Detective Sergeant Ally Brown, a man with a knack for thinking outside the box, had also been enlisted.

On top of that the Armed Response Team were on a discreet standby, imaginatively housed within the actual confines of the greenhouse which had not gone down well with either their commander or his team given the soaring temperatures within.

For his part, at bang on midnight Sushi had to drop the details of the dagger's new location and his contact details in a closed container underneath a bench outside the giant Victorian greenhouse. Then all the waiter had to do was vacate the gardens before he came eyeball to eyeball with Tariq's representative. Sushi had been well warned that he could not afford to linger and thus put the operation in jeopardy, The bottom line of the op being to place a tail on Tariq's man that would at last give them something to work with.

At 23.55 Sushi walked up the path, fag in mouth. He felt the sweat trickling down his back and wondered how he had found himself playing a major role in trying to prevent the biggest terrorist incident the city might ever see.

Thirty yards from the bench and he was aware of a slight trembling in his legs. "Get a grip," he told himself, furtively glancing over his shoulders to see if he had any company. Apparently he did not.He tried hard not to let his eyes linger on the hydrangea bushes that flanked either side of the path, in which he knew Hardie and Thorough-good were hidden.

As he approached the bench Sushi admired the impressive greenhouse. It was a place that had provided Sushi with a lot of pleasure. It was here in the late nineties that he had found his first love.

An afternoon of sunbathing on the immaculate lawns of the Botanics was a popular past-time for West Enders and the teenage Sushi and his mates had often made a beeline for it during an unusually balmy summer.

'When was it? '97 or '98?' he asked himself. He remembered his first meeting with Laura, an English and Classics student.

He gazed at the left of the greenhouse where she had sat, all poise and class, the first time he had clapped eyes on her. Man, they had made some sweet music that summer. He wondered where she was now?

It was in the Botanics too that he had first come across Thoroughgood, while working on the Sally - short for salmonella - fast food van that had been outside the main entrance back since anyone could remember. The DS's penchant for spicy food had meant the pair often banged into each other at the West End's more exotic eateries from then on.

Those early meetings were what had ultimately brought him to this moment, that and the fact that something had to be done about Tariq and the evil he and his men were spreading. To Sushi it still beggared belief that they could have pulled off the bombing at Braehead. As for the murders on Dowanhill, they made Sushi sick to his core.

Every time he left his front door, hostile eyes were directed his way. The panic the events had caused led to the organisation of an emergency meeting of the Mosque

170

Council. The elders agreed that something had to be done.

He still could not get his head around the fact that Tariq was prepared to jeopardise the lives of the thousands of Muslims living across Europe to augment the forces of terrorism in al-Qaeda and the Taliban.

Maybe the invasion of Afghanistan and Iraq was illegal, but was financing the mass slaughter of innocents, and spreading vitriol against the West, the way to redress it?

For Sushi, a devout Muslim, it was impossible to square Tariq's version of Islam with that espoused in the Koran. He fished into the pocket of his bomber jacket, feeling uncomfortable encased in the Kevlar bulletproof vest he wore underneath, and pulled out the container holding the message details. He prayed to Allah it would be seized upon by Tariq's men and provide a trail to the Imam himself.

Looking closely at the bench he noticed a commemorative silver plate – 'In loving memory of Elsie Harris (1930-2001) for whom this spot provided many happy hours. Donated by her loving husband Frank.'

Sushi felt a wave of emotion well up inside him.

Then the bullet smashed into his head and he toppled over Elsie's bench. The container fell out of his hand onto the path.

Thoroughgood and Hardie had been positioned on either side of Sushi at a distance of around 30 feet, lying under the cover of bushes. As soon as the crack echoed out they knew it had come from a sniper's rifle. As Thoroughgood screamed a warning to the waiter, the bullet impacted into the rear of Sushi's head. His blood began to trickle slowly down the path he had just climbed.

171

The silence was shattered for a second time by Hardie's voice howling a single word. "Bastards!" Without a care for his own safety, the DC was out of cover and heading for Sushi as quickly as his stubby legs would take him.

Thoroughgood was frozen in shock. It was they who had been set up and not Tariq. The sniper was almost certainly the same one from Dowanhill. He was unlikely to pack up and head home when he could get two birds for the price of one.

Hardie was almost certainly in his sights and that meant only one thing to Thoroughgood – his mate was about to meet his maker. Suddenly a giant flash of light erupted over their heads, shining in the direction of the rooftops where the shot had come from.

A second crack echoed out but this time it was followed by the smash of glass, underlining that the sniper had been unsighted by the spotlight aimed in his direction.

Approaching Sushi's body and the heaving figure of Hardie, who had dragged the waiter behind the bench for cover, Thoroughgood could already hear the voice of the Tactical Firearms Unit Commander calling in the police helicopter and directing them towards the rooftop of Glasgow University's Dalrymple Hall of Residence.

Arriving at the bench Thoroughgood was met by Hardie's enraged gaze. "He's dead Gus. I'd say we're well and truly fucked now."

Thoroughgood's silence indicated that for once he and Hardie were in total agreement.

24

IT WAS almost 2am when Thoroughgood arrived back at his flat, emotionally and physically exhausted. He ached for sleep. As he put his key in the security door his mind was relentlessly replaying the events of the last couple of hours and asking what they could have done differently.

Despite an extensive search no traces of the sniper – apart from two spent cartridges – had been found. The cartridges had almost certainly been left as a calling card.

Thoroughgood had updated Tomachek by phone. The apoplectic superintendent had confirmed that the 11am meeting with Willie Stratford was still on, leaving Thoroughgood in no doubt that the Botanic Gardens fiasco would result in Strathclyde Police being hung out to dry after the further loss of civilian life. Tomachek had warned the DS that he, Thoroughgood, would shoulder full responsibility. For his part Thoroughgood had been too tired and desolate to argue the toss.

While Tomachek had applied the verbal hairdryer to Thoroughgood, Hardie had gone into overdrive; making sure a full entry was on the Holmes Major Inquiry system and leaving notes to the great and the good, including the Head of CID and the ACC Crime. Full statements had been taken and a precise briefing note for Tomachek to take to the meeting later that morning had been written.

As Thoroughgood pushed the heavy door open he did not know whether he had the strength to undress before letting sleep claim him or, conversely, the ability to stop his mind flaying him with guilt over Sushi's demise.

"Detective Sergeant Thoroughgood," said a female voice from behind him. Exhausted he turned slowly, trying to keep the door open and gain a good line of sight out into the night.

"It's Aisha, Professor Farouk's daughter. I just wanted to speak with you."

Thoroughgood hardly felt welcoming. However guilty it made him feel, though, Aisha had entered his thoughts on more than one occasion since they had met.

"Yeah, sure, come in," and he beckoned Aisha to follow him up to the flat. Ushering her into the lounge he was conscious that it was here that he'd last seen Sushi and now, thanks to him, the waiter was dead.

Slowly his mind filled with guilt. 'Why didn't you blow your brains out on Sunday morning? No balls? The only thing that you have ever been any good at is turning the lives of those around you to shit. If you had, you useless bastard, Sushi would still be here.' He realised that the curtains had not been drawn day or night since that morning. 'No point in opening the drapes now mate,' added the helpful voice in his head.

Clearing his throat he gestured to Aisha to make herself comfortable on the settee. He noticed that his grandfather's revolver was still perched disconcertingly on the mantle piece, the old man's bible and an empty whisky glass keeping it company.

'Shit! How the fuck had Hardie failed to spot it?' he wondered.

He opted to pursue a 'silence is golden' policy and stammered an apology. "Sorry about the mess, the last couple of days I've hardly had time to draw air never mind keep the place tidy." As discreetly as he could, he tipped the revolver into his inside jacket pocket.

But Aisha wasn't about to let the evidence in front of her to go unremarked. "An empty whisky glass and a revolver! An interesting combination, Detective Sergeant Thoroughgood."

He smiled weakly. Her eyes felt like they were peering into his soul but thankfully she did not pursue the topic further.

Edging towards the door he said, "Listen, I could murder a drink. Fancy a glass of red? I think I have a decent bottle of Malbec."

"Yeah, that would make a nice nightcap," she agreed.

When he returned there was definite warmth in her smile. 'What have I done to deserve that?' he asked himself. She took the glass of red and sipped.

Thoroughgood rifled through his CD drawer without thinking.

Watching him with interest Aisha said "Maybe I shouldn't have come by so late but I came off back-shift and went for a couple of drinks with the girls up at Cottiers. My father told me where you lived because I wanted to thank you. I know you guys in the CID don't keep regular hours – just like us."

She sipped from her wine glass, the redness of the Malbec giving her lips a heightened fullness that was proving a powerful antidote to Thoroughgood's exhaustion.

He put on *How Can I Sleep With Your Voice Inside My Head?* by A-ha, then without a word he slipped into his favourite armchair and grabbed his wine glass, his nervousness making Aisha frown in puzzlement.

"So, DS Thoroughgood, are you ok with a female visitor at this time of the night?"

He attempted to smile that he was, but guilt was starting to seep through him. 'You're a charlatan, Thoroughgood. One minute you're playing Russian roulette, forever heartbroken and the next you've got the 'Night Nurse" here, mentally undressed and bedded in five minutes.' As he battled his internal demons the silence drew on.

Aisha could sense all was not going according to her plan. "I'm sorry; I know it's late. I don't make a habit of this, it was a bad idea. I'll finish my wine and head home. I'm sorry, this was all very selfish of me."

Her words acted as a metaphorical bucket of water and the vision of Celine that had been about to replace Aisha's svelte dark features, disappeared.

"No, I'm sorry. We've just had a disastrous night ending with the murder of a good friend. I don't know if I want to lay all my problems out before you. Can I just say things have happened in my life over the last few months that I'm still struggling to come to terms with."

"You mean Celine?"

And that was it, the floodgates opened and out it all poured. Her words hit him like a freight train and his tears came. He cuffed at them with his hand and jumped up, stormed over to the curtains, opening them to look out at Partickhill Road glowing eerily in the moonlight.

Aisha spoke. "I know what happened, Gus, I know about Declan Meechan. I know about Celine and how it all came to an end for you two. God, it was all over the papers and it dawned on me today, after you left, exactly who you were. All I can say is, I want to help, if you'll let me."

He leaned forward and planted his forehead on the window pane, sobbing his heart out. Then his legs seemed to give way and he slumped to his knees.

Immediately he felt the encircling embrace of her arms around him. "It's okay, okay, let it go Gus, let it all go." Slowly he turned round and buried his head in her shoulder, aware that this had been the first time since Celine's death that he had sought any real comfort from another human being.

Her proximity, her smell, her warmth were a heady intoxicating brew, preying on his heightened state of emotional anxiety. Again he was wracked with guilt for allowing any emotion other than desolation to permeate his being. He was aware of her leading him over to the settee. "Sorry," he repeated, over and over.

She cradled his head in her hands and kissed his forehead and for once in his life Gus Thoroughgood was at a complete loss over what to do next. Her brilliant, azure eyes penetrated his and she could have done with him what she wanted at that moment, so laid bare had he become.

He became aware that she was speaking softly, adding to the sensuality of the moment. "Do you want me to leave you alone tonight Gus?"

Staring into her eyes he moved closer to Aisha and her lush ruby lips. They kissed.

In the background Morten Harket sang *Summer Moved On.*

He woke that morning alone but with the smell of her still fresh on his sheets. Squinting at the red figures on his alarm clock he saw that it was 9am. In just two hours he faced one of the most important meetings of his career – if he still had one.

A debrief in which he would have to fight a rear-guard against an incandescent Tomachek reeling at the embarrassment caused to Strathclyde Police by the Botanic Gardens incident and Sushi's murder, in front of the Head of MI5, Sir Willie Strafford, one of the most powerful figures in British intelligence.

The creak of his bedroom door opening brought him back to the here and now. With it came the almost overpowering presence of Aisha. She was carrying his Partick Thistle mug filled with steaming coffee and a plate with a couple of slices of toast.

But it was what she wore that threw him. She was wearing his shirt from the night before, just as Celine had always done, and his initial smile faded fast. This wasn't lost on Aisha as she set the mug and plate down.

"Is it the shirt, Gus?" she asked in the slightly accented voice that added to her allure.

He decided, in the wake of what they had shared last night, that honesty was the best policy. "Yup. Why is it that the women I go for always take ownership of my shirts like some kind of trophy?"

She smiled and leant forward, cupping his jaw in her hands and kissing him – lightly at first but with a slow increase in pressure that forced him to use all of his powers of self-control.

She drew back, picked up the mug and took a sip of his coffee, perching on the side of the bed, legs crossed in

a pose that sent his senses through an emotional stratosphere.

"Is that what I am to you Detective Sergeant, one of
the women you go for?" she asked.

He chuckled, enjoying the fact he didn't feel guilty
for the moment of mirth. "Correct me if I'm wrong, Staff
Nurse Farouk, but surely it was you who went for me?"

With time against them, he felt he needed to firm up
just where last night had left them.

"Aisha, I'd love to see you again. But I have a nightmare debriefing this morning and I just don't know how
things are going to go for me after the Intelligence boys at
MI5 take over the enquiry."

She leaned back and sighed: "So what you are telling
me Gus, is that you would like to see me again but don't
know when you will have time?"

Thoroughgood cleared his throat awkwardly. "I guess
that is the bottom line, and all because of this little baby."
He pulled out Saladin's dagger, the superb ivory and bejewelled handle crowning the vicious curved blade.

He placed it on the bed between them and they both
looked at it.

Aisha was first to speak. "Wal, the ceremonial dagger.
800 years of history lying on your bed. Do you know this
dagger was used by Saladin against the butcher Raynald
de Chatillon? I guess its role in destroying Chatillon and
the winning of the battle of Hattin which allowed Saladin
to reclaim Jerusalem and the Al-Aqsa Mosque are why it
is so revered."

She picked it up and held it in the palms of her hands
in obvious awe, reading the carved words on the handle
out loud. Immediately Thoroughgood chorused them with

179

her. Then, as she grimaced when their meaning hit home he said:

"Somehow we have got to stop Tariq taking any more 'infidel' lives and make sure he never takes possession of the dagger."

Aisha nodded. "That is so. Yet at the same time the dagger is your best hope to lure Tariq into daylight. It is a dangerous and difficult game you are playing Gus."

25

THE DOOR to Tomachek's office was open and the smoke billowed out into the corridor as Thoroughgood and Hardie entered. Tomachek was not alone. In the corner, leaning nonchalantly against the archaic filing cabinet and drinking a mug of coffee was Sir Willie Stratford, head of MI5.

As Thoroughgood entered he took stock of Stratford's imposing figure, his immaculate pinstriped navy blue suit and his Harlequin's Rugby Football Club tie which hinted at a sporting past. He exuded casual authority.

"These must be the two fellows I have been hearing so much about. Pleased to meet you," drawled Stratford in a smooth English public school accent.

Stratford straightened up and, adjusting his double fold cuffs, strode over to greet Thoroughgood and Hardie. Tomachek, his subordinates noticed, sat silently fuming on his walnut pipe which was blowing smoke at an incredible rate.

Stratford offered his hand and his introduction in unequivocal fashion. "Sir Willie Stratford at your service, gentlemen, and damn good to meet you both at last."

After a round of handshakes that would have graced

any masonic lodge meeting, Thoroughgood and Hardie took their customary seats opposite Tomachek aware that their superior officer, relegated to the role of subordinate by the imposing presence of Stratford, had still failed to find his usual voice.

That soon changed. Tomachek removed his pipe and tapped the head onto his ashtray.

"As you know gentlemen, this matter has now gone well beyond our remit. Sir Willie is here to take overall control of the enquiry. I have brought him fully up to date with all of the events since the Braehead explosion, right up to the Botanics last night."

Tomachek belched like some venerable silver-backed Gorilla, intent on making a statement of primal reaffirment that this was still his turf. Then he ploughed on: "But now you need to hear what Sir Willie has to say from his side of things." With that statement Tomachek appeared almost satisfied at his walk on role and gestured for his visitor to continue, "Sir Willie if you care to take things on?"

Sir Willie slurped on his mug of coffee and placed it down. "Don't mind if I do, Tomachek. Well, we have a real problem here as I'm sure you are aware and one I am not going to be able to offer much positive input to.

"At present we have thirty-five Islamic terrorist networks within London alone and sundry others throughout England and Wales, while in Scotland right now there are twelve.

"The terrorist threat level is currently severe, the second highest on the Reichter scale, so to speak." Sir Willie rubbed his hand over his shiny dome a couple of times then levelled grey eyes that had a hint of cruelty in them at Thoroughgood and Hardie.

"Most of these networks comprise of two or three activists, with a few numbering up to six. The members become radicalized and melt into their own communities as sleeper agents, maintaining contact with each other at Friday mosque prayers and waiting for instruction.

"Their deep cover is protected by the normality of their daily jobs as academics, doctors, schoolteachers etc. All the time they observe our society for weaknesses and flaws they can capitalise and exploit."

Stratford took another slurp of coffee and carried on. "These are the networks that spawned the 'shoe bomber' Richard Reid and the London 7/7 bombers. Some of them train in Pakistan before returning to Blighty as sleeper agents.

"These people are resourceful and they pursue training on these shores in remote areas like the Brecon Beacon Mountains and suchlike to be ready for their big day. I fear most wholeheartedly gentlemen, with all due respect to the victims of Braehead, that we have an even bigger 'day' coming in Glasgow."

Thoroughgood cleared his throat, acutely aware that to interrupt a man of Sir Willie's stature was risky, and spoke into the temporary void he had created. "If I may?"

Stratford nodded.

"I take it that you have analysed all the data and evidence from the atrocities at Braehead, Dowanhill and the cache at St Vincent Terrace?"

"Indeed," Stratford replied curtly.

Despite the dismissive tone of his reply Thoroughgood continued, "Don't you have most of the mosques in the UK under surveillance? Why didn't you know about the increasingly radicalised nature of Tariq's preachings and his growing followers?"

Stratford sipped his coffee slowly to underline the fact he would provide an answer on his terms. "My dear fellow if only it were as easy as that," he said in a slightly patronising tone before continuing. "Look Detective Sergeant, I see what you are driving at, but even when you know a Jihadist cell is in operation, taking action against it is not an easy thing, pre-emptively speaking.

"You do know – I sincerely hope – that neither MI5 nor MI6 have the power of arrest?"

Hardie interjected. "Buggered if I did, Sir. But surely in an age of global surveillance you must be able to keep your suspects under scrutiny 24/7?"

Stratford turned his slate grey eyes on Hardie, clearly irked at the blunt nature of his question. "The intelligence community works closely with the police to ensure arrests are made but then you have these infuriating human rights lawyers challenging every arrest on the slightest bloody pretext.

"So the process, gentlemen, is exhaustive and expensive in terms of both manpower and finance. As for surveillance, every predominantly Muslim area in the UK including Glasgow is subject to surveillance from cameras using fibre optics that can pick up to 50 individual traits and track a potential terrorist along a street or in and out of a building."

Sir Willie was in full flow now. "We have one network devoted to automatic licence plate recognition that goes from snapshot to target recognition in the blink of an eye."

Hardie snapped, "So, if you've got all of that technology, all of that global surveillance, then how in the name of the wee man did a team of Jihadists wash up in auld Glasgae toon without a hint or a trace on your feckin' radar?"

Thoroughgood added his dissent. "And how has Tariq been able to recruit and develop terrorists in our city? Surely he must be known to you? You must monitor all cellphone use, emails etc. and share intel' with the CIA, Mossad and the like, especially after all the bad press that MI5 had."

Stratford's face was a mixture of anger and frustration. "That is just it gentlemen; we thought we were well versed on what Tariq was up to until very recently. Our man on the inside has disappeared and so has our intel'. In any case it would now appear that intel' was for the most part fabrication."

"Rogue?" boomed the previously calm Tomachek.

"We have been aware of Tariq for around six months and an agent was inserted to ensure a steady flow of information. We got just that initially but of late it became irregular then went dry and our man has, or should I say had, disappeared off the map."

A previously gnawing concern now suddenly made sense for Thoroughgood. "Of course! Your man on the inside was Doctor Mustafa Mohammed who has been identified among the dead at Braehead."

Stratford nodded resignedly. "That is the case. It appears that Tariq had managed to wave his messianic spell over Mohammed. Clearly it is vital we find Tariq and his henchmen quickly but we also have two other pressing needs."

Stratford placed the filofax from St Vincent Terrace onto Tomachek's desk before continuing. "Firstly, when you add the 'Nikah', begging your pardon, or wedding email to the anonymous location, you have two parts of a jigsaw of terror. Gentlemen, we are running out of time to work out the location and date of the impending nuptials.

"Secondly, we have two high-profile hostages with very little time left and at this precise moment we don't have the damnedest clue where they or their captors are. So you are correct gentlemen. Despite this age of global surveillance, we do not have a foggy where Tariq is."

It was all too much for Tomachek; his colour had been rising as the seconds passed and at last he blew. "I don't believe my own ears. You have millions of pounds worth of technology at your fingertips and you wouldn't have known if your own agent was alive or dead without a lucky break with his dental work. Well I have news for you, Sir William." The use of the intelligence chief's full name was not lost on Thoroughgood or Hardie. "It is obvious to me and my colleagues that your man in the field did indeed turn rogue and had been shovelling you a pile of shite. And we're left in the middle of a chain of terrorist atrocities in Glasgow just because you lot think the world ends at London's city limits."

Stratford stammered nervously in the face of Tomachek's onslaught. "I can assure you Superintendent Tomachek, all measures are being taken and we will have the matter in hand as soon as possible."

Thoroughgood tried to press the intelligence chief from a different angle. "If you're not picking up sufficient chatter from Tariq's team via cellphone, email and the like, then they must be communicating by other means surely? Have the mosque and Tariq's apartments been bugged? Surely you have something that will help us locate him or identify someone who can?"

"That is not the case, largely because our man on the inside fed us a diet of duff information."

Hardie chipped in, "What if there are two parts to Tariq's group? Firstly the home grown Jihadists; cultivated young, sent away to train then returning to take their place in apparently normal domestic life – like your man Mustafa? Secondly, guns for hire, 24 carat Jihadists using specialist equipment to take out punters on the streets.

"If that is the case," Hardie continued, "then as well as trying to locate Tariq we have another twofold investigation and very little time."

Thoroughgood continued where his sidekick had left off. "Listen, there are two ways forward. Firstly our contact Professor Farouk is an elder on the mosque council and views Tariq's rantings as anathema, and he may well not be the only one.

"Tariq is likely to have sympathisers on the council and I'm pretty sure that Farouk will have a good idea who they are. So we locate them through Farouk and then it's over to your agents, Sir."

Stratford nodded his approval while a slight smirk appeared at the corners of Tomachek's mouth.

The DS continued. "Secondly, Farouk attended a meeting at The Half-Moon bookshop earlier this week at which Tariq basically announced Jihad and flaunted his AK-47 toting terrorists.

Farouk will be able to give us names of those in attendance and the bookshop owner. With your surveillance vans in situ' surely to God we would get something."

Hardie interjected, "There is another angle that I think has real potential. The kidnapping at One Devonshire Gardens was obviously based on inside information. My betting is that background checks will point to at least one member of staff there being part of a sleeper cell. After the checks they can be brought in on anti-terrorist legislation and we can surely get a spin-off."

Stratford looked unconvinced. "I'll have every member of staff at the hotel vetted and once we have some sort of association they will be placed under surveillance. But I would suggest they would be more use to us being monitored in the field rather than in the cells at Govan Police Station saying nothing and with briefs and human rights activists crying wrongful arrest, injustice and racial harassment."

Tomachek pitched in, "I concur with Sir Willie on that one. We have to maximise the chances of turning over a lead that will take us to Tariq. It is vital we have as many riders and runners to pursue over the course as possible."

"We also have the dagger," added Thoroughgood.

"I propose to take it with me on a visit to the Half-Moon and let them know I have it in my possession. That should allow us to draw out some kind of response."

Sir Willie lifted his coffee cup up and peered into it for a moment before putting it down. "Well, gentlemen, time is against us but this is how I propose we go forward."

"Detectives, you will liaise with Professor Farouk immediately and obtain a list of those who may be associated with Tariq and privy to the information we need. When you get that list I want it emailed to Chief Intelligence Officer Malcolm Etherington ASAP. He will forthwith be the main liaison officer between our two organisations.

"Then I want the Half-Moon visited and once more gentlemen, everything you have from that visit emailed to Etherington. At 6pm today we will have a further meeting in this office."

Sir Willie continued, "In the interests of time I have

taken the liberty of having this meeting recorded. Our surveillance operation officially starts from now and before you get to the bookshop we will have a van situated near by monitoring it.

"I must also advise you that there is a conduit opened with the anti-terrorist branch at Scotland Yard. Every potential terrorist target in your city is now under our scrutiny. You have my word that the protection and safety of the citizens of Glasgow are firmly at the top of Her Majesty's Secret Agents' agenda.

"If there is nothing else gentlemen, I suggest we be about our business. It is a pretty mess and we are going to need the help of the Almighty and more than a bit of good fortune to clear it up in time."

Hardie couldn't help himself. "You can say that again."

Sir Willie walked out the office leaving the three detectives in a state verging on shell-shock.

26

TARIQ PACED the damp confines of the room that had become his HQ, listening to the words of his trusted lieutenant. The intelligence services had arrived in Glasgow. It was Tariq's intention to have their whereabouts and activities monitored by the army of informants he had cultivated from his days of street corner preaching.

He knew that he had inspired great loyalty in his men but he was also acutely aware that they did not have the training to defeat the technical capabilities that would now be brought to bear against them.

Beside him, Naif appraised the Imam. "There was a meeting earlier today in the city centre police office between local police and Sir William Stratford, the Head of MI5. We are now going to have the full force of the infidel unleashed against us.

"Yet everything is in place and now all you need to do is make and broadcast the film to ensure we keep our brothers and sisters safe while we inflict destruction on the infidel."

Tariq nodded his head at his second in command. Naif had been crucial to him in enlisting and radicalising young impressionable members of the community with his tales of the war against first the Soviets and then the 'crusaders' in Afghanistan.

Naif's tale of how he came about his ruined white eye in a fire fight with the devils of the SAS in Kandahar was a major attraction. But it was the fact that Naif had been in the company of Osama bin Laden and been able to recount his dignity and serenity and his devoutness to the word of Allah and the five pillars of wisdom, which had brought the volunteers flocking to Tariq's meetings. Ultimately, these volunteers had left for the Jihadist training centres of North West Pakistan before returning to take up places in Glasgow's society in different communities and professions. Trusted and valued people, waiting for the time when they would be needed.

That time had come.

Tariq inclined his head towards Naif and said, "All is good. If we want to make sure our plans are completed in the way that will enshrine our names alongside that of Sheikh Osama and Ayman al-Zawahiri we must make sure that there are no loose ends."

That was why using cellphones and any other electronic devices that could be traced to his whereabouts was strictly forbidden.

Naif met his gaze steadily. "That is as I am sure Imam. Your will shall be done. Praise Allah."

But Tariq needed further assurance from Naif that success would be guaranteed. He said: "I have your word brother, that the target you have selected will cause maximum impact both physical and mental?"

Naif met his demand with his usual assuredness. "Yes Imam. We have selected the Buchanan Street Underground Station because it is at the very heart of the city."

Naif continued, "This station is surrounded by offices and shops and sure to be busy. No one will be able to stop us and when our truck impacts at the entrance it will kill all those inside or within a radius of 100 metres. It will also show how futile the safety methods the infidels have been boasting about since Braehead are."

Tariq almost purred with delight at the thought of the destruction he would wreak, yet still he wanted more detail. "Can we be sure that there will be no premature explosion before the truck reaches its target?"

Naif smiled. "Have no fears Imam. We have used a mixture that is tried and tested and sure to produce the desired result. Hasim, Allah rest his soul, had produced a supply of devices of the highest quality before he entered through the gates of Paradise. Do you wish me to go into more detail, Imam?"

Tariq stroked his black beard for a second before nodding almost imperceptibly that he did.

Naif went on, "The ingredients, TNT, aluminium nitrate and aluminium powder, were mixed most carefully by Hasim in my presence Imam. The mixture was placed in boxes used for containing fruit and vegetables which have all been wired to batteries.

"We have 1,500 lbs. of explosives in the delivery truck plus a number of gas cylinders also wired up to the main connection. This, Imam, means that when the explosion occurs there will be a fragmentation process that will provide a deadly rain of shrapnel, tearing through the air and slicing through the bodies of any infidels in the vicinity. In short, carnage.

"This method was used in the attacks by our brothers on the American embassies at Nairobi, Kenya and Dar esSalaam, Tanzania in 1998 to great effect. I am confident we will enjoy similar results in Glasgow."

Tariq smiled cruelly. "Excellent, Naif. All is in hand and we can turn our attention to spreading panic through the unbelievers whilst warning the faithful of what is to come."

Tariq planned to take a chance by broadcasting a film that would echo a famous speech of bin Laden's and so by association, he hoped, insert himself into the consciousness of the greater Islamic world. The film would be posted via the Al-Jazeera website to ensure there was no technical trace obtainable from it. Puffing out his cheeks Tariq took his place on the simple seat at the end of the room.

"Naif, I want you to stand behind me at my right shoulder. Your presence is known throughout the mosque now. You are the man who defied the SAS and was introduced to and honoured by sheik Osama and broke bread with him in the caves of Tora Bora.

"You are an inspiration to our young and it is time we come out from behind our masks and let the world know who is behind the Jihad in this city of the damned."

Naif responded with pride. "Imam, it will be an honour. I will stand behind you just like I watched sheik Osama's back these summers past."

Looking at the camera, his head held proudly, Tariq spoke. "We are living in dignity and honour, for which we thank God. It is much better for us to live under the ground or under a tree or even in a wasteland than to live in comfort at the behest and under the shadow of the infidel's patronage.

"Even in a land that is Godless we must make sure that

we, the true believers, continue to adhere to the shahada, to worship and obey the words of Allah at the appointed time and also follow the prophethood of Mohammed. If the believer does so he or she will come to no harm.

"The time is come; we have brought Jihad to these shores in this Godless city of the infidel and forced him to feel the pain, experience the fear that he has wrought upon our defenceless communities for all these years. I ask you the devout to join us in the World Islamic Front and to bring home the words of the sheik Osama with all your power."

Then he concluded, "Jihad is everyman's duty – fard ayan."

With that the recording ended and Tariq returned to his office to wait for the next stage in his Jihad to be waged.

27

IT WAS 10.00hrs Friday morning and Sergeant Hugh Campbell had just started the third cup of coffee of his twelve hour tour of duty. He was the officer in charge of the 'ring of steel' encircling Buchanan Street Underground and neighbouring Queen Street Station and he was bored shitless.

Everyone had seen the video of 'that nutjob' Tariq broadcast on the main news channels and his threats and his calls to the believers to unite under the colours of the World Islamic Front. 'The big difference is that this time we are ready for you,' Campbell thought as he picked up his coffee which had been balanced on the butt end of his Heckler and Koch.

The morning rush hour over, things had settled down. Buchanan Street, as he looked down it, was a lot quieter than it usually would have been on a pleasant autumn morning – as good as it gets for the retail therapy junkies of the city and its suburbs.

Trussed up in the cumbersome poundage of uniform and bulletproof vest, with the additional weight of his weapon, Campbell sweated profusely and cursed silently.

Normally, at this time on a Friday morning he was sitting with his body armour off, enjoying a fag and a coffee in his office at the airport, perusing the security cameras away from the fearful gaze of the Glaswegian public; a public who were almost in a state of meltdown despite all the assurances that, this time, Glasgow was ready and that Tariq and his Jihadists would be caught and brought to justice sooner rather than later.

Looking round his detail Campbell checked that the lads were all awake and not dozing in the sunlight.

"All right Jimmy you got your finger on the trigger – but not too itchy I hope? Keep your eyes peeled boys, these bastards are cunning, cold-blooded killers but they ain't doin' any bleedin' killin' on Shug Campbell's watch. Comprendez?"

"Yes Sergeant!" was the chorused response.

Campbell checked his watch; nearly 10.30hrs. His mind was already straying to the weekend which he would spend up on the golf course at Dougalston. A late-comer to the game, Campbell and his best mate Albert would spend Saturday afternoon engaged in a barely amicable tussle on the course he considered to be the city's toughest north-west of the Clyde.

Shuggie had developed a strategy he was sure would bring him a rare victory over Albert and guarantee him the mythical sub-90 round he had been unable to produce in five years up at 'Dougy'.

As if by magic his text message alert went and he gazed at the screen. The name 'Uncle' – his not so affectionate nickname for Albert – appeared and he scrolled down to the message.

All right bawheid? You up for another spankin'? Winner buys beers and grub at the Burnbrae. Up ye!

A typical pre-match wind up from 'Uncle'. But this time Shuggie was going to make sure some selective iron play, as opposed to his usual driver 'Russian roulette', would provide him with the accuracy to enjoy a rare afternoon of triumphalism.

Campbell replied, *Bring yer cheque book nanny. Yer mine.*

Campbell's ears picked up the shrill tones of youthful voices filling the air. Turning to his left he observed a group of school kids led by two teachers making their way out of the underground entrance. He smiled benignly as the party of about 60 drew level with his men and the lead teacher, a middle-aged female, approached him.

"Hi Sergeant, all quiet I hope?"

He nodded before adding reassuringly, "Yep. Lovely day for a school outing, Miss. Where are you all heading?"

The teacher – identified by her name badge as Mrs Fabien, an attractive if slightly prim brunette – smiled back and Campbell thought, 'Amazing the effect a uniform and a firearm has.'

She gushed, "Oh, we're off to the Museum of Modern Art today. An ideal outing for P7 kids."

Campbell smiled again. "Have a nice day now."

But the sergeant's attention was soon elsewhere as a shouted warning from Jimmy to his left registered. "Sarge, we've got incoming! Looks like a delivery truck for Sainsbury's. It's comin' right up Buchanan Street – that cannae be right?"

Campbell saw the delivery truck proceeding up Buchanan Street at a casual pace, letting pedestrians make way as it drove.

The lack of any great haste on the part of the driver provided some reassurance to Campbell. Twenty-three years police service told him not to jump the gun (he smiled inwardly at his pun) when making a judgement on the threat level being presented. But that judgement was complicated by the presence of the school party in the possible field of fire.

The group had already started to file through his men down into Buchanan Street two-by-two, led by their teacher. Taking stock of his increasingly complicated position, Campbell knew that safety and caution had to come first. He had to get the school party out of the position which placed them potentially as the filling in a lead sandwich. On top of that there was civilian pedestrian traffic milling about.

Campbell knew he had to get beyond the school party and put himself and some of his men between them and the delivery van.

"Okay boys swing 'em into ready position. Jimmy, you and Shaun follow me. We need to get in front of the school party and make sure there is no threat from our lost delivery driver. The rest of you make sure your full attention is on me and act upon my signal."

Only half of the school party had gone beyond Campbell's position and he strode purposefully but calmly down the left side of their line. As he did so he registered, with a shudder that went right through his powerful frame, that the Sainsbury's van was picking up speed. Pedestrians were diving out of its way as it shot up Buchanan Street heading straight for Mrs Fabien and her group of fresh-faced school kids.

Campbell had no doubt what that meant and translated

his fears into a concise order to his two subordinates. "Right lads at the double, we have to get beyond the kids. Van oncoming and picking up speed. Clear and present danger oncoming, fire at my command."

Campbell and his men ran down the line until they were level with Mrs Fabien and he barked out a command to the startled teacher who was slowly becoming aware of the danger coming her way.

"Miss, kids, stop right there!"

Thankfully she did as she was bid despite her obviously raw fear and instantly ordered, "Children, stop!"

Campbell and his two officers had now gone beyond the school party and his responses were driven by an auto-pilot from years of training and drilling.

He barked out the command, "On me!" aware that the sound of youthful chatter was now being replaced by a mixture of shouts and screams.

Campbell strode in front of his officers and raised his hand in a gesture to stop that he already knew the van driver would ignore.

The distance was less than 100 yards and he could make out a white cloth bandana wrapped around the driver's head. The van's speed had increased and Campbell knew he was about to take the ultimate gamble. He was going to command his men to open fire on a truck that was almost certainly carrying mass death.

The van was now only 50 yards away and heading straight for Campbell and his men, the school party and the underground entrance. There was no time to move the kids. If the van was packed full of explosives and a stray bullet hit them a few yards would make no difference to the children's survival. Likely as not the delivery van carried a pay load that would wipe out everything and anything in Buchanan Street that morning.

"This is it boys. Aim for the driver and pray we hit him. Fire!"

The three Heckler and Kochs opened fire simultaneously. The air filled with screams and shouting.

But the van kept on coming.

"Eat lead, you motherfucker," Campbell spat through gritted teeth as he pumped lead from his firearm into the cabin of the oncoming van.

Still the driver remained untouched by the rain of vicious projectiles splintering through his windscreen.

Campbell could make out the driver's lips moving and his look of dripping evil.

'Shit, thirty yards to go before impact; it's going to take a fuckin' miracle now, come on Big Man, do us a turn,' Campbell pleaded with the man upstairs.

He could feel the grip on his rifle becoming cold and clammy as the realisation hit home that he and everyone else in Buchanan Street that morning were about to meet their maker. Anger ripped through him. But anger was a wasted emotion at a time like this and he forced his breathing to even out and sighted the driver's head, aiming for the scrawled writing he could now see on his headgear.

He pulled the trigger again. "Buy it, you bastard, buy it!" His heart seemed to stop beating as time stretched into a new dimension.

At last Campbell's prayers were answered and the driver's head smashed forward into the steering wheel as the sound of the vehicle horn punctured the air. But the driver's death brought a new and potentially even more disastrous scenario to the fore as the van began to zigzag wildly out of control.

Campbell knew the vehicle had to be brought to a stop as quickly as possible. "Aim for the tyres lads," he barked and a triple payload of lead was unloaded into the tyres. The front two rubber spheres burst under the volley.

It was a gamble; although this might ensure the van did not plough right through his men and the school party, the now deflated tyres might lead to a collision and therefore a detonation of the cargo of death he had little doubt was packed inside.

But as the van continued to slow Campbell knew he had got lucky. The driver was dead and somehow none of the repeated rounds his men had pumped into the cabin had penetrated the rear of the vehicle where he assumed the explosives were packed.

Now he needed to make his own luck.

"Jimmy, take this," he said, quickly throwing his H&K to his number two before adding, "Get the school party back inside the underground entrance if you can." Jimmy nodded and Campbell sprinted towards the van's driver's door.

Drawing level he launched himself at the half-opened window and latched on. The driver's head was buried in the steering wheel. Forcing his hand through the window Campbell tried to grab it to straighten the vehicle's course. He knew he had to get inside the cab and somehow bring the vehicle to a stop, aware that any form of collision would mean carnage.

The van's speed had decreased significantly and Campbell realised it could not have been going at more than 20 mph. The shuddering coursing through the cab and the screeching of metal on tarmacadam was testament to the fact it was running on wheel rims rather than rubber. But still he had to bring it to a halt.

Quickly he felt inside the door, located the window's handle and wound it down. He forced his body through the window and on top of the driver's corpse. Just out of reach lay the handbrake he needed to pull. Campbell grabbed the driver by his bandana and yanked him back into an upright position while simultaneously shooting out his free hand to pull on the handbrake, using the other to hold the steering wheel straight.

The vehicle shuddered once more and then slowly, agonisingly, ground to a halt. Campbell breathed again. But he knew full well his work was far from done.

His ears picked up the harsh sounds of barked commands from Jimmy's familiar voice.

"Clear the area immediately; clear the area immediately."

"Thank Christ," he thought. Jimmy had been alive to the danger that although the driver had been killed and the van brought to a halt the vehicle was still full of 'live' explosives that could blow at any minute.

Disengaging himself from the driver's corpse Campbell eventually managed to get himself out of the cabin. As he did so he took pride from the way his men had fanned out and were automatically clearing Buchanan Street of pedestrian traffic in a steady and calm manner, showing little concern for their own safety. He also saw that the last of the school kids had just disappeared down the underground entrance.

Looking over at Jimmy he saw his number two was in the process of calling for bomb disposal back-up and, given that an army unit had been centrally located for just such an event, Campbell took some comfort from the fact it would be here momentarily.

Placing an armed cordon around the delivery van, there was nothing more Campbell could do but wait. As he tasted the salty sweat slipping into his mouth the sergeant had to admit all his prayers had been answered by what he silently told himself had been 'the miracle on Buchanan Street' that Friday morning.

28

THOROUGHGOOD AND Hardie had just finished an impromptu pit-stop for 'light refreshment' as Hardie put it when they heard the news bulletin on Radio Clyde detailing the attempted suicide bombing in Buchanan Street.

It didn't take long before they were piecing together the implications. Hardie was first to offer his thoughts. Almost before completing a large mouthful of the McDonald's quarter pounder meal he said, "Fuck me, that must have been a close one. I bet that Sergeant Shuggie Campbell must have been on the verge of a serious Code 21 brown broadcast. Took a few chances didn't he though? I mean what are the odds on shredding the cabin of the delivery van with lead and not one bullet making it through to the payload of explosives?"

Thoroughgood, his window down, sat with one arm dangling over the rim of the driver's door staring aimlessly into the passing traffic.

"Tariq is cute though. That video broadcast basically warned the Muslim community that if they were at prayers they would be safe. 10.30am Friday is the holiest time for the devout to be about their business at the Mosque," advised Thoroughgood.

"Makes you wonder what's next on the hit list don't it?" demanded Hardie. "I mean that's a shopping centre, street assassinations, and now an underground in the busiest pedestrian shopping street in Scotland. So much for the targets all being shopping centres. It would appear there is no pattern to them other than maximum impact and the only way to find out what they are is to decipher the asterisks in that bleedin' filofax. You've got to admit the bastards have done their homework. But where the feck does Johnny Balfour and his bum chums fit into all of that? For me that is one piece in the jigsaw that just don't fit."

Thoroughgood met Hardie's inquisitorial gaze with a nod of agreement.

"Aye, yer right on both counts. Regarding Balfour, the only thing I can come up with is that he must have intimidated the Muslim community in some shape or form, or maybe he was contaminating it with a supply of drugs? The bottom line is that we've got to start turning the heat up on Tariq. He's the one setting the agenda and we aren't doing enough to disrupt him. It isn't gonna be easy with Vanessa bleedin' Velvet and Jim Fraser set to lose their heads in 24 hours time. We need a break and fast, but we've got to do more to make it happen..." Thoroughgood cut off his summation of where they were as his attention wandered to a figure at the corner of the street.

Hardie's eyes followed his gaffer's until they too rested on a beggar. "Bloody beggars, seem like they're everywhere these days," opined the DC.

The beggar in question was a swarthy male wearing a faded Adidas tracksuit. As his gaze met that of the two detectives he scuttled around the corner into Maryhill Road and blended in with the pedestrian traffic.

Hardie's eyebrows shot up quizzically. "Bit strange that one gaffer. Call me paranoid but did the beggar boy there seem to be taking a bit more than a passing interest in us, or was he just scavenging for scraps of my McDonald's?" Hardie emptied the last remaining French fries from his poke into the cavern that was his mouth.

Thoroughgood remained nonplussed. "You're losin' it you old git. Just because I refused to order you a Happy Meal and you're missing out on the toy the whole world is against you. He's just another junkie with a sheriff's warrant to apprehend on his head who's just woken up to the fact he's been eyeballing 'the Rozzers'. We've got a lot more important things to be worrying about right now. . ."

But Thoroughgood got no further because his ring tone erupted into life. His mouth turning up in a frown, he picked up. "DS Thoroughgood, who calls?"

It was Professor Farouk. Within 10 minutes they were sitting in the academic's office having answered their invitation to talk by the distinguished scholar.

"Gentlemen, I heard about the attempted suicide bombing in Buchanan Street. I have to be honest and say that I thought Tariq may have planned something this morning but in some way I still couldn't believe he would."

Thoroughgood seized an opportunity to take the moral high ground. "You mean our mutual friend tipping off the true believers that if they remained faithful to the shahada at the appointed time they would remain safe?" Thoroughgood's green eyes burned straight into Farouk's.

Observing his gaffer's intensity the thought struck Hardie that his superior officer was at last returning to the detective he would ride shotgun through the gates of hell for.

Farouk, guilt written large over his features, cleared his throat. When he spoke his voice was soft and clearly weary. "I'm impressed Detective Sergeant. My daughter has told me that she believes you can help us save the Muslim community in Glasgow from the disaster that Tariq is bringing upon it. Perhaps she is correct."

Hardie, mystified by this unforeseen interlude, went on the attack. "Now wait a minute Professor, with all due bleedin' respect, if you suspected there was some sort of coded warning in Tariq's broadcast then what the fuck were you doing sittin' on your hands?"

Farouk was now firmly on the defensive. "I am sorry but. . ."

"You would be a whole lot more sorry if that Sainsbury's van had detonated and taken everyone in Buchanan Street with it. Don't you know a party of school kids en route to the Modern Art Museum came out the underground entrance just as the bomber put his foot to the floor and went for it?" fired Thoroughgood.

"I'm sorry, I truly am. But I have not, as you say Detective Constable Hardie, been sitting on my hands this last hour or so. I think I may have uncovered the route that will take you to the Imam and bring this lunacy to an end before there are more lives lost and there is not a street in Glasgow a Muslim can feel safe on."

Hardie remained unconvinced. "And that would be?"

Farouk steepled his hands. "It is something called Hawala."

Hardie barked a laugh out loud: "Forgive me Professor but I haven't seen that one on the menu at India's recently."

"For crying out loud faither, let's hear what the professor has to say. Before we think about bringing him in on anti-terrorist legislation as aiding and abetting an act of terror," added Thoroughgood threateningly.

But Farouk had recovered his resolve. "Hawala, detectives, is an ancient system in the Muslim world which provides money transfers which leave no trail.

"I assume that you have failed to trace any financial transactions to Tariq that could be used to pinpoint either him or his confidantes?"

The silence was all that Farouk needed by way of an answer. He continued. "This is a financial system that is hundreds of years old and is the perfect means for Tariq to receive a continuous flow of funds from every Muslim that has answered his call to support jihad. It is also used widely by the World Islamic Front and Osama bin Laden."

Hardie's elongated whistle penetrated the room, underlining the importance of the information that the professor was giving them.

Farouk moved swiftly on. "It is a simple system and foolproof. It was created by Arab traders on the Silk Road, stretching . . ."

Thoroughgood interrupted impatiently, "From China to Europe. For your information Professor, I was a Medieval History student so if we could keep the history lesson to a minimum that be great. May I remind you that for a variety of reasons time is not on our side."

Rebuked, Farouk carried on. "Indeed. At the system's centre are the hawaladars. Every Muslim community has its quota of these 'brokers'. They come from a variety of occupations be it taxi driver, shop keeper or indeed even Imam. But all are sworn to secrecy and no one can be admitted to the system until he is vouched for by another hawaladar.

"The key, gentlemen, of the system's secrecy and dependability is that there is only one rule. Trust. Substantial sums of money are transferred through it. The slightest breach of trust and the breaker of the bonds is expelled and branded a disgrace and a traitor within his community. His reputation blackened beyond redemption in short, unforgivable," Farouk took a break for breath.

"Bloody hell, the possibilities are endless," opined Hardie.

"Indeed they are Detective Constable. It seems likely that the majority of Tariq's funding, and al-Qaeda's for that matter, comes via Hawala and through the acts of the hawaladars.

"All Tariq or his minion would need do is to make a visit to a hawaladar, hand over the sum of money he wished to donate and leave his name and the location of the recipient. The hawaladar would then add his fee – maybe half a percent of the sum to be transferred - then contact a hawaladar at the destination using his personal code. The recipient's broker then knew that next time he and his correspondent broker did business, when the process would be reversed, he would recover the money he had paid out."

Aware that the two detectives were hanging on his every word Farouk ploughed on. "This is a system, gentlemen, that operates on such a high level of trust that no formal banking system can come near it. It offers, as you now understand, complete anonymity within the system."

Thoroughgood tried to keep his excitement in check.

"Okay the opportunities this could bring us are endless. But first we need to know who is acting as Tariq's hawaladar. If we can get his identity then we can force

Tariq to set up a meeting and we've got him. But given what you have just said about anyone breaking the code being effectively ostracised from your community how are we going to get someone to run the gauntlet? Basically you are talking about someone being prepared to be shunned by his community almost a form of excommunication from the Muslim faith."

Farouk's brow creased in a frown. "We are now at a stage Detective Sergeant where if we do not do anything about this then the Muslim community in Glasgow, perhaps even throughout the United Kingdom, will no longer be able to exist. It is my belief that if I can bring all of that to bear we may be able to convince the hawaladar in question to break the code for the sake of his fellow 30,000 Muslims here in Glasgow."

Hardie interjected, "It's a big ask of anyone. But I'm sure you can make the person in question see that the price for doing nothing is even greater. You will be aware, Professor, that there are already reports of racially aggravated violence on Muslims in the city starting to escalate. The unease is only going to grow. I shudder to think how bad it would be if that delivery van had detonated in Buchanan Street this morning.

"You know who Tariq's hawaladar is, Professor, if I'm not mistaken?"

Farouk hesitated slightly before answering. "I think I do know who the hawaladar is, yes, although I can not confirm it, as yet. Surely if you have him watched his actions will confirm my suspicions?"

Thoroughgood was not convinced that Farouk was telling them everything he knew and he was in no mood to hold back. "You're right, Professor, there is now a strong

MI5 presence in Glasgow and if you give me the identity of the man you believe is acting as Tariq's financier we'll have him put under surveillance immediately."

Farouk shrugged his shoulders. "This is not something I do lightly but I know it is for the best. His name is Dhiren Rahman; he is a banker with the United Arab Emirates Central Bank. I believe he may also have links to the Russian Mafia and Tariq and his group may have been armed through him. I believe there may be something even more sinister that Rahman has helped finance."

"This just gets better and better. The Russian Mafia, feck me, what next – Osama bin Laden making a guest appearance with half the bleedin' Taliban in tow marchin' down Sauchiehall Street?" said Hardie in disbelief before adding, "Stone the soddin' crows. I just cannae get my heid round this."

When he spoke the anger in Thoroughgood's voice betrayed that he had got his 'heid round it'. "Let's cut to the bottom line, Professor. I think you know a whole lot more than you are letting on. That right? If it is then you need to spill or we will be walking out your door and you can kiss your cosy little life in the bosom of alma mater goodbye."

Farouk's composure at last deserted him.

"Detectives you must realise that I am an honourable man and that is why I am speaking to you at this moment. But I find myself feeling that whatever I say I will betray someone."

But Hardie's patience had snapped. "For fuck's sake will you just spill? With respect Professor, of course."

Farouk knew that he had no alternative. "Last week I arrived early to the mosque for a meeting of elders so waited outside the meeting room. I had heard voices

211

within the Imam's chamber which is opposite the meeting room; The Imam was talking to Rahman."

Farouk took a breath then added, "Large sums of money were discussed and I believe they were talking about material that could be used to make a 'dirty bomb' with a target in Scotland in mind. At the time I thought it was all talk but as each day goes by with each new atrocity I now believe they may have the capability and the materials here in Glasgow to carry that out."

"You've got to be having a laugh Professor. Why the fuck haven't you said anything before now?" demanded Hardie.

Farouk's shame was clear. "I was in denial, I could not bring myself to believe the evidence of my own ears. But after Braehead, Dowanhill, the death of Sushi and what almost happened this morning I had no option to tell you before it is too late."

"Too fuckin' late? Too late for whom? Those who lost their lives at Braehead, the four killed in Dowanhill or our friend Sushi who had his bloody brains blown out because he had the balls to do something about that maniac Tariq and didn't give a damn about being ostracised. Because that is the bottom line Professor, you put your own position and self-importance before the lives of the innocent and even preserving the Muslim community's place within our society."

A proud man, now humbled, Farouk held his head in his hands and begged for forgiveness over and over again. "I am so sorry, may Allah forgive me."

29

"IT IS barely believable fine fellows, barely believable, I tell you," said Sir Willie Stratford in a state of apparent bewilderment.

Into the silence that followed Chief Intelligence Officer Etherington spoke.

"If you forgive me, Sir. I am afraid it is more than believable. Do you remember the intelligence we came across via our friends in the French DST internal intelligence service that suggested Mossad had been secretly trying to buy up fissionable materials from the Russian Mafia – namely the Rising Sun gang?"

"I do indeed Etherington. If memory serves, that was just before the July bombings in London. But I thought that was all squared away between the frogs and our friends in the Mossad?" said Stratford.

Observing the relationship between the two intelligence service members from the other side of Tomachek's office, Thoroughgood had to admit to himself he was impressed by the candour with which Etherington, from under the shock of a blonde thatch of hair that reminded the DS of the Tory dandy Boris Johnson, addressed his boss.

"That bombshell, if you pardon the pun sir, came to light shortly after a raid on a Paris apartment by the DST. That came via an intelligence source we now believe to have been a double agent from within the Rising Sun that five grams of enriched uranium and possibly a quantity of another even more lethal substance called Caesium 137, which is both extremely soluble and reactive, had been removed from the building by the Rising Sun gang's operative. Who, of course, was the double agent behind the tip off."

Turning to the detectives, Etherington swept them with a cold assessing stare and continued to explain, "Detectives, the bottom line here is that the quantity and quality of this substance is enough to make a 'dirty bomb'."

"Balls and buggery!" exploded Tomachek: "What you mean is between Farouk's info and the fact that some enriched uranium and what not has gone missing, it could be tucked up nice and cosy under the mad Imam's pillow somewhere in Glasgow?"

Etherington applied the straight bat. "Exactly Superintendent."

"Would you mind if I provided you with some background to the impasse I now believe we find ourselves in?" he asked, coolly.

"Be my guest," said Tomachek.

"The Rising Sun are the most powerful gang in what is loosely referred to as the Russian Mafia, and they don't care whether they supply Israel or al-Qaeda with fissionable material. It is strictly business with whoever is the highest bidder.

"But before Mossad could buy it 'out of the market', so to speak, the DST swooped and that was where the role of Mossad started to emerge.

"What we later learned was that although the DST acted upon intelligence that correctly informed them of the presence of the enriched uranium, though the presence of the Caesium 137 was never confirmed, the substance was never truly intended for the Mossad – they were double-crossed."

Hardie's incredulity was revealed in one word. "What?"

Etherington offered a faint smile. "Yes, I know it sounds like something out of a Le Carré novel but I'm afraid that is the world in which the security services operate."

"Hold on Mr Etherington," Thoroughgood interjected, "Correct me if I'm wrong but you're saying the Rising Sun had set up a deal with Mossad they never intended to honour? So would it be fair to suggest it was the Rising Sun operative who tipped off the French intelligence service with information concerning the location and substance that was up for grabs that was also less than wholly accurate?"

Etherington nodded. "Indeed they did Detective Sergeant. What we now suspect is that the Rising Sun tried to make it look like they had managed to get the uranium smuggled out ahead of the apartment being raided by the DST. Further that they had done so after acting on information received via a tip off themselves. But we believe it has since been sold to and was always going to be sold to al-Qaeda."

Sir Willie contributed his thoughts on the whole sorry mess. "Obviously gentlemen, in the wake of the London bombings we have been moving heaven and earth to locate the uranium, the identity of the Rising Sun double agent and where his deal with al-Qaeda took place."

Etherington resumed his monologue. "Quite so Sir. Going back gentlemen, as you can imagine we became somewhat deflected from the pursuit of that intelligence in the immediate aftermath of the terror attacks on London. Before you brought it to the surface again with the information from Professor Farouk it had, to all intents and purposes, gone underground."

"Sounds like a case of Tinker, Tailor, Soldier, bloody Spy to me," quipped Tomachek.

Thoroughgood remained unconvinced. "It's still a quantum leap to put all the pieces of the jigsaw together and place the enriched uranium in Glasgow and in Tariq's possession, surely?"

Etherington did not agree. "I'm afraid not and doubly so after your conversation with the professor. In the short spell since what we are referring to as 'the Glasgow Terror' we have moved the whole focus of our attention onto what is going on in your city. Gentlemen, we have had further intelligence from Mossad. Who as you can imagine are far from happy."

"Go on," said Tomachek.

Etherington duly obliged. "The name of the Rising Sun operative who got away in Paris is Declan Meechan. The reason we have not been able to trace him and gain any intelligence of his transaction with al-Qaeda is because the Mossad have sanctioned a Kidon death squad to terminate him.

"We believe the reason he has not been located is because he has been shielded within the al-Qaeda network as a hawaladar, a money lender based on an ancient Muslim system that demands total trust and secrecy. But his true importance to them is as the provider of the substance they are desperate to utilise for a showpiece atrocity. Despite that, it would appear that Meechan had his own agenda all along and that was a Glaswegian agenda and that is where the Imam Tariq and the Spear of Islam come in. I believe, gentlemen, his is a name very well known to you."

Hardie's long rising whistle was the only sound that punctured the silence but at that moment all eyes locked on Thoroughgood. His heart pounding in his ears, he felt a cold bead of sweat starting to glisten on his skin and the oxygen in his lungs drained. He stood up, opened the door and walked out.

His worst nightmare had returned.

30

TOMACHECK WAS first to speak after the Detective Sergeant's exit. Eyeing Hardie, who was half way out of his seat, he said, "Let him go Kenny. He's going to need time to get his head around this and he isn't the only one."

Turning his attention to the intelligence officers he asked, "I assume you are aware of the local intelligence we have on Meechan and the level of personal enmity between him and DS Thoroughgood?"

Stratford nodded before answering. "Of course Detective Superintendent. I must stress at this stage we do not know if Meechan is back in Glasgow." He looked for confirmation from Etherington, who provided it with a brief nod, before he continued, "But all the intelligence agencies have been sent his last known description and the importance of the substances he may be in possession of."

Etherington re-enforced his boss's message, "Indeed Sir. Interpol have issued a warrant for Meechan's immediate arrest. There is also an 'all ports' lookout for him in place and the Police Service of Northern Ireland, given his roots, are also on alert.

"Regarding Dhiren Rahman, gentlemen, I will have a team of 'watchers' placed on him to conduct round-the-clock surveillance. We will install electronic listening equipment everywhere he is likely to frequent. If Rahman is the hawaladar who has established a liaison with Meechan he can lead us to both Tariq and Meechan. More importantly he can lead us to the enriched uranium and/or Caesium 137. So, gentlemen we have already made it a priority to ensnare him and let him lead us to our prey."

Almost before Etherington had completed his final sentence Stratford interrupted, his hunger for a successful conclusion to the whole affair obvious. "Bang on Ethers, bang on! At last we have the lead we need to bring 'the Glasgow Terror' to an end."

Hardie took great delight in bringing the head of the secret service back down to ground. "If I may be so bold Sir, there are a couple of other things that we need to take into account.

Firstly, the hostage situation. What have you done regarding Tariq's demands and the fact we have 24 hours left on the first deadline? "Secondly do we have any intelligence yet on the staff at One Devonshire Gardens and the Half-Moon bookshop?"

"Etherington?" boomed Sir Willie providing a crystal clear pointer as to who the buck stopped with.

"Sir," acknowledged Etherington flatly, before continuing to address both Tomachek and Hardie. "We have placed the bookshop under scrutiny and some very interesting results have been obtained." Etherington's clipped tone and the slight trace of a smirk implied all was well now that the real professionals were involved.

The intelligence chief continued. "An informer we have brought with us from England visited the shop and purchased a selection of interesting literature both in written form and on CD. After being translated from Arabic and Urdu the material proved inflammatory in extremis. It has only recently arrived in Blighty, almost certainly smuggled in from Islamabad by UK-born jihadists.

"With genuine British passports they can pass freely in and out of the country. The CDs were disguised as popular Pakistani music but inserted neatly between the tracks were messages of hate. On translation the messages were revealed to be instructions on how to make and release cyanide within enclosed public places." Pleased with his revelation Etherington took stock of its impact on the two detectives and his boss.

"Well fuck me," was the best Hardie could do. Tomachek for his part remained hanging on Etherington's every word.

Etherington carried on with gusto, "The bookseller is now on a watch list and under surveillance as we speak. Listening devices have been inserted in his vehicle and within the Half-Moon bookshop itself. Every meeting Friend Omar has is being watched and logged and if there is any contact between him and Tariq or his underlings we will have full intelligence on it.

"As for One Devonshire Gardens, we believe that the kidnap was set up by information provided by the junior manager and one of the porters who are both members of the Central Mosque. Both have been on trips to Waziristan, in the North West Province of Pakistan within the last 18 months. They too are under surveillance. Gentlemen, the net is closing."

"But just how fast is it closing? We're up against the clock here Mr Etherington," said Hardie.

"Don't you think we are aware of that Detective Constable Hardie?" demanded Stratford, adding, "Damn it fellow, it is all a balancing act. We need to draw out more intelligence from them before we roll things up. Move too quickly and Tariq is tipped off we are onto him and what happens then?"

Etherington quickly backed up his master. "I am entirely confident that through either Rahman or Omar, or one of the hotel staff we will have a route to Tariq within the timescale for the executions."

"However, we are going to use a little ruse to try and trap Tariq," he finished.

"And just how do you propose to do that Mr Etherington?" demanded Tomachek.

Etherington smiled benignly. "The individual Tariq wants released from Guantanamo Bay will to all intents and purposes be freed and a video detailing this will be posted to Al-Jazeera. But of course his freedom will be a total sham. He will remain, naturally, under water-tight FBI surveillance and should he contact Tariq he will be helping to lead us to him.

"After we secure the release of Miss Velvet and Mr Fraser the released detainee will be rearrested on fresh terror charges.

"If, however, Tariq fails to honour his side of the bargain and double-crosses us we will at least have done everything possible to avoid the resulting grisly outcome, should that be how the situation pans out for the two hostages.

"You must learn to trust us detectives. Your work here is over now. We will debrief Farouk and see if we can gain any extra intelligence beyond that which he provided for you."

"Can we be of any further assistance?" asked Tomachek dryly.

Once again Stratford took control. "Most importantly, where is that damned dagger we have been hearing so much about?"

Hardie replied, "Detective Sergeant Thoroughgood has the dagger, we've not had time to lodge it as a production with everything that has been going on."

"Ah yes, your man Thoroughgood, is the poor fellow going to be okay?" Stratford enquired.

Once again Hardie had the answer – almost. "Sir, I'm really not sure. How do you fix a broken heart?"

Stratford's over ample eyebrows shot up. "Quite," was the best the head of MI5 could do.

31

THOROUGHGOOD COULD not remember how he had reached The Rock but it seemed to him that he had been in some kind of a trance ever since Etherington's revelation about Meechan. Meechan, the puppet master, pulling the strings all along as he implemented his plan to wreak mass destruction on the city that had vanquished him.

Staring into his pint Thoroughgood recalled that Meechan's departure from UK shores had allegedly been on a Russian trawler. Meechan's friend Brendan O'Driscoll was an assassin regularly used by the Russian Mafia. The resurfacing of Meechan within the hierarchy of the Rising Sun made perfect sense now.

Thoroughgood took a swig from his glass, his mind running riot. So was Meechan back in Glasgow for vengeance? If he was then he had to be in the company of either Rahman or Tariq himself. Obviously part of their deal had been the massacre of Balfour and his associates, leaving a vacuum at the top of Glasgow's underworld which Meechan would fill on his return. The chance to avenge Celine was coming his way at last.

It was a tantalising prospect but with the security services now so heavily involved and the personal enmity between him and Meechan so well known it was not going to be easy to get in a position to make payback. Lost in his emotions, Thoroughgood was oblivious to the voice repeating his name.

"You alright Gus?" asked Hardie.

The DS looked up at his mate. "What do you think?" was the best he could do.

Hardie sat down and placed his own pint on the table. "Who would have thought it? Meechan behind the whole shootin' match? At the same time you wouldnae put it past him. Feck me, if someone had told me he had turned up in the Celtic dugout to manage the Totty Howkers at Ibrox next week I wouldnae have said no to takin' a tenner on that!"

Thoroughgood smiled but his face lacked any real warmth. He said nothing but Hardie needed no words to read his thoughts. "Listen Gus, I know what's going through your mind and if I was in your position I would be thinking the exact same. How are we gonnae get Meechan?"

Thoroughgood's gaze lifted and he met Hardie's jaded eyes grimly leaving his subordinate in no doubt that if there was a way to Meechan he would find it.

"We'll finish these and sack it for the night. Get some kip and reconvene in the morning. I think it's time we went and did some sniffing about at the Mosque. You never know who might be hanging around but there has got to be someone there who we can put the heat on. Second we visit the UAE Bank in Sauchiehall Street and see if Rahman is about."

"Fair enough to me," replied Hardie.

Thoroughgood stared at the red numerals on his alarm clock for the hundredth time. The sleep he craved so much would not come. Round and round the wheels of his mind revolved, replaying the moment he had found Celine at Meechan's mansion, dead. Her contorted face; so beautiful, so still. The life he considered more precious than his own extinguished for ever.

He shut his eyes again and tried to blot her tortured face out of his thoughts. The woman he loved, the woman he had always loved, the woman he could not stop loving. Not then, not now, not ever.

Eventually Celine's face was replaced by that of Meechan's. Cruel and sneering, promising him death as they had fought in hand-to-hand combat around the poolside at Tara. 'Why didn't I take him out when I had the chance and then she would still be here?'

But now, through Meechan's twisted need for revenge on the city he had almost owned, the death wish Thoroughgood had made himself over and over was almost within his grasp. The chance to avenge Celine in the only way that would ever ease his pain; to put the full stop on Meechan once and for all, might soon be his.

The alarm clock read 23.30 and he needed sleep but still it would not come.

The doorbell sounded and broke into his tormented thoughts. He padded into the hall not caring who awaited him outside.

Had Meechan come back to finish him once and for all?

The door opened and he found himself staring into Aisha's opal eyes. "Can I come in?" she asked but her features were cold.

225

"It's getting to be a bit of a habit, your night visits," said Thoroughgood with a smile that showed he had no complaints.

But Aisha's manner was different from before. Her jaw was tight, bringing a hardness to her face Thoroughgood had not seen before.

She sat on the settee and focused a searing gaze on him.

"So Gus, you met with my father and obtained information that may lead you to Tariq but at what cost to my father?"

Confusion swept across Thoroughgood's face. "Sorry," was the best he could do.

"Not as sorry as my father. Do you know the shame he bears for betraying Rahman as a hawaladar and the dilemma he feels – torturing himself over betraying his community to stop Tariq and bring an end to this madness?" Aisha demanded.

Thoroughgood leant back into his armchair. Before he could help himself the words were out. "Look Aisha, with respect I don't give a fuck about your father's high-minded moral dilemma.

He had the chance to provide us with information that may have led us to Tariq before these atrocities started piling up. I'm not saying we would have got to Tariq before Braehead or Dowanhill or even stopped the hostage taking but it would have given us a shot.

"The bottom line is the hostages lives are still in the balance and all these other lives are over and there could be more to come unless we get our hands on Tariq tout suite. So forgive me if I don't shed a tear for your old man's angst."

Aisha jumped off the settee and covered the small gap

between them in a sudden explosion of movement. Her hand stung his cheek with a slap that took him totally by surprise.

"You bastard. You've just used him and now you don't give a fuck. My father is an honourable man. He has put everything else before himself to provide you with information and you couldn't give a damn about the repercussions he'll face within the Muslim community."

This time it was Thoroughgood who moved with an unexpected suddenness. He vaulted to his feet and stared down at Aisha, who refused to move an inch.

"Repercussions from the Muslim community? That's a laugh! There wouldn't be a Muslim community in Glasgow any more if he hadn't climbed down off his moral high horse. So forgive me if I don't buy all of this outcast and shame shit."

Thoroughgood picked up a flicker of movement from Aisha's hand as she attempted to repeat the stinging rebuke of earlier. He grabbed her hand before it had reached shoulder height.

"That's quite a temper you've got there Nurse Farouk. But let me fill you in on the value of the information your dad has been holding back, while going through his bout of ethical hand-wringing," shouted Thoroughgood.

He spotted her other hand moving and slapped an iron grip on it. "That information from dear daddy has just allowed MI5 to place a crucial piece in a jigsaw that suggests there may be material in this city with which Tariq intends to explode a dirty bomb."

He could see from the tremor in her face that she knew exactly what he was talking about and continued relentlessly.

"It has also allowed us to piece together a network of conspirators that stops with the Russian Mafia who have been supplying Tariq with his explosives and arms, and it has identified Declan Meechan as the organ grinder behind our bunch of crazed Jihadists and that fuck Tariq."

Aisha's eyes burned with fury and she tried with all her strength to break free from his grip.

"Let me go you brute. . ." she screamed at him.

But their proximity and the intensity of the emotions that were in the mixer at that moment were too much. Her rage gave Aisha a magnificent allure that Thoroughgood could not fight and all of a sudden his lips were locked on hers and she did not resist them.

Now their bodies intertwined in a passion that had to be spent.

His hands seemed to be on automatic pilot as they ripped her clothes from her and now Aisha reciprocated as they staggered in their mutual passion into the lounge.

Their bodies slammed onto the Chesterfield settee as the pain and heartache of their worlds collided in a moment of intensity that neither would ever forget.

Thoroughgood realised that Aisha was talking as his mind slowly slipped back into gear.

"How can it be that I came round here to let you know exactly what I thought of you and now I find myself in your bed – again?"

"The best laid plans . . ." Thoroughgood replied.

Aisha continued, "I visited my dad at his office and, whatever you think about him and the redundancy of his moral dilemma, he is in bits. But he also had more information for you and asked me to pass it on. I thought doing so would give me the ideal opportunity to put you in your place. I must be honest, I almost refused to act as his messenger but then who would that help?"

"Thank God for that," sighed Thoroughgood. Leaning up on one elbow he added, "Go on."

"My dad has sent a message to Rahman that he must speak with him urgently at the Central Mosque tomorrow. Rahman has replied that he will be there."

Thoroughgood exhaled a sharp breath.

His eyes burned into her intensely. "Do you know how important this information is? This could be our first chance to get to Tariq and more importantly, Meechan."

Aisha nodded. "Can I ask one thing Gus?"

"Be my guest," said Thoroughgood.

"Do you still have Saladin's dagger?"

"I do. It's in the lounge. With everything that has been going on I keep forgetting to lodge it. Why do you ask?" enquired Thoroughgood.

"It has great significance to our community and it just annoys me that it is going to be boxed, labelled and stuck in a strongroom indefinitely. For an artefact that played a key part in one of the most important episodes in Islamic history to be locked away in a strongroom and removed from its place in our culture is not right," said Aisha.

Thoroughgood laughed disbelievingly. "Until we have Tariq bang to rights and this whole mess is sorted whoever has the dagger is going to be in danger. Wherever it is Tariq is going to be looking to get his hands on it. Nope, first thing once we have done our rounds the dagger is being taken into protective custody and mothballed for the safety of anyone who has been handling it. That is if it is all right with you Nurse Farouk?"

Aisha smiled but Thoroughgood was convinced that she was far from happy with his answer.

But right now, right there, gazing at her in such close proximity was overpowering. "Christ, you are beautiful Aisha," and with that Thoroughgood abandoned his self-control all over again.

32

BEFORE DRIVING over to the Central Mosque Thoroughgood phoned Tomachek, informing him that Farouk had made contact with Rahman and a meeting between the two had been set for 11am.

The detective superintendent had been sceptical about allowing his two subordinates to go after Rahman on their own. At the same time, irked by the arrogance shown by Stratford and Etherington, Tomachek decided to allow his boys the chance to grab the glory.

The detective superintendent's words down the line had provided mixed messages. "Are you sure you trust Farouk? That is the bottom line. Remember we've been set up already and lost a civilian and everywhere you two go death is your neighbour. I don't want any more bodies piling up, least of all yours."

Hardie muttered, "How touching."

"I heard that Hardie. I'm tempted to have TFU back-up deployed to the mosque and these blighters at MI5 brought up to speed with your meeting with the ...What was it they called Rahman again?" demanded Tomachek.

Hardie's voice piped up again at the other end of the phone. "Hawaladar!"

"That's the bugger," agreed Tomachek.

But Thoroughgood had something to ask of his superior. "Boss, have five got any intelligence from One Devonshire Gardens yet?"

"I don't know," was Tomachek's honest answer, "But what I do know is that I want a clean-cut apprehension and Rahman brought in so he can lead us to either Tariq or the puppet master himself. Is that clear, dear boy?" demanded the Detective Superintendent.

"Crystal," replied Thoroughgood and heard the line go dead.

The journey over the Clyde had been surreal as the two detectives immersed themselves in small talk to keep the mounting tensions at bay. Hardie was for once happy not to mention Meechan's name ahead of an arrest he knew Thoroughgood hoped would lead him to his nemesis.

In time-honoured tradition the DC turned to his specialist subject. "So, Gus, surely you cannae be prepared to suffer any more self-inflicted abuse by going back to Firhill, for Pete's sake. Isn't it time you found some other trivial pursuit?" inquired Hardie, not bothering to hide the impish delight he took in teasing his mate over his footballing allegiances.

Thoroughgood's face momentarily creased in a frown before he replied, "For a start, I don't suppose I am going to be taking my seat in the Jackie Husband stand anytime before we've got Tariq under lock and key, and smoked out his hornets' nest of jihadists.

"But the other thing you fail to take into account, my rotund friend, is the outstanding value for money I now get for my season ticket. Glasgow Warriors rugby team have recently moved to God's own Football Stadium and

I can see myself takin' in a rugga game on Friday night since there are various double-header weekends available to combine both rugga and footie for the price of one. But like I said, that isn't gonna be anytime soon," admitted Thoroughgood.

"Not like you to be looking for a bargain, gaffer. Rugga, eh? A game played by gentlemen with oval shaped balls," said Hardie as sarcastically as possible, before quickly adding, "er, so they tell me."

The DC moved onto his next point of verbal attack, "Speaking of Firhill, if memory serves, you have a bit of a penchant for takin' your birds up there for some X-certificate viewing, so does that mean that Nurse Aisha will be following in the footsteps of, what was she called? Ah, that's it, sexy Sarah the very civil servant?"

Thoroughgood shot his number two a withering glare but it failed to deter Hardie.

"C'mon Gussy boy, I saw the curtain in your bedroom windae twitch when we left and I noticed that you'd kept Glasgow's version of Night Nurse concealed while I was waiting on you." Hardie erupted into a deep rumbling laugh.

"Bog off faither," was Thoroughgood's final word on the matter.

Trying to distract Hardie the DS added, "Anyway, how's the missus? Has she been out for any retail therapy or is she still too badly shaken?"

Hardie seemed less than inclined to open up on the subject of his beloved Betty.

"Look I'm sorry mate, I can well appreciate it if she is still in a state of shock but it could have been a helluva a lot worse," said Thoroughgood attempting to show some sensitivity.

Hardie found his voice, albeit somewhat sheepishly. "Betty is bloody fine. It's the damn chickens that are the problem."

"What?" asked Thoroughgood, gobsmacked.

"Well a couple of months back she wanted to get a couple of chickens in, to lay our own eggs, and I knocked her back – obviously. But after Braehead she started banging on about them again and well I . . . er . . . couldnae refuse," revealed Hardie.

"Chickens in a semi-detached in the middle of Knightswood? Are you off your bleedin' chomp?" asked Thoroughgood dissolving into a fit of uncontrolled mirth.

Hardie was far from happy with his predicament. "Aye, two chickens and a bloody hen-house the missus bought off eBay and guess what? We've already had the feckin' thing attacked by foxes. I didnae get a wink's sleep last night for them howlin' or barkin' or whatever they do at the moon."

Recovering his composure with some effort, Thoroughgood wanted more. "What happened mate? How did you fight the cunning Mr Fox off?"

"I didnae. But my boy David decided he was gonnae hang out his bedroom window and turn the back garden into a bleedin' shootin' gallery. All because the missus wants to play at The Good Life!"

"Aye I can see you as the Richard Briers type! Let's hope we don't discover any fowl play at the mosque," added Thoroughgood sarcastically.

As the impressive shape of the Central Mosque came into view Hardie's relief at the end of his interrogation was palpable.

The main place of worship for Glasgow's Muslim community was situated south of the River Clyde in the Gorbals, an area that had been famous for 'razor' gangs and tenement slums but had been transformed into affordable 'des res' for young professionals by the mid nineties.

Parking the Focus half up on the pavement outside the Mosque grounds they alighted to be met by a beggar.

Hardie looked at the man, sitting cross-legged outside of the Mosque gates, his cap on the ground between his knees. To no one in particular the DC let rip with his indignation. "Fuck me, not another one. It's about time we set up a task force to deal with these spongers. It ain't right."

Thoroughgood laughed. "Ah come on faither, have a heart," and tossed 50p into the beggar's hat.

"Gratitude," came the accented reply. Thoroughgood noticed the beggar's eyes seemed to simmer with an unusual intensity far from the usual puppy dog eyes of the imploring. But his rags were as soiled and ancient as any the DS had seen on a beggar.

As the two detectives walked along the path leading to the Mosque entrance their attention was immediately hooked by the impressive minaret; a translucent, almost diamond-shaped dome placed centrally on the roof above the main prayer hall. The minaret was perfectly placed to let sunlight stream through, allowing those praying below to do so in the luxury of natural light. The main entrance was arched with etched glass doors imprinted in a floral design. Hardie admitted he was impressed with the building.

"This isn't what I was expecting. Don't know about you gaffer but I've never been anywhere near a Mosque on business or pleasure."

The DS replied, "It's not the Mosque we want but the Imam's residence." He turned to his right and pointed to the two-storey red sandstone house sitting 100 feet away, "I'd say that would be it."

The area around the mosque baked in the unexpectedly warm autumn sun and as they made their way to the Imam's residence Thoroughgood loosened the silver tie that had been his one exception to his habitual black, to let fresh air circulate around him. Hardie, resplendent in his anorak, sweated. The red sandstone house stood in a silence that had the hairs on the back of the detectives' necks standing on end.

Hardie articulated the tension they both felt in a barely audible voice. "I'm wondering if we are here first or second gaffer."

"An interesting question, Hardie," whispered the DS hoping the traffic in the background would mask their voices. "Either way we err on the side of caution."

"Comprendez, mon gaffeur," echoed Hardie.

There was no reply to repeated knocking but when Thoroughgood tried the handle it gave way helpfully.

The DS nodded to Hardie to draw his police issue ASP baton although they both knew that it was an act of complete futility should they come up against the gang of AK-47 toting fanatics at Tariq's beckoning.

Slowly they moved through each room in the two-storey house making sure that there was no company waiting for them. But the building was eerily empty and the signs were that someone had vacated the premises in a hurry.

The detectives' interest centred on the study. It appeared to be the core of the Imam's theological and spiritual world. The study had also been the designated place for Farouk's bogus meeting with Rahman. But despite subjecting the the room and its contents to severe scrutiny there was nothing of any interest.

Settling into the desk chair Thoroughgood pushed it back and tossed the ivory handled dagger onto the desk's leather writing surface.

"Well my dear faither, I'd say whoever was here before us has taken everything we might have wanted to get our paws on. I get the feeling that Rahman has been tipped off that we would be waiting for him. Your thoughts on where we are with this whole bloody mess?"

Hardie's eyebrows raised involuntarily before he began his discourse. "I'd say you're right, and who have we got to thank for that? Who has been torturing himself over turning in one of his own and betraying some ancient system and ruining his standing within his treasured community? Bottom line – who supposedly set up Rahman for us?"

Thoroughgood stated the obvious. "Farouk."

Hardie had not finished. "So, we are hours away from the beheading of Vanessa Velvet and Jim Fraser. We are carrying around some kind of religious artefact that our jihadist friends want back at any cost. We've found out that Meechan is tickling the strings behind Tariq and is intent on detonating a dirty bomb sometime bloody soon within the city."

As Thoroughgood attempted to interrupt, Hardie held his hand up to indicate he had not finished. "But to top all that I'd give you an honest tenner that we have been set up . . . for a second bleedin' time at that." Hardie rifled his jacket pockets only for a look of disgust to spread across his portly features as the packet of Silk Cut he pulled out proved empty.

He took a breath and ploughed on regardless. "All we seem to do is go down dead ends. Look at what happened with poor Sushi. Now we are here and Farouk has given us a bum steer. We better radio in and have an all ports and stations lookout placed on Farouk because ten to one the good professor will be looking for a fast camel out of here. I just hope these stuck up sods in MI5 are working for their inflated pay packets."

Thoroughgood had pulled out his radio and broadcast the lookout for Farouk as well as barking instructions out to have the academic's work and home addresses checked.

Completing his broadcast Thoroughgood returned his attention to his number two. "Okay, there appears to be nothing here. Next port of call has got to be the UAE bank in Sauchiehall Street. We've got to get Rahman." Looking at his watch Thoroughgood winced. "Time is just slipping away. Don't know about you faither but I just have this feeling in my bones that the worst is still to come. Braehead was a dress rehearsal and if Meechan is involved you can bet your hairy arse that the mother of all bangs is coming our way."

Hardie agreed. "Definitely sometime soon. I'd hazard a guess at somewhere in that bleedin' filofax but somewhere beginning with feck only knows. Christ I sound like when I was a kid in the back of my old man's Vauxhall Viva playing eye spy!"

Thoroughgood's smile was fleeting and did nothing to discourage Hardie who rumbled on, "But going back to the Filofax and the email we lifted off Mustafa's computer. I think they have got to be connected. Just maybe the target is actually not a shopping centre – or maybe not even in Scotland?"

Thoroughgood offered a half-hearted smile "By God I got it wrong when I let you talk me out of Castlebrae!" But the DS knew his pal was onto something and the conundrum had been eating away at him too.

"OK, so say it is not a shopping centre our friends have targeted for the big bang. What could the link be with the Nikah mentioned in the email between the 15th and the 25th? We got any royal weddings coming up?"

Hardie's eyebrows arched in disbelief.

"Nope, I think you are barking up the wrong metaphorical tree there Gus. Nikah is code for some sort of public event where the impact of a big bang would be the carnage Tariq and Meechan are clearly after. Something even bigger than blowing up a shopping centre. But just what is the event and how the fuck do we find the place?"

Thoroughgood nodded in reluctant agreement, "Okay faither, you've made your point. But correct me if I'm wrong, terrorism is a matter for MI5 or MI6 or maybe bleedin' both but the one thing I am sure of is that this is way beyond our remit."

Hardie growled back. "After the mess they made of the intelligence from the FBI warning them of London 7/7 would you trust 'em to score in a brothel?"

Thoroughgood indicated he would not.

"Aye damn right. As much chance of Thistle making it back to the SPL this season," concluded Hardie.

Thoroughgood ignored him and said, "The old man clearly has as much faith in our pair of London fops as we do. It's like he can't bear the thought of the intelligence agencies cleaning up the shite on his own doorstep. We put together the whole hawaladar thing and outed Rahman as the link between Tariq and the Rising Sun and more importantly that bastard Meechan. But with what happened to Sushi we haven't exactly covered ourselves in glory."

Thoroughgood paused to let his words find their mark before adding, "But that isn't our problem mate. Bottom line is, this is too big for us; it's time to let the spooks earn their corn. Nope, what we need to do once we've finished up at the UAE bank is take that feckin' dagger back to the old man and get him to hand this whole shootin' match over to the intelligence communities before it's too late."

"What about Meechan?" asked Hardie.

"Look, you know I want nothing more in this life than one chance to take the bastard out but come on . . . In the cold light of day getting that chance seems unlikely. I mean how is he going to get back into the UK carrying a substance as lethal as enriched uranium? Or if the Mossad have put a Kidon on him? Nope, this Meechan thing is fantasy and I need to take a reality check on it. I need to put Meechan behind me and concentrate on the job in hand which is apparently spoon-feeding our friends from London to the extent that even MI5 can't cock it up."

The DC replied, "We don't even know if Tariq's gang of gunmen are from these shores or foreign imports. Or both. That's what really worries me. How many sleepers do they have in Glasgow? Christ, Farouk could be one for all we know after this wild goose chase.

"What bugs me is the fact that we don't seem to have a bloody clue where Tariq is holed up but he always seems to be one step ahead of us. It is like he is the one having us watched rather than the way it is supposed to be.

"Feck me Gus, how can you have a gang of tooled up

jihadists running around Glasgow toting AK-47s and yet they manage to melt into the shadows without a trace. They are out of our league mate and it looks like they're out of those numpties from MI5's league too. I wish someone would turn this whole thing over to the SAS."

Thoroughgood could not help himself laughing at his partner's thoughts on the matter.

Hardie continued his monologue. "You remember that the sniper's rifles from Dowanhill and the Botanics were Russian made? And now our jihadist gang are supposed to be kitted out with more Soviet-style hardware. Then Balfour and his boys are whacked. It all adds up now, don't it, with Meechan on the payroll of the Rising Sun. Christ, and I thought it was mere coincidence Gus. Nope, this is way out of our stratosphere."

Thoroughgood held his hand up. "No more. Let's just get out of here and up to Sauchiehall Street pronto. Hopefully Rahman doesn't know what is coming his way. That said if Farouk has stitched us up here then who is to say Rahman isn't on that feckin' camel as well and the pair of them are on their way to Timbuk-bleedin'-tu! Fuck, I better post another lookout for him or he'll have flown the coup. I think you're right faither, the one thing we must do is keep ourselves right in all of this. If the shit hits the fan I am not getting covered in it for Tomachek, or anyone else for that matter."

Hardie though was clearly still amazed by his gaffer's sentiments. "Never thought I'd hear those words. I mean, come on Gus, you sure about forgettin' about Meechan? You've always been one for the adrenalin ride and this is the biggest story to hit . . ." Hardie's voice faltered almost immediately as a footfall sounded outside the study window.

241

"Company," was all Thoroughgood had time to utter before the staccato of automatic gun fire smashed through the room window sending a spray of splintered glass through the air into the space previously occupied by Hardie.

33

THOROUGHGOOD WAS already on his knees with the dagger in his hand. He crawled round the desk, making for the hall with Hardie in hot pursuit as the bullets continued to pour into the study.

They made it into the hall and Thoroughgood immediately noticed a hatstand located inside the front door. He made a grab for it just as the door opened and a shadowy figure swathed in black linen lunged in.

Thoroughgood toppled the stand and the male crashed over it onto the carpeted floor.

Seizing his moment Hardie smashed home a right foot volley into the head of the prone gunman. "Aye, Ally McCoist would have been proud of that one." But it was the most fleeting of triumphs because in the darkness the two detectives heard voices speaking in a foreign tongue and they had no doubt that death was the currency they had come to deal in.

Grabbing the AK-47 Thoroughgood gestured to Hardie to head for the house stairs. "Up, faither, for feck's sake!"

They climbed as if their very lives depended on it, which neither was in any doubt was the case.

The detectives got to the first landing before the window crowning it was shattered by a hail of lead. Thoroughgood turned and fired the AK-47.

"Feeding time you bastards." The weapon spat out its deadly volley as the first of three males reaching the bottom of the steps went down with a grunt.

The detectives continued their furious ascent of the stairs and saw that there were three bedrooms leading off the top-floor landing.

Hardie, puffing badly, shouted, "Left!" and they burst in.

The clatter of footsteps suggested that their pursuers were now on the first landing although the murmur of their voices indicated that the shooting of their colleague had imbued them with a caution they had not expected to need.

Hardie pulled two heavy blue curtains apart and looked out the window while Thoroughgood kept the AK-47 trained on the door which he had shut behind them.

Seeing a single bed in the corner of the room the DS shouted at his mate, "Help me get this up against the door, that'll buy us some time while we come up with Plan B. It ain't gonnae be long before our friends try and shoot us out of here."

After slamming the bed against the door Hardie quickly provided a Plan B. "Look, the mosque roof ain't that far away, if you can keep these bastards busy I'll rip the curtains off and tie them into a lower we can get ourselves out of this place. There's a side building only 30 feet below the window."

"Fuck me, makes you feel like Butch Cassidy and the Sundance kid about to meet their makers," said Thoroughgood.

"Always thought Lee Van Cleef would have made a better Butch than old blue eyes Newman any day," quipped Hardie as another round of sharp cracks splintered the door.

"Fuck's sake faither, just do it. Now get the bloody hell down will you . . ." was as far as Thoroughgood got by way of reply because right then there was a thud through the bedroom door that jolted the bed back quickly followed by a renewed hail of lead.

Hardie had ripped the curtains off their hooks on the way to the deck and now he attempted to tie them together. But what with? Quickly his brain clicked into gear and he removed his tie and set to work making knots.

The door splintered again as twin AKs emptied their rounds of death into its frame. Although Thoroughgood responded with his own fire he was aware that time and ammunition were running out.

Then the DS heard another thud, this time from behind and saw that Hardie had opened the window fully and was throwing the curtains out.

He crawled over to the window and said, "Right old man, you get out first, here – take the dagger. I'll cover you and jump when I'm ready."

Hardie knew there was no point in arguing the toss and belied his portly appearance by quickly jumping onto the window frame, grabbing the thick fold of curtain hanging over it and with a wink he was down the other side. Thoroughgood took the strain but knew he needed to anchor the curtain on something and fast.

The dresser at the side of the room, two feet away, was perfect. He did his best to tie the end of the curtain around it while trying to keep the AK47 trained on the door.

'Anytime soon the end is nigh," said the voice in his

head. Out loud he said "Come and get me you bastards!" and they did not disappoint.

A volley of lethal projectiles splintered the door into a set of unseemly shards and the impact of whatever the terrorists were using knocked the bed clean away from its position behind it.

Thoroughgood jumped onto the window frame facing the fast disintegrating room door, AK47 slung over his shoulder and began to lower himself as the Keffiyeh-sheathed figures entered at pace. He counted three of them before dropping down the wall as quickly as he could cradling the AK in the nook of his elbow and pointing it upward at the receding sight of the open window.

Twenty feet away was the flat roof that was the adjoining side building of the mosque. He knew that if he let go of the curtain he'd land in an uncontrolled fashion, a sitting duck for his pursuers who would empty out the contents of their magazines into his prone body.

'No, if you go down, you go down fighting son.' Aware that his body was shaking with the sheer effort of his descent and the growing certainty that he was about to keep the grim reaper company, he slowed his drop and waited for heads to appear out of the window.

Almost immediately the first linen-wrapped head jutted out. Thoroughgood pulled the trigger. The agonised scream was proof of a hit and he concentrated everything on reducing the gap between him and the flat roof as quickly as he could.

Ten feet now, and he gambled and made the leap. The impact jarred up through his ankles but his balance, honed by endless hours on the squash court, was good. He steadied and rolled as a series of high velocity impacts smashed onto his landing point. Their impact was like torrential rain drops throwing up dirt, moss and other debris.

Thoroughgood knew one hit would bring about his end. Quickly he was on his feet and sprinting in a zigzag, making his way for what he realised was the glazed dome of the minaret.

A thud behind him was followed by a second and he knew he had company. Then a voice shouted, "Gus over here!" It was Hardie and thankfully his mate had chosen the same point of cover that was now just 20 yards away from him.

"C'mon son, you're clean through with the yellow and amber hoops on, put the fuckin' foot down!" screamed Hardie in encouragement.

But he was aware that footsteps were closing in on him, his lack of conditioning again letting him down. He turned to see that one of the Jihadists was less than 15 feet away.

He dropped to his knees and slung the AK into the ready position and pulled the trigger. Click. The magazine had run empty. "For fuck's sake," raged Thoroughgood. He threw the empty AK-47 at his attacker as he closed the short distance between them.

Observing from his crouched position next to the mosque dome 15 feet away Hardie watched in horror as the disaster unfolded before his eyes, helpless to aid his mate. 'Not quite mate,' and he reached into his pocket and pulled the ceremonial dagger out shouting, "Gus! Incoming!" and launching it along the ground to Thoroughgood where it skated across the flat roof.

Thoroughgood grabbed the ivory handle and shouted. "Get tae, Faither . . ." then the Jihadist was on him.

247

He took the impact as he rose from his crouch and had not managed to bring the gleaming blade to the level as the terrorist's full sprinting body weight hit.

Thoroughgood felt himself flying through the air, his assailant's hands grabbing his wrists and he landed with a thud. The male's eyes exuded fiendish hate as he encircled Thoroughgood's wrist with both hands and tried to force the dagger free from the DS's grip.

Automatically Thoroughgoood smashed his hand off the side of the turbaned head and a piece of the male's Keffiyeh came loose. 'Perfect,' said the voice in his head. He yanked it with all his power, the pull unbalanced his attacker and his grip loosened enough for Thoroughgood to force the blade home with all his strength.

A groan escaped from the terrorist but it was not the only noise in the background. Over his shoulder Thoroughgood could see a second male closing fast on him. He knew that the last thing he could do was roll away from his previous attacker as that would make him an easy target for his second pursuer. Instead, retaining his grip on the dagger but with both hands also on the limp male he pushed him up, ramming his own body in an upward motion behind and into the terrorist and using the increasingly lifeless body as a shield.

The manoeuvre clearly confused his second pursuer who stopped for a minute, unsure whether to unload lead into the body of his comrade, who was still alive although far from kicking.

Slowly, Thoroughgood shuffled back holding onto the inert body of his attacker, the dagger, still in his hand, protruding from the side of the body, warning the second terrorist that Thoroughgood was still armed and dangerous. The male charged across the roof and closed in on Thoroughgood and his dance partner. The cop launched the lifeless figure at his second pursuer but he seemed to anticipate the move and applied a side-step that allowed his previous brother-in-arms to collapse onto the roof, bleeding out in his death throes.

The male stopped five feet from Thoroughgood and unwrapped his head to reveal a familiar face. Dark beard and curly hair but most familiar was the white eye.

"This time I make no mistake. This time you die, kafir," he spat. He dropped his AK on the ground and slipped his hand into his kameez to withdraw his own blade. "I gut you like a pig and leave you to drown in your own blood."

"Gratitude," said Thoroughood sarcastically and readied Saladin's dagger to once more bring death.

Naif charged. But Thoroughgood was ready for this dance of death. As Naif slashed down with his own steel the DS brought his up and the sparks from the clash shot into the air. The two blades remained locked together as Naif used all his strength to force Thoroughgood's blade – and the DS with it – down.

Aware that he was slowly being overpowered Thoroughgood backed off. He realised he was almost up against the geometric glass dome but also that Naif was trying to move to the left, away from his right hand and the blade.

Naif flashed a mocking smile and began to toss his own blade from one hand to another. "There is no one to save you. Renounce your God, the false crusader god, and I will give you merciful Dawa – in your words that is the true faith, kafir. Don't be shy, don't run. Do you know that the last time I had work for my blade it gutted one of your SAS devils? Do you think you, a mere cop, are going to beat Naif in a knife fight? Are you scared of death, kafir, now that it is here?" Naif continued his mockery, attempting to goad Thoroughgood into a rash move but he made none.

His failure to draw any kind of reaction angering him, Naif burst forward, this time lunging directly for Thoroughgood's midriff. The DS rammed Saladin's dagger upwards as powerfully as he could and the force of his motion smashed Naif's own blade out of his hand and it clattered across the roof. Such was his momentum the terrorist smashed into Thoroughgood and the two of them cannoned off the glass dome.

A sickening sense of déjà vu washed over Thoroughgood as he thought back to the last time he had tangled with his assailant – over the bonnet of a parked car. But this time he was the one holding the ivory-handled knife, Saladin's death blade. The irony seeped through his mind that he was using it to try and kill one of the great Sultan's own, centuries after it had been used to gut the most infamous crusader of them all Raynald de Chatillon.

But Thoroughgood could feel energy draining as Naif did everything he could to prize the dagger from his grip.

With both hands wrapped round Thoroughgood's wrist Naif smashed the blade off the geometric dome time after time as he attempted to break it free. Weakened from his previous efforts against the other jihadist Thoroughgood could feel hope as well as strength slipping away from him fast.

At the third attempt the blade broke free from his grip and as he pushed off Thoroughgood, Naif smashed his right fist into the cop's guts. Bent double by the power of the blow Thoroughgood was in no position to try and stop his attacker taking possession of the ceremonial dagger and as he straightened up he could see the gleaming blade dancing in the sunlight, his tormentor smiling in cruel delight.

"At last I have Saladin's blade back and now, kafir, your life is also in my hands. Prepare to make your way through the gates of hell unbeliever," he spat and began his killing move.

Realising he had to play for time Thoroughgood tried to engage his would be killer in dialogue. "Why are you doing all of this? What on earth are you trying to achieve in the name of your God? You can not tell me that anywhere in the Koran it encourages the followers of Allah to butcher innocents? Tell me where suicide bombing fits in with the teachings of Mohammed and the words of your Holy book?"

Naif leered but seemed incensed by Thoroughgood's attempts to undermine the purpose of his mission.

"You waste your time, infidel pig. If any member of the true faith dies when they are killed in the cause of Allah they are doing the right thing. It is not called suicide, it is called shahada: martyring, because if the only way to hurt the enemies of Islam is by taking your life for theirs then it is allowed. The person who hinders Allah's rule, this man must be eliminated."

He smiled and kissed the gleaming steel of the blade. "Enough talk. I am not scared to die, kafir, but you, it is clear, are almost drowning in your own shit. I will not allow your presence to defile this Holy place any longer and deflect me from my mission. Salam, infidel."

With that Naif advanced, dagger in hand, intent on death.

Thoroughgood caught a flicker of movement behind him. Ten feet away, and removing the AK-47 from the prone figure of the dead terrorist, was faither.

"Stop, you bastard. It's time you met your maker," and as Naif turned to meet his tormentor Hardie pulled the trigger and emptied the entire contents of the AK's magazine into him.

The terrorist whiplashed back with frightening violence. His body jerked in a single macabre movement and smashed into the dome. The toughened glass, glowing with soft green light didn't take his body weight and with one vicious crack Naif plummeted through the dome and down into the main prayer hall.

"How appropriate," was all Thoroughgood could say.

Slowly the DS sank to his knees and shook his head. "Do you fancy dear faither, telling me what the fuck we are doing slap bang in the middle of this mess?"

Hardie smiled. "Maybes aye, maybes naw. But that is the second time I have saved your life in a week and it's gettin' feckin' boring."

A wail of sirens filled the morning air but there was complete silence between Hardie and Thoroughgood. The enormity of the threat now facing Glasgow and Scotland rammed home to them as never before.

"So what now, Gus? We may have wiped out their death squad but how do you fight an invisible enemy? The sleeper cells are a job for the intelligence services and there's no way Tariq is placing all his money on red so to speak."

"I don't know and I'm not sure I want to know. Let's just hope there have been some positive developments with Etherington and his cronies. It is going to be like Apocalypse Now with the media.

"Four terrorists dead after a gun fight on the Glasgow Central Mosque roof and all in broad daylight. Jesus H Christ, think of the impact that is going to have in terms of unrest between the natives and the Muslim community in Glasgow."

"Fuck me, it is like we have half-done the fanatics job for them. Midday prayers are only half an hour away. Bloody hell, I hope uniform get here pronto otherwise the shit is gonnae hit the fan in a matter of minutes. Can you imagine what it is going to be like when the faithful and devout come to prayer and find their mosque has been turned into a morgue, and now a crime scene?" asked Hardie.

Thoroughgood winced. "That isn't going to be our problem. Look there's the first Panda pulling in. Once we update the uniform and allow them to get down to business we need to be heading for the UAE bank ASAP. It might be a long shot that Rahman is still there but it is one we have got to make. By then hopefully we will have some intel' on where Farouk is.

"But our first priority after putting the wooden tops in the picture has got be a call to Tomachek. The news about our little gun fight will be winging its way to the Chief Constable like a rogue Exocet. After all this, faither, there is going to be no let up until the final throw of the dice and by the looks of it that ain't far away."

"What about the dagger Gus?" asked Hardie bringing the conversation back to earth with a bump.

"Right now, whatever the significance it has to the Muslim community, there is no way anyone else can have it because it's clear that these maniacs will stop at nothing to get it back. It is also a piece of evidence after I used it to take care of one of our friends back there. Nope it's Stewart Street nick for Saladin's razor blade!"

A mutual smile of relief swept over the detectives' faces but it was fleeting.

34

AS THEY pushed their way out through the growing crowd of passers-by and the devout gathering for prayer, both detectives realised how lucky they were that they did not have to deal with the fallout of this latest episode.

Hardie had managed to get the Mondeo out from the kerb despite the crowd and turned back round towards the city centre. He mouthed quick clarification on direction of travel to Thoroughgood. "Sauchiehall Street?"

Thoroughgood was nursing a frown that showed he was undecided, though it had initially seemed so clear that pursuit of Rahman was the logical next move.

"Nope, I think we head for University Gardens and an impromptu meeting with Professor Farouk," he said.

"Okay," was all Hardie had the energy to say, and as the DC looked at his mate he had to admit it would have been hard to tell who had been left more exhausted by the events at the Mosque.

As was his wont Hardie couldn't help himself articulating the maelstrom within his mind. "I'm fucked, pure and simple. Eight years until I pick up my pension and at this rate I have as much chance of making it to the golden

handshake as Thistle have of winning the Scottish bleedin'
Cup."

"Charming!" replied Thoroughgood before turning to
the issue at hand. "You aren't the only one in that particular boat now, are you faither?"

Hardie frowned in acknowledgement before Thoroughgood continued. "I think Farouk is the key to tying up
some loose ends and that is why we are heading back up
to the Uni. The bottom line is that he either arranged the
meet with Rahman and then cancelled it in a fit of mis-
guided conscience, or he sent us there without ever having
made contact with our friend the hawaladar. Which do
you think it was?" asked Thoroughgood.

Hardie, by this time fag in mouth and elbow leaning
over the driver's window, had no doubts. "The former.
You saw the lather the professor was getting himself in
over his big dilemma. I think he made contact and then he
reneged on it and warned Rahman off and that means it's
time we took the old boy into custody and made sure he
gives us Rahman bang to rights on a silver platter."

"Eloquent as always," said Thoroughgood just as the
Mondeo pulled into a bay outside the department of Middle Eastern Studies.

On entry into the department the detectives were met
by Farouk's secretary who informed them emphatically
that the professor had taken himself over to the West
Quadrant for a bit of fresh air to clear a blinding headache. The mention of the quads had Thoroughgood recalling halcyon days as he and Hardie crossed University
Avenue on foot.

"It's amazing, considering I live half a mile away and
drive up and down University Avenue virtually every day

that I have never set foot in the quads since I graduated best part of 15 years back," said the DS.

"Fascinating," commented Hardie with dripping sarcasm.

"Aye, July 7 was the big day. I graduated with my MA Hons and enjoyed the old shampoo on the lawns within the quads. I'll never forget it because it was the last time my mother and my old man were together in this life and they spent the whole day bickering. They may have been apart for almost 20 years before it but they went at it hammer and tongs and it wasn't helped by the fact that my bird at the time made it clear it was the last place on the planet she wanted to be. Aye, happy days as you might say faither!" concluded Thoroughgood.

Hardie's surprise at his superior's comments was clear in the habitual raised eyebrow. "You know that is about the first time I've ever heard you mention your folks Gus. Your old man is dead ain't he?"

Passing the security guard at the entrance with a quick flash of his warrant card Thoroughgood was already mentally back on the job. "Long gone. Now up the stairs and turn left and hopefully Professor Farouk is sitting on the verge at the back of the quads, enjoying the view out over the Kelvingrove and the Art Galleries and getting himself together 'cause we are going to need him lucid for what he has coming his way."

They climbed the old, worn stone steps that would take them up past the Bute Hall – where the young Thoroughgood had spent many excruciating hours studying the demise of the Capetian dynasty and comparing the importance of Wallace and Bruce – and into the West Quad.

Hardie, shivering as the autumn sunlight gave way to a

chilly shade, could not help himself moaning, "Feck me, did you graduate with long johns on? It's Baltic in here. Where are all of the student spongers?"

Thoroughgood smiled. "Lunch time my dear Hardie. The GU beer bar and the QM will be packed. Aah the mammaries, sorry, memories, this place brings back. You know I've never told anyone this but I was going to ask Celine to marry me here, in the University Chapel."

Hardie looked shocked but before he could find any words Thoroughgood added, "That's right and you know who I was going to ask to be my best man?" Clearly from the unchanged look on his portly chops Hardie did not.

"You, dear old faither."

But as he scanned his side-kick's face Thoroughgood saw that the cause of Hardie's speechlessness was not his revelations but a body swinging from a cloister 30 yards to his right. As he turned to take in the sight Thoroughgood's thoughts were once again articulated by Hardie.

"Jesus H Christ it's Farouk. The poor sod's gone and hung himself."

35

THE BMW drew to a halt outside the giant iron gates which had been shut for months. The passenger's window rolled down to access the remote control and the gates swung wide. The vehicle drove along the estate road, eventually sliding to a halt on the white stones. Two men jumped out and made for the the imposing oak doors.

The driver, a swarthy man attired in an immaculate Armani suit, watched as his companion inserted a key in the door, softly saying, "Ah, Tara, it's good to be home." Meechan turned to the driver adding, "You'll be glad to know, Mr Rahman, that the drinks cabinet has been kept well stocked. A glass of Talisker?"

"Thank you," replied Rahman in his accented English and he followed Meechan through to the drawing room.

Drinks poured, the two men sat down and Meechan cut to the chase. "Are we on course for the Nikah?"

Rahman smiled thinly before replying. "Farouk is dead, Mr Meechan, and the balance of the sum agreed has been paid into the Swiss bank account you stipulated. The Imam has one more little diversion planned for your friends before the Nikah is carried out."

Meechan looked at the golden-brown liquid for a moment, swirling it in the glass before taking a draught and sighing in appreciation.

"I had this house built as my family home. I planned to fill it with the voices of my children and the woman I loved. I was this close," Meechan held up his thumb and a forefinger almost touching, "until these bastards ruined everything and I was left with nothing."

Again Rahman's sleek smile; clearly he was interested in the circumstances behind Meechan's flight from his homeland and his desperation to return to Glasgow.

"Your circumstances interest me Mr Meechan," he said. "We have talked for many months in order to make this business happen and to cheat the Jews out of the enriched uranium but business has always come first ..." he finished, giving Meechan the option to elaborate.

Meechan raised his glass in salute. "First, a toast to the ancient system and right of the Hawalidar. For without it, you and I would not be sitting here anticipating the realisation of our respective dreams."

"The Hawalidar." They both raised their glasses but yet the discomfort and distrust between them was mutual.

Rahman had rarely experienced the level of Meechan's intensity, even when dealing with the religious fervour of Tariq and his Jihadists. The thick dark beard and mane of hair framing his ghoulish grey eyes gave Meechan an intimidating appearance that left Rahman feeling threatened. The banker had done his homework and knew of Meechan's expertise in killing to order, extortion and intimidation, of his meteoric rise within the Rising Sun after his way in was paved by his associate O'Driscoll. It was said his rapid rise was down to the personal interest of the Russian Mafia's leader Omar Youssef Tipsarevich himself.

Appraising the banker with icy fire burning from his

eyes Meechan could smell fear and enjoyed the sensation.

"All of this and almost all of Glasgow was mine, Rahman. Almost within my grasp until I found out that the woman I loved was in love with a copper. She claimed the baby she carried was mine but I could not believe her and that meant that she had to die."

Meechan finished the sentence in matter of fact manner leaving it hanging in the air.

Rahman sipped nervously at his whisky before replying, "As you say, Mr Meechan, I am no more than a hawaladar, a banker. I thank Allah himself that your path has led you to us and our arrangement which I hope will be most profitable for both parties."

Meechan sneered then continued, aggression and anger bubbling near the surface of his voice, "This is not about money for me, Rahman, it's about revenge on the people and the city that spat me out. Total revenge starting with the death of Balfour and his hangers-on and from which there is no way back. The execution of the hostages is no more than a sideshow. I hope for your sake and your friend the Imam's that it does not jeopardise the Nikah. Do you understand me?"

"Perfectly," said Rahman.

Meechan got up and headed to a large oil painting at the back of the room. He pulled it away from the wall, twisted the combination lock and the safe door opened.

He removed an attaché case and placed it on the table between them.

"This, Mr Rahman, is what you paid seven figures for. The key substances needed for your Holy Grail, the dirty bomb that al-Qaeda have been so desperate to get their hands on. And it's all yours." Meechan barked out a harsh laugh. "The weapon the West have been pissing themselves over for years; smuggled in on a Russian Trawler. It's laughable Rahman, is it not?"

"Nevertheless you have taken a great risk to get it here and we are grateful. May I ask where you brought it onto the mainland?"

"Oh, we washed up on the Isle of Barra then shipped down to a wee cove near Oban which I'm told used to be a smugglers' haunt. The rest is history." Meechan added, "Now it is up to you and your organisation to make history of your own." The smile that had temporarily lit his face was gone and the calculated viciousness returned.

"It is almost unbelievable," stammered Rahman.

"Unbelievable maybe, but, with regards to this case, the proof is in the pudding. Your responsibility is to get it to the secure location without being intercepted. The Caesium 137 in the second vial is extremely soluble and reactive. You are confident that you have the expertise to help it, shall we say, reach its full potential?"

Rahman shifted nervously but smiled that he was.

For a moment Meechan seemed about to lose his temper. "Because I can assure you that if you fail it will matter not whether you are incarcerated or not, your life will be over."

Meechan took a quick slug of his Talisker but his cold eyes never left Rahman's.

He continued, his Northern Irish accent becoming markedly more pronounced, "You are aware that Mossad have sanctioned a Kidon squad to terminate my life for double-crossing them? That the Rising Sun are denying all accountability and that, at least in public, the blame will be all on my head?"

Rahman nodded.

"So you can see that the price I will have to pay for the revenge I want your organisation to help me achieve is very high."

"I appreciate all of that," said Rahman, running his fingers over the suitcase, "I know how hard it must have been to procure the substances. I can assure you that it will not go to waste. We have men ready to make sure the bomb achieves its intended purpose."

Meechan smiled. "Good. Very good," and he ran his fingers through the beard that had so altered his appearance since he last left Tara.

But he had not finished. "Tell me about Professor Farouk? I believe he got cold feet?"

Rahman finished his drink and stood up. "I can assure you Mr Meechan that he has been dealt with. The last loose end has been well and truly tied up and the police and MI5 have no route to me. Tariq's headquarters are underground and will not be traced. We have an army of well paid observers watching the security services as they try to watch us. In short, we know what their moves are almost before they make them."

Meechan raised his glass in salute. "You know that there can be no contact between us via cellphone or email from now on? How do you propose to circumvent that?"

Rahman surprised Meechan with a sneer of his own. "All communication with the Imam has been outwith both these channels for sometime now. We are aware that MI5 are monitoring everything and that is why we reward our trusted street runners so well. Do not worry, Mr Meechan, we will remain in contact with you as needed."

"Remember this and remember it well Rahman. I am

here to settle a personal score as well as a business one and I will allow no one to stop me achieving both."

After Rahman's departure Meechan poured another Talisker and took himself on a tour of his property. The experience left him with mixed emotions.

As he walked round the empty pool the memories came flooding back. The knife fight that should have ended Thoroughgood's life but instead confirmed what he had dreaded all along. That Celine would never truly be his and that somehow Thoroughgood would always find a way to come between them. That was why she had to die.

He opened the French doors and took his whisky out to the lochan, sitting on the grassy verge which overlooked it. Losing himself in its cooling blue hues, he knew that these moments of reflection at the estate would be the last he would spend at the place he had once called home.

As his eyes swept the panoramic beauty of the Campsies, sheathed in the noon sunshine, he knew he had nothing to lose. The threat of a death squad had condemned his life to one of anonymity spent in the shadows – if he chose to live. To risk that marginal existence by exacting the revenge the desire for which burned his every wakened moment was no risk at all.

He would not leave without Thoroughgood's complete destruction. Raising the glass in the air Meechan spoke into the silence, "Count your hours Thoroughgood because they will be your last."

36

THE DOOR creaked open and a man entered. He pointed at Fraser and spat two words: "Get up."

Fraser struggled to his feet and a few stammered words left his bloodied mouth, "For pity's sake please ..." But the handle of the man's pistol smacked off the side of his jaw and knocked him into the cavern wall. As he staggered a powerful hand gripped his shoulder and he was dragged towards the door by a second shadowy figure.

"What are you doing? Where are you taking him? Stop it! Stop it!" Vanessa screamed at her captors.

"Shut the fuck up bitch or I come back here and make you beg to join him," their captor said gesturing towards his genitals, leaving Vanessa in no doubt about what he had in mind for her.

Fraser was dragged out into the corridor and propelled along it towards the main chamber. He knew about the medieval city that existed underneath present-day Edinburgh but this had a more industrial feel to it. Perhaps they were still in Glasgow, he did not know; his period of unconsciousness had distorted his perception of time and its passing. As his mind ran over the possibilities he was thrown to the ground in front of Tariq.

He was restrained on his knees. Craning his head round he saw that he had been returned to the same chamber that had been used for the ransom video. A shudder of cold fear wracked his body and mind.

Tariq spoke in a measured tone, "So, Mr Fraser, your moment of truth has, I'm afraid, arrived."

"What do you mean?" demanded Fraser, his voice shaking.

"I mean that, despite the pathetic attempts of the infidel pigs in the FBI and MI5 to fool us, we know our brother has not been freed. Now you must pay for their lies and treachery with your life."

Fraser felt rough hands dragging him to his feet and in front of a huge banner emblazoned with Islamic writing. Once again he was forced down onto his knees and as he saw one of his captors start to film him, he knew that the last grains of his life were slipping away.

"Stop, please stop," he sobbed. "Look, I can get you whatever you need, just let me help you," he spluttered through his broken mouth.

Tariq looked at him dispassionately, his dark eyes pulsing with contempt. "But Mr Fraser it is not I who needs help, it is you who is the one in need of divine intervention."

Tariq reached down and picked up the long curved blade before he looked at the camera and spat a string of words in the language of his faith.

The Imam moved towards Fraser and stood behind him before speaking to the camera again in his thickly accented English, "We demanded the release of our brother but instead you sought to deceive us with a film of his faked release. For that you have brought death on this godless son of a whore."

Fraser felt a sharp rush of air on his cheek and caught a glint of metal. He knew what was coming next. "No! Wait!" he screamed as Tariq's words filled the background and the scimitar began its downwards sweep.

"I despatch you into your hell, unbeliever."

The gleaming steel sliced through sinew and bone and the Leader of Glasgow City Council lost his head for the last time.

"Allahu akbar," shouted Tariq and his followers took up the chant with him.

In her cell, snivelling in the dirt, Vanessa heard the chant cascading along the corridor and her awful certainty at what it meant sent a shudder through her body. The door to her room burst open and a second shudder of raw fear went through her.

Tariq stood in the doorway and smiled viciously. "So, capitalist whore, what do I do with you now? That is the question."

For a moment Vanessa's former pride stoked a fire of hate. "Go to hell!" she shouted.

But Tariq had other ideas. "I believe that will be your final destination, not mine, Miss Velvet, but I wonder should I take some pleasure from you before I send you there?"

He closed the few steps between them with a languid movement. He grabbed her jaw with his hand forcing her to her feet.

"Those painted lips are faded and dirty. All your beauty is nothing now, Jezebel. What does your life mean now that it has turned to shit?"

Tariq's face hovered an inch away from hers and Vanessa felt sure he was about to kiss her.

His eyes burned into hers and he rolled his tongue out of his mouth and along his top lip.

"Tell me bitch, should I despoil you in the name of Allah?"

Vanessa began to sob uncontrollably. For once no words came to her, such was her sense of hopelessness.

Tariq uttered one word. "Quiet." His lips clamped on hers, cruel and hard. Their dryness and the harshness of the kiss were repellent.

Then, to her surprise Tariq recoiled and spat on the ground at her feet.

"No, painted harlot, I have other delights in store for you. But first I have more important matters to attend to. For now I will leave you in the company of my men. Maybe they will take pleasure from you. But know this, Miss Velvet. I will return and when I do you must prepare to meet your fate."

With that Tariq laughed and left the room. Even after he shut the cell door she could hear his cackles of vicious delight slowly receding down the corridor.

37

THE DIRECTOR of MI5 shook his head as the video of the Leader of Glasgow City Council losing his head came to an end. But the voice that punctured the silence in the conference room on floor five of Force Headquarters came from the other end of the table and from a far less illustrious mouth.

"Jesus H Christ!" cried Detective Constable Kenny Hardie. "Please tell me you have managed to get a trace on this?"

Sir Willie Stratford smiled uncomfortably at the assembled meeting and then broke the awful truth. "Sadly we have not been able to decipher the backscatter. It is impossible to tell when these things are posted on Al Jazeera web sites like that. But it seems our ruse did not work."

Detective Superintendent Tomachek, robbed of the comfort of his pipe due to the relocation to Force HQ, could not contain his anger any longer. "With all due respect Sir William, Chief Constable and the rest of you gentlemen, if you haven't managed to get anything from the army of listeners you have deployed and all your technology then what is the point? You are aware that this video will have brought public faith in both the police and the intelligence services to an all time low. This is the last thing we needed so soon after the London bombings."

"Quite," replied Stratford but before he could respond fully Tomachek was on him like a butcher's dog after a stray sausage.

"This bloody well isn't good enough. The leader of Glasgow City Council is not just some nobody. He is … was … one of the most public figures in the city if not the country and he has just been executed on a video that will be all over the web by the time this meeting is at an end."

Tomachek was only warming up. "If Vanessa Velvet's pretty little head rolls too she'll end up canonised while our careers will be over."

Stratford snapped under the relentless pilloring of the second generation Pole. "Now listen to me Detective Superintendent Tomachek, I am aware of that. Everything possible is being done to locate Tariq's lair and Miss Velvet. Etherington will explain exactly what is being done to facilitate that."

But before his second-in-command could speak Stratford was challenged again, this time by Thoroughgood.

"Sir William, do we have any further information on the whereabouts of Meechan or Rahman? If they have a dirty bomb then they must now be our top priority."

Etherington tried to deflect the line of verbal fire from his boss. "Everything within our power is being done to trace Meechan on the continent and all UK Ports have been circulated with his description. Rahman's addresses are all under surveillance but he is nowhere to be found. I am being kept updated on both searches. I must stress that we still do not have confirmation that they have met, or that the device you refer to has changed hands."

But Thoroughgood had not finished with the beleaguered head of MI5. "What about the jihadists we killed at the Mosque? You must have gleaned some intelligence from their bodies? Surely the male with the white eye who spent the last fortnight pursuing me and Saladin's dagger is known to you."

Etherington provided the answer. "He is the only one known to us, or rather, our friends in the CIA. His name is Naif and he is known as the Lion of Waziristan. He is a veteran of Afghanistan who was once a bodyguard of bin Laden. He's famous within al-Qaeda for having defeated and killed three members of the SAS in a firefight. He has been used to whip up radicalism within mosques in the West. He was on our American counterparts most wanted list. So Detective Hardie deserves great credit for terminating him."

"Indeed he does, excellent work Hardie," said ACC Crime, Graeme Cousins.

Etherington moved on, "As for Naif's counterparts we are having their visuals circulated to friendly intelligence centres across the globe. But that is the problem with Jihadists, for the most part they are law abiding people who have never come to the attention of authorities anywhere in their lives.

"What I will say is that not one of them was recorded on our surveillance equipment outside the Mosque. So we are talking about recruits from abroad, probably Pakistan.

"So, right now we don't know what capabilities the Spear of Islam still have at their disposal. Tariq seems to be acutely aware that he can afford no communication via cellphone or email. He has pre-empted our every move and has gone to ground, God knows where."

Etherington took a deep breath and continued his tail of woe. "One thing we are now sure of is that Professor Farouk did not commit suicide but was murdered. He was strangled prior to being strung up in a rather crude attempt to mimic suicide by hanging."

Hardie interjected, "Poor sod."

Thoroughgood challenged the intelligence officer, "Tragic but perhaps not surprising, given that Rahman failed to turn up for his meeting with Farouk at the Mosque. What of the bookshop owner and the staff at One Devonshire Gardens? Surely you must have turned up something from them?"

A new voice, possessing total authority, spoke into the ensuing silence; that of George Salmond, Chief Constable of Strathclyde Police, known less than respectfully as 'slippery' to the rank and file. He was not a happy man.

"Indeed, Sir William, I echo Detective Sergeant Thoroughgood's concern over your organisation's continual inability to track and locate these terrorists. As far as I can see these amateur fanatics are leading you on a merry dance as the bodies pile up."

Sir William tried to interject but Salmond raised his hand and carried on. "In my building I abdicate the floor when I have finished, Sir William. You will do well to remember that I want to say one thing. If you do not provide the intelligence and the means to end this carnage within 48 hours I will be on my private line to the Prime Minister and I can assure you we will not be talking about our former schooldays at Fettes College."

Stratford's skin mottled and he fidgeted with his Harlequins RFC tie but he was rescued by Etherington.

"With respect, Chief Constable," the chief intelligence

officer said, "we have made significant progress. Firstly, we turned our attention to the staff at One Devonshire Gardens. The porter and the duty manager who we had brought in for questioning are no more than impressionable fools. They were basically asked to supply the names of the great and the good to Tariq so that any sensitive trysts could be used for financial blackmail. Beyond that they know nothing and certainly had no idea what the information they provided was going to be used for."

"Sham-bloody-bolic," muttered Hardie under his breath.

Etherington forged on. "The bookshop owner is different. He's in custody at Govan Police Station being interviewed by one of our expert interrogators."

There was an abrupt metallic scrape as the chief constable slammed his chair back and drew himself up to his full 6ft 4inches. He cast an incinerating gaze on the shaken and clearly stirred members of Her Majesty's Intelligence Service.

"I don't care who you are Stratford! This is my city and you will get this mess sorted out by whatever means, or you are finished. Believe me."

With that Salmond and his entourage left the room.

Thoroughgood and Hardie followed but as they left Etherington called,

"A word if I may, Detective Sergeant Thoroughgood?"

Thoroughgood and Hardie turned in unison. The DS responded, pointing at an adjoining empty room, "In there? Looks ideal for the privacy I imagine you'll want this conversation to take place in."

"Indeed," said Etherington and walked into the room behind the DS.

As the door shut Hardie said, as sarcastically as he could, "Fire away Ethers."

Etherington winced but carried on. "Look gentlemen, I know how bad this whole thing looks and it will undoubtedly be the end of Stratford, but we can still get our men. More importantly we can, and will, prevent further carnage. The means to that is through Omar."

He was met with silence but was not deflected. "It is my belief that Omar knows all about Rahman, Tariq and of course Meechan. Certainly that is the impression our interrogator is getting. I have no doubt that he is aware where the mad Imam is located but if we want that intel we can't afford to play by the Marquis of Queensberry's rules."

Aware that he had their attention now, Etherington continued, "My proposal is that we take matters into our own hands and keep those further up out of it. You will be aware that sometimes in the world we operate in, unsavoury methods are employed when needs must. Regrettably within our timescale we have to take what measures we can to prevent merry hell erupting."

"About fuckin' time," rapped Hardie.

"Gentlemen, I would like you to join me at the former Partick Police Station to view at first hand a unique form of interrogation which you will know as waterboarding. The time for niceties has long gone detectives. Are you with me?"

Thoroughgood and Hardie exchanged a glance before the DS said, "All the way. Whatever it takes."

Etherington smiled thinly. "Excellent. Your destination, as I said, is the old Partick Police Office where friend Omar has been relocated. I believe the building is also known as the Marine? As the form of interrogation we are planning is somewhat indelicate, the fewer who know about it the better. Right now, however, the ends justifies the means – and it's a damned pity that my superior could not see it that way. It is now 3.32pm. I suggest a 4pm rendezvous at the location mentioned?"

"No problem," agreed Thoroughgood.

Hardie was the voice of doom. "I just hope we aren't too late."

38

AS THEY parked the Mondeo at the rear of the famous old police station, originally built in 1853, the memories swept back over both Thoroughgood and Hardie.

"Aye, bricks and bars; the old place hasn't changed much since it closed for business," said Hardie, looking at the intimidating back wall of the station which looked exactly as it had done upon its opening.

"I remember coming back in off the street right at the start of my service in a pea-souper and expecting Dracula to jump me. On a dark pissin' night this place used to scare the shit out of a good few. God knows what delights we have waiting for us now M15 have commandeered it for this bit of business."

"A case of 'for what we are about to receive . . .' if ever there was one," added Hardie.

Making their way round to the arched doorway in Gullan Street the two detectives could not quite believe that they were heading into the building that had played host to so much of their past. Each half-expected the solid wooden doors would be barred as they had been since the Marine closed for police business in 1993.

But after Hardie had banged the door with the traditional polis seven rap knock, Etherington's face appeared from behind it and they were beckoned in.

"Welcome to our new home from home. A step back into the past but one that will facilitate the giant step forward we need to avoid more disaster."

They passed two suits in the foyer as they followed in Etherington's wake. Both detectives heard voices that indicated these were not the only spooks currently stationed in the Marine. They walked through black iron gates and up a set of concrete steps into a corridor caged in iron mesh.

Halfway along the corridor Etherington stopped at a black steel door and inserted a key into its ancient lock. Thoroughgood was convinced the scene could have come from a Bram Stoker novel.

Before Etherington turned the key he spoke. "Gentlemen, this is the last chance to turn back if you are squeamish or concerned that anything you may witness is unacceptable. Anything you witness can, and will, be denied. What we are dealing with now means human rights are no longer a prime consideration."

Thoroughgood provided confirmation the detectives were on side, "Let's go in."

Etherington opened the door.

Immediately opposite them, caged within the observation cell was a dark figure, full-bearded and spitting venom.

"Meet Omar al-Rahim al-Abidin, gentlemen," said Etherington.

His hands clinging to the bars of the observation cell al-Abidin glowered at them with pulsing hatred. "You think that you can get away with this, pigs? All your pathetic efforts will count for nothing, for you are too late," he said and spat through the metallic mesh that filled the spaces between the bars.

The spittle landed just short of Etherington's brogues. He looked down at his shoes and tutted his displeasure, "Dear me, Omar, that was a bit close. Your punishment awaits."

"Follow me detectives," he said.

They exited the observation room and followed Etherington along the damp and chilly corridor until Etherington turned into cell number 10. Occupying the centre of the floor was a two plank wooden bench supported by trestle legs at either end. At a signal from Etherington the two suits who had obviously prepared the bench left the cell.

"A couple of moments, gentlemen, I have a feeling that Omar will not come willingly," admitted Etherington.

After a moment the detectives heard sounds of a commotion, reminiscent of the years when the cells within the Marine had been fully functional.

"Get your hands off me scum! I am an innocent man!" They heard Omar shout, then there was silence.

Moments later the two suits half-dragged the semi-inert body of the bookshop owner into the room, bound and hooded. He was slammed down on the bench and secured by straps across his ankles, shins, waist and chest. His hands were already strapped to his side.

An interrogation light hovered around 12 inches above him.

Having secured Omar to Etherington's satisfaction, the suits stood on either side of the book shop proprietor, one holding a plastic canister filled with what appeared to be water.

There was no doubt whose show this was and Etherington gestured to Thoroughgood and Hardie to move to the side of the cell, beyond the prone figure.

"It's time we got to work. Excuse me."

Neither Thoroughgood nor Hardie knew what to say. But in their minds they questioned why they had been singled out for the viewing of such a command performance.

Etherington addressed Omar. "You are about to experience something that is very uncomfortable. In fact I am reliably informed it is quite shocking. A practise first used by the Japanese Army and perfected by our American cousins in the CIA. May I say that this goes very much against the grain, but I'm afraid your chums in the Spear of Islam have left us with no choice. Can you hear me Omar al-Rahim al-Abidin?"

Despite the hood covering his mouth an indistinct voice could be heard cursing, "Go to hell infidel pig!"

"That's the spirit!" said Etherington before continuing, "I am now going to place a piece of wood in each of your hands. When this process gets too much and you feel like a chat – drop them. If not, your agony will continue, I promise you, until I get the information I need. Have you heard of the interrogation process known as waterboarding? It is proving very popular with your brothers at Guantanamo Bay."

"Fuck you, scum," was the muffled reply.

"Excellent, I can see you are still in fine fettle," said Etherington as agreeably as if he had asked Omar if he was ready to take his place at the crease for the local village cricket team. "Now, my dear man, I will give you one last chance. Are you ready to furnish us with all that you know about the Imam Tariq, Dhinir Rahman and Declan Meechan; including their whereabouts and plans for future atrocities?"

"Your mother sucks cocks in hell, you crusader devil!" spat Omar.

"She most certainly does not. A bit naughty that one, Omar," Etherington cracked a back-handed slap across the hooded face.

He continued, "Now, listen to me, Omar. We know all about your CDs and their coded messages of Jihad. We know about the meetings addressed by Tariq but I think you have more to tell us and now you will. Gladly, believe me . . ."

With that Etherington grabbed the canister, took the top off and began to pour water liberally onto the hood, alternating between the areas covering Omar's mouth and nose.

As he did so Etherington counted slowly, "One . . . two . . . three . . . four . . . five. . ." By the time he had counted to twelve the bookshop owner had dropped both pieces of wood but Etherington continued to pour. As Etherington's count reached fourteen Omar's linen trousers turned dark as he pissed himself and he screamed, "No more! No more, I tell you!" At last Etherington stopped.

"How dammed decent of you," said the intelligence officer and stooped over Omar before ripping the covering off his head.

Clearly in a state of distress, Omar coughed and spluttered as he spat water out of his mouth.

Etherington gestured at the suits. They moved over to

Omar and started to unstrap him leaving only his ankles and hands still bound.

Watching Etherington, the detectives clearly saw a cruel grin curl at his mouth but the intelligence officer said nothing. He swept Omar with a gaze intent on assessing whether the detainee was truly genuine in his state of distress.

As Omar's rasping subsided and his face was wiped clean, the room was filled with another pungent aroma. Omar had emptied his bowels. This was confirmation enough for Etherington that his man was broken.

He produced a tape recorder and held it close to Omar's face. "As you know we don't have time for a formal interrogation; that will come later, believe me. I want you to answer all my questions clearly and concisely into the tape recorder. Do you understand me?"

Omar nodded.

"Okay, I am going to stick to the essentials. Where is the Imam Tariq at present? Does he still hold the hostage Vanessa Velvet with him?"

Omar's eyes shone defiance but his mouth opened. "He is in Glasgow. I do not know where, but I believe he is underground. I believe the bitch is still with him, awaiting her death."

Etherington smiled thinly. "A half-truth if ever there was one, Omar. We will come back to that. Does the Imam have another atrocity planned for Glasgow, or anywhere else?"

Again the hatred burned from Omar's features but evidently his fear of repeated torture was compelling. "He does. But I know not where or when, other than it is in Glasgow and that it is referred to as the Nikah."

"The 'wedding'; how very cryptic. I warn you Omar,

you are not giving me enough and that will mean a second session. Next, have you any knowledge of a male called Declan Meechan or of the Hawalidar Dhinir Rahman. Do you know what they have been contracted to bring into Glasgow by Tariq?"

"I know nothing," said Omar and spat with all the force he could muster, straight into Etherington's face, "and if I did, you devil, I would rather burn in hell than tell you."

Omar looked over at Thoroughgood and shouted, "The police pig who has Saladin's dagger! Your days will soon be at an end, unbeliever! You commit sacrilege by possessing a relic of such importance. You will pay with your life."

Stunned by the tirade directed at him, Thoroughgood remained silent. He did not know what else to do.

Etherington took a step back and the suits moved forward, grabbing Omar by his arms. The chief intelligence officer pulled a monogrammed hanky from his trouser pocket and wiped the spittle from his face. "Restrain him gentlemen," ordered Etherington calmly.

Before the subordinates sheathed Omar's head once more in the sodden hood he spat more defiance, "I tell you nothing, Satan spawn! You will count the bodies piled high before this week is out and the Imam Tariq will have claimed vengeance on behalf of Islam."

Etherington's eyebrows rose sardonically. On the bench the bookshop owner writhed in a desperate attempt to avoid being tied down for his second bout of waterboarding.

"Why don't you take a couple of minutes to think about all of that Omar? I'll be back shortly." Etherington gestured for Hardie and Thoroughgood to follow him out of the cell.

Standing on the rusted steel flooring in the corridor Thoroughgood was first to speak, "So the next atrocity is due before the week's out and the bodies will pile high. Plus he says Tariq is underground."

"Interesting information," chimed Hardie.

Etherington smirked. "Indeed gentlemen, with more revelations to come I promise you. It's a distasteful business, waterboarding, but a mixture of the sensations of drowning and being asphyxiated is a powerful persuader and one our friends at the CIA have put to good use in Guantanamo Bay and beyond.

"Nevertheless, we now have two lines of enquiry which you can pursue while I complete Omar's interrogation. I believe we are not far away from snaring our quarry, but speed is of the essence."

Thoroughgood offered his hand in gratitude. "We'll stay in contact via mobile, as and when. I think the underground aspect could be crucial. Where to start is the question."

Shaking the DS's hand Etherington underlined his belief in Thoroughgood's ability to provide the answers. "I have every faith in you both.

"Happy hunting, gentlemen." Etherington returned to Omar's cell.

"Mitchell Library?" asked Hardie as they took their seats in the Mondeo.

"Where else?" Thoroughgood levelled the accelerator. As he did so he felt the ivory handle of Saladin's dagger handle protruding into his ribs and the replay of Omar's words it triggered sent a shiver down his spine.

39

RAHMAN WAS met at the disused tunnel entrance by Aaban, the man Tariq had appointed to organise the street beggars and rag-tag army of the homeless and the desperate whose lives had been given purpose by their conversion to Islam following Tariq's street sermons. But now through Aaban's efforts they were a silent and well organised, all-seeing but unseen, group. An army of the shunned who were positioned throughout the streets of Glasgow, ignored and despised but whose job it was to inform the Imam of the authorities' every step.

Aaban smiled. "You have it!" He gestured at the silver case with the handgun held tightly in his hand and Rahman nodded. The sentry opened the gate replacing the handgun in his tracksuit pocket which did little to reduce its visibility. The implied threat was very real; Rahman knew that the group Tariq referred to as 'my eyes and ears' were all armed and ready to deal with any circumstance with utter ruthlessness.

The stench of urine was nauseating as Rahman followed the beggar in his grimy white tracksuit along the tunnel, holding tight to the precious case.

As he followed his silent guide, despite his queasiness, Rahman marvelled at the strong columns that had been used to stabilise the tunnel. It had been a masterstroke by Tariq to use the long forgotten city institution to once again outsmart the authorities. One that brought an extra satisfaction to the hawaladar.

Absorbed in appreciation of this glimpse into a forgotten world Rahman staggered as his foot landed on an old drain which gave way slightly. It crossed his mind that his foot must have been the first one to disturb the spot since the building was built over 100 years before. Cursing, he exhaled, "Allah be praised."

Alerted by Rahman's stumble and then his exclamation Aaban turned in alarm. "You are good?" he asked, his stilted English not surprising the hawaladar, given his guide's Yemeni origin. Rahman replied with a thumbs up but felt himself clutching the case even tighter, aware of the potential disaster that could erupt if he dropped his deadly and unstable cargo.

The constant dripping of water became more and more disconcerting and Rahman heard a scraping sound close by. His guide turned and flashed a smile. "Rat. Don't worry, not long now, maybe 100 metres."

As Aaban led Rahman round a bend in the tunnel the acoustics changed remarkably. The sounds of the modern world above dulled down. A glimpse of light up ahead proved the beggar guide to be correct.

As they approached the light Rahman noticed other silent figures in the shadows. One of them offered a greeting. "Assalamu alaikum."[5]

Aaban flashed a smile and replied. "Wa alaikum as-salam wa rahmatu Allah."[6]

Rahman felt pride swell his breast as he continued in Aaban's footsteps. In his hands was the means to the end that they had all worked for. The ultimate act of vengeance on behalf of their brothers, all those thousands of miles away.

Rahman's chance association with the Rising Sun, leading to his meeting with Meechan and their hatching of a plan that would allow both parties to achieve their mutual goal of mass destruction, had elevated his status in Tariq's Spear of Islam organisation.

When this was over and they had made good their escape they would be received and revered as the men who had achieved what al-Qaeda had failed to do in the toothless years since 9/11; the procurement and detonation of a dirty bomb in a major city in the West. For that, in no small amount due to Meechan, Glasgow was perfect.

Sunlight flooded through the open vents above and bathed the ethereal underground world in a wan glow. Rahman followed his guide up a set of stairs. Rickety rotten wood had been reinforced in places with fresh wood, no doubt down to the current occupants. They arrived at a raised cement platform that he realised with satisfaction must sit only a few metres below Great Western Road. Rahman marvelled at the silent, abandoned world from

---

5   "Peace be with you."

6   "And to you be peace, together with God's mercy."

the past from which – within a matter of hours – would come a deadly attack on the present to scar Glaswegian society forever more. Rahman could see that the platform he stood on still showed signs of fire damage inflicted by some long ago inferno. The staircase was not the only part of the man-made cavern that had been the subject of fresh renovation. There were also new doors on anterooms he assumed must have a new purpose replacing their previous Victorian use.

His reverie was punctured by a familiar voice and there at the top of the stairway stood Tariq. "At last Dhinir, Salam akhee! So you have come with the most important present for our Nikah I see. The family will be so glad." Then Tariq laughed long and loud, the sound reverberating across the platforms and seemingly down the tunnel into the darkness.

Rahamn watched wide-eyed as a line of figures ran out and stood erect on an opposite cement bank. The air was filled with voices shouting, "Allahu Akbar!"

Tariq had turned at the top of the stairs and began to speak to his gathering.

"My friends, the time is almost upon us when we will fulfil the destiny of our Jihad and repay the infidels for the pain and hurt they have inflicted on our brothers in Afghanistan and Iraq. The time when the Crusader pigs will know the meaning of hell and all its agonies." Turning to Rahman, Tariq gestured for him to pass the case. Taking hold of it he lifted it above his head. "At last I have the prized present for the Nikah. The means to bring the faithful the joy we crave. Allahu akbar!" finished Tariq and his shout was chorused once more by the figures on the opposite platform.

The Imam raised a hand for quiet and the believers

287

were stilled instantaneously. "Now I want those who will be attending the Nikah to return to your homes and families and prepare for tomorrow and the answer to our prayers. The rest of you know what is required of you. May Allah and the prophet Mohammed be with you."

The gathering began to melt away down the tunnel, back into the shadows, and Rahman tried to puzzle out where they would be in relation to the modern world above. Two worlds running in parallel lines with only one aware of the other.

Rahman felt a strong hand take grip of him. "Come Dhinir we have much to talk about and little time left to do it," and Tariq guided him thorough a door into a room that could not have been inhabited in 70 years until, like the rest of this forgotten world, it had been given new life and purpose by Tariq.

Tariq placed the case on the table at the centre of the dimly lit room. He ran his fingers lovingly across its silver surface. "Small enough to fit into this do you think?" He lifted a black rucksack onto the table and slotted the case inside. "Excellent. Fit for purpose is the appropriate saying, I believe!" The elation on Tariq's face was something that Rahman had never seen before and found strangely at odds with his usual unreadable countenance.

"Tell me Dhinir, how was Meechan?" asked the Imam.

Rahman flashed his thin smile. "Burning for revenge on this city and certain individuals within it, and grateful for payment; yet a man who knows that the sands of his life are slipping away fast, Imam."

"Explain," demanded Tariq.

"He has paid a high price for the revenge he has manufactured for us to wage, Imam. The double-cross on the

288

Mossad has led to the sanctioning of a Kidon squad. Not even the Rising Sun can save him."

"Indeed," said Tariq. "Does that make him, in your opinion, a danger to us? Could he lead the Kidon squad to our door?"

Rahman shook his head. "No, Imam, Meechan does not know where that door is."

Tariq smiled benignly and rose slowly pulling the rucksack off the table and in so doing revealing the revolver in his hand. "I am sorry Dhinir but we can have no weak points." Rahman's eyes opened wide in shocked realisation that his end was nigh. That he was expend-able. He started to push the chair back but the Imam was already around the table at his side and pushing him down with the aid of that vice-like grip. He felt the icy cold of the revolver's barrel end placed against his temple and be-fore Rahman could beg for his life Tariq pulled the trigger.

The hawaladar's head exploded and his body smashed down onto the table where his precious cargo had been just moments before.

Leaning over the inert form, Tariq said a brief prayer and finished with one word. "Gratitude." On the eve of his longed for triumph no chances could be taken.

Tariq watched dispassionately as Rahman's body was dragged out of the room. He sat staring at the shiny metallic case which he had retrieved from the rucksack. He opened it, aware that the thrill was akin to that which he had experienced as a small boy, receiving a longed for present and not quite being able to believe it was his. His mind surfed tidal waves of elation as his eyes slipped over the key components of the bomb, marvelling at the intri-cacy of the wiring. At last he had acquired the dirty bomb that had been sought so desperately by al-Qaeda all over the globe. They had failed, but now he had the lethal prize sitting right here in front of him. A cargo of death located metres underground and no one knew he had it. No one except Meechan, whom he now knew had no knowledge of its, or his location. He examined the two 20 cm vials intently. They were sheathed in lead for added protection. One was labelled RA 226 the other C137.

He knew that it was the latter's powdered state and solubility that made it more dangerous than the uranium, and smiled malevolently at the thought. It was worth exposing himself to the radioactivity for the few seconds of deep satisfaction it had afforded him. He eased the case shut.

As he looked at his watch he saw that they were within 24 hours of detonation and with it his elevation to a position that would place him only behind the Sheik Osama as the pre-eminent Jihadist and champion of Islam against the tyrannies and corruption of the West.

A small smile played across his face at the thought of the triumph he was now so close to savouring. But, the job was not done . . . yet. The complication caused by the pursuit of Meechan by a Kidon was something he had not foreseen. That was why Rahman, Meechan's only link to him had had to be terminated. There were still other loose ends to tie up. Most importantly, how to dispose of Vanessa Velvet to maximum effect and what to do with Professor Farouk's daughter Aisha.

Try as he might to dismiss the latter as soiled and immoral, Tariq had been captivated by her from the moment he had first set eyes upon her and knew full well he was not the only one at his mosque who had come under her spell.

Tariq wondered where she was and how she was coping with the grief caused by her father's death. She was wanton and would not adhere to the fundamental tenets of Islam he demanded from the devout and this angered him. But she had been helpful. . .

The Imam was quickly shaken from his thoughts by the door opening. Aaban entered, slight and inconsequential, his dark skin shining.

"Asalaam Alaykum," said Tariq and Aaban responded in pre-conditioned kind. "Wa 'Alaykum Asalaam."

"Sit," said Tariq, "and I will give your instructions." Tariq pushed the case within the rucksack towards Aaban and levelled his most intense glare upon him.

"The day that we have been waiting for is almost upon us. In that rucksack is the means to bring about the result we have all dreamt of. The chance to realise the dream of Sheik Osama.You are the man who will turn that dream into reality.

"I trust that no suspicion has fallen upon you and the other brothers, and that you will be able to take your place within their ranks as normal?"

"It is so, Imam," responded Aaban.

"Before I go further tell me, how is the girl?" asked Tariq.

"She grieves for her father, Imam. They were close and she has no other family. She . . ." the male faltered.

"Go on akhee (my brother)," demanded Tariq.

"She seems to have come under the spell of the kafir detective Thoroughgood. She has stayed the night at his residence on more than one occasion. This is the infidel pig who killed Naif and the other brothers at the Mosque. The one who we believe still possesses Saladin's dagger."

Tariq was saddened by the confirmation of the intelligence that had already been hinted at by his network of beggar informants. "Then her fate is interwoven with his and the die is cast. I trust the others have been tasked with making their arrangements?"

"Your will, as always Imam, is my command. The arrangements are made and the dagger will be in your possession once again Imam. God's will."

Tariq stroked his beard for a moment and silence dominated the room as he struggled to control his conflicting emotions. He did not want her to die, yet there was no other way for she had cheapened herself and defiled her religion by her behaviour. There was no other option. Tariq forced himself to focus on what was important and banish his human frailties.

"You know the exact location and time to deposit the rucksack and how to detonate it?" he demanded.

"I do Imam. A call from the disposable cellphone you have given me will be the means by which the bomb is detonated. Allah alim."

"Your place in paradise will be guaranteed and your passage there will be instantaneous, praise be to Allah. Take the rucksack and guard it with your life Aaban, until it is ready to serve its purpose. May Allaah have mercy upon you, Akhee, and rain down his mercy and blessings upon you such that were each a mere raindrop from the sky, the world would be flooded many times over. Amen."

Aaban stood and strapped the rucksack to his back, just another beggar about to walk the streets of Glasgow. "Ma'assalama," he said.

"Fi aman Allah," replied Tariq and the door slammed shut behind Aaban as he left and took with him everything that Tariq had planned so long and hard for.

Judgement day was almost upon them and there was no turning back. "Allah alim,"[7] said Tariq out loud over and over again.

Vanessa choked on the gruel she had been almost force fed. She had lost count of the hours and then the days, and now she felt that she had begun to lose all hope of ever seeing daylight again.

She supposed she must still be in shock from Fraser's decapitation. She had no doubt that a similarly grisly fate awaited her.

The guard sneered at her and waited for her to finish the disgusting semi-solid slop. Placing the empty bowl on the small wooden table next to her mattress she felt the guard's iron grip around her wrist. "Maybe tonight, whore, I take my pleasure with you? You like it for sure," he laughed.

It had become a cruel ritual that with every meal time he would taunt her but as she wallowed in her self-pity Vanessa heard another voice in the background.

"Ihfaz alayka lisaanak!"[8] said the voice, "Get out." Vanessa saw that Tariq had once more honoured her with his presence. His smile danced malevolently in the shadows on his face and he surveyed her ragged and filthy appearance with apparent delight.

"Your time has nearly arrived. Just one more night and

---

7   "God's will,"
8   "Hold your tongue!"

then, with the dawn, you will be consigned to oblivion forever. How delightful that all your vanities will be laid bare before your adoring public at the moment of your death. For, my dear Miss Velvet, by the time we have finished with you, you will clamour for death. And all the while your humiliation and agonies, your final breaths, will be shown on film; displayed on the websites of the faithful all over the globe. Another example of how the West, and one of her whores, can be brought low and subjected by the faithful. By the power and will of Islam."

Vanessa said nothing. Exhausted, all resistance had left her and she was resigned to her fate.

After a while she realised that Tariq had ceased talking but was continuing to sear her with his gaze. She sat with her knees up to her chest and her arms wrapped tight around them thankful for the heat that radiated from the wall torch.

"So, you have nothing to say to me, Miss Velvet? Where is your pride now? Just another snivelling plastic bitch. As you say in the West, all show and no substance." He laughed once more.

Vanessa shut her eyes and prayed he would leave but her horror was intensified when he softly sneered in her ear, "What do you think Miss Velvet, should I give you to Najeeb so he may at last indulge his base desires?"

Vanessa sobbed and her whole body ached with the motion.

Tariq whispered once more, "No? I thought not. You may have a final night to reflect on your sins and iniquities, Miss Velvet. Tomorrow they will be cleansed once and for all." The Imam administered a backhanded slap that knocked her flying, leaving her sprawled on her soiled mattress.

Utterly bereft of all hope, and certain in the knowledge that a fate beyond her worst nightmares awaited her, he left her broken and hysterical.

40

THOROUGHGOOD AND Hardie scanned through the online material at the Mitchell looking for references to abandoned underground sites. The city and the West End in particular was sitting on top of a long-since forgotten memorial to the Victorian engineers who had constructed the Glasgow Central Railway.

Thoroughgood turned to the librarian who was hovering behind them. "Do you have an anteroom, Miss Morris? It would be more suitable for scrutiny of the material that concerns us."

"Follow me," she said and led them to an empty wooden-panelled reading room with a slightly musty atmosphere.

Before she left the detectives to their study she favoured Thoroughgood with a smile, providing Hardie with a source of mirth.

"Looks like you're the academic bird's perfect piece of crumpet." Jumping on the chance to crowbar his way into Thoroughgood's tortured love life he continued, "While we're on the subject of romance, how is Alicia?"

"For Pete's sake, you're like a butcher's dog … and it's Aisha as you know full well. I'm seeing her tonight;

her dad has just gone to meet his maker under suspicious circumstances, so how do you think she is? Now, can we return to the purpose we're here for?"

"Sorry gaffer," said Hardie shamefacedly and reabsorbed himself in his subject matter. Running his finger along the route of a railway line he almost shouted, "The Botanic Gardens Railway Station!"

Thoroughgood looked to where Hardie was pointing. "I've heard of it. Burnt down and unused for God knows how long."

Hardie read out the information in front of him. "The station was opened on August 10, 1896, by Glasgow Central Railway. Although the station building was on ground level, the actual station platforms were underground, beneath the Botanic Gardens themselves. The station closed between January 1, 1917 and March 2, 1919, due to wartime economy then closed permanently to passengers in 1939. The line itself closed in 1964."

Thoroughgood's scepticism was obvious. "No doubt bricked up and cemented over long since. How are a gang of gun-toting fanatics going to get in and out of there without being spotted? Nope, I'd say you are barking up the wrong tree there, faither."

Hardie carried on, "The station building was an ornate red-brick structure with two towers sporting a clock and the Caledonian Railway monogram. Topped by domes reminiscent of a Russian Orthodox church it was a well known landmark along Great Western Road. Too bleedin' right."

Thoroughgood's drumming fingers showed his impatience as Hardie's history lesson continued. "Designed by the renowned Glasgow railway architect of the period

– James Miller – who also designed the interiors of the famous Clyde Built ocean liners, the Lusitania and the Aquitania in 1914. Hints of features in these more famous designs could be found in the Botanics Station itself. What a pity it's gone."

"But it is gone, my dear Hardie, which is why we are wasting our time here. We need to do our digging elsewhere," said Thoroughgood. As an afterthought he added, "Okay, how did it all go belly up?"

Hardie read out loud, "After the line closed in 1964 the station building was transformed into the Silver Slipper Café. Okay boss, here we are. An Evening Times article from 1970.

"'A fire started after a Battle of the Bands contest had been held in the nightclub. It was primarily the roof space that burned, resulting in the decision of the Fire Brigade to pull down the two domed towers for safety reasons the following day.'"

Hardie's features changed. "Apparently the café owner's German Shepherd went to the great kennel in the sky after dying of smoke inhalation," he said, a lump in his throat.

"You and your bleedin' animals. At least no one bought it." Thoroughgood said taking over scrutiny of the plans. "Right, here we go, the bottom line."

"'Despite the outer walls of the building remaining intact and the damage confined largely to the roof area, the decision was taken by the then Glasgow Corporation not to undertake repairs and instead to completely demolish the building and leave the site derelict. At the time of the fire, plans were being considered to demolish the building as part of a controversial scheme to widen Great Western

Road and this may have been behind the decision not to repair the building despite its prominent and recognisable presence in the West End for seventy-four years.'"

Thoroughgood couldn't help himself: "Yup, old Jamesy Miller and the hound of the Botanics will be turning in their graves."

But Hardie ignored his sarcasm and grabbed the faded copy of the Glasgow Central Railway plans he'd been looking at earlier. "Look at the plans, Gus," he demanded. Hardie's finger traced its way along the lines. "Here we are; old stations at Partick West, Kirklee, the Botanics, Kelvinbridge. It's all there. Don't you think we should make a site visit before casting it aside?"

Thoroughgood considered, "You might have a point, faither. Looking back to the shootin' in the Botanics, I thought something wasn't right the way our sniper managed to take him out and then vanish into thin air."

"Plus the business in Dowanhill. And One Devonshire Gardens is in the West End too. Most of the action is taking place this side of the Clyde and each time the terrorists disappear without a trace. Too bleedin' easily in my book, Gus."

"You've got a point. There may be a way into the underground at some point along the line. How many stations are there?"

"Eight in total. Partick Central, Partick West, Crow Road, Hyndland, Kelvinside, Kirklee, Botanics, Kelvinbridge," answered Hardie adding, "There must be access points along the way that will be away from the public eye. Why don't we start at Crow Road?"

"No, too far away. We want to start at one of the stations next to the Botanics. And we can't go right in with-

299

out stirring up a hornet's nest, we need observations first. That's if this isn't a whole bleedin' wild goose chase."

Hardie asked, "So either Kirklee or Kelvinbridge? Kirklee?"

"Gotta be. It's far closer," said Thoroughgood, his excitement showing in his voice, "Just maybe we've nailed it, faither."

"We gonna inform Tomachek or Etherington? Or both?"

"The auld man needs to know about this even if it's just a reccy. After the reccy we can drop in at the Marine and let Etherington know."

Twenty minutes later, having negotiated the West End evening traffic, the Mondeo drove through Kirklee crossroads. Hardie punctured the silence, "That's it, stop there, where the old Callender's Mercedes garage used to be."

Thoroughgood looked surprised. "I used to work at that garage as a security guard back in the mid-eighties. It's long gone now though."

Hardie's head was buried in his documents from the Mitchell. "It says here that the station buildings were constructed from red sandstone and straddled a bridge connecting the line to the mouth of the Botanic Gardens Station tunnel. We need to leave the road and head off into that foliage running towards the Botanics. Can you cope with your Sherman suit and Loake brogues getting mucked up? I know how particular you are about your appearance," laughed Hardie as both men got out out of the car. Thoroughgood's back was the only answer he got. The DS crossed the road, vaulted over some fencing and went down a bank with Hardie in not-so-hot pursuit.

The DC shouted, "Hold on Gus, you're just passing

what would have been Kirklee Station's booking office. It was built on the legendary 'Three Trees Well' and allegedly, a popular spot with young Victorian lovers."

Exasperated, Thoroughgood turned and saw Hardie was stuck, half-over the fence. He offered him a hand. "Look faither, all that Victorian stuff is fantastic but can we just stick to the here and now? The light's fading and I want this reccy done and dusted."

Hardie, puffing and flustered, folded his map into a tight rectangle and continued in a more business-like fashion. "Okay, I would say the concrete under the foliage will be the remainder of the Kirklee platforms. Over there looks like a bricked-up bridge and the trackbed runs towards the Botanics which is where we want to be heading."

The detectives walked along the old railway trackbed, passing the ruins of an ancient sleeper. "There it is," called Hardie and pointed 100 metres down the trackbed. "The old tunnel mouth!"

"Will you keep the noise down, for feck's sake," whispered Thoroughgood adding, "We're going to have to be bloody careful from now on. We could be 200 meters from Tariq's lair which is likely to be full of AK-47 wielding maniacs. Now, let's hide in the foliage behind me."

Hardie followed Thoroughgood to the side of the trackbed and dropped to one knee out of view. Thoroughgood took out a pair of binoculars and pointed them in the direction of the tunnel. The DC whispered, "You see anything?"

Thoroughgood answered, the binoculars still pressed to his eyes. "Yup! There's definite movement beyond the iron railings. Let's see if we can get a bit closer. I think I have the beginnings of a cunning plan!"

"Okay, you let Etherington and the auld man know where we are and what we suspect."

Hardie looked suspicious. "You?" he asked.

"Look, let's keep it simple, you head back to the car, make the calls and then come back. I just want to take a closer look and see what I can come up with. Nothin' heroic, just a bit of snoopin'."

"Come on Gus, you're playing with fire."

Thoroughgood attempted a mollifying smile but had a far-away look Hardie recognised from the encounter with Felix Baker and the fight on the mosque roof.

"Like I said, I just want a butcher's," the DS reassured Hardie.

Hardie was not buying it. "Pull the other one! You're up to something and you don't give a damn what the consequences are for yourself and we both know it."

"Like it or not, faither, this is a one man reconnaissance mission and the sooner we both get on with what we've got to do the better," said the DS, rising and stretching out his hand. "Adios amigo!"

Hardie shook his mate's hand but before he could offer any further argument Thoroughgood had disappeared into the foliage. Staring into the semi-darkness Hardie wondered if he had seen his mate alive for the last time.

41

THOROUGHGOOD APPROACHED the mouth of the tunnel, thankful for the increasing murkiness that was now masking his progress.

The metal fence across the face of the tunnel stood around 10 feet high. Using the binoculars' night sights he could see that, although most of the railings were rusty, one section appeared unweathered. It had obviously only recently been installed to provide a smoothly opening entrance that neither creaked nor jammed.

He noted a copse of decaying silver birches that had been semi cleared to provide an unobstructed area outside the tunnel.

He crept closer to the fence. A pin prick of light glowed in the darkness behind the railings; a cigarette being inhaled. Obviously, someone was on guard within the blackhole of the tunnel mouth and Thoroughgood decided he needed to draw him out if he was going to have an effective reccy.

The obvious means would be to rattle the railings and wait for the guard to come and investigate. Reaching into his jacket he felt the ivory handle of the dagger protruding. He grabbed it and, leaving the cover of the foliage, planted it on the ground a few feet in front of the railings.

He picked up a broken branch before taking cover again around five feet away from the dagger.

He clattered the railings with a succession of stone throws and, sure enough, the glow of the guard's cigarette moved closer. When he drew closer Thoroughgood recognised him as the beggar from McDonald's a couple of days ago.

The guard opened the gate and stepped forward, flicking the cigarette from his fingers onto a damp sleeper.

Even in the murky darkness the male could not fail to notice the bejewelled ivory handle of Saladin's dagger. He made straight for the relic.

As he passed Thoroughgood's hiding place the DS saw a handgun protruding from the male's hoody pouch. Ignoring it, he smashed the branch down onto the back of the guard's head and was rewarded with a grunt and a thud as he pitched forward onto the sleeper. "No need for a ten-count, matey!" said Thoroughgood to himself.

The DS dragged the body into the birches where he cuffed the guard to a tree and gagged him with the Burberry scarf that had been wrapped around his neck. He was out cold and no longer an issue. Taking the revolver Thoroughgood also helped himself to the hoody. He wedged the dagger into his belt, slipped through the railings and began to make his way tentatively through the blackness of the tunnel.

Despite the night sights Thoroughgood made slow progress along the debris-filled tunnel. The constant dampness chilled him and icy water slopped over his brogues. Slowly he continued to edge along the wall of the tunnel, revolver in his hand, hood up and the binoculars now hidden inside the hoody.

As he approached the bend he could hear voices speaking in Arabic. They were coming his way. Thoroughgood knew that his options were limited and that soon he risked an exposure that would be fatal.

The flickering of torchlight began to sweep the tunnel wall above him and he dropped to his knees just as two males came round the edge of the bend diagonally opposite him. One of them said something and they laughed, then he continued his progress along the tunnel while the other remained stationary for a while and then started to walk back.

The figure on his way towards Thoroughgood seemed likely to be the relief for the guard at the entrance. A voice in Thoroughgood's head summed up his predicament. 'If he makes the tunnel entrance and finds matey gagged and bound, you're on a one-way ticket down shit creek without a paddle. But it's one-to-one now he's detached from his neighbour. Fair game.'

As the male walked past Thoroughgood's hiding place the DS tripped him. The minute he went down Thoroughgood was on him with a punch that cracked off his jaw and caused a cry of pain. A double fisted salvo administered from atop the prone figure put his lights out. Thoroughgood grabbed the guard's dropped AK-47 and was once more on his way. So far, so good.

But, as he passed the curve in the tunnel, Thoroughgood could see a further gateway and the male who had turned back standing in flickering light.

The use of torch-light surprised Thoroughgood momentarily, then he realised there would be no electric or gas supply to the old out-of-use tunnels.

Taking stock, the voice in his head went into overdrive.

'What the fuck is this? Your very own suicide mission? What are you going to achieve? A bullet in the brains? For cryin' out loud you've got your confirmation that this is Tariq's lair and there's a body sittin' outside waiting to be taken into custody. Time to get out.'

But in the blackness Thoroughgood heard his own voice speak out loud. "For what?" He edged towards the inner gateway.

Thoroughgood could clearly make out open vents overhead and, beyond the gates, he thought he could discern platforms in the flickering light. The thought hit him that Vanessa Velvet could still be alive in a chamber or vault only yards away. 'Better late than never,' said his inner voice, 'but how you gonna get past the guard?'

Thoroughgood remembered he was wearing the dispatched guard's hoody, which should at least give him an advantage. His mind made up Thoroughgood decided to brazen it out. Pressing on, he emerged out of the dark. Hood up over his head, he walked down the tunnel. His figure was now clearly outlined by the flame light from behind the gate guard.

As he approached the gate Thoroughgood kept his head down, hidden by the hood. The AK-47 was slung over his shoulder, while he placed the handgun inside his belt and took the, dagger in his grip inside the pocket. There was a clunk as the gate opened and a voice offered him a greeting he didn't understand, "Das-salaamu 'alai-kum," Thoroughgood replied in the only way he could, "Salam." He walked through the gate, head bowed.

He understood the next words, "Stop brother! You disrespect me!"

Thoroughgood took in the twin platforms and the hive

of activity. There was only one way to get out of this. He turned back towards the guard and walked slowly up to him. At the last minute he looked up and flashed a wicked smile that brought a confused look to the male's face. He rammed the dagger into the guard's midriff.

"How does it feel to be turned into a kebab, mate?" he said, shoving his free hand over the guard's gaping mouth and forcing the crumpling figure back through the gate and into the blackness of the tunnel.

Thoroughgood pulled the dagger free from the dead guard and closed the gate, praying that he had not been observed. But what now?

The only way he was going to get what he wanted was by creating chaos. Looking around Thoroughgood noticed two elaborately carved parallel stairways leading to a footbridge crossing over the disused track. He also spotted a burning torch pinned to the wall. It would provide him with an easy means to ignite the largely wooden station.

Before he did that, though, he had to find Vanessa.

The sound of voices approaching filled Thoroughgood with fear. He turned his face towards the blackness of the tunnel, holding the AK-47 in a manner that suggested he was the guard.

He listened to the conversation. "No brother. The Imam says that the bitch is not to be despoiled. Instead, I have to deliver her last supper. Maybe I make her show some gratitude though, eh?" Both males laughed.

They were en route to Vanessa's cell and, by the sounds of it, Thoroughgood was just in time.

The DS half turned and saw that the males had gone in different directions. One had turned towards a stairway at the top of the platform, the other, who was carrying a bowl, had continued down an adjoining corridor lit by further torches.

Thoroughgood followed the second guard.

The guard stopped outside a door, placed the bowl on the ground and put a key in the lock. As he pulled the door open he bent down to pick up the bowl.

Thoroughgood smashed the butt of the AK-47 down on the back of the guard's head and kicked his inert body into the room, quickly following it inside.

Huddled in a corner of the room on a putrid mattress was Vanessa, almost unrecognisable, barely covered by a ripped shirt, wild-eyed and filthy.

Thoroughgood spoke quickly, "I'm here to get you out. Just stay calm." He placed his knees on the back of the prostrate male and ripped his linen head gear off before using it to tie the male's hands behind his back.

As he concentrated on the job in hand Vanessa asked, in a barely audible voice, "Who are you?"

Thoroughgood looked up into her eyes which were brimming with tears. He answered, "Detective Sergeant Thoroughgood, Strathclyde Police CID. But you can call me Gus. I'm here to get you out."

"Thank you," she said in trembling reply.

"Don't thank me until we are out of here, Vanessa."

A weak smile lit up her face with a trace of hope.

"Look, you're going to have to trust me, there's only one way out of this place for us. By creating chaos. We are going to have to set the place alight. Here, take this," Thoroughgood ripped off the guard's shirt and threw it to her. Vanessa pulled it over the torn remnants of Fraser's shirt.

The DS rifled through the guard's remaining clothes and pulled out a lighter. He ripped up some of the linen and emptied the lighter fuel over it before picking up the bowl and a glass. He filled both with the soaked linen shreds.

"Right, here's the plan," he said as casually as he could. "Stick right behind me and do what I tell you. Carry these," he handed her the bowl and glass. Vanessa smiled weakly, part of her amazed at how compliant the situation had made her. Yet she knew this slightly crazed looking man represented her only hope of making it out of her underground hell alive.

Thoroughgood took her hand, felt her trembling fingers and reassured her. "Listen, help is on its way. We're gonna be fine. You ready for this?"

She looked into his blazing green eyes and said, with some semblance of conviction, "Go for it!"

Thoroughgood wrenched the burning torch off the wall and led her out of the cell, the AK-47 levelled in front of him. They reached the corridor's end without being challenged.

Peering round onto the platforms Thoroughgood realised their best hope was to make for the disused railway track and head back where he had come from.

From the sound of raised voices coming from the tunnel the skewered guard had been discovered. Their chances of making it out alive were receding fast.

Any escape now would have to be by following the tunnel towards the city centre and taking their chances with whatever awaited them. There was more shouting and Thoroughgood realised the voices were directed at them.

"Stop, kafir!" shouted a figure swathed in flowing linen. As Thoroughgood turned towards him a volley of gunfire smashed off the wall of the corridor in which they stood.

Thoroughgood pulled back and pushed Vanessa against the wall behind them. Their close proximity and her imploring blue eyes stirred something in him as he pressed up against her.

"What now, Detective Sergeant?" she asked pleadingly.

"The tunnel has just gone out of bounds. Time for Plan B. We need to make the stairs at the right-hand side of the platform. They must lead up to the original over ground part of the Botanics Station. If we can get to the top there must be a hatch," he said matter-of-factly. She smiled at him and he could see exactly why this woman seemed to be able to control everybody around her.

"You make it sound easy!" she said.

A further rake of gunfire on the wall opposite proved it was going to be anything but. Looking out onto the platform Thoroughgood saw a pile of smashed wood and kindling on the concrete floor.

"Look, this is how we play it. Give me the glass and bowl." Vanessa handed them over and Thoroughgood lit the fuel-soaked cloth in the vessels with the torch. He was rewarded with shooting flames.

He ducked out of the corridor and lobbed the glass at the group of males who were gaining ground towards them. The vessel smashed just in front of them and a sheet of flame spread across the floor, engulfing two of the figures in it. Thoroughgood lobbed the bowl and a second explosion of flame enveloped the left bank of the platform in searing heat.

He opened up with the AK-47, pumping its contents into the two burning figures, putting them out of their misery and sending the others scurrying for cover.

Thoroughgood ducked back.

"That'll give the bastards something to think about. I'm going out there to unload as much lead as I can into whoever else is coming our way. You come out behind me and," he handed her the torch and changed the weapon's magazine, "lob that into the pile of crap over there and then make for the stairway as quickly as you can. I'll be right behind you and we will take it from there. Okay?"

She nodded her agreement.

"Right we go on 'three'. Three!" He ran out onto the platform and unloaded the AK-47 into three figures who were less than 20 yards away. The male in the middle went down first. Vanessa sprinted behind him and the crackling of wood indicated she had lobbed the torch onto the pile of debris and it was already catching light.

Gunfire now spat back at the DS and he dived behind the burning wood pile pulling Vanessa with him. He grabbed what looked like the leg of an old chair from within the pile praying the other end was on fire. It was.

He peered out from behind the fire and opened up with the AK. Then he was up and running for the stairs, dragging Vanessa in his wake. As he reached the bottom step he pushed her up. "Keep going to the top and then take cover." He ducked as a hail of bullets splintered the old wooden banisters.

The increased intensity of the firepower indicated to Thoroughgood he was being fired on from more than one direction. He jammed the burning chair leg into the banister hoping it would set the staircase alight then turned round. "Come and get it, you bastards!" he screamed and let rip.

The odds were stacking higher against him by the moment. He heard Vanessa's voice from above him shout, "Gus! On your left!" He turned just in time to see a bearded man take aim with a handgun. Thoroughgood dived onto the bottom step as the single projectile smashed off the wooden railing he had been kneeling next to. Feeling the increasing warmth of the flames as the fire took hold of the staircase, he crawled up the steps heading to the overhead platform, bullets thudding into the stairs all around him.

Reaching the landing he saw that Vanessa was unscathed. "Listen, you ever shot a handgun?" he asked and tossed the revolver to her before she had answered. "First time for everything, Miss Velvet, isn't there?" Her eyes locked on his with a hint of mischief he liked.

Looking down, he saw that there were at least six males on the platform taking orders from the black-swathed figure who had missed him with the revolver shot moments earlier. He supposed it must be Tariq himself.

Looking above him, Thoroughgood saw a hatch and hope sprang in his heart that a way out was at hand. He shuffled along the landing to take a closer look. "Shit, it's concreted in. No way out there."

"That is the least of our problems, Gus," said Vanessa, "they've split up."

Peering over the wall Thoroughgood saw that three of the males had jumped down onto the disused trackway and were climbing onto the other platform.

They had to make their move immediately. "Okay Vanessa, we need to go." He grabbed her by the hand and pulled her along to the top of the other side of the stairs. "The flames are taking hold off the staircase we came up and that will keep them back. We need to get down this side, onto the track and into the tunnel pronto or we're fucked. You wait at the top of the stairs until I give the word. If anyone comes anywhere near you fill them with lead. Once I tell you, come down and jump onto the track and run. Stop for nothing. Understand?"

She smiled. "Thank you Gus. Whatever happens, thank you!"

Thoroughgood shook his head and charged down the staircase. At the bottom he knelt down and levelled the AK-47. Two males were still on the track but the other was halfway up onto the south platform and Thoroughgood took him out with a quick burst of fire. He shouted, "Now, Vanessa!" and heard her footsteps coming down the rickety steps behind him. The whole staircase opposite was now engulfed in flames which were spreading right across the balcony landing. He pulled the trigger and unloaded the remainder of the AK-47 into the two males on the trackbed and they toppled over with anguished screams.

He grabbed Vanessa's hand and they both jumped onto the trackbed. "Get into the tunnel and run for your life," he barked at her. She leant forward and kissed him. Then she was gone.

As he heard more shouting from the north platform Thoroughgood tried frantically to change the AK magazine and discovered that he had no spare ammo.

A guard jumped down onto the railway bed and charged at him screaming, "Allahu akbar!" his teeth bared and his eyes searing through Thoroughgood with hatred.

The DS closed the ground between them as quickly as he could. At the last minute he lifted and rammed the barrel of the semi-automatic into the terrorist's guts then smashed his forehead into his face. The male went down, poleaxed.

Thoroughgood heard more footsteps yards away from him and looked up. Grinning in savage delight, Tariq aimed his revolver straight at Thoroughgood's head.

42

"DETECTIVE SERGEANT Thoroughgood, I believe," said Tariq with a venomous smile.

"I guess you must be the Imam Tariq," replied the DS breathing heavily. "Can't say it's a pleasure."

"You have been causing me problems for a while now, but at last I get to apply the full stop on them. Doing it personally will be so much more satisfying. Don't you think, kafir?"

In the background Thoroughgood could hear voices and more gunfire coming from the Kirklee end of the tunnel. Hope grew afresh within him. "Sounds to me, Imam, that you have a whole lot of problems coming your way. Don't fancy your chances of putting a full stop on them."

"They will be taken care of," replied the cleric and Thoroughgood saw a group of Tariq's minions hurrying towards the tunnel.

"There is no escape for you or the Velvet bitch. Tomorrow, I will showcase your execution alongside hers. The hero policeman minus his head and his world turned to shit. Who do you think you are, Thoroughgood? Bruce Willis?" Tariq laughed long and loud.

His revolver remained levelled at Thoroughgood's

head as sparks and splinters started to shoot all around them from the staircase, which was starting to disintegrate above. A huge chunk of burning wood detached itself from the staircase and shattered into the soil yards away but Tariq's focus remained on the DS.

Thoroughgood tried to stall for time. "Why? What is all this for? The suicide bombing in Braehead? The murder of innocents? You can't tell me that a religion known for its kindness and compassion can endorse the carnage you've wreaked on your adopted city? That this is how Islam repays those that welcome and show hospitality to its followers?"

"You know not what you talk about, dog. You will not turn my mind from its purpose with worthless empty words. For the thousands of innocents who have died in Afghanistan and Iraq because of your Crusades there has to be vengeance. Sheikh Osama has warned the West that they would pay the price for their wars with the blood of their own people. I have taken the Jihad to your shores and now I have the device that will turn this city into a mausoleum for the masses and allow me to take my place in Paradise."

"So it's true you have a dirty bomb?" demanded Thoroughgood.

"You will find out soon enough, my pathetic little policeman," replied Tariq.

"Where in the Koran does it say that butchering innocents is the way to heaven? You're the fuckin' cleric so why don't you quote me chapter and verse," raged Thoroughgood, his self-control deserting him.

Tariq flashed a malevolent smile. "Before I kill you, Detective Sergeant, I want to let you know what you will be missing. In 12 hours time we have a celebration planned that will cause a level of destruction that will make 7/7 and perhaps even 9/11 seem petty."

"The Nikah," stated Thoroughgood.

"Very good, Detective Sergeant. But where it will be held, you will never know." said Tariq.

Thoroughgood's mind went into overdrive. Standing a hundred metres underground with his surroundings burning down all around him and Tariq pointing a pistol at his head, he felt like he was already in a highly personalised version of hell.

The gunfire in the tunnel was intensifying and with it screams of agony. Thoroughgood tried to focus his mind on the matter in hand. It dawned on him. "Ibrox. You are going to blow up the Old Firm game, you crazy bastard."

Tariq inclined his head. "What does it matter where the joyous event is held? But before I kill you, I want something from you. Give me Saladin's dagger," he demanded.

Thoroughgood smiled, aware that the gunfire was creeping closer. "Oh yeah, the dagger! The one that signifies its owner will unite Islam, the one that you have tried to have me killed for and that you hope will elevate you above bin Laden, you delusional bastard. Do you think I am stupid enough to run about with it on my person?"

Tariq's smile was venomous. "But of course you are, Detective Sergeant. My information comes from a most reliable source and one that has recently become very close to you."

Thoroughgood could not help a look of surprise breaking over his face. "Aisha?" he said.

Tariq grinned. "Your pretty little nurse? Funny how that chance meeting in the hospital has led to an arrangement that has proved so convenient to me. Do you think that Aisha would have given herself to an infidel pig like you for any other reason than to serve the true faith and protect our Jihad?

"Her father was a traitor who realised too late that he had betrayed all that was right. The revelation of the hawaladar's identity was tantamount to sacrilege. It was right that he paid for that with his life."

Thoroughgood was left incredulous. "And Aisha was happy about you butchering her father, you madman?"

"Aisha has become an important instrument of the Jihad. Sadly, she too must pay the price for her sins. Now give me the dagger, Thoroughgood. The time for your death is upon you. Try and meet it like a man."

"What have you done with her, you murdering son of a bitch?" demanded Thoroughgood.

"It is of no importance to you. Now give me Saladin's dagger." Tariq ordered, his patience coming to an end.

Thoroughgood flicked a resigned smile and pulled the blade from his trouser belt, holding it in front of him and examining it with apparent reverence. "So this is the legitimisation of your reign of terror? A crazed perception that you will unite Islam and become a successor to Saladin? Jesus H Christ, you want it all don't you?"

"Your words are hollow, kafir. Give me the blade before I kill you," ordered Tariq holding out his free hand.

"My pleasure," said Thoroughgood and smashed the blade upwards into Tariq's hand. Thoroughgood threw himself at the Imam, knocking him over.

As they hit the ground the DS grabbed Tariq's pistol-holding hand and repeatedly smashed it into the ground. Their free hands were locked in a deadly battle for the dagger.

The revolver eventually broke from Tariq's grip and

scudded across the trackbed. Both men put everything into gaining control of the dagger.

Being on top, Thoroughgood had the benefit of his body weight pressing down on the Imam but Tariq was the bigger man. The cleric's hate seemed to give him extra strength. The dagger began to inch closer to Thoroughgood's face forcing him backwards and upwards.

"Now I gut you, kafir pig," spat the Imam and he surged upwards in a powerful movement that knocked Thoroughgood off him, slamming the cop down on his back and wrenching the blade from his grip.

Tariq advanced on Thoroughgood who attempted to slide back across the ground but he was soon brought to shuddering halt when his back hit the solid concrete of the platform side.

"Nowhere to go, policeman. Now at last, after all this time, Saladin's blade is once more to be used for its true purpose. Time to take your place in hell," the Imam spat and lunged at Thoroughgood, the blade glinting in the flames that raged around them.

Thoroughgood spotted metal glinting on the track bed and in a movement given extra speed by his desperation ripped an iron linchpin from the debris on the ground. As Tariq loomed over him he rammed the wicked two pronged railway remnant into the Imam's eyes.

Tariq staggered backward screaming and holding his face. The force Thoroughgood had exerted had rammed the twin two-inch pins deep into his face and the Imam toppled onto his knees, dropping Saladin's blade on the ground.

Thoroughgood grabbed the ceremonial dagger and screamed, "Go to hell you murdering bastard!" but before he could administer the coup de grâce with the Imam's cherished blade, Tariq's throat gave a final gurgle and the cleric pitched forward and lay face down on the soil, motionless.

Thoroughgood staggered back. He sat on the edge of the platform and placed the bejewelled dagger down staring through it unseeingly. Although Tariq was dead his plans for Armageddon to hit Glasgow were very much alive. And what of Aisha?

He pulled his mobile from his pocket but he had no reception and felt a wave of helplessness wash over him. Whatever she had been guilty of he had no doubt that Tariq had used every means in his power to coerce her. Almost certainly he would have used the life of her father as a means to get her to do his bidding.

A voice spoke his name and he looked up to see the dishevelled figure of Vanessa standing three feet away. "You made it Gus. You got him," she said.

Thoroughgood looked into her face and felt tears roll down his cheeks, his emotions in turmoil. "I may have got him but this is far from over, Vanessa, believe me. Are you okay?"

She smiled a smile that made all the grime, ripped clothing and her stress-worn face fade into insignificance. She took his face in her hands. "I owe you my life, Gus." For the second time that night she kissed him.

This time there was no rushing their parting.

The morning dawned, cold and grey, and Aisha knew she had to get over to Thoroughgood's place and make everything all right with him.

Her mind was in meltdown, her grief raw with the

death of her father and the shock that it had been murder. She had been wrong to betray Thoroughgood to Tariq but what could she have done with her father's life on the line?

Thoroughgood, the man she had tried to lure into a death trap, had turned out to be the type of man she had hoped fate would bring her. His haunted melancholy and sadness was similar to her father's after her mother had been taken by cancer five years back. With Thoroughgood there was also desperation, anger and a vulnerability she found amazingly appealing.

She knew that he was still cut up over the death of Celine. She knew he had contemplated, if not actually attempted, suicide. The evidence of the revolver and the bible on his mantle-piece proof that he was far from fully healed from the agonies inflicted by her murder.

Aisha found herself increasingly wanting to be there for him. To be the one to make his hurt go away and aid his mental healing. Was she falling in love with him? She didn't know, Aisha had never loved anyone but her father.

Riven by guilt over her father's murder, knowing that he had been right about Tariq months back when he had branded him 'a killer and a religious despot', Aisha knew that she too was vulnerable to heightened emotions.

As she descended the stair of her tenement flat an on-going worry niggled her. 'How can I compete with a ghost if he is still in love with Celine?' But she knew she had to try, had to make things good between them.

As she came out of the tenement door she saw little Jimmy from across the landing sitting astride his bike and smiled at him. "Be careful, Jimmy, no cycling on the road. Your mum letting you go to the paper shop on your bike?"

"It's my first time cycling there Auntie Aisha. You goin' to the hospital?" the ginger-haired 10 year-old asked.

Aisha smiled. "Something like that Jimmy. You take care." As she watched him cycling down Oban Drive's steep hill she couldn't help thinking about the possibility of having her own kids. But first she had to make Thoroughgood believe in her.

She opened the Fiesta door and sat in the driver's seat, fastening the seat belt and smiling sadly to herself as she inserted the key in the ignition and turned it.

The explosion ripped through the car and instantly shredded the vehicle. It was suddenly nothing but a hollow melting metallic shell.

At the bottom of the street Jimmy heard the blast and felt the heat sear the back of his neck, the air trembling. He turned and saw wide-eyed that where the car Auntie Aisha had been sitting in moments before there was now nothing but flames.

He screamed.

43

HOURS LATER, sitting in the Mondeo, Hardie brought
Thoroughgood up to speed with the chief constable's
briefing from which he had been excused. Thoroughgood
shook his head in disbelief. "In the name of God, why,
when we have the intelligence that Tariq has the means to
cause devastation and the perfect event to stage it, has the
Old Firm game not been called off?"

Hardie cleared his throat awkwardly. "That's just it
though Gus, we don't have a specific admission from anyone that Ibrox is that target, despite the fact Etherington
has been interrogating Omar around the clock."

"What about the filofax? Braehead was just a decoy,
like Sushi said, it was only the first act but the grand finale
was still to come. We have been duped into thinking it
was going to be a series of bombings in shopping centres
when all along the ultimate target was Ibrox. That is why
they had the words asterisked out, so that we would go
barking up the wrong tree after they blew up Braehead!
It all fits now, faither. Surely you rammed that down their
throats? For fuck's sake are you so desperate to see the
Queen's eleven blown to smithereens and Ibrox incin-
erated? 'Cause that is what we are talkin' here," raged
Thoroughgood.

"Come on Gus, don't shoot the messenger. Don't you think I made that case this morning, with Tomachek backing me to the hilt? You know what it's like. The idea of an Old Firm game being cancelled in Glasgow because of a terrorist threat? You'd think it would be the end of civilisation itself. Christ, we got the whole 'the show must go on' stuff. I thought the Chief Constable was gonna break into a rendition of The White Cliffs of Dover and Vera Lynn was about to serve us tea. You'd have thought I was the bloody bomber the way they reacted."

"But we're talking 50,000 lives on the line . . . it just beggars belief," said Thoroughgood in a resigned voice.

"They just kept coming back to the bottom line. The only person who knows the target now is the bomber and we don't have a fuckin' scooby who he or she is. Therefore, there is no conclusive proof Ibrox is the target. So 'the show must go on'," Hardie mocked.

Before Thoroughgood could interject Hardie was off and running again. "Oh, and here's the icing on the cake. The First Minister will be in the director's box to oversee the whole anti-bigotry campaign!"

After an incredulous silence the DS recovered his voice. "What about the search of Tariq's hideout, surely they must have found something evidence wise? Bomb-making material or something?" he asked.

"Not yet. The search hasn't finished but if the dirty bomb exists, it's on its way to the target or already there. Who took it and how it got there are details we don't know," admitted Hardie.

"I don't suppose we have had any sightings of Meechan?" the DS enquired.

"Zero. But never mind that, the top brass are none too

324

happy that you killed Tariq, self-defence or not. You know what they're like, arseholes who don't know or remember what it's like to walk a beat. But the bottom line is Tariq had answers we needed that are now gone forever," said Hardie.

As Thoroughgood searched for an indignant answer Hardie held his hand up. "Sorry, that was out of order, but there's something else I need to tell you mate, before we head for Ibrox."

"I'm all ears," said Thoroughgood.

Hardie took a deep breath and delivered the death message in monotone. "It's Aisha. She was blown up in her car this morning."

Thoroughgood desperately searched Hardie's face for some clue that he had misheard or misunderstood his words.

"There was no suffering. Death was instantaneous. Look, I don't know what was goin' on between you but we both know she was involved with Tariq and his organisation. Virtually everyone that has come in contact with the bastard has ended up dead. She was gonna have some pretty tough questions to answer mate," Hardie said.

Thoroughgood whispered, "I'm not sure what was going on with us either. Maybe she was just usin' me …" he trailed off.

Hardie put his hand on Thoroughgood's shoulder. "Just maybe there was something there for you. I'm sorry Gus, I really am."

"It's no' your fault, faither." Thoroughgood rested his head on the window pane.

"Gus, you were exhausted. You can't go blamin' yourself, you got the bastard that's been holding Glasgow to ransom, and you can't be in two places at one time."

"No, I guess not." Thoroughgood's voice was barely audible.

Their conversation was interrupted by a text message alert on Hardie's phone. The DC relayed the message. "It's Etherington. He has something important for us. We're to meet him at the Albion car park at Ibrox, pronto."

"One hour before kick-off? Whatever it is, he's cutting things a bit fine. Still. . ."

"We better get our arses over there, you never know what MI5's finest has turned up. Let's just hope he's got some kind of lead out of our friendly local book dealer," said Hardie adding, "It never ceases to amaze me, but the minute the brass think that some kind of Armageddon act is going to take place they seem to want to be there. Like moths around a flame. I tell you, if Ibrox is the target then we are going to have half the senior command of Strathclyde Police wiped out!"

"Listen mate, most of them are taking their seats there every other weekend so what's the difference whether they're on or off duty," replied Thoroughgood.

As they made their way to Ibrox the increased police presence was clear. "Don't know about you, Gus, but I've never seen so many armed cops in my puff. Didn't even know we had that kind of capability. The brass were right, if someone is going to try and penetrate the ring of steel they've erected around Ibrox they'll have worked a miracle," said Hardie.

"You're no' jokin'," replied Thoroughgood though his mind was clearly elsewhere as his eyes stared aimlessly out of the window.

Aaban took his place among the 'yellow jackets' and waited for his briefing. The rucksack was nestled safely between his feet as he sat in the main stand. Within moments his baggage would be deposited at the target site, ready to wreak destruction and death here in Glasgow and immortalise the Imam Tariq and his followers when it detonated.

It had been hard to remain focused on the job when he had heard the news on the radio of Tariq and the other's deaths. Aaban knew that his mission was even more precious now.

He was the last of Tariq's followers left and so the most important, entrusted with ensuring that the last act of the Imam's Jihad was a signal to the western world that no city was safe from those who waged Jihad.

He checked his watch, 11.45am, less than an hour before the first Old Firm derby of the season was scheduled to kick-off.

Aaban said silently, "Allahu akbar."

Thoroughgood and Hardie arrived at the Albion Car Park which had been commandeered by Strathclyde Police. They located the green Land Rover Etherington had described in his text and parked next to it.

They climbed into the back of the vehicle.

"Detective Sergeant, well done with your heroics last night," said Etherington in his usual plummy tones before adding, "I'm afraid it's too early to break out the champagne. The game is still very much afoot but, at last, we have a lead!" he revealed.

"Thank Christ for that," said Hardie in evident relief.

"Yes and no, Hardie. The problem is that we have a lead but we've had scarcely any time to follow it up. Correct me if I'm wrong, 28 minutes to kick-off?" asked Etherington.

"Yup. Go on, sir," responded Thoroughgood, shivering from sheer physical and mental exhaustion.

"Indeed. You will notice heightened security around the ground. I'm confident that should there be an external, secondary threat we will deal with that, and credit to your lot on that front."

Etherington continued, "Unfortunately, information from Omar strongly suggests the threat will come from an internal source. We believe there is a bomber already at large within the stadium posing as an employee. We don't have any more than that because friend Omar was not in Tariq's inner sanctum."

Hardie responded, "Okay, if your target is maximum impact you want access-all-areas if possible. You need to be in a position where you're under the radar of natural suspicion."

"Hardie's correct," agreed Thoroughgood. "The bomber has to be a member of the emergency services on duty today."

"Exactly," Hardie interjected. "Shouldn't be too hard to get the various duty rosters checked to bring up backgrounds on everyone on duty."

"First class," said Etherington. "Logan!" Instantly a man appeared at the vehicle door. Etherington issued him with orders to liaise with the Police, Fire and Ambulance services and obtain the required backgrounds.

Etherington pulled out his mobile. "Please attend at the vehicle, Major."

Seconds later a male in his mid forties, prematurely greying and wearing army fatigues climbed into the Land Rover. Taking a seat he shook the hands of all three occupants. "Major Niall Munro, counter terrorism unit. Pleased to meet you, gents."

They nodded and he got straight down to business. "A lot of what I'm going to say is hypothetical. We don't know how big the bomb is and what it consists of explosives-wise. A dirty bomb is a crudely-made device that combines a simple explosive with radioactive material. The idea is that the blast disperses the radioactive material willy-nilly. You with me so far?" asked Munro.

The rapt attention of his audience was answer enough.

The ATO continued. "The dirty bomb is perhaps the least understood of all terror weapons. It is sometimes called the 'poor man's nuclear weapon'. Whereas the aim of a nuclear bomb is instant and outright destruction, a dirty bomb would have an entirely different effect. It wreaks panic in built-up areas, contaminates large areas and results in long-term illnesses, such as cancer."

Thoroughgood interrupted. "Sorry Major, but may I ask what the worst case scenario is?"

Munro frowned. "If such a dirty bomb was exploded at Ibrox, there would be massive panic and disruption. Obviously the more conventional the explosive used, the bigger the initial blast. Thereafter radioactive dust would settle on people, buildings, and roads. Wind, rain and air conditioning in buildings would spread the radioactive dust even further. Although the radiation would not be effective in killing people directly, it could cause a huge public panic leading to potentially fatal accidents. Living conditions in the area would be contaminated indefinitely and there would be disruption to the local economy."

"Sweet Jesus, your worst feckin' nightmare," groaned Hardie, putting everyone's thoughts into words.

"Thank you, Major," said Etherington adding, "How many of your men are on duty in the stadium?"

"There will be four of us, one situated within each stand and all linked via headsets. We also have two sniffer dogs trained in nosing out conventional explosives."

"Excellent," said Etherington, handing comms equipment to the detectives, "We'll be on the same secure communications. Salmond's aware of our internal op. I'll remain in close liaison with the police match commander who has also been briefed. Is there anything further we need to discuss before assuming our positions?"

Thoroughgood grabbed the opportunity, "I think it's odds on the attack will be in the main stand. If the First Minister's sitting in the directors' box, that has got to be a target."

Munro responded, "That's true, Detective Sergeant. We have 24 minutes before kick-off and I anticipate hearing from the dog handlers momentarily on the search results. It's a pity we had such short notice."

"Too feckin' right, Major. You've no idea what it's like dealing with the brass when their pride is in danger." raged Hardie.

Munro nodded in a world weary way that confirmed he knew all too well what Hardie meant.

"Talisker mate, make it a large one," Meechan requested. Drink in hand he took his seat and trained his eyes on the big screen beaming the Old Firm game live to The Rock.

Taking a slug of whisky Meechan let the sense of excitement tingle over him as the wonderful spiciness of the iconic malt aroused his palate.

His concerns had been heightened by the radio and TV reports that Tariq had been slain and his underground lair exposed. But the fact there had been no mention of a bomb plot had reassured Meechan that Tariq had taken the precaution of making sure the lethal substances were elsewhere.

That place could only be Ibrox.

This was it. Revenge on a scale he could never have dreamt of when he had left. Now, here he was, about to enjoy entertainment that none of the Old Firm fans filling the Rock with their colours and age-old taunts could ever dream of. Prime time carnage about to erupt right here, right now, or at least in the next 90 minutes.

Meechan took another slug of the malt and gave all his attention to the giant screen as the first whistle blew.

44

AABAN MOVED silently through the crowds of supporters, smiling benignly. His package had been placed in the target area and now all he needed to do was punch in the code on his mobile phone at the designated time and carnage would ensue.

That time would be when the referee's half-time whistle blew. Aaban listened to the roar of the crowd from outside the stand. The game had kicked off and there were 45 minutes until the final act of the Imam's Jihad was completed.

He was sad that Tariq would not be here to enjoy the fruit of his labours but he knew his master, who had welcomed him into the Glasgow Central Mosque from war-torn Somalia, would be congratulated in Paradise by the prophet.

His mind swept back to the car bomb he had laid for the girl Aisha. He felt more regret for her death than he would for his own and the kafirs who would enter hell in the moments ahead. But then her relationship with the detective had made her a source of concern which could not be allowed to disrupt his mission.

After today the fear that would grip every major city

in the west would be a hundred-fold greater than that wreaked by 9/11.

He, Aaban, would be enshrined and elevated in the consciousness of the faithful.

The detectives approached gate twenty one and were met by a burly female security steward. Cherry-red unruly hair dropped from under her yellow baseball cap. She was none too impressed to see them.

Hardie flashed his warrant card. "Detective Constable Hardie and Detective Sergeant Thoroughgood with Major Munro. Would you mind letting us in, doll?"

Cynicism swept across her face. "Don't 'doll' me, mate. If I had a fiver for every copper trying to get in through this gate for free I wouldnae be sitting here in this ridiculous luminous jacket would I? Naw mate, you and yer muckers can go and pay at the turnstiles like everybody else."

Thoroughgood's self-restraint snapped and he pushed passed Hardie. "Listen to me, I don't give two flyin' fucks whether you think we are takin' the piss or not, we are comin' in. Radio your superior officer and tell him to speak direct to the Strathclyde Police match commander. Do you understand me?"

It was all too much for the steward and her indignation melted in a stream of tears. "There's no need to take that tone, I was just trying to do my job. You polis are always at it. How am I supposed to tell when you're genuine?"

Faither tried to calm the trembling steward, "Listen darlin', it's kinda important we get into the stadium. We're lookin' for someone and we need to get a hold of him quick."

333

The Major's face said it all. If this was the first line of stadium security after the police cordon what hope was there?

Etherington's voice broke through their headsets. "Bad news gentlemen. All emergency service commanders have reported back. No suspect persons within their ranks. Repeat no potential suspect persons within their ranks. You are open all mics. Thoughts, please."

In the background the steward was now speaking into her radio, presumably making a complaint to her supervisor. Hardie spoke up. "What if we are looking at the wrong emergency service?"

Thoroughgood's eyes wandered to the still plainly upset steward. "That's it! The bomber has got to be a member of the stadium security staff. He can gain access to almost anywhere unseen, trussed up in his yellow jacket. He'll no doubt have been working with the security company and doing match days at Ibrox for months so his knowledge of the lay-out will be spot on."

Hardie broke in. "It's gotta be. The vetting for these companies is pathetic. He's gotta be a steward and ten to one he is on duty in the main stand."

Munro added his voice to the deliberations. "Mr Etherington, I'm switching all my resources to the main stand. If the detectives are correct we may have only a matter of moments to intercept the bomber."

Just then the sound of raised voices came from the direction of the fast food outlet. A posse of yellow jackets were coming their way.

"I don't believe this," said Thoroughgood. An angry female voice behind him said, "That'll teach you to throw your weight about, you ignorant polis bastard."

Hardie turned to Thoroughgood. "Let me deal with this."

"Just who do you think you are upsetting my staff and reducing her to tears?" raged the security supervisor.

Hardie raised his hand in a placatory gesture. As he did so Munro and Thoroughgood traded nods and the Major made his way unnoticed down the corridor behind the yellow jackets.

"Look sir, I can appreciate your anger but can we talk about this over here?" said Hardie attempting to usher the supervisor away from the growing crowd of Rangers fans who were taking an amused interest in the confrontation.

"Look mate, you need to listen and then I'm gonna need your help," said Hardie in his most conspiratorial fashion.

The supervisor wasn't having any of it. "What? You verbally bully my staff and now you want my help. That'll be right." His radio went off and he listened to his controller barking a set of instructions that brought a look of outright shock to his face. The supervisor handed Hardie the radio.

"There, that wasn't too difficult, was it, mate?" Hardie spoke into the radio. "DC Hardie here. How can I help?"

"Jim Smith, match controller, Total Security, here. We have been brought up to speed by Mr Etherington and believe we may have the male in question on duty within the stadium," said a no-nonsense voice. "His name is Aaban Mansour. He is on duty within the main stand."

"Description?" demanded Hardie.

"I believe he is of Middle Eastern appearance and wearing a yellow jacket."

"Fuckin' amateur," shouted Hardie and he threw the

radio back at the head steward. "Satisfied now? Get out of my way."

The detectives marched forward through the bustling red white and blue legions that had assembled for the contretemps. Turning right they faced the main stand's first level stairs.

"We've gotta check the directors' box first. What time you make it?" asked Thoroughgood.

Hardie checked his watch as they climbed. "Nearly 12.55. We're 25 minutes into the game. Shit, this all depends on the optimum time for the detonation to have maximum impact."

Reaching the landing they passed the members' lounge and came out the vomitory just below the directors' box. But they had already been beaten to it.

Major Munro was being met by a torrent of verbal indignation from the exalted inhabitants of the box comprising of club directors, the First Minister and his entourage. But there was one face in the box that was even more familiar to Thoroughgood and her eyes met and locked on his.

Standing next to his mate Hardie heard one word escape Thoroughgood's mouth. "Vanessa."

Hardie's incredulity was apparent. "How the feck did she get here? Christ she scrubs up well mate and she's comin' your way by the look of it."

Hardie was right, the reality TV-star-turned-business woman was out of her seat and descending the stairs from the directors' box, her blonde hair, savaged by Tariq's barber work, unevenly protruding from a black velvet fur-trimmed hat. The eyes of every male she passed transferred from the field of play to her svelte form descending the stairs in a figure-hugging red trouser suit.

"Hi Gus, we keep bumping into each other! What are you doing here?" she asked.

In his peripheral vision Thoroughgood saw Hardie and Munro descending the stairs two at a time.

"I'm sorry Vanessa it's a long story and I'm gonna have to go. Take care." Before he left she leant forward and kissed him and he felt something being pressed into his jacket pocket.

"Go and do what you've got to do, Gus." She winked at him and turned on her three inch heels and climbed the stairs back to her VIP world.

Hardie was back. "Directors' box is clear. I've gotta hunch the Major reckons is worth a check."

As they made their way back to the main internal stair case Hardie filled him in on his theory. "There's a book-ies on the second floor which shuts before kick-off and re-opens at half-time. If our man has been in with the rest of the security staff then he'll have had time to place the device in there before the bookies' staff came in. He'll also have been able to return before the staff are back in at half-time and prime it.

Munro chipped in. "That's 13.10 hours. We have five minutes to find him or his device if you're right. Jesus, we're leavin' it late."

Inside the main stand Thoroughgood swept his eyes over the individuals in front of him. The corridor was still pretty quiet as hungry punters and those desperate for the urinals hadn't dragged themselves away from the action yet.

337

Munro was also searching for the bright yellow jacket that would locate the renegade steward then the thought hit him. "Shit! What if he's taken off his luminous jacket and is in civvies?"

But the DC's attention had now been drawn by something that riveted him to the spot. "Got him. There, 20 yards to your left. Male, sticking a high-vis' jacket in the bin."

The DS reacted, "Right, this is it. Major, get behind the urinal entrance and wait for my signal. If he spots a uniform we're fucked. Hardie, we split up, I take the left flank and you the right and whatever happens we have to take him before his hands get anywhere near a pocket. If he has a remote on him then he is about to make for the exit and press the button when he gets out of the stadium but if we alarm him he's gonna do it on the spot.

"Major, the minute we have him immobilised it's up to you to get in the bookies. There's no way this is coincidence. The bomb is in there and he is walking away ready to blow it during half-time. You were right faither. Okay gents, this is it. Good luck."

"God save the Queen," said Hardie and they were off.

Aaban rammed the high-vis' vest and cap into the bin. So far so good. The bomb was primed on a timer, which meant even if he failed to detonate it manually for some unforeseen reason it would still explode within 10 minutes. Either way it was long enough for him to be out the stadium and well away from the blast radius.

He'd been patient over the weeks assembling the key elements of the bomb. It had taken nerve but every home game he was on duty he would bring the rucksack with him, a deadly cargo of fertilizer, acetone peroxide, nails or explosives concealed under his packed lunch. His experiences in the Yemen and Somalia had made it easy for him to link up the elements of the bomb before the bookies opened that morning. Final check done he'd started to make his way for the exit knowing that, one way or another, carnage was on its way.

As he turned from the bin Aaban was hit by a violent blow that smashed him against the concrete wall opposite the bookies.

His face filled with panic as he looked into a pair of furious sea-green eyes. He tried to get his hand into his jacket pocket to the detonator.

"You fuckin' bastard, keep your hands out of your pocket!" shouted the fiend who had locked his left hand. But his right hand was still free as the duo rebounded off the wall and dropped to the ground. His attacker was now on top of him, his head coming straight at him. Aaban felt the smash of the male's forehead on the bridge of his nose which exploded in a spray of blood. Another blow rammed into his left hand side but his hand was still free and going for his jacket pocket.

"Noooooooo!" screamed the man. He grabbed Aaban's head with both hands and smashed it off the concrete floor of the corridor. The terrorist's lights went out.

Thoroughgood spoke into his head set. "Major, you're on. Suspect immobilised, make your way to the bookies immediately."

Thoroughgood rifled the terrorist's jacket pockets. He found the control he was looking for and slowly removed it, aware that if a digit slipped the game could be well and truly over.

Turning his gaze to the bookies he saw Hardie and Munro booting in the wooden door. As it gave way Munro surged in and Hardie looked over his shoulder towards the DS who gingerly held the remote aloft.

Hardie gave a thumbs up then drew his warrant card from his breast pocket and walked away from the door. "Police. Please clear the area. Clear the area."

Thoroughgood placed the remote on a window sill and slapped cuffs on the unconscious male. As he did so, he noticed two figures in green army fatigues sprinting through the startled crowd, making for the bookies. The Major had summoned his subordinates and Thoroughgood could only hope that whatever awaited the ATO within the bookies they would be able to diffuse it.

Standing up he added his voice to Hardie's. "Police, back off and clear the area." It took a moment for the detectives' instructions to hit home but slowly the surprised punters retreated as an increasing number of fluorescent uniforms began to filter through. Within minutes a police cordon had been set up clearing the area either side of the bookies for fifty yards and gradually advancing to clear the whole floor.

Another green-uniformed figure joined Thoroughgood.

"Afternoon sir! Major Munro ordered me to attend. You have the control," the ATO stopped in mid-sentence as he saw the control on the window sill. "Very good sir. If you move away I will deal with it."

"Be my guest, mate," was all Thoroughgood could say.

The DS was joined by Hardie and the pair shook hands warmly. "Well done Gus, sad to say the job is only half done. The rest is down to the Major." They looked over to the bookies where one of the attending ATOs was handing a minute wire cutter through the doorway.

340

"Brave men these ATOs," said Thoroughgood. "Without Munro and his men we'd be fucked."

Their gaze remained transfixed on the doorway.

Munro lay prone on the concrete floor as he removed the fascia of the bomb. The luminous red digits flickered. 240 and descending. He had four minutes to disarm the bomb or Armageddon awaited.

"Wipe," he ordered in a calm measured voice and his lieutenant removed the moisture from his glasses.

"Crude but deadly, looks like our bomber has spent time in the Yemen," said the major to his subordinate.

The bomb had been placed in a wooden box that in turn had been inside a locked cabinet under the counter. As he eyed the explosive and the wiring linking it to the vials the awful truth was confirmed to Munro that they were indeed dealing with a dirty bomb.

The timer reached 120.

A voice in Munro's head offered reassurance. 'Yemen trained, come on you've diffused these bastards' best efforts before. They keep it simple so little can go wrong, which means one connecting wire. Where is it though? Bastard's concealed it.'

"Where, where, where?" Munro realised he was thinking out loud.

"There you are," he said. There were two suspect wires, one blue and one green. Cut the wrong one and it was all over.

Thousands of deaths on his tombstone and a one-way ticket to oblivion.

He had 32 seconds.

Munro's hand hovered and he could not stop the tremor in his arm shuddering down to the instrument he held poised in his right hand.

Twelve seconds and he was frozen. The counter reached single digits and descended and Munro remained paralysed in fear and indecision. Seven, six, five . . .

"Come on man, find your balls!" shouted the Major and clicking the incisor he put all his money on green.

The blades seemed to take an eternity to slice through the wire. Munro saw the timer reach two and realised he had left it too late.

Then the wire broke under the attack of the twin blades. A click sounded as the timer froze at one.

He'd done it. They were safe. Munro lowered his head onto the cold concrete of the floor and breathed again.

"You've fuckin' done it Major, you've done it sir!" shouted his lieutenant and Munro felt a pat on the back.

It was over.

Thoroughgood and Hardie had heard the words, "You've done it," shouted from the bookies and a shudder of relief broke over them.

Munro's grey head popped round the door and with it came the thumbs up sign.

"Mission accomplished, gentlemen!" he shouted.

"Amen to that," said Hardie and, his self restraint melting, the burly DC bounded over to Munro and shook his hand furiously. Thoroughgood was next in the queue.

"Thank God for you, Munro, you've saved our bacon," said Thoroughgood.

"I can't take all the credit, mate, you didn't do too badly yourselves," replied Munro, adding, "Christ I need a beer!"

"Can I suggest the Burnbrae in Milngavie? Excellent selection of real ales, good pub grub and a Ned-free zone,

342

Major. That tickle your fancy?" enquired Hardie before adding with wolfish relish. "But before beers and debriefs and all that, though, think I could take a wee butcher's at the game?"

Nodding his head Thoroughgood replied, "You know what mate? Someone else can take our friend here to the cells. I reckon there are two seats in the directors' box with our names on them."

45

THOROUGHGOOD RETURNED home at 5.30pm. As he opened the door the euphoria and adrenaline that had got him through the last few hours drained away and exhaustion hit hard. Even an hour's sleep would be a blessed relief. He made his way into the lounge and walked over to the window, looking out at the street as his mind relayed a picture of the day's events and the part he had played in them.

Tariq was dead and Glasgow was safe but at what cost? Plenty of good people who had been caught up in the crazed Imam's madness were now dead. Farouk and now Aisha emotionally blackmailed and coerced into Tariq's crazy world of religious lunacy. Both dead.

His mouth was bone dry and he felt emotion gripping him as thoughts of what might have been raced through his mind. He made his way into the kitchen and helped himself to an ice cold bottle of Carlsberg Export before returning to the lounge and sitting in the armchair. He took a sip of beer and closed his eyes.

This was it. Alone again.

He heard the agricultural roar of a diesel engine outside and automatically registered that a taxi had pulled up. A voice he recognised said, "Thanks, and keep the change."

A tell-tale clicking of heels on the pavement outside followed and his intercom buzzed.

He walked into the hall and spoke into the voice box. "Yes?"

"Fancy some company, Detective Sergeant?" asked Vanessa.

"Do I have a choice?" he retorted.

"No, Detective!" she replied and a moment later he opened the door and looked into her beautiful blue eyes and at the blonde hair he could not wait to run his fingers through.

There was a slight dishevelment about her and Thoroughgood guessed the hospitality had been good. He opened his mouth to speak but she silenced him with her lips. They both stumbled back against the wall with the intensity of the moment.

Thoroughgood's hands worked their way down the buttons of her velvet jacket and they soon found themselves in his bedroom as the passion of the moment took over.

Thoroughgood raised himself up on an elbow and checked his alarm clock. 7pm. "Bollocks," he said and was met by a slight murmur from Vanessa. She rolled over and smiled up from behind the tousled blonde tresses that wreathed her face.

"Christ you're beautiful, Vanessa," Thoroughgood said involuntarily.

"Why thank you, Detective. What's for dessert?" she asked playfully.

"Eh, well …" stuttered Thoroughgood, "You see I've gotta be somewhere in an hour."

She feigned anger. "So you have your wicked way with me and then want to throw me out afterwards. I thought you were a gentleman, Detective Sergeant," she pulled him to her and once again their lips locked.

As their passion reached its zenith a sharp crack rapped out. A micro part of Thoroughgood's mind registered it as a handgun. The sound of the flat door being booted open and banging into the hallway wall was unmistakable.

As he turned to the bedroom doorway his worst nightmare was confirmed.

There, framed in the doorway, stood Meechan. The revolver in his hand aimed at Thoroughgood's head.

"Did you think I would ever forget you, Thoroughgood?" said Meechan matter of factly.

"It didn't take you long to forget Celine, I see. Miss Velvet, I believe?" He turned his attention back to Thoroughgood. "I thought you had better taste than some fake media tart, Thoroughgood."

Thoroughgood's mind swarmed as Vanessa, fear writ large over her face, quickly pulled up the covers and wrapped herself in them.

"Listen Meechan, you're right. We have unfinished business but it's between you and me. Leave Vanessa out of this, there's been enough innocent people killed in this mess. I know the concept of innocence is beyond your grasp but for Christ's sake, Meechan it's me you want, not her."

Meechan laughed loud but his icey grey eyes retained their feral fascination on Thoroughgood. "Get out of the bed both of you," he shouted, "Now!" He unloaded a bullet into the wall above the headboard.

Vanessa screamed and Thoroughgood grabbed her. Slowly they shuffled through to the lounge where Meechan forced them to sit on the settee. He settled himself into the armchair.

"It's almost déjà vu Thoroughgood. You remember your uninvited visit to Tara and your waste of my malt?"

Thoroughgood said nothing but pulled Vanessa tight to him.

"Get your slut to pour me a whisky before I decide whether to end her life before or after yours, you worthless piece of shit."

"For fuck's sake Meechan ..." began Thoroughgood but stopped as his nemesis jumped onto his feet, grabbed Vanessa and jammed the revolver barrel against her head. "Don't piss me off, Thoroughgood, or her brains will be all over your carpet."

He sniffed her hair and whispered in her ear, just loud enough for Thoroughgood to hear, "How are you gonna tweet this you vain bitch? I assume the good detective keeps his malt over in that cabinet. From past experience I imagine there may be a bottle of Lagavulin in there? I seem to recall that when it comes to malt you're into the peat? One last drink for the condemned man, eh?" Meechan was clearly enjoying the mayhem he was wreaking with their emotions.

He pushed Vanessa towards the antique cabinet with such force that the bedclothes that had been covering her fell to the ground revealing her ample curves for his viewing. Meechan admitted his appreciation. "Still got it, hasn't she Thoroughgood? Was this the start of something beautiful, something to make Celine go away forever?"

The DS couldn't help the anger in him spilling over.

"What do you care you bastard? You're the one who had her killed."

Meechan gritted his teeth as he attempted to control his rage. "I had her killed because you had murdered our love once and for all. Taken the only thing that ever mattered to me. For that you will pay, and so will Miss Velvet. There can be no happy ever after for you, Thoroughgood, not while I still draw breath."

Vanessa appeared at Meechan's shoulder with the whisky and he took it from her. "A new experience for you, Miss Velvet, having to wait on someone else hand and foot?"

Anger over-riding her fear Vanessa shot back. "I don't know who you are or why you are doing this but you will never get away with it, you bastard."

Meechan jumped to his feet and backhanded her viciously. She stumbled onto the couch where Thoroughgood put his arms around her.

"Be careful what you say Miss Velvet because it may hasten your impending demise." His attention was caught by the bible above the fireplace.

Before Meechan could say anything more Thoroughgood spoke, "You've been behind all of this haven't you Meechan? It was through you that Tariq was supplied with his weapons and ammunition all ex-Soviet and stock in trade for the Rising Sun. That, in return for the death of Johnny Balfour and his cabal. But the enriched uranium? You've taken it too far this time. Do you think the Mossad will ever forget about you ripping them off? No chance, you'll spend the rest of your miserable life looking over your shoulder."

Meechan had finished his whisky and was leafing

through the bible, all the time keeping the revolver levelled on Thoroughgood and Vanessa.

He read out loud. "Presented to Mr David Thoroughgood from the Kirk Session in appreciation of his services as Treasurer. Your father or grandfather, Thoroughgood?" he demanded.

"What's it to you Meechan? There's no room for any God in your world," raged Thoroughgood.

But Meechan's attention was back on the bible. "Ah ha! How appropriate, a handwritten prayer. Fitting, I think, that we end your lives with a prayer from the good book your grandfather so cherished. Stand up as I read you your last rites, the broken-hearted copper and his new harlot." They hesitated and Meechan screamed. "Do it!" They jumped to their feet.

Holding the bible in one hand but keeping the revolver levelled on Thoroughgood Meechan walked across to the bay window reading aloud. "The Grace of the Lord Jesus Christ and the love of God and the communion of the Holy Ghost be with you all."

He slammed the bible shut and threw it onto the armchair. He turned to level the gun at Vanessa. "You first, bitch," and his trigger finger started to move.

Thoroughgood shoved Vanessa back onto the settee and threw himself over her as the shot cracked out. But no bullet penetrated him.

He looked up as Meechan pitched forward, his head exploded, brain and blood spraying over the detective.

Thoroughgood sprinted towards the smashed bay window through which the deadly projectile had been fired and saw a black BMW burning rubber as it ripped down the street.

349

He turned to Vanessa who sat sobbing on the settee. "The Kidon," he said in a gasp of relief.

Thoroughgood walked over to the body of the man who had ruined everything good in his life for the last decade and said one word.

"Amen."

Acknowledgements

FIRSTLY, THANKS to you, the reader, whoever you may be, for without you there would be no point.

As always, thanks to my darling wife Arlene; a lady who has the patience of the saint, and has needed every ounce of it!

Thanks also to my daughter Ava and my mother Margaret for keeping me in check.

For helping me realise my dream of being signed to a Scottish publisher, and for giving Thoroughgood and Hardie the second outing they deserve, my undying gratitude to Clare Cain, CEO at Fledgling Press. Also to Zander, founder of Fledgling, both have given hope and opportunity to aspiring Scottish writers.

Next, my gratitude to Flora, editor of *The Hurting*. Her ability to provide a different perspective has been vital.

Thanks to Graeme Clarke for maintaining my website www.rjmitchellauthor.co.uk, and for his technical expertise.

Gratitude to my *Evening Times* colleagues; Mick Brady for the excellent cover illustration, and Martin Shields for his imaginative photography.

Also to Brian McIntyre, general manager of W.H Smith, Argyle Street, for his encouragement and support.

As always, thanks to my old chums from the cops, Kenny Harvey and SupaMalky, for keeping me from straying off the radar. My gratitude to Major Niall Moffat for his technical expertise and advice on forms of terror used by the Jihadist. I also appreciate the Time Lapse Glasgow website's virtual tours.

Thanks to the Daily Telegraph, a treasure trove of information on the Jihadist.

If I have forgotten anyone, please accept my sincerest apologies.

Enjoy!

For David Jones and Martin Kaney
You may be gone but you will never be forgottten